I HAD TO STOP THE SEARING, ALL-CONSUMING ITCHING on my neck, and there was only one way. I felt a pure certainty about this—kind of like before with the shower—one that was growing with every minute of agony and every step I took.

I reached the edge of the lapping water. MoonGlow reflected on the surface, blackness beneath.

I kicked off my shoes, thinking at the same time, *I just drowned here*, but then my toes touched the water's edge and though I felt little aching spikes from the cold, I also felt a sudden rush of calm.

Tiny soothing shocks seemed to be reaching my wounds. Water erasing my pain. I looked up to the sky in relief and took a deep breath—

But it didn't work. The breath passed over my teeth, my tongue, and then stopped in my throat, like it had run into a wall. My chest locked up, nothing getting in.

And something felt different about my wounds. They felt open, strange, almost like they were moving. I clawed at the bandages, tearing them away. My fingers scraped my neck and I felt the flaps of skin quivering, like my wounds were creatures coming to life.

I felt there, felt the wounds. . . .

That weren't wounds at all. They were—

Gills.

THE
LOST CODE

BOOK ONE OF THE ATLANTEANS

KEVIN EMERSON

 KATHERINE TEGEN BOOKS
An Imprint of HarperCollins Publishers

Katherine Tegen Books is an imprint of HarperCollins Publishers.

The Lost Code: Book One of the Atlanteans

Library of Congress Cataloging-in-Publication Data
Emerson, Kevin.
    The lost code / Kevin Emerson. — 1st ed.
        p.   cm. — (The Atlanteans ; bk. 1)
    Summary: "In a world ravaged by global warming, teenage
Owen Parker discovers that he may be the descendant of a highly
advanced, ancient race, with whose knowledge he may be able to save
the earth from self-destruction"— Provided by publisher.
    ISBN 978-0-06-206280-2 (pbk.)
    [1. Science fiction.   2. Identity—Fiction.   3. Camps—Fiction.
4. Environmental degradation—Fiction.   5. Atlantis (Legendary
place)—Fiction.]   I. Title.
PZ7.E5853Los   2012   2011053348
[Fic]—dc23   CIP
                                                              AC

Typography by Torborg Davern
13 14 15 16 17   LP/RRDH   10 9 8 7 6 5 4 3 2 1
❖
First paperback edition, 2013

For my parents,
who have always supported my creative pursuits
and also sent me to summer camp

Before the beginning, there was an end
Three chosen to die
To live in the service of the Qi-An
The balance of all things
Three guardians of the memory of the first people
They who thought themselves masters of all the Terra
Who went too far, and were lost
To the heaving earth
To the flood.
Three who will wait
Until long after memory fades
And should the time come again
When masters seek to bend the Terra to their will
Then the three will awaken, to save us all.

PART I

Good night, Mother Sea,
Good night, Father Sky,
Hide from sight the sunken homes,
The faces floating by.
—TRADITIONAL GREAT RISE LULLABY

We'll go down to SoHo,
Shop for antiques in a rowboat.
—THE TRILOBYTES, "NEW MANHATTAN LOVE SONG"

1

THE MORNING AFTER I ARRIVED AT CAMP EDEN, I drowned for the first time. I was three-quarters of the way through the cabin swim test when the cramp that had been tightening in my side the whole time finally twisted into a solid knot. I seized up, my legs shut down, and I sank.

Kick! I thought desperately, but the order didn't make it past my abdomen. The cramp was like a fist, clenching tighter, white pain radiating from its grip. I reached wildly for the surface but found only water and bubbles. I kept thrashing, trying to get my cabin mates' attention as they swam by above, but none of them noticed.

I never should have been in the water, never should have even taken the test. I knew that, but I'd tried it anyway, because of her: Lilly, the lifeguard and one of the counselors in training. You didn't impress someone like Lilly by being too lame to tread water and swim a few laps. And up on the dock, impressing her had seemed like maybe the most important thing.

I saw her now, a blur of red bathing suit, standing there watching us. Well, watching everyone else. I guess I hadn't made enough of an impression for her to notice either.

And that was nothing new for me.

I slipped deeper, into colder depths. My arms started to slow, the muscles too tired, the pain from the cramp blinding. Pressure on my ears. The light dimming around me.

A feeling began to ache in my chest, a certainty: *Owen, it's time to breathe.* The order was matter-of-fact, like there were little technicians inside my body, wearing yellow jumpsuits and monitoring all of my functions on glowing screens. That was how I always felt, like others were in charge of me, like I was just along for the ride.

The technician watching my heartbeat whispered to his neighbor, who was in charge of my blood-oxygen levels. Her screen flashed ominously. A persistent beeping made her shake her head. *There's not much more I can do,* she said. *We're going to need air.*

The urge grew, a balloon expanding in my chest. Like I *had* to breathe. Exhale. Inhale. Even if there was water outside of my mouth. It didn't seem to matter.

That's all I've got, chimed in another technician, watching the last blips of oxygen leave my lungs.

No! I couldn't . . . But the body is a simple machine. It doesn't plan for you being underwater when you need air. It figures you wouldn't be that stupid, I guess. And if you were, well, then there were three billion other humans out there who probably wouldn't make the same mistake, so your genes clearly weren't worth passing on. Survival for the fittest, that was the plan. Then again, there had been *ten* billion people on the planet. Not sure losing seventy percent of the species was really part of that grand design. Maybe it was time for the genes to go back to the drawing board.

I'm hitting the intake override, said another technician.

Has to be done, said the blood monitor.

No . . . No . . . Pressure everywhere. I struggled to hold my mouth shut. I could get the cramp under control, then swim up. . . .

BREATHE!

No! Had to hold on, had to—

But my mouth opened anyway.

The air burst free in oblong bubbles. I watched helplessly as they made their wobbling dash toward the surface. Water poured in to fill their place, and there was a feeling of cold—*cold!*—icy pain and weight, pressing me down, my lungs filling, and for just a second it all hurt so much—

Then it didn't. The pain was gone, leaving an immediate silence, like that strange way that the lightning rains back home would suddenly be over, and in their aftermath there would only be this sense of quiet, no more rumbling, no more wind, just the pop of cinders in scorched earth and the hissing of rocks.

Calm. I was so calm. When had I ever felt like this? No

more worry, no more panic. Was this what death felt like?

I sensed everything in my body slowing down. The technicians were studying their screens in mild surprise. *Well, that was unexpected,* said the lung monitor, surveying the flood with dismay.

The woman watching my brain activity shook her head. *Probably a few minutes more,* she reported, *then that will be that.*

I knew what she meant. I'd read that the brain could live for about four minutes without oxygen. Even longer if the water was really cold, but the lake here inside the EdenWest BioDome was kept at 22°C, which was supposedly the ideal temperature of summers past. I knew lots of facts like that, but being smart had done me no good. Better muscles, an abdomen that didn't malfunction—these were the things that would have made me more fit to survive.

I drifted down into the shadows. My feet touched muddy bottom, making clouds of brown particles. Slippery plants clutched at my ankles, the fingers of unseen creatures of the deep. I keeled backward, my back settling into the cold muck.

The surface looked like another world. There were my cabin mates, sliding by in loose lines, their hands and feet smashing the shimmery mirror top of the water over and over. The white-and-red lane lines vibrated in their wakes. Some were finishing the test now, hauling themselves up onto the floating dock.

High above, I could see feathery white SimClouds gently

drifting across the hazy blue of the TruSky, the afternoon brilliant in the warm glow of the SafeSun lamps. Another perfect summer day in the temperate forest, just like it had been half a century ago, before the Great Rise, when global warming and climate change spiraled out of control. The soaring temperatures and savage depletion of the ozone layer turned most of North America into a desert. The rapid melting of the world's ice caps caused the oceans to rise up and devour the coasts. The old technopolises of New York, Shanghai, and Dubai drowned, and billions of people around the world became climate refugees, displaced and doomed to die in the wars, plagues, and chaos that followed. The only safe havens were the thin rim of land in the Habitable Zone above sixty degrees north latitude, and the five Eden domes, where people could still live as they once had.

Yet with the murky filter of the water, I could see through the illusion, to the distant ceiling of EdenWest. When I'd arrived last night, getting off the MagTrain after the all-day trip from my home out at Yellowstone Hub to here in what used to be Minnesota, the dome had looked even more impressive than in the pictures I'd seen: an endless curve of perfect white, an impenetrable guardian of the people inside. But from down here, I could see the black burn marks where the dome had been damaged by the increasing solar radiation. Some of the triangular panels were new and shiny white, but most were gray and spotted.

I could also see the monitoring station in the center of the roof, a pupil in the dome's eye that constantly kept watch for solar flares, dust storms, or lightning rains.

There were rumors back home that all the Eden domes were failing. The Northern Federation worried that it was only a matter of time. Then, the modern cities inside would fall, but instead of submerging, the Edens would bake, and this little lake would dry up just like all the rest. When it did, maybe they'd find my bones in the cracked mud.

One more minute, said the technician monitoring my brain. I tried one last time to move my arms, my legs, anything. No use.

Just about everyone was out of the water now. Everyone else passing the test, and here I was, dead. Had any of my cabin mates even noticed I was gone yet? What about Lilly? Could she have forgotten about me already? What about our moment on the dock?

"Hey there, you gonna be okay?" Lilly had asked, just before the swim test. All ten of us in my cabin were crowded in front of her on one end of the dock, which was shaped like a wide H and stuck out from a small brown beach. Inside the lower half of the H was the shallow swimming area for the little kids. Strung inside the top half were the lane lines. This was where the test took place. Every older camper had to take it to get a swimming level, from Tadpole to Shark. You had to be a Shark to do any of the cool things on the water, like sailing, kayaking, or swimming out to the big blue trampoline raft where the CITs hung out and did acrobatics.

I hadn't even realized that Lilly was talking to me. I'd been gazing out across the water, still getting used to the sight of trees everywhere, to the feel of air that was heavy, moist, and thick with scents of flowers and life, and also to all these healthy, well-fed Eden kids around me, who acted like being in a place like this, feeling like you were *outside* on a summer day, was no big deal.

But I guess I'd also been worrying about the test, and it showed.

"Hey," Lilly said again.

Finally I glanced over and saw she was staring right at me. Another reason I'd been looking away was so that I wouldn't just be gawking at her the way the rest of my cabin was. She was dressed in baggy green shorts and a red bathing suit, the thin straps indenting her smooth shoulders. Her braided dark-brown hair had streaks dyed lime green, and her sandstone skin was tinted lavender from NoRad lotion, which we'd all been instructed to wear during midday. She wore mirrored sunglasses, sky-blue flip-flops, and her toes glimmered with pearl polish. She stood there with her hip cocked to one side, one hand on it and the other spinning and unspinning a whistle around her index finger. It seemed impossible that she was only a year older than us.

"Huh?" I replied, my voice cracking slightly.

This made a group of my cabin mates laugh. They were the central unit in our cabin, a tight knot that had formed almost immediately around a kid everybody called Leech.

Lilly ignored them. "Just making sure you're okay."

"Oh, I'm fine," I said quickly, trying to meet her silver-rimmed sunglasses through the glare of water and sun and make my gaze say, *Yes, I can do this,* even though I was pretty sure that I couldn't.

I had taken swim lessons when I was a kid, back when there was still enough water to fill the one pool out at Hub. I wasn't great at it, but I did okay. That was before I got a hernia last year, which is like a lame old-man thing to have. It didn't surprise me that I'd gotten one, though, because it seemed like if you could get an injury doing something, I did. Temporary asphyxiation from the cave mold spores in our classrooms? Check. Sprained wrist from paddleball? Check. The hernia probably started when my whole class was forced to try cave diving, Hub's most popular sport. It always felt like my body was made of weaker stuff, or like I'd been built for something different from everything I normally had to do.

Technically, a hernia starts with a tear in your abdominal wall. You can get them without really knowing it, which was what happened to me. I guess it slowly grew wider, until one day all I did was bend over to pick up the sandwich I'd dropped on the way to a lunchroom table and a chunk of my intestines popped out, and then there was this weird bubble beneath my skin and so much pain.

I had to have surgery to sew it up. "You'll need to exercise some caution with strenuous activity for a while," the doctor informed me. And after that, I got bad cramps whenever I had to exert myself.

Dad put it on my camp application, but apparently word hadn't gotten down to the lifeguards. And now here I was, not telling Lilly.

"The Turtle is roadkill," said Leech from nearby. The group around him laughed again, just like they laughed at all his jokes. Leech just grinned his slopey grin, his thin eyes squinting and making his dark freckles bunch into blotches. Looking at him, you wouldn't think that he would be the ringleader of our cabin. It wasn't like he was some amazing athlete or seriously good-looking specimen or anything. He was short and pretty skinny and covered in freckles and had uneven eyes that always seemed half closed. But he had one thing that none of us had: he had been at camp the previous two sessions already that summer, and for as many years as you could be before that. And just because of that, he was the king, and one of his royal duties was handing down nicknames.

Like Turtle, which barely made any sense, and yet because Leech said it, it was so, and his minions thought it was hilarious.

But Lilly just frowned at him. Apparently, Leech's powers didn't extend to the CITs. "Are you—," she started to say. "Oh, wait." She nodded dramatically, like she was solving a big mystery. "You're trying to be funny."

A laugh rippled through our whole cabin. Leech's buddies jabbed him with elbows, and he smiled weakly. "I am funny," he said, but the comeback was halfhearted. It was the first time I'd heard him sound that way.

Even he felt that whatever-it-was that Lilly had. Like she had her own Eden dome around her, some kind of force field. And it even felt like, when you were near her, that force field extended to you, made you safe. Like right then, when Beaker, whose real name was Pedro and who was one of the few kids who had it worse off in our cabin than I did, actually laughed out loud in these big silly chuckles.

"Shut up," grunted one of Leech's pack, and immediately shoved Beaker into the water.

Lilly's hand flashed out and snatched her whistle, midspin. "Whoa, what's *your* name, tough guy?"

"Jalen?" he answered, as if Lilly had made him question his own name. Jalen was the tallest of all of us, with muscles that made him look older. They weren't the ropy, taut things you'd see on the stronger kids out at Hub. Instead Jalen's muscles were smooth, easy-looking, like he'd just been given them without having to work, like he'd been pumped up with an air compressor. He tried to push out his chest now, to look like he wasn't scared.

Lilly scowled at him and looked past us. "Hey, Ev!" she shouted.

Another CIT, Evan, turned in our direction. He brushed the mop of white-blond hair from his eyes and squared a set of shoulders that made Jalen's look like beginner models. "What's up, Lil?"

Lilly pointed at Jalen. "Put this kid in the box for me, 'kay?" We'd already learned that the box was the square of shade beneath the wooden lifeguard chair. "Start walking, scrub," she said, glaring at Jalen. "Enjoy your time with the other babies." The little campers were playing on the beach all around the box, running and squealing and throwing sand.

"Whatever," Jalen muttered. "This is stupid."

"Hey! Don't make me ask Ev to hurt you," said Lilly, "'cause he'll do anything I say."

Jalen looked like he had another comeback, but then thought better of it. He trudged off toward shore.

"Have fun!" Lilly called after him. She turned back to us. Everyone was dead silent now. "You okay?" she called to Beaker, who was dragging himself up onto the dock while we all watched.

"Fine," he said like he wasn't.

Lilly flashed a glare at Leech, then looked at me. "So, you're gonna be all right with this?" She waved her hand, indicating the water.

"Yeah," I lied, trying to sound confident.

"What's your name?"

"Owen Parker."

Lilly grinned. "I'm not your math teacher. You don't need to give me your whole name."

"Sorry."

She raised an eyebrow at me. Her eyes were a mystery behind her sunglasses, and I figured she thought I was a lost cause, except then her gaze stayed on me and her smile remained and I felt like it was suddenly really hard to stand there and not do something stupid like try to say something funny, or throw myself into the lake.

I wondered if maybe I already loved her, in that at-first-sight kind of way that was the only kind of love I really knew. The kind you could just have without ever actually telling someone, without them even knowing you. The kind that was perfectly safe, that you didn't have to do anything about.

Her gaze left me, and I looked away and found Leech staring at me with a squinty sneer like now I was on his list for what had happened to Jalen.

"So, where were we?" said Lilly. "Right: the test. It's pretty simple. Five minutes treading water, then freestyle, backstroke, breaststroke, and butterfly, two laps each. To be a Shark, your form has to be perfect. Got it?"

We all nodded slightly. Yes. Perfect form. Since Lilly had led us out to the end of the dock, I'd noticed everybody trying to stand with better posture and constantly checking their hair. I had been, too, though I'd tried to do it less.

"All right, then," said Lilly. "In you go."

We lined up and jumped off the dock. The water was a shock, cold wrapping around me, seeping in, and it had this weird, slightly tangy taste, a little bit like putting your tongue against something metal. It was different from the chemical flavor I remembered back at the Hub pool.

We spread out to start treading water.

Lilly held up a stopwatch from around her neck. "Go."

I started kicking my feet, circling my arms and thinking, *Come on, you can do this,* but I already felt the cramp beginning. And yet, when Lilly blew her whistle, my head was still above water.

"All right, not bad, guppies. Now swim over and start your laps."

I grabbed the side of the dock and tried to will my stomach to relax. *You should get out, now,* I thought. But I didn't.

"Next," said Lilly. Three at a time, we pushed off and started the freestyle. And again, somehow I got through those laps, and the backstroke, and even the breaststroke. I could feel my side cinching tighter, but amazingly, even though I was sinking too deep with every stroke, I was almost there.

But in the end it was the butterfly, the strange and inexplicable butterfly, with the weird kicking where both feet stayed together and the lunging with the flying arms that did me in. Why did we even have to swim like that? It was like a test to weed out the weakest. I kicked, I lunged, my side failed, and down I went, to my quiet, dark tomb.

○ ○ ○

I blinked, feeling the pressure of deep water on my eyes, the ache in my ears, the cold of water in my nose and throat, the heaviness of liquid in my lungs. Everything numb. There was a distant whine, like of machinery, and the faint warble of voices far off on the surface.

Now that it was too late, all I could think was that it really stunk to be dead. It was just unfair and stupid, and I hated it. I hadn't even wanted to come to this camp in the first place! But I'd gone along with it, and now this was what I got.

Darkness crept into my vision, like a fog over everything. The technicians were checking the monitors one last time. *That's about it, then,* said one, watching my heartbeat slow to a stop.

The surface began to dim, fading to black.

Good-bye, Lilly, I thought.

Shut it down, said the brain technician.

Nice working with you, one said to another, shaking hands.

They flicked off the light switches, closed the doors. Everything went dark.

For a while.

Then there was a small light in the distance. It was pale blue, struggling through the murk.

Owen.

Yeah?

The light seemed to pulse. Maybe this was the final message from my dying mind, the one you were supposed to think was the light at the end of the tunnel. Or maybe it really was that light. Maybe I was about to lift up to heaven, or be picked up by the vultures who brought the dead into the embrace of Heliad-7, that sun goddess they worshipped in the South.

But this seemed more . . . actual. Like my eyes were really open, and that light was slithering around in the green water above me. It had a long, fluid shape, almost like it was alive.

You are not at the end, it said.

I'm dead, I thought back.

No. This is just the beginning. It sounded like a girl. *Find me. In the temple beneath the Aquinara.*

The light moved closer. It seemed to have features. A face. Maybe a beautiful face . . .

Temple?

What is oldest will be new. What was lost shall be found.

What?

Find me, Owen. . . .

The light faded.

Black again.

For a while.

Hey, Owen. . . .

Who are you?

"Owen."

I opened my eyes. Blinding daylight. Cold was now warm. The squish of the lake bottom had become hard, coarse sand; the press of water now the nothing of air.

I was lying on the beach, the campers crowded around me.

And that calm feeling of an ending ended with a huge, awful cough. Water erupted out of my body, burbling out of my mouth, a brown swirl of lake water, vomit, and phlegm, spilling onto my chest and down to the sand.

There was Lilly. She had her hands in a fist on my sternum. Her head was lifting away like—

CPR, I thought, which meant her mouth, and my mouth—

Stop thinking about that! What about how you're not dead?

But it was weird: the fact that I wasn't dead didn't seem like much of a surprise. I sat up. Everybody shuffled back. Muck from my insides dripped down my chin. It smelled sour, hot.

"Let me through," an adult voice called from beyond the kids.

I looked down at myself. There were long, tan plants still wrapped around my legs, my arms. I saw now that they ended at little plastic bases. Fake. My body was covered with splotches of mud and the spray of lake puke across my abdomen.

I fell back on my elbows. Tried to speak, but my voice just croaked at first, like a reptile. "Whu . . ."

Lilly leaned close to me. Her wet braid brushed across my arm. "Don't try to talk yet."

But I had to. I hacked up another slick of water and phlegm. "What happened?" I asked.

"You—," Lilly began, but now the sea of kids parted and my counselor, Todd, appeared. Behind him was Dr. Maria, the camp physician.

"Okay, let us in." They flanked me.

I looked at Lilly. Her gaze was still so odd. . . . Then she quickly leaned in. "No matter what happens in the next couple days, don't tell them anything. Especially not how long you were down there."

"What? How long I—," I said.

She leaned even closer, her lips brushing my ear, pressure of her warm breath into my ear canal. "You were on the bottom for ten minutes."

"Ten?" I croaked. "But how—"

"Excuse us, Lilly." Dr. Maria knelt beside me.

"Don't worry," Lilly whispered. "This is just the beginning. Trust me." She pulled back and stared at me.

This is just the beginning. I focused on her eyes. Sunglasses gone, they were pale, sky-blue disks woven with threads of white. I nodded to her. I would trust her.

And then Dr. Maria was leaning down over me and Lilly was pulling away and the SafeSun made me squint and I coughed out more water.

"Just lie back, Owen," said Dr. Maria. She held a small rectangular electronic device above me. It had a single glass dot that started to glow green as she moved it closer to my face.

I closed my eyes against all the brightness and my head seemed to come unglued and everything faded out again.

2

THERE WAS MORE DARKNESS, AND THEN I HEARD VOICES.
Fragments of a broadcast:

*Good afternoon, this is Teresa Alamos. Turning now
to the latest EdenNet news . . .*

*New images from EdenCentre of the fires sweeping the
French Desert . . .*

*Fighting continues on the American-Canadian Federa-
tion border, as the Nomad Alliance has mounted new
coordinated efforts to breach defenses at the sixtieth
parallel and cross into the Habitable Zone. . . .*

*The latest report released by the Northern Federation
Climatology Council indicates that the rate of sea level
rise lessened slightly this past year. The study shows
that the reasons are simple: there's not much ice left in*

Greenland, and after the big ice-shelf collapses that we saw in Antarctica, the main continental ice appears to be remaining stable. Still, though the worst of the Great Rise seems to be behind us, its aftereffects continue to wreak havoc, especially in Asia. Today, EdenEast is reporting more violence on the edge of the People's Corporation of China, just north of the current shore of the Indian Ocean. Salt intrusion continues to ruin farmland in the region, causing still more suffering for the half-billion remaining climate refugees from the former subcontinent. And an outbreak of a lethal new strain of Supermycin-resistant cholera-D is sure to worsen the situation. . . .

Now voices from close by, speaking quietly.

Dr. Maria: "He seems to be recuperating fine."

And a man's voice: "Have you determined exactly what happened?"

"From what his cabin mates said, it had to be at least a few minutes, if not more. He definitely drowned, but I ran an mPET scan, and his brain activity seems fine. I think we dodged a bullet."

"What about the physical injuries?"

"Just the neck lacerations that—"

The man cut her off. "Right. Sounds good. I'll read the report. Send him to me when he's feeling up to it. Thank you, doctor."

For local climatic conditions, let's get a report from Aaron Cane, chief of operations up in the Eagle Eye observatory. . . .

Thanks, Teresa. Well, more of the same from up here. Today's external temperatures are topping out at forty-six degrees Celsius, and that's likely only the beginning of what July has in store for us. Doesn't sound like too much fun for humans, but as you can see, the pronghorn in these shots seem to like it just fine.

My eyes finally opened, and I found the screen in the corner of the room. The face of Aaron Cane, youngish-looking with thick-rimmed glasses and short black hair, was replaced by an outdoor view. The camera zoomed down the outside of the dome wall, its surface streaked with tan dust and black solar burns, then out over the concentric rings of thousands of gleaming solar panels to the barren, cracked earth beyond. A herd of pronghorn roamed on the flat wasteland, grazing on bits of grass underneath ledges of gray shale rock, oblong sections of upturned pavement, crumbled house foundations, and the picked-over carcasses of cars. The only smooth line among the fractured topography was the curved path of the MagTrain tunnel roof, its snake back punctured now and then by boxy air vents.

Pretty creatures, but not the ones your great-great-grandparents used to hunt here in Minnesota.

Turning to solar monitoring, it looks like we've got calm conditions for the next few days, so I expect UV Rad levels to be holding steady. Dome integrity is still rated at eighty-six percent, but we've got a deteriorating ozone forecast for the weekend, and we can likely expect elevated Rad levels and maybe a half percentage point off the DI, though RadDefense says they're in the process of replacing two of the OzoneSim panels, so maybe we'll hold steady. That's the report from up here.

My eyes fluttered shut and I lost track of things again.
Owen . . .
Dark water, something curling in the shadows, flickering blue . . .
Find me. . . .
"Owen."

I looked up to find Dr. Maria leaning over me. "He's back," she said with a smile that felt friendly. She had long black hair that was streaked here and there with gray. It was held back in a clip. She wore a classic white lab coat over a collared flannel shirt and jeans. The outfit was retro, pre-Rise, even with an unbuttoned collar so that her neck was exposed. A doctor out at Hub would be wearing the standard LoRad pullovers and pants, which were dark colors with shimmery surfaces that reflected sunlight. The neck would be zipped high, the wrist cuffs tight, but here inside the safety of the dome, retro was part of the look of the camp, and apparently you could relax a little.

"Hi," I croaked. Talking hurt.

Dr. Maria adjusted something on my neck. I reached up to find thick bandages there. The area beneath them itched faintly. The feeling surprised me. I didn't remember hurting my neck. I started to scratch, but she stopped my hand. "Careful," she said, "these are delicate wounds. You need to try not to touch them." She sat back and her brow wrinkled. "So, Owen, do you remember what happened?"

I tried. Things were murky in my head. "I got a cramp," I said. "I couldn't do the butterfly."

"Mmm." Dr. Maria smiled and shook her head. She picked up a computer pad from the table beside my bed and swiped her finger over its glass surface. "I always thought that was a weird stroke," she said. "You'd see it in the Olympics and think, Why would someone ever choose to swim like that?"

"Olympics?" I asked her.

"Oh, sorry," said Dr. Maria. "Showing my age. Yeah, back before the Rise, there were a lot more countries, and there used to be these games where each country sent their best to compete. They tried to keep them going, but too many countries were either in chaos or too much debt. I think I was about ten when the last one happened. Anyway, they swam the butterfly. It's weird to think that with everything that's been lost, something so silly has lived on." She sighed. "But, then again, that's the goal here at EdenWest, to make everything just like it was." I almost thought I heard a note of disapproval in her voice as she finished, but I wasn't sure.

She held a stethoscope to my chest and listened for a moment. "Sounding good. So, any idea how you got those neck wounds?"

"No, not really," I said.

"Maybe you got tangled in the lane lines or something, before you went under?"

I just shrugged. "I don't think so."

Dr. Maria pushed a loose strand of hair back behind her ear and held a light to my eye. "Well, they weren't deep enough to need stitches, so I gave you a topical antibiotic." My left eye went blind in the flash of white. She checked the other. "I'd like you to come by tomorrow for fresh dressings. And you really shouldn't go in the water again until they heal, although I bet that wasn't first on your agenda, anyway." She smiled.

"No," I said, smiling back. That sounded fine to me. The more I thought about the wounds, the more they itched, simmering, like the skin was cooking in there.

"Maybe something got on your neck on the lake bottom," said Dr. Maria. "Lake Eden is supposed to be a fully functioning ecosystem—you know, real fish and leeches and things. That's probably not what you want to hear."

"No," I said. I thought about the fake plants that had been on me. But that didn't mean there weren't real creatures too, like in an aquarium, and if I had really been down there ten minutes, like Lilly said . . .

Lilly.

I remembered her lips against my ear. What was with her? What did she mean, "No matter what happens in the next couple days, don't tell them anything"? What exactly did she think was going to happen? I drowned, maybe got my neck munched on, and got pulled out in the nick of time. Except, ten minutes wasn't the nick of time. Wasn't there basically no way I should have survived that? Maybe Lilly had been exaggerating. Dr. Maria had said it was only a few minutes. Kind of a big difference, in drowning terms. But then there was something else. . . .

Find me, Owen. That light, that voice. What had that been? Probably just some kind of hallucination, my brain tripping on a lack of oxygen.

"I think it's okay to take this off," Dr. Maria was saying. She bent over my left arm, where a clear tube emerged from my elbow and led up to a bag of fluid. She unhooked the line, then grasped my forearm. "You might feel a slight sting." She pulled and the tube slid out, chased by a drop of blood. It stung, but the feeling faded quickly.

"There we go." She placed a sticky round bandage over it. I noticed her black fingernails, which seemed a little fashionable for a camp doctor, and as her smooth, almond-colored fingers pressed against my arm, I thought of Mom. She would do things like that. The extra bit of fashion. Dr. Maria was maybe a little older. Then again, it was hard to remember. The mom in my head was from eight years ago, when she left. She'd look different now. Wherever she was. She'd never told us. For a while she'd sent letters, but they never had any kind of location or date information. And then, about three years ago, she'd stopped writing altogether.

"Okay," said Dr. Maria. "I think we're good to go. If you promise to keep your hands off those neck wounds, I can release you to your cabin."

"I can't stay?" I imagined my cabin mates leering at me from their bunks like waiting predators as I walked in, ready to harass their little drowned Turtle.

Dr. Maria fixed her hair again and sighed. "Sorry, Owen. They're a tough bunch, I take it."

"Sometimes."

"Well," Dr. Maria continued, "the first few days of a session are always the hardest. A lot can change in a month. You'd be amazed the kids who end up as friends by the time a session's all over." She tapped on her computer pad. "Oh, once you're dressed, the director would like you to stop by. End of the hall. See you tomorrow, okay?" She smiled and stepped out.

"Okay."

Someone had brought over my shorts, T-shirt, and sneakers. I got out of bed and started taking off my hospital gown. My chest hurt, my ribs aching with each breath I took. My right side, the cramp side, was still sore. I ran a finger over the pink, four-centimeter scar from my hernia operation, just below my waist. Its warped skin was raised, smooth.

There was a mirror in the corner, and there was my uninspiring self, skinny, a child of the rations, nothing like these Eden kids, but also nothing like the kids you saw camped out on the ACF border. I may not have had much muscle, with clavicles and ribs kinda showing, but you weren't seeing shoulder sockets and hip edges. Having a father who worked for the Hub's geothermal heat company meant there was enough food. His genes, not hunger, were more the reason I was skinny. That and the fact that the things that gave you real deltoids or pectorals were also the things I never seemed to be any good at.

Dad would say to me, "You could always work out more at the school gym, or join the cave-diving team." I knew he meant well, and he was probably right. I could probably get some better muscles if I tried, but it seemed like it would take forever—almost like, to get some sort of physique, you already had to *have* a good physique. And I never felt farther from having one than on that mandatory school day when everyone had to put on a skintight neoprene slick suit like the cave divers wore and try the sport. I hated being on display like that. Being in a bathing suit this morning had been just as bad. I might as well have been a different species from someone like CIT Evan, who got a single-syllable nickname from Lilly.

I got my clothes on, being careful as I pulled my T-shirt over my neck. The bandages looked like a neck brace. I grazed my fingers across them, and just that slight attention seemed to ignite the itching underneath. My nails started scraping around the bottom edge, digging up under the soft fabric, desperate to scratch. *No, stop. She told you not to.* I pulled my fingers out. The tips were shiny with blood. I wiped them on my gown, leaving streaks. The itching increased, pulsing in waves. I tried to ignore it as I left the room.

Outside, the hall was painted a cheery peach color. Framed black-and-white photos of pine-forested hills hung at regular intervals on the walls. There were five other clinic room doors, all open. I heard Dr. Maria speaking softly in one of the rooms, but I couldn't make out what she was saying. To the left, the hall ended at a solid red door with a keypad lock. It looked odd and modern compared to everything else around. Kind of like seeing the panels of the dome from underwater, a glimpse backstage. To the right was an antique-looking brown door with a square frosted-glass window. I headed through it, into a dark room with warped, wood-paneled walls.

There was a door in each wall, each with a similar window. One led outside. The others had gold, stenciled lettering that read OFFICE and DIRECTOR. The one I'd come out of said INFIRMARY. There were cracked leather chairs in the corners, and coffee tables piled with old paper magazines.

It was like being in one of those exhibits that you'd find in the history museum back in Yellowstone, the ones that explained about the United States pre-Rise, before the War for Fair Resources when the United States invaded Canada and created the American-Canadian Federation. That name was supposed to sound peaceful, like the two countries had happily joined forces, but my dad said the name was a lie. The invasion and occupation had really been bloody and terrible.

I pushed through the director's door. There was a wide desk on the far side of the room, a tall black chair behind it, and two fabric chairs in front. The desk was antique, but its top had been replaced with a glass table monitor. Files glowed on it. On the wall behind the desk, a bulletin board was covered with maps that looked like they were expertly hand-drawn, showing intricate coastlines and mountain ranges. I wondered if the director had drawn them himself.

There was a large fireplace in the left wall, built from giant gray stones that were scarred by black soot. The head of something I was pretty sure had been called a bison was mounted above it. Along the right wall were high shelves of frayed books and a leather couch. The room smelled like soot and pine, a scent I vaguely remembered from my clothes and sheets back during the Three-Year Fire, which erased the last forests of the American West. It had started when I was four, and during the middle year and a half of it, we barely saw the sun.

The wall behind me was covered with framed photos on either side of the door. They were all-camp photos. Each one had a year beneath it. The earliest ones were in black-and-white, then they switched to faded color. Groups of wild-haired boys and girls. Not much separated the decades, except the size and color of the kids. They went from skinny and mostly white to chunkier in the middle, with more varieties of skin color. Then, in recent photos, the kids got thinner again. And in the last few photos they were no longer sun-bronzed, their skin instead tinted purple by NoRad lotion.

"Fascinating, isn't it?" A man was peering through the door. He stepped in and extended his hand. "I'm Paul. I'm the director. And you . . . You must be Owen." He said it almost like I was a celebrity or something.

"Hi," I said, shaking his hand. It was cool, the skin smooth-feeling.

He was a little taller than me and old, maybe in his fifties. Like Dr. Maria, he was dressed retro, I guess like the director of a summer camp would have been, in jeans and a blue button-down shirt and a black vest with the overlapping *E*-and-*C* EdenCorp logo embroidered on it. Everything was relaxed except for a striped tie that was done up tight, the knot perfect. He had wavy gray hair and a thin face, lots of freckles and dark spots on his tanned skin from time spent in the sun.

The only thing about him that was modern were his

square, black-rimmed glasses. Their lenses flickered in a tinted shade that indicated Rad protection. I was pretty sure that the tint could be turned off on glasses like that, or at least lightened, but Paul still had it full on, even though we were indoors, and so I couldn't see his eyes. He seemed to be smiling, but the glasses made the smile strange, incomplete.

He closed the door and pointed to the photos. "Almost two hundred years of campers have come to this very spot—well, not counting the fifteen-year break while the dome was being built."

"Oh," I said.

"They used to call it Camp Aasgard," Paul continued. He spoke in a low voice, all his words flat and even. "It had a whole Viking theme because of the archaeological finds near here. Lake Eden actually used to be part of Lake Superior, before the big lake receded. Imagine, Vikings right here."

"That's pretty cool," I said, thinking that it was. It was interesting to me to try to imagine a place like it looked to the people who came before, like how Yellowstone used to be full of people just driving around in big homes on wheels, peering into the trees looking for animals, not a care in the world.

"Indeed," said Paul, and it seemed like my interest excited him a little. "They apparently traveled up the waterways from the Atlantic, and also down from Hudson

Bay. Most people don't know that," he added mildly. "But most people don't know most things."

"Huh," I said, and saw that all the photos to the left of the door had *Camp Aasgard* in funny letters above the photo, with Viking hats on either side. The photos to the right of the door said *Camp Eden.*

"And that's not all," said Paul. "If that kind of thing interests you, then Eden has some other surprises."

"Like what?" I asked, still interested but also trying to sound polite.

"Well, for starters, there are copper mines in this region that are over ten thousand years old," said Paul. "It makes you wonder: Who was here, back then, and what were they up to? I find those kinds of questions most intriguing."

"Wow." There were old towns out by Hub, all abandoned, but that stuff was only about forty years old. You could still picture the people being there, like ghosts, living the pre-Rise life with cars and lawns and stuff. Our life was mostly underground, but it was still similar. We still had technology like video channels and subnet phones and electric lights at least some of the time, and even some of the newer stuff, like holotech.

"Then there's our own little archaeological study right here." Paul pointed at the camp photos. "The world outside has changed so much, as I'm sure you're well aware, but life in this spot has endured. Just a bunch of kids smiling, enjoying life. It's nice to know that's still possible. . . ." He turned toward his desk. "If you do what it takes." He sat down in his chair and motioned to me. "Have a seat."

I sat. Paul had put his fingertips together and was gazing at me, but didn't say anything right away. After a few seconds, I wondered if he was waiting for me to say something. He was so still, just sitting there. It bothered me that I couldn't see his eyes. I started to feel weird, like I was being examined.

"Dr. Maria told me to come see you," I finally said.

"Yes," said Paul. Another second passed, just staring . . . but then he sat up and twisted around. He picked up a metal pitcher and cup from a cabinet behind him. The pitcher's sides were foggy with condensation. "Bug juice?" he offered.

"Sure." The bug juice was just fruit punch. Typical powdered juice drink, like we'd have back at home. There were more flavors here, though, each a different bright color, and they sorta tasted different, but really all just tasted in the end like bug juice. I'd had this one before. It was purple and called Concord Explosion. I heard one time that a Concord was a type of grape, but they took the word *grape* out of the name because they didn't actually use any real grapes in it anymore, and maybe it didn't even really taste like a grape—not that I would have known, since I'd never had one.

Paul handed me the cup. I took a sip. More tangy than sweet. Still kinda the same as all the others. Fine, though.

"Thanks," I said.

"Don't mention it." His face became motionless again. Smiling maybe, sort of. It was impossible to tell with those glasses.

Then he leaned forward again and swiped at the glass monitor top of his desk. Files slid around. "So, Owen, the main reason I wanted to see you was to say that I am truly sorry about what happened to you today. Everyone here at Camp Eden is glad you're okay."

"I'm fine," I said.

"Apparently." Paul was studying a file. It looked like a chart of numbers. "Your tests all seem normal, even"— his finger touched the file and part of it zoomed in, but since it was upside down, I couldn't quite make out what it said—"*better* than normal. You have noticeably high levels of hemoglobin."

"Is that weird?" I asked. I didn't remember ever hearing that in past doctors' visits.

Paul didn't answer right away. He kept reading, files flicking across his glasses. Then he sat back and stared at me again. "No," he said, "totally within the expected range. And you feel normal other than those neck wounds?"

"Yeah," I said.

"Good. Well, you can rest assured, we spoke to the lifeguard who lost track of you. Made her aware of her error."

"It wasn't Lilly's fault," I said immediately. "I got a

cramp." I didn't want Lilly to get in trouble over this, over me.

"Right," said Paul. "And to be fair to young Miss Ishani, she hadn't been informed of your condition." Paul ran a finger over another file. "A hernia. . . . Again, my apologies. This information should have made it to the lifeguards."

"I wanted to be a Shark," I said.

Paul nodded. "Of course you did. And I like your spirit. Not afraid to take a risk to get what you want."

I wouldn't have described myself that way.

Paul tapped at the monitor again. "I spoke with your father and let him know what happened, and that you were fine. He seems like a nice man."

"Yeah," I said. I wondered if Dad was worried, and for a second I thought, *Serves him right.* It was his idea to enter me in the drawing to come here. He kept saying how a month at Camp Eden was a month I didn't have to spend scraping by out at Hub, a month when I didn't have to help him with his breathing issues, the nebulizer packs and the beige phlegm that never seemed to get all the way down the drain, a month when I could have fun like people used to. I hadn't really wanted to apply, but I saw how much he wanted me to, and besides, the odds of actually winning were terrible. Except then I won.

"You two get along well?" Paul asked.

"Mmm." I nodded. We did. "We don't talk much," I said, "but not in a bad way."

Paul seemed to smile again. At least his mouth widened. "Fathers and sons often don't," he said. "Sounds like he doesn't put much pressure on you, though." Paul's smile faded. I wondered if he was thinking about his own dad.

"Nah," I said. "We just sorta do our thing." It felt weird answering questions about my dad. I felt almost like I was defending him, or something. And I didn't need to do that. Sometimes Dad got on my case, but we never really fought. Most nights he got home pretty late, and his breathing was always the worst then, and he'd be tired. I usually made the frozen dinners for us. I wondered what night tonight was . . . Tuesday. Pizza night with the Arctic League football game. I remembered looking ahead at the schedule and seeing that it was going to be Baffin City and Helsinki Island. Dad always missed the first half, so when he got home I'd give him a summary of the key plays. He'd have to figure it out himself tonight. I hoped he could make his dinner fine, and that his cough wasn't too bad.

Paul checked my file. "And it's just you and your dad, I see."

"Oh. Uh-huh." That comment made me feel weird, too. Like Paul was pointing out flaws. I didn't want him to know all this stuff, but of course my whole situation was laid out for him right there on the screen. Maybe he was just trying to be sympathetic, to connect, like adults sometimes tried to do.

"There's no contact information for your mom here."

"We don't have any." Saying that caused a squeeze in my stomach. That was the feeling that thinking about Mom always seemed to create.

"My parents split up when I was about fifteen," said Paul. "I'd seen them fighting, so it didn't surprise me, but it was still challenging. It's hard to accept that our parents are just people, and sometimes it's even harder to accept who those people really are."

"Yeah," I said, but I felt defensive again. Sure, I had thoughts about my mom leaving, got angry about it sometimes, but I didn't like the idea that Paul might be judging her. Then again, maybe he wasn't. His tone was so flat, and I couldn't tell what he meant without seeing his full expression.

We both sat there for a second. "Challenging living out there at Hub," Paul offered.

"I guess," I said, really not wanting to talk anymore. Maybe he was right, though. I thought about life back home. Living in an apartment in the cave complex, the fluorescent lights dimming every hour as the geothermal charge faded. School was fine, pretty normal, but only compared to what I knew. Lots of kids had asthma due to the fumes, but I actually didn't. I hadn't really considered my life and family to be that bad, but I guess it was, compared to things here.

Paul clapped his hands together in a sharp, flat smack that echoed in the room. "Well, Owen, these are all good reasons to finally have you here. You are exactly why I started running the drawings to invite kids from outside EdenWest to be a part of our camp."

"Thanks," I said, but my defensive feeling only grew. I didn't like being one of the charity cases, the poor wastelander being given a golden chance.

"No, thank *you*," he said, his tone level, almost like he was being sarcastic, except I figured he wouldn't be. "Now listen," he continued, "it may not seem this way right now, but your time at Camp Eden can really be life-changing. In fact, in your case, I'd go so far as to guarantee it." Another smile. With each one I felt more like I wanted to leave.

"Okay," I said.

"So . . ." He shuffled the images on his desk. "I've reassigned you to Craft House for the electives hour. You'll be with some younger kids, but it will be fine. And I've noted exemptions in your file for any of the rituals that could pose a problem for you, like polar bear swim. We don't want you going out there and getting damaged."

I had no idea what he was talking about. Polar bears? They'd been extinct for almost thirty years. Did Eden have one here? Maybe it had been in the Camp Eden brochure, but I hadn't really read that. And why was he talking about me like I was some prized piece of merchandise? Maybe he didn't mean it that way, but that was how it sounded.

"Well, that should do it." Paul pressed his fingers

together again. "Dr. Maria noted that you're due back in for a follow-up, tomorrow."

"Yeah."

"In that case, you can head back to your cabin now."

I nodded and stood. Paul did, too.

"Listen, Owen," he said. "I may be the director here, but I also want to be your friend. If there's anything you need, or anything you're concerned about, anything at all . . ." He stepped around the desk and over to me. "You'll come to me first, won't you?"

"Um, sure," I said, just trying to end the conversation.

"Especially," said Paul, and then his voice lowered to almost a whisper, "about these . . ." He reached out, his fingers extending toward the bandages on my neck. They grazed the fabric gently. The wounds seemed to ignite with simmering itching, and I flinched and stepped back.

"Sorry," he said mildly, and I had no idea if he was, but his smile was its widest yet, like he wasn't actually sorry at all, and suddenly I needed to get out of there.

"I should go," I said, and stepped toward the door and yanked it open, trying to stay calm but really wanting to run.

"Of course." Paul didn't stop me. "Owen?"

I turned to see him standing casually, hands in his pockets. "Just remember, I've seen it all. The more you share with me, the more I can help."

"Okay, um, thanks." I hurried out.

3

OUTSIDE, IT WAS EARLY EVENING. THE TEMPERATURE was balmy, the breeze like a soft hand. The moisture in the air made my skin feel sticky. It was still a strange feeling, but a relief compared to being with Paul.

The SafeSun lamps had been dimmed to orange, the SimClouds tinted purple. The wind had been turned down, and the insects were making a bunch of different sounds: drones and screeches and blips. Out at Hub, we only had the usual insects that could've cared less about the Great Rise, like ants and flies, and the cockroaches that had adapted to become hand-sized so they could compete with the snakes for the rodent supply.

EdenWest was supposed to contain all the animals that used to live in this part of the country except for the mosquitoes and biting flies, which they'd thoughtfully not included. I was passing tall bushes of purple flowers by the dining hall, ones that Todd had called rhododendrons, and I saw yellow-and-black bugs buzzing around. Bees. Actual bees. That made sense. You'd hear stories of how they had things like real honey in the Edens, just like they had up north in the HZ.

I stopped to watch them work, floating to a flower, then flicking their delicate leg structures and abdomens to gather pollen. It seemed so amazing that creatures like that, so small and complex, were the work of the same world that offered massive things like oceans, or a Three-Year Fire, or even this soaring dome.

Something bounced on the air, closing in on the bush like it was being controlled by a puppeteer. I flinched, then saw that it was a butterfly, another creature that was only memory out at Hub, and in most of the world. Its wings were powder blue and jewel green with black curling patterns. It flittered around the bush, like it was looking for a free flower. I stuck my arm out near it and the butterfly wobbled, then landed right on the top of my wrist. I could barely feel its feet.

I moved it closer to my face to get a better look, its wings flicking up and down slowly, its feet readjusting so that it almost seemed to be looking right at me. It had a long, straight abdomen trailing behind it, two delicate antennae, and shiny eyes. Except, I saw that there was actually only one eye. And it wasn't even an eye. . . . It was a camera. Now I recognized a tiny humming sound, and clicks as the legs moved.

A robot.

Its tail was actually an antenna. I looked up at the lavender TruSky, and wondered if there was someone up there in the Eagle Eye who controlled this thing. It lifted off and fluttered away from me and the bush, not actually needing the flower nectar.

I started down the hill to the playing fields. The itching on my neck was acting up again, getting hotter. Despite Dr. Maria's warning, my fingers found the outside of the bandages and started rubbing softly. It helped a little.

The boys' cabins were on the south side of camp, in the woods between the playing fields and Mount Aasgard, which wasn't really a mountain like out West, but it was a high hill with a naked set of rock ledges at the summit that reached out and almost touched the curving dome wall. The granite sparkled in the pink sunset light.

I entered the pine trees, my sneakers scuffing along a wood-chip path. The forest was still except when I passed near an air blower. A steady chord of insect noises hummed in the background, but I wondered now if that was real or instead broadcast from hidden speakers.

I reached the clusters of boys' cabins. The girls' cabins were on the other side of the fields, near the beach. Each cabin was named for an extinct creature, and I could hear the wild calls and thumps from mine, the Spotted Hyenas, before it was even in sight.

I got to the door and felt the usual flutter of nerves. I hated this place already, and I felt pretty sure that there was no way I was going to have the amazing transformation that Paul and Dr. Maria talked about.

I walked into the front room. Todd was lounging on his bed, the curved brim of his dirty white cap pulled low over his eyes. He was reading a paper book. Another part of the costume of this place.

"Hey, Owen, good to see you back," he said. "You feeling okay?"

"Fine." I passed him and walked through the doorway into our bunk room. There were wooden bunk beds built into the walls, a small window beside each bed. Another wall was lined with cubbies. Everyone was messing around, some kids playing dice on the wooden floor, others joking, some sitting, legs hanging off their perches. I headed straight for my bunk, which was in the far corner, by the side exit door.

I was just reaching the little ladder up to my bed when a balled-up, sour-smelling sock whipped past my head and smacked against the wall.

"Check it out: the Turtle lives!"

I looked over to see Leech staring down at me from his bunk, where he was leaning on his elbow, lounging like royalty, giving no indication that he'd just thrown the sock. Everybody stopped when they heard him and turned to look at me.

"We thought you were dead," said Jalen, sounding disappointed.

I wanted to say something, but what? Leech was the undisputed ruler, there was no use fighting it. When we'd all first walked in, each dropping our bags onto our bare bed and sliding our trunks underneath, Leech's top bunk had already been decorated with posters, photos, and drawings, his stuff already hung in cubbies. He'd been wearing the hand-dyed T-shirt from last session that was signed by the other kids and even the counselors, like an endorsement of his king status. He'd already shown that he knew everyone on the staff by name, and they all knew him. Even the kitchen cooks gave him high fives.

He'd started handing out the nicknames during the first dinner, the night before. I'd been busy eating real wheat pasta for the first time, and also this leafy plant called spinach, which was greener than anything I'd ever seen and tasted bitter and smelled like wet rocks. People were giving welcome speeches to the whole camp, when I heard Leech begin.

"How about . . ." He scratched his chin with his index finger and thumb, a scientist hard at work. To either side of him, Jalen and Leech's other freshly minted minions were already leaning in close. "Ooh, I know," he said, and then he pointed dramatically to the two kids at the opposite end of the table. "Bunsen and Beaker." Leech's gang laughed, though I'm not sure any of them knew what those nicknames were from. I didn't. "Who else?" said Leech, scanning the table with his squinty gaze. It landed on me. He nodded and grinned. "Turtle," he said. More snickering laughter.

"What?" I said back to him, because I didn't even know what he meant by the nickname. I figured I didn't look turtlelike in any way, since I wasn't overweight, so I wondered if maybe it was because of how the tortoises out in Yellowstone lived in burrows and how I lived underground, too.

"Turtle," he snapped back at me, and I guess it was the fact that I'd dared to question him that suddenly made his grin curl downward. "That's you."

The reason for the nickname turned out to be even dumber than I'd thought. I learned later that night that it was just because I had been *wearing* a turtleneck shirt. And nobody called those shirts turtlenecks anymore. I'd never even heard of the word. It was just a LoRad pullover like anyone else might wear back at Hub. They were part of the dress code at my school, where Rad levels were a daily issue.

And the reason Leech even knew a retro word like *turtleneck* was because he was a Cryo. He'd been frozen during the Great Rise and put safely inside EdenWest by his parents, who couldn't afford to move in themselves. After things settled down, the Cryos were awakened in batches. He and the others lived at Cryo House, which was like a foster home over in the main EdenWest city. All the Cryos came to camp, but then the rest of the kids here were apparently normal, the grandchildren of EdenWest's original inhabitants, and so this was just another part of their life of luxury. Not that I blamed them for that. It wasn't their fault they'd grown up in here. They couldn't be expected to know what it was like outside, to treat the sun like an enemy, to never have tasted spinach.

I ate that first dinner quietly, thinking, *Great, twenty-nine days left and I've already been identified, categorized, and labeled*. And things only got worse as dinner went on. I sat there mostly quiet except when Todd would ask me a question, and watched as friendships formed around me, everyone gravitating to one another, the natural thing that people did, except for me, a satellite off in my own orbit. It was just like so often back at school, and I never knew how it happened, how you did that magic thing where you became part of a group, and it seemed like, once again, it was already too late before it even started.

There were ten of us in the cabin. We'd gotten the basics out of the way the first night: Leech, Jalen, and Xane were the Cryos. Mike, Carl, Wesley, Bunsen, and Beaker lived with their families in EdenWest. Noah and I were the outsiders. He was from Dallas Beach, along the Texas coastline. It was kind of like Hub: a little satellite state of the ACF, which basically meant that, other than the military units that came and went to escort supplies, it was on its own. You'd think that would have made us natural friends, but Noah had already made his intention clear to join Jalen and Mike as one of Leech's minions. I suppose I could have done the same, but it never really occurred to me, and it had been obvious even by the end of dinner that first night that no more invitations for the Leech club were going to be available. Also, I was pretty sure I didn't like him from the first moment I met him.

Leech and Jalen had immediately started bonding by referencing ancient TV shows and comic books and junk from way back in pre-Rise, talking in code and making the rest of us feel inferior. When Leech had started tossing out nicknames at dinner, Jalen was the only one who laughed. Xane got the jokes but didn't really join in. He was the one who'd told me what Turtle meant, later.

"What happened to your neck?" asked Beaker as I reached the ladder to my bunk. He had the bed below mine. Leech had two cubbies, even though we were only supposed to take one each, and so all of Beaker's clothes and shoes were stuffed under his bed.

Just the mention of my neck made the slow itching seem to get stronger.

I was about to answer when Leech's voice boomed across the room. "Beaker! I thought I told you: no speaking!"

Beaker sighed quietly and his shoulders slumped.

"Good Beaker," said Leech.

It had been established that Bunsen and Beaker were on the lowest rung of the cabin food chain, where everything you did made you a target. I seemed to be up on the second level, where you were more just invisible, enough so that you could drown without anyone noticing.

"You can talk if you want to," said Bunsen quietly to Beaker. He was lying on the next bunk over, typing up a letter on a computer pad, the blue light reflecting on his big round glasses. The cabin only had one computer. You weren't allowed to bring your own, to preserve the experience. But you could write a letter home on the cabin pad, and then the camp would send the letters out over the gamma link each night.

"Hey, bed wetter!" Noah snapped, looking up from an old board game called Stratego that he was playing with Mike. He was talking to Bunsen. Jalen claimed that he'd seen Bunsen crying and changing his sheets in the middle of the night. No one could confirm this, but Leech and his gang had decided it was fun to believe it, and so it was. "Shut up and try not to piss yourself!"

"You—," Bunsen began.

"Careful, bed wetter," warned Leech.

I climbed up into my bunk and lay down, staring at the ceiling. My neck was starting to really burn. I rubbed at the bandages with my knuckles.

"All right, guys." Todd appeared in the doorway. "Time to head to the dining hall."

Everyone stopped what they were doing and started out.

I sat up but then felt a wave of dizziness and lay back down. The itching rose like a wave.

"Owen, how you feeling?" asked Todd.

"I don't know," I said.

"Dr. Maria said you might need to rest. If you want to skip dinner, that's fine with me."

"Okay, yeah."

"We'll bring you back some food."

"Thanks."

I listened to them leave, a commotion of shuffling footsteps, jostling shoulders, and laughing and shouts. It faded. The insect drone seeped through the window, the cabin now silent and still.

I fell asleep for a little while, but the burning in my neck woke me up. I needed a distraction, so I grabbed the computer pad and lay back down. I started a letter to Dad:

Hey Dad,

Things are okay here. Guess you heard about my swimming accident but I'm mostly okay.

I stopped, not knowing what else to report. I didn't want to tell him about my neck. Not because of Lilly's warning not to tell anyone, but because I didn't want him to worry. I wondered if I should tell him that things were basically terrible in my cabin? That would probably make him worry, too.

It's Tuesday. How was work? How was the game?

I tried to think of more to write, like maybe ask him what he had for dinner. Thinking about Dad and how he'd manage on his own made me think of how Mom always made fun of him for not liking to cook. She used to say that he'd be lost without her. Except she didn't seem to think about that when she left.

The itching was getting worse, so much so that I could barely think straight.

Okay, write back soon.

Owen

I sent the message and put the pad down. I lay back, trying to keep my hands off the bandages. Maybe if I thought about Lilly, about her lips on my ear as she whispered to me, about the closeness of her leaning over me and the view I'd had of her bathing-suited figure—and that made things start to burn in other places. . . . But even that couldn't compete with the searing in my neck.

I ran my fingers over the bandages. Hotter. And I was starting to have this weird urge. I didn't get what it was, I just knew that I couldn't lie there anymore. I had to get up. Had to do something. It was almost like I wasn't in control of myself.

I climbed down off my bunk, wincing now, gasping at the pain, and started pulling off my clothes, while at the same time wondering, *What are you doing?*

Don't worry, said a new technician in a bright-red jumpsuit. *You want this itching to stop, right?*

Yes, that was what I wanted. So badly.

Okay, he said as he busily assembled a new monitor screen, *then just do this.*

I stripped down, grabbed my towel from my cubby,

wrapped it around my waist, and headed for the bathroom.

I turned on the shower, cold water only. Dr. Maria had given me explicit instructions: stay out of the water. But I wasn't thinking about that. Or anything, really.

Keep going, the new technician advised.

The water hissed out of the showerhead. I got in. The second the stream hit my chest, I felt this huge shiver, and then a rush of calm. Like everything was relaxing. My wounds still itched, but less.

Don't touch them. That was Dr. Maria's other warning. But instead I started clawing at the tape that held the bandages on. I peeled it up and unwound the fabric. At the end, the last few layers resisted, stretching away and then finally breaking their dried-blood bonds with snaps of pain. The burning surged. I leaned out, tossed the crusted bandages into a sink, then dunked my head into the shower spray.

Water poured over me, down over the wounds, and the itching suddenly ceased. Like my nerves had been shut off. Relief spread through me.

There we go, said the new technician.

I reached back up to the wounds. My fingers came away with thick crimson blots. Drops of water dabbed the blood away. But the wounds didn't hurt. They didn't itch. And the blood wasn't bothering me. Not since the water had starting falling on me. There was blood and water and wounds, and yet I felt calm, that strange sense of peace like I'd had on the lake floor, returning.

Other technicians were shrugging. *I can't explain it, sir,* said one.

None of this made sense except the undeniable relief. *Okay,* I told myself, *think like a normal person. If the wounds don't hurt, then this blood is just 'cause the bandages pulled off some scabs on the surface, or something. The wounds must be almost healed. Fine. So we rinse them off and cover them up again.* I stuck my head back into the shower stream and turned to the side, exposing the wounds. Water hit them directly and the calm feeling increased, the pain barely a memory.

Then I coughed. Took a breath but coughed again. Wait—there was a weird feeling, like water in my throat. Tightness in the back of my windpipe. I couldn't breathe.

I lurched away from the stream of water and slapped at the dial. The water stopped, but my balance was off. Spots bloomed in my vision, and I tripped and fell sideways, tearing down the shower curtain and landing on the cement floor.

I lay there, staring at the wooden ceiling with its single naked lightbulb, trying to breathe, but I couldn't, like nothing worked. Everything stuck.

Um, we really need air, said a technician. He jabbed at the glowing button that should have opened my mouth, but my mouth was already opening and closing, gulping at the air but getting nothing.

Don't panic, said the new technician, working busily.

Oxygen is running low! shouted the technician monitoring my blood.

The edges of the world grew dark again. I was back on the lake bottom. . . .

Owen, this is just the beginning.

It was her again. The voice from the lake. Who was she? *Stop thinking about that! You are drowning again!* But that didn't make sense. Oh, maybe she was like a sprite, or a nymph, or one of those other creatures from old stories about shipwrecks and sailors. Mermaid? Siren? *There are no sirens in the lake!*

The sound of other voices broke me out of my thoughts. From outside, getting closer. My cabin was coming back.

I tried to breathe again, tried to suck in air—

And it worked. I felt my throat burst open, my lungs ballooning, and then I coughed out a huge breath. Whatever had been keeping them from working—blocking them, it felt like—had stopped.

I scrambled to my feet, untangling from the nylon curtain. Had to not be naked when my cabin got back. I grabbed my towel from the hook and threw it around my waist. I had just secured it when that gagging feeling like I'd felt at the lake came back and I staggered to the sink and threw up a slick of bile, shower water, and blood. Looking up into the mirror, I saw my dripping chin, my shuddering naked body, and the wounds on my neck—

Whoa.

They were way worse than I'd imagined. Two long, red gashes on each side of my neck. They didn't seem to be bleeding at the moment. I reached toward one with a finger and found that the red separated, and for just a moment my finger slipped inside the wound—*way* too far—and there was blinding pain and white spots. I grabbed the sink to stay on my feet.

The wounds had looked feathery inside. Like there were flaps of skin. These didn't look like bites, like parasites feeding or whatever. What had happened to me? An infection? Was this that flesh-eating bacteria that you heard about at medical clinics along the ACF border? Or that cholera mutation that was ravaging south Asia?

The screen door slapped open. I could hear laughing. Okay, the wounds were really weird but seemed stable. I had to move. At any moment, the bathroom door would slam open and Leech or one of his crew would pop in and find me with this mess everywhere and come up with some amazingly stupid yet funny-to-them way to harass me for it. I looked at the shut door, then the broken shower curtain. First, my neck. . . . I grabbed the bandages from the sink. They'd gotten damp, but they'd have to do. I wrapped them back into place. The tape was gone, so I tucked in the end and hoped it would hold.

Feet clomped into the bunk room. I turned on the shower to wash away the blood, whipped paper towels out of the dispenser, tearing them free. Turned the shower off, dropped to the floor, wiped the blood from around the shower drain. I got most of it, threw the towels in the trash, tore out more, and threw them on top of the bloody ones to cover the mess. Then I grabbed the shower curtain. A few of the rings were broken, so I tossed it over the rod. Turned back to the door. It would have to be good enough. . . .

A few seconds passed. There were shouts, more laughing, then a heavy thud. I cracked open the door and peered out.

Leech had Bunsen in a headlock. His chubby legs were flailing uselessly. "I told you not to talk! Stupid bed wetter! You smell like piss! It's cleaning time!"

Meanwhile, Mike and Noah were on Bunsen's bed, stuffing his blankets, sheets, clothes, and pillow out the tiny window beside his bunk. Closer, Beaker was sitting on the floor, holding his knees to his chest, his face red, trying not to cry. Jalen was just finishing up giving his bed the same treatment. Jalen looked down at Beaker. "That's for getting me put in the box," he taunted.

I shuffled quickly over to my bunk, glad to be invisible by comparison. I kept my chin down, but nobody even noticed my wet bandages. I climbed up the ladder and found a metal dining hall plate on my bed. It was piled with some kind of noodle casserole, but there was dirt all over it.

"Oh, Owen, dude, sorry," Xane called from across the room. I turned to see him shrugging apologetically. "We got that for you but it got knocked on the ground on the way back." He sounded sorry, but not too much, and turned back to his conversation with Carl and Wesley. I took the plate over to the compost container and slid the food in.

The group moved on from tormenting Bunsen and Beaker to a game of Monopoly. The cabin quieted down.

Later, Todd came in and read to us. It was this old book with a long title by some author named Edgar Poe from, like, two hundred fifty years ago. It was apparently a cabin tradition, and it was weird, being read to, like we were innocent children instead of a bunch of savages, but it was also maybe cool, 'cause you could just lie there and picture the words, or not. It had seemed like it would be kind of a boring book, but then the main character, named Pym, was almost getting killed every chapter. He and the other two survivors on this lost boat were just deciding which of them they were going to cannibalize when I started to doze off.

I closed my eyes and felt the faint twinge of the strange wounds on my neck. They weren't burning anymore. No pain since the shower, just a slight hum. Why had water made them feel better, when Dr. Maria had said to stay away from it?

Soon the cabin buzzed with slumber, light snores and heavy breaths, and as I drifted off to sleep, I thought of Lilly's words. *No matter what happens* . . . Maybe this, these weird wounds, was what Lilly had meant. Maybe she was the one I needed to talk to.

4

WE WOKE THE NEXT MORNING TO THE REVEILLE horn. It was a recorded trumpet sound, hissing from speakers in the trees. My wounds had awakened me a few times in the night, sizzling lightly, then calming down. In between, my dreams had been strange, dark, full of water and blood, the kind of dreams where you were convinced they were real the whole time, and yet I couldn't remember any specifics, and so I just felt slow and fuzzy as everyone hopped up around me. The wounds were humming faintly now, not bad, just a prickling reminder that they were there.

Todd came in, wearing boxers and a dark-gray Camp Eden T-shirt with the sleeves cut off. "Good morning, ladies," he said, stretching like he was giving us a furry armpit show. "We leave for flagpole in ten minutes."

That was enough time for everyone to get dressed and for Jalen to run over to Beaker. "Wake-up wedgie!" he shouted like he was half our age, and yanked Beaker off the ground.

"Everybody make sure to put this on," said Todd, reappearing and passing around a stiff plastic bottle of NoRad lotion. "Arms, legs, face, and neck."

"Don't forget your balls!" said Leech. "Can't be too careful." He looked toward Bunsen, Beaker, and me. "You guys probably don't need to worry." He and Mike slapped hands.

"Okay, enough," said Todd, but I saw him smiling a little.

I slipped my pullover carefully over my neck. It didn't quite zip over the bandages. When the bottle got to me, I rubbed the greasy, metallic paste onto my face, my hands, and my ears. It always tingled a little as it sank in, and you heard rumors that it was bad for you in its own way, but I'd seen the effects of extreme UV radiation out at Yellowstone: the purple melanomas etched into boiled skin, the whites of eyes burned brown, the lost fingers and noses. Apparently, there were regions of the world—in some of the Habitable Zone, a pocket over central Asia, parts of the Pacific—where the ozone layer was still thick enough that you could step outside without any kind of NoRad, at least for a few minutes. It hadn't been like that anywhere near Hub for over fifty years, though.

We trudged out the side door and followed Todd toward the flagpole at the edge of the playing fields, where we met before each meal for announcements. On the way out, I noticed that Beaker's blanket and sheets were still lying in the dirt. He'd apparently decided it was easier to just sleep without them.

We filed down the path, and I ended up walking next to Xane. "So, dude," he asked me, "what was it like?"

Xane was from a place called Taipei, which had submerged in the Rise. The People's Corporation of China had refused most of the refugees, so his parents had gotten him into Eden as a Cryo. I'd heard that when you were accepted as a Cryo, Eden got to choose which center you'd be placed in, based on space, so he ended up here instead of EdenEast. Xane's parents, and most of the Taiwanese, had emigrated to Coke-Sahel, which was formed when the Coca-Cola company merged with Walmart and then purchased twelve West African countries. Even now, they were constantly advertising out at Hub for new employee-citizens.

"What," I replied, "drowning?" I tried to remember. "It hurt, until I blacked out."

"No, not that." Xane turned and slapped me on the shoulder. "Getting mouth-to-mouth from Lilly. That's what I'm talking aBOUT." Xane always did that, making the second half of a word really loud.

"Oh." This was a chance, I guessed, to earn some points. I could talk it up, and everyone in my cabin would think it was awesome. They were all trying to flirt with the oldest girls' cabin, the Arctic Foxes, but nobody was getting anywhere, and here I was, having had actual lip contact, though not for the right reasons. But apparently it counted. Still, the thought of talking about that, of bragging about it or whatever, just made me want to be silent instead.

Luckily, I could answer Xane's question with the truth: "All I remember is waking up and throwing up."

"Wow," Xane sighed. "That's sad. A girl sucked your face and you don't even reMEMber."

Noah heard this and turned around. "I would totally drown to get mouth-to-mouth from Lilly. She's HiRad for sure."

"Easy, too," added Leech. "She gets down with all the CIT guys is what I hear."

"Duude," said Xane softly, like he was imagining this. "Owen, man, you must have gotten some swEET views when she was all bending over you saving your life and all that." He started sliding his hands up and down through the air, drawing idealized girl shapes.

"Look, I drowned," I snapped. "It wasn't a turn-on, so forget it." The truth was obviously different: not that drowning was a turn-on, but that Lilly was, and that I'd definitely had all kinds of thoughts like that, though the part about her and other CITs was hard to hear, and it just reminded me once again that someone like me was not going to have a shot with someone like her.

Leech's freckled face squinted at me. He shook his head slowly. "What a waste."

We got to flagpole and sat on a long bench made from

half a tree trunk. We were in the last row. Behind us, a short hill rose to the tall glass windows of the dining hall. All the campers were there, except the CITs, who didn't have to do kids' stuff like this. The activities coordinator, a lady named Claudia who wore a camp sweatshirt over her wide body and khaki shorts that showed off her purple-coated knees, welcomed us and then said good morning to each cabin. When she said it, each cabin had to say some kind of cheer. The littlest kids took it really seriously, but then the effort faded with age, with a huge drop-off when it finally got to us.

"And good morning, Spotted Hyenas!"

Groans and sighs. We couldn't have hated this more. Todd's idea for a cheer had been "Sssssneak attack!" because today we were playing capture the flag. It trickled out of our mouths in a sad mumble.

"Okay," said Claudia with obvious disappointment. "And goood morning, Arctic Foxes!"

"Balance!" half the Foxes shouted in eerie female unison.

"Support!" called the other half.

"Strength!"

"In numbers!"

The girls, despite being oldest like us, seemed to take some sick pleasure in being super coordinated and enthusiastic about these kinds of things. They also always seemed to look great for flagpole, like they'd been up for hours, while us boys had our hair pointing every which way. They all cheered and clapped to themselves when their routine was over, and all the boys around me had their heads hanging sideways watching.

"They're going to the ropes course today," Beaker said quietly from beside me. I hadn't even realized he was there.

Claudia started making announcements about the day. "I've checked in with Aaron up in the Eagle Eye and he reports that midday Rad levels will be slightly elevated, so everyone follow the two-hour application cycle."

Out of the corner of my eye, I noticed Leech rubbing his hands all over his chest, like he was putting NoRad on girl parts, and making ecstatic faces while doing it. Mike and Jalen and Noah were cracking up.

The show was mostly for the Arctic Foxes' ringleader, Paige, who was smile-glaring at Leech from across the aisle. She flipped her sandy blond hair like we'd already seen her do a hundred times in two days, and then made a big show of whispering something to her friends that made them all laugh hysterically. Then it was Leech's turn to do the glare-smile thing.

Paige and Leech had apparently been going out last session, and now, even though there had only been one day off between sessions, it was suddenly this big will-they-or-won't-they-date-again thing for reasons that nobody really knew, and you had to wonder if the two of them were just doing it to keep all the attention on themselves.

I saw other Arctic Foxes looking at our cabin and whispering, sizing us up. I figured the kid with the clumpy white bandages around his neck probably wasn't going to interest them.

When announcements were over, one of the little girls' cabins, the Lemurs, did a skit about something to do with always remembering to wear your NoRad lotion, and we were released to breakfast. Everybody walked up the gravel path to the dining hall in a mass. Leech and his gang mingled with the Arctic Foxes, and there was lots of pulling sweatshirt hoods over each other's heads, and then when we got into the dining hall there were lots of whispers across the aisle between Leech's end of the table and Paige's. I was at the other end, and noticed that there was a similar quiet end at the Foxes' table, too.

There was bread and margarine waiting on the tables, along with metal pitchers of bug juice. Today it was bright yellow and was supposed to taste like something called a pineapple. There were jokes about how it looked like pee, about how Beaker was drinking pee. Tables got called by age, youngest to oldest, so we had to watch tray after tray of millet pancakes and scrambled synth eggs go by. The food at each meal was still good, and there was plenty of it, but since that first night, there had been no sign of real wheat, or delicate leaves of spinach.

Now a piece of bread smacked against the side of Leech's head. "Oh no!" he said, looking over at Paige, who was glaring wickedly, like she was auditioning for the part of "bad girl" in a school play. Leech scanned the table, grabbed a square of margarine, pressed it onto the tip of a knife, then flicked it back at her. She ducked and it hit a poor girl named Sonja, who you could tell had a life in her cabin like Beaker had in ours. The margarine bounced off her cheek and fell down the front of her shirt and she started grabbing at herself, and all the girls cracked up and the boys went nuts.

"Knock it off, Carey," said Todd, using Leech's real name.

"That's bloodsucker to you, mammal!" Leech shot back.

Todd leaned forward, slapping both hands on the table. "Watch it, kid, or you'll be missing electives today."

Leech glared back at him, smile unflinching. "I think Paul would say that was unfair," he said, like because he'd been here so long, he and the director were best friends.

"Not if I explain your behavior." Todd's eyes narrowed; his jaw set.

"Try it," said Leech.

Todd kept staring at him . . . then looked away. "Food time," he said, and everybody at the table knew who had just won.

We headed across the busy dining hall. I was glad to get away from all that table stuff, but also for the chance to walk by the CIT area. They owned one whole end of the dining hall. They had a normal dining table, but then also couches along the walls, and a Ping-Pong table. The CITs were all there, spread out over the surfaces like someone had tossed them carelessly, and yet placed them perfectly, legs in sweatpants hanging this way and that, heads covered by sweatshirt hoods or backward mesh baseball caps. They leaned on each other's shoulders, their toes painted, their ankles and wrists wrapped in woven bracelets. They were like a portrait of perfection, like the ideal of youth that you'd see in holotech environments, who had that plastic feel and smiled at you and talked to you about the products they were wearing. Except the CITs weren't smiling, and they were more real, unnerving, almost dangerous feeling. You could imagine them never even having to speak, lounging there, communicating in glances and scents like the Turkish lions that roamed the deserts of France and Germany.

And yet one pair of those silent eyes was looking at me, sky-blue irises peering through green-streaked bangs. She was sideways on the couch, legs draped over the armrest, her head against the fortress shoulder of Evan, who was reading a video sheet. CITs didn't have to go the whole "no technology" route, like the rest of us.

Lilly's gaze made me freeze, and then almost trip, and I looked away quick, hating that she was seeing me with these ridiculous bandages on my neck, but then I glanced back, and she was still looking at me, and she nodded, or at least I thought she did. I wondered if I should nod back, or do nothing, like I was playing it cool, or—

"Lil!" someone called from the Ping-Pong table, and she looked away.

I hurried into the kitchen. On my way back with my food, I caught a glimpse of her playing in a doubles game. She was wearing someone else's purple-and-white mesh cap, maybe Evan's, her sweatshirt sleeves pushed up, her gaze across the table intense. She didn't look at me, and I told myself not to stare.

Breakfast dragged on, and as we were finally getting up to leave, Todd said, "Owen, you're supposed to go see Dr. Maria?"

"Oh, yeah."

"Meet us down on the fields when you're done."

I headed out of the dining hall and across a dirt road toward the infirmary. I didn't mind the idea of seeing Dr. Maria. She'd seemed nice. And I wondered again whether or not I should tell her more about what was going on with me. Maybe she should know about last night with the wounds and the shower. She was a doctor, after all. And yet, going to the infirmary also meant the possibility of running into Paul. That was something I definitely wanted to avoid.

"Hey! Owen!" I turned and saw Lilly pulling away from a little cluster of CITs, including Evan. "Just a sec," she said to them, and hurried over to me. "Hey, I've been thinking about you."

She had? When? Where? What about? Wait, she was still talking—

"How are you feeling?" Lilly was asking.

"Oh," I said quickly, "you know, better. Fine."

She nodded. "Cool, and what about your neck?"

"Oh, that," I said, flapping a hand against my bandages like they were no big deal, except that movement made the wounds cry out and so then I tried not to wince. "Something must have gotten tangled around me on the bottom, or a parasite got me or something. Did you, um, see anything when you found me?"

"No." Lilly looked around, almost like she as checking to make sure no one was listening. "So, that's it?"

"It?" It sounded like she was expecting me to have more to report. There was the whole thing with the shower. "Well, actually—"

"Lil!" Evan called. He tapped at his wrist. "We gotta go!"

"Right," said Lilly. "Gotta get down to the docks. Okay, listen . . ." She touched my arm. I looked down at that happening. She had teal-green nail polish with little glitter stars. "We should talk," she said, starting to step away, "about your neck and stuff."

"My neck?"

"Yeah, can you find me during elective time today? I'll be guarding free swim."

"Sure, okay," I said.

"Cool." She smiled. "Hey, until then"—she nodded over my shoulder—"mum's the word with *them*, okay?"

I glanced back at the infirmary. "Oh, yeah. Right."

"And listen, if you get any strange urges," said Lilly, "just go with it."

Strange urges—what was she talking about? But I just nodded. "All right."

"Good." Lilly hurried back to her group. I looked down at my arm, where her fingers had been. I could almost feel little heat impressions there.

I turned and headed to the infirmary, thinking about what Lilly had just said. We were going to talk. She knew something about what had happened to me. It was already killing me not to know what.

Inside, I found the office door and Paul's both closed. I could hear a low, muffled voice in Paul's office, like he was speaking to someone. I hurried over to the open infirmary door.

As I walked in, I heard the strained sound of vomiting. I found Dr. Maria in one of the exam rooms, sitting on the bed beside a little Panda girl who was bent over a plastic basin, her face red. Strands of her black bangs had gotten stuck by the corner of her mouth. There was brown goo on her pink teddy bear T-shirt.

"It's okay, Colleen," said Dr. Maria gently.

"It hurts," Colleen whispered, her voice hoarse.

"I know. Just try to breathe and it will be over soon." She

rubbed the little girl's back, then glanced at the computer pad lying beside her. She looked worried.

"Hey, Dr. Maria," I said.

She looked up. "Oh, Owen, hi. How are you—"

Colleen lurched over and barfed again, the liquid splattering into the basin. She coughed a little, then looked up, staring off into space. Vomit dripped from her nostrils.

"Is it over?" Dr. Maria asked gently.

Colleen exhaled hard and nodded. "I think so."

"Okay." Dr. Maria helped Colleen lie back on the bed.

Without really meaning to, I glanced into the basin, and looked away fast. But I'd seen that the vomit had red swirls of blood in it. I backed away and stayed by the door.

Dr. Maria pulled the covers over Colleen. She moved quickly over to the counter, and returned to Colleen holding a little gun-shaped tool with a needle at the end and a clear glass vial mounted on top. "I'm going to take a quick blood sample. Just look toward the window and you'll feel a slight sting."

Colleen turned away. Dr. Maria stuck the needle in her arm, and blood splashed into the vial. "Okay, that's it. Just rest for a bit, sweetie. I'll be back to check on you soon, okay?"

Colleen nodded, her eyes already drifting closed.

Dr. Maria put the syringe back on the counter, grabbed her pad, and tapped the glass a few times. She put that down and picked up the vomit basin. "Just a second, Owen." She hurried around the bed into the little bathroom. There was a sound of pouring and flushing.

"Now let's take a look at you." Dr. Maria smiled at me as she walked around the bed, but she also glanced worriedly back at Colleen.

We crossed the hall to another room.

"She seems pretty sick," I said. I'd been thinking about my incident the night before, throwing up some blood, too. Was something going around? Did Colleen have the same condition I did? But her neck had looked fine.

Dr. Maria sighed. "Yeah, the poor kid. Could be some minor food poisoning. I think she just needs to rest." But Dr. Maria sounded more worried than that.

I sat on the bed, and Dr. Maria snapped on new rubber gloves. She sat down on a rolling stool, untaped my bandages, and started unwrapping them. The attention caused fresh itching. "Things any better with your cabin today?" she asked. She was looking at me with a smile that felt genuine, like she cared.

"I guess," I said, thinking, *Not really.* But they hadn't gotten any worse.

She pulled off the last layer. The fabric stuck again and caused a fresh throb of pain. She threw out the bandages and returned with a small exam light. "And how are these doing?"

"Fine," I said. "They itch, but less today. They—" I paused, thinking of my talk with Lilly. It was almost like she knew something about these wounds. And even though Dr. Maria seemed like someone I could trust, too, I wanted to talk to Lilly first. "They just get kinda sore," I finished.

Dr. Maria leaned in and ran her finger gently over the wounds, but didn't try to separate them like I had. "Well," she said, squinting, "they are looking a little better." She rolled to the counter and got a little square towel that she used to wipe gently around the wound edges. "There's some blood here, but not as much. Do you remember any more about getting these?"

"I don't," I said, a truth, but I also felt the weight of the unspoken lie, about being under for ten minutes, and now I'd added to it by not telling her about the shower.

"You sure?" Dr. Maria asked, and I worried that she was onto me, but when I looked over she was just tapping on her pad, like her question was routine.

"Yeah."

"Okay, well, I'm going to put fresh bandages on your neck and then I'll just need a quick blood sample. Does that sound all right?"

"Sure," I said. "Is that to check for an infection or something?"

"Oh, the blood?" Dr. Maria was turning away as she said it, getting bandages from a drawer. "Yeah, we just want to, basically, just keep an eye on things."

"Okay."

Her answer sounded vague, almost like I was a little kid

who couldn't understand the details. And then I wondered, were there unspoken lies on her side, too? I thought about little Colleen. Maybe.

Dr. Maria gently put on the bandages, then rolled over to get a new vial and needle for her syringe gun. She clipped them on and took my hand. "Just push up your sleeve."

The needle stung, the blood leaped into the vial, and then it was over.

"Miss Maria?" It was little Colleen, calling weakly from across the hall.

Dr. Maria got up and put her supplies on the counter. "I should get back to her. See you tomorrow, same time?"

"Sure," I said.

She rushed out.

As I left, I heard Colleen wretching more, and I wondered again if our conditions were related. It would be Dr. Maria's job to notice that, wouldn't it? And she hadn't said anything. Except we'd both had the blood samples taken. And what were those for?

More questions. I had to get to electives and talk to Lilly.

5

ELECTIVES WERE RIGHT AFTER LUNCH. ONLY AS WE left the dining hall, Todd turned in the other direction. "It's time for a special tradition," he said.

"Oldest cabins get a tour of the Eagle Eye!" Leech finished for him, grinning big.

"This way," muttered Todd.

And so instead of me seeing Lilly, we met up with the Arctic Foxes in a paved area with a security checkpoint, by a set of large metal double doors where I'd entered the dome two nights ago. I followed along in the back, so annoyed that I'd missed my date, well, not *date*, but meeting time. My neck started to itch more, almost like it agreed.

Leech, Noah, and Jalen started joking around with the Foxes. I hung back by the edge of the group, away from where the girls and boys were mixing.

"Good afternoon, kids." We turned to see Paul approaching. He was wearing a black hat with the Eden corporate logo on it. Despite the shade that the brim cast over his face, his sunglasses were still on and as dark as ever. He didn't slow down as he neared us, and we parted to let him by. "Right this way," he said over his shoulder.

We followed him to a rectangular metal column, an elevator shaft stretching straight up until it was lost in the SafeSun glare. "Open," he said, and the doors slid apart.

We all crowded inside the metal box. Elbows and shoulders jostled, and I found myself against the back wall, right behind Paige and two other Arctic Foxes. The doors slid closed. There were narrow windows in them. I had to get on my toes to see out.

The elevator shot up, the force pressing me into the floor. I saw other kids wobble.

"This is quite the privilege," said Paul. "A look behind the curtain. It may feel like we are breaking the illusion here—some of you probably forgot you were even inside a dome—but knowing what really makes the insides of this living facility work is the true magic."

I felt like there hadn't been a single moment when I'd forgotten where I was. Maybe it was easier to accept Eden's illusion if you'd always been here.

We watched the tiny cluster of wooden camp buildings shrink, getting lost among the treetops. The lake spread out away from us, sparkling, and in the distance I caught a brief glimpse of shining towers and glass, the EdenWest city, but then we were up into the first misty layer of SimClouds. You could see them being spun by little jets on the dome wall. I tried to keep my gaze out the window, but sometimes I had to stare at the floor. I'd never been up nearly this high in anything.

The elevator came to a stop and there was a series of clicks. The car stayed vertical, but shook slightly and began ascending at an angle, following the curve of the wall. I stumbled a little and brushed against Paige's back. She turned around, her magenta-streaked ponytail flipping over her shoulder. She was chewing a thick piece of gum. It smelled like the Citrus Blast bug juice and combined with a soapy clean smell that always seemed to be around the Arctic Foxes. She was tall and glanced slightly downward at me.

"Sorry," I said immediately.

The two girls to her right were looking back at me, too. Pairs of eyes ringed by thick blue and lavender makeup.

Paige spoke in between chews. "It's all right." She squinted at me, almost like she was trying to figure out what I was. "What happened to your neck, anyway?" She kind of scowled when she said it, like my wounds were a bad fashion choice.

"It's from when I drowned," I said quietly, thinking that I shouldn't feel embarrassed but then feeling that way anyway.

She turned away. The three Foxes ducked together and conferred. The girl next to Paige, her black hair striped with glittery teal and held up in a swirl by two sticks, shot a glance back at me again with her thin, dark eyes.

More huddling, then they all cracked up. I looked around for a place to move, but we were packed tight.

The girls turned back around. Paige looked me up and down while talking to the others. "I don't know. . . ."

"What?" I asked.

"Mina thinks you have CP," said Paige, cocking her head at the girl beside her. Other Arctic Foxes cracked up now. She looked me over again. "I guess it's *possible*. . . ."

"Him?" Leech suddenly called from nearby. "That's the Turtle!"

Paige whipped around to him. "You are so mean!" she snapped, but with a smile, and she punched him in the shoulder and then she and Leech were the center of the universe again, and I was alone in my slice of space against the back wall, having no idea what Paige had meant.

"CP means 'Cute PoTENtial,'" said Xane from nearby.

"Oh," I said.

"Lucky," he added.

Knowing what that meant only made my nerves hum faster. I felt my face startingto burn. What did you do if you had CP? Were there ways you were supposed to act? Things you had to start saying? Was I now expected to work my way up to "real" cute? It felt like another thing I had no idea about and I wondered if I'd been better off when I thought I was invisible to the Arctic Foxes.

A blinding light speared through the windows, making us all squint. We were passing a bank of SafeSun lamps, ten enormous round bulbs. You could see the heat shimmering around them.

Above that, things got darker. The roof of the dome arced overhead, and now we could see the giant triangular panels and the crisscrossing girders. We were above the hazy atmosphere of the place. The ground was lost from sight. The light up here was pale and electric and almost reminded me of being back underground at Hub.

The elevator slowed and stopped. The doors slid open and we stepped out into a metal-floored room. To our right were clear doors. We had just filed out when a tiny tram arrived. We boarded, and the tram shot ahead. Out the front window, I could see the little track, suspended in a steel superstructure that hung down from the dome roof.

"EdenWest was completed in 2056," said Paul, extending his hand toward the window and sounding moderately bored. "It took fifteen years to build, a colossal effort, like we were the Egyptians building a pyramid. But, that's what happens when you get enough people who want to save themselves"—Paul said this with more interest—"and a board of directors with a *vision*."

"How big is the dome?" Noah asked.

"The base is six kilometers in diameter," said Paul. "It's home to two hundred thousand people, not including those currently enrolled in our Existential Services program."

I wondered what this was. Then I heard Leech explaining it to Noah: "When you're gonna die in Eden, you can opt to be frozen until we figure out how to cure diseases and live forever and stuff."

I thought about back at Hub, where everybody got cremated when they died. People either had their ashes donated to the struggling gardens, or scattered off the caldera rim by full moon.

I'd heard that in the Edens, and up north in the Habitable Zone, life expectancy was still in the nineties, if you were born there. Out at Hub, it was down near fifty-five, and that was higher than the worldwide average, which was closer to forty-five. Those numbers were partly because nobody could get advanced treatment for cancers, partly because of infant deaths due to malnourishment or the toxic plumes that hit the water supply now and then, but also because every ten years or so, one of the new resistant plagues would sweep through and shave off the old and young and weak. There were no Existential Services when the plagues came.

We sped past a series of hanging cranes moving a new triangular dome panel into place. "As you can see," Paul continued, his voice flattening out to a nearly sleep-inducing disinterest, "we are constantly upgrading the OzoneSim panels in response to atmospheric radiation levels."

I vaguely remembered my view from the lake bottom, of the roof panels having burn marks. All the panels around us up here looked spotless and white, free of damage. I wondered if what I'd seen had been some trick that the water had played on me. Or maybe they worked harder to keep this part of the dome looking good for visitors like us.

"My parents are worried about the dome integrity," said Sonja quietly.

"They make her wear one of those deflector helmets around town," added Paige, half laughing.

Sonja's face got red.

Paul shook his head, his tone like a weary teacher's. "All your parents need to do is follow our standard protocol based on the DI Index. There's no reason to worry."

The tram kept speeding forward, then finally slowed down.

Ahead was the round Eagle Eye observatory. It hung down below the dome roof like the bottom half of a ball. Two rings of windows looked out over the whole of EdenWest. An enormous spiky antenna array extended down from beneath, its end brushing the tops of the SimClouds.

The doors whooshed open and we all filed out into a short hallway. "This," said Paul, "is where we monitor every aspect of the Eden experience."

Another set of doors opened to a wide, round room. There were three ringed levels, getting smaller and stepping down toward the center. Each level had banks of computer screens. Workers busied from one monitor to the next. It made me think of how I pictured the technicians inside me. Like EdenWest was a giant organism itself.

Paul looked over the bustling room. One of the workers

stopped in front of us. She stood up straight and smiled big. "Oh, hello, Mr. Jacobsen, it's nice to—"

Paul talked over her like he hadn't even heard what she was saying. "Aaron Cane."

"Oh, sure, right. Um . . ." The worker turned and began scanning the room, hopping up on her toes.

"Here!" Aaron was standing among a group of workers, surveying a set of monitor screens. "Now, does everyone understand that *this* is the readout for the humidity controls and *this* is the meter for vapor control, not the other way around? I'd appreciate it if we had a long and happy life of me *not* having to remind you of that and you *not* screwing it up anymore. Got it?"

The workers around him mumbled in agreement.

"Good," Aaron said with a dramatic sigh. "Thank you." He stepped away from them and walked up the steps to us.

"Aaron, I told you the guests would be here now," said Paul. His tone was still ultra-calm, and yet there was maybe an annoyed edge to it.

"Right." Aaron looked at us, fixing his glasses and rubbing his hands through his short black hair before shoving them into his pockets. "How could I forget the lovely children? It's not as if I spend every waking minute of my day ensuring the operation of an entire living habitat." I could see us all flinching at this, hating being called children, and also thrown off by the sarcasm, as if Aaron couldn't have wanted less to do with us.

"Aaron," said Paul, like a parent lecturing a child, "please show the campers around."

"Right, okay." Aaron glanced about. "Let's see, what could your half-formed brains comprehend . . . ? Actually, probably not much less than my capable staff here." Aaron said this just as two workers were walking by, maybe for exactly that reason. I saw them scowl to themselves once they were past him.

"Follow me, lemmings," said Aaron. He led us down a set of steps and around the first ring of workstations.

I heard whispering and saw some Arctic Foxes pointing excitedly at the seated workers we were now passing. One was looking at a map of the entire complex, lit up with tiny green dots moving around. A close-up screen showed one of the mechanical butterflies. The woman typed in a command, then slid her finger on a touch pad, moving the creature around. Small windows displayed wobbly, curved views: what the butterflies were seeing. It made me wonder: were the butterflies a form of surveillance?

Beside her was a man doing the same with hummingbirds, then a woman who seemed to be configuring bat wake-up times. A falcon, a trio of deer. All fake. And all possibly keeping watch. With that many cameras, there wouldn't be much that could escape Eden's eye.

"Over here," Aaron was saying up ahead, "is where we're monitoring internal and external atmospheric conditions. You can see here, inside the dome it's a comfy twenty-four degrees Celsius, and outside, a french frying thirty-eight. Humidity in here, sixty-eight percent; out there, nine percent."

I was half listening, but the itching had started up in my neck again. I tapped my knuckles against the bandages.

"From here," Aaron continued, "we control all the weather in the dome. Want to see it rain?"

"Totally," said Leech.

This idea seemed to actually excite Aaron. "Okay." He tapped at the monitor and slid a few bars up and down. He looked up and gestured with his chin. "Look out that window to the right, everyone. . . ."

We did, and saw a dark gray cloud start to spin itself into existence off in the distance. It grew, up and out, and then a blur of rain began to appear beneath it.

"And there we go," said Aaron. "Just call me God."

"Can you do lightning?" asked Leech.

"How about making the moon come up?" asked Paige.

Aaron smiled. "Of course I can do all those things, even reverse the constellations, or make new ones—"

"And yet I think we wouldn't want to alarm the people far below," said Paul from behind us.

Aaron's face straightened back to normal. "Right." He moved his fingers, and the rain cloud began to feather apart and dissipate.

"You should show them this," Leech called, sounding like a know-it-all because of his previous visits. He had moved across the aisle and was pointing at another screen.

"Can you please"—Aaron rushed over and pushed Leech back from the consoles—"keep the greasy fingers off the equipment."

Leech stumbled back and I saw him look at Paul, like he was hoping Paul would say something in his defense, much like he'd bragged about so many times. But Paul was quiet. "Jeez, watch it," Leech mumbled, but it lacked his usual edge.

"Nothing broken or soiled," Aaron was saying, looking over the console. "Sure, I suppose everyone can see this."

We moved over and saw five camera views displayed. They showed panoramic views of the outside world, flicking from one angle to the next, always down the side of a dome. Labels beneath identified each Eden location.

"Wow, cool, a pyramid!" said Mike, pointing at the camera marked EdenEast. For a moment, we all saw the giant stone structure, perfectly pointed and immense, before the camera switched. Now, we could see a large statue like an animal sitting, though it was nowhere near the size of the pyramid.

"Guess we can't expect any of you to know that's the Great Pyramid at Giza," said Aaron. "And the Sphinx."

I actually knew what they were, but had no interest in telling Aaron that.

"What's that?" Xane was pointing at the view in the EdenCentre camera. Far below, on the burned brown plains, stood a series of tall stones in a circle.

"That would be Stonehenge," said Aaron.

"It's believed to be an ancient astronomical clock," added Paul.

"The other domes are near cooler stuff," said Jalen, like he was disappointed that EdenWest wasn't.

"Yes," said Paul, "my counterparts in the other Edens have much nicer things to look at." I thought about how Paul had said there were Viking ruins near here. I figured he'd mention that, but he didn't.

"What about this one?" Bunsen was pointing at the screen for EdenSouth. It was blank.

"Aaron," said Paul, "why don't you show them something else."

"What happened to EdenSouth?" Noah asked.

Leech punched him in the shoulder. "Shut up."

"Ow, okay, fine."

"Yes, let's go find something else to amuse you," said Aaron.

I had heard that EdenSouth was destroyed in an attack by the followers of Heliad-7. Nobody knew much about them. There were rumors that they were some kind of sun-worshipping cult modeled after ancient religions.

"How about this?" Beaker asked. He was looking at the next bank of monitors. I was near the back of the group and could see what he saw. It was a circular grid of triangular spaces. Most were colored green, many were yellow, and a few were red.

"That there, my young and curious friend . . . ," said Aaron, his teeth gritted as he darted over and slapped at the screen, making it go dark, "was not what I asked you to look at, was it?" He threw up his hands. "This is a workplace, not a nursery!"

"Sorry," Beaker mumbled.

A loud beeping sounded throughout the room.

"Mr. Cane," a young woman called from a nearby console. "We have another fail in arc segment fourteen."

Something boomed in the distance, and the entire Eye shuddered. Everyone stumbled, grabbing tables and railings for support. For a second I wondered if the Eye was going to drop free, and imagined us falling to our deaths, but the shaking subsided.

Another alarm began beeping. Aaron glanced at Paul. "You want to take them out?" he asked.

"They are old enough to know the true dangers that we face," said Paul, "and to see our response."

Aaron scowled. "Fine. Kill the alarms and bring it up!" he called.

A large video projection illuminated in the center of the room. We all saw the dome wall and a triangular panel that had caught fire. Black smoke billowed from it. Chunks were melting off and falling in little molten streaks.

"Okay, scramble air units," said Aaron, moving around us and tapping on a monitor. Screens flashed beneath his flying fingers.

"And now let's open the arc fourteen emergency vent."
A vibration shook the room again, and on the screen we saw a large, multipanel section of the dome slide completely open. The smoke immediately began to siphon out of it, up into the blinding real sky.

Meanwhile, two small helicopter-type vehicles were soaring toward the fire. They each had two short wings with propellers on the end. As they neared, the blades rotated to vertical, making the two-person craft hover. Streams of pink fire suppressant burst from their underbellies, coating the burning panel. The flames died out.

"Give me a heat reading on the surrounding panels," said Aaron.

"Stable," called out a nearby worker.

"Close vents," said Aaron. He stopped typing. "Deploy RadDefense to replace that tile." He turned and looked at us. "And that, children, is how it's done."

Leech and Paige and a few others burst into applause.

"Thank you, Aaron. We'll leave you to your work," said Paul. He motioned us toward the door. "Can everyone please thank Mr. Cane for his time?"

We all mumbled thanks and headed out. As we walked up the hall and onto the tram, I started scratching gently on my bandages. The heat had been growing inside throughout the visit.

"How are you feeling, Owen?"

I looked up to find Paul right beside me, looking down,

or at least, it seemed like he was. I wanted to step away but we were crowded in the hall. I tried to just be calm, normal.

"Oh," I said, lowering my hands. "You know, getting better."

"You've been on my mind since yesterday," he said. "Is your neck still giving you trouble?"

"Not really," I lied, hoping it sounded sincere. "No big deal."

"No side effects?" Paul asked.

"Nah," I replied. "Dr. Maria says they're healing right up."

"I see," said Paul.

We arrived back at the tram, and everyone filed in.

"Well," said Paul, "just remember: you know where to find me."

"Sure," I said, trying to sound like I thought that was a fine idea.

"Good." Paul patted my shoulder as I boarded. As I moved to a seat, I saw Leech watching me. He was looking around Paige, who was sitting on his lap. It was a weird look, like he was studying me, like he was trying to figure something out. I waited for the next wise comment, but it didn't come.

"I'll be staying behind," Paul said to the group. "Have a nice afternoon." He turned and walked briskly inside.

As we rode back to the elevator, I heard Bunsen saying to Beaker, "If panels keep going out like that, they won't be able to replace them fast enough."

"I know," said Beaker, "and did you see that map I found, and how many panels were red?"

Bunsen nodded. "I think the dome is screwed."

"Hey, Bunsen!" Leech shouted. "How many times do I have to tell you: shut the hole!"

"Quiet down," said Todd from the front of the tram. He sounded stern, sullen, like maybe he was thinking the same thing that Bunsen and Beaker were.

Soon, the flirting started back up again and led to all kinds of loud laughing and whispered jokes as we descended back to camp.

I thought about the panel fire. How often did that happen? What kind of danger was this place really in?

But my thoughts were drowned out by the burning in my neck. The sensation had been growing through this entire visit, and now I almost couldn't stand it. I felt like I wanted, needed, water again. I tucked my chin down and moved my head back and forth, making the collar of my pullover scratch against the bandages.

It helped, but it must have looked weird, because Noah said, "Hey, Turtle, what's with you?"

"Nothing," I muttered. I glanced at him but then looked away. The last thing I needed right now was to have to deal with anyone from Leech's pack. I leaned back against the tram window, hoping the itching would stop.

6

BUT IT DIDN'T. NOT ALL AFTERNOON, NOT AFTER dinner. By the time we got to bed that night, I was rubbing my knuckles against the bandages nonstop. I'd thought about trying to ditch dinner again, thinking maybe the shower would help, but I was still constantly hungry from having thrown up and missed eating the day before. I saw Lilly from a distance in the dining hall, but there was no chance to talk to her.

While my cabin spent the night playing games and tormenting each other, I was just lying in my bunk, burning up. Todd read more to us, and everyone eventually fell asleep, except me. Hours passed, and I kept thinking, *Come on,* but I was stuck awake, neck scalding.

I don't know what time it was when I finally sat up. I gazed around at the sleeping faces in the cabin. Everyone looked younger, their brows round instead of sharp, their closed eyes making straight lines. Leech's mouth made a little *o* as he snored. From the other room, I could hear

Todd sawing away. There was a chorus of breathing, ins and outs, a peaceful, musical sound compared to the steady whir of the air compressor in my dad's nebulizer.

It wasn't soothing me, though. The burning was worse than ever. I couldn't stand it anymore. And I had a feeling, a certainty, that there was something I needed to do.

I got up and slowly climbed down my ladder, slipped off my sweatpants, and put on my bathing suit. I had that weird feeling again, like with the shower, of just doing things, and not really knowing why. All that mattered was stopping the pain.

You're doing great. The new technician was back again.

I slipped on my sneakers and pushed open the side door. It squeaked, but no one stirred. I slid out onto the steps and slowly let the door close. It locked from the inside, a fact that Todd had pointed out to us for precisely this reason.

"Try to sneak out, and the only way you're getting back in is through the front door," he'd said. "And I'm a light sleeper." His rumbling snores seemed to refute that.

I headed down the dark, winding path through the trees, shivering. The night air had been cooled to fifteen. Above, an owl called.

I crossed the fields. The grass was bathed in MoonGlow. The moon itself was halfway up the wall, being projected at three-quarters full, and the stars were sprayed across the ceiling, a faint river of Milky Way meandering between them.

Cold wet seeped through my sneakers from the dew, and there was a strange smell, kind of like flowers but tangy. I looked down and saw tiny rectangular segments clumping on my sneakers. Cut grass. I'd never seen it before. My feet made swishing sounds in the chopped plants.

Neck burning, I kept moving. Ahead was the beach. The lake sparkled with little diamonds. The sand caked over the layer of grass already coating my shoes.

Why am I here? I wondered.

Just relax, we need to do this, said the new technician. And I felt like, yes, we did. Had to stop the searing, all-consuming itching on my neck, and there was only one way. I felt a pure certainty about this—kind of like before with the shower—one that was growing with every minute of agony and every step I took.

I reached the edge of the lapping water. MoonGlow reflected on the surface, blackness beneath. The dock's rusty hinges creaked. Little plunks echoed as water sloshed in the shadows between its Styrofoam floats.

I kicked off my shoes, thinking at the same time, *I just drowned here*, but then my toes touched the water's edge and though I felt little aching spikes from the cold, I also felt a sudden rush of calm. Water around my ankles in little icy shackles. Even more relief. I pulled off my T-shirt and tossed it back onto the sand, walked out until the water reached my knees. My muscles twitched, cramps quivering in the arches of my feet, my arms and chest sprouting goose bumps. But at the same time, tiny soothing shocks seemed to be reaching my wounds. The pain ebbed further. It was the shower all over again. Water erasing my pain. I looked up to the sky in relief and took a deep breath—

But it didn't work. The breath passed over my teeth, my tongue, and then stopped in my throat, like it had run into a wall. My chest locked up, nothing getting in. I could hear myself making gagging sounds.

And something felt different about my wounds. They felt open, strange, almost like they were moving. I clawed at the bandages, tearing them away. My fingers scraped my neck and I felt the flaps of skin quivering, like my wounds were creatures coming to life.

Breathe! It was happening again. I was sinking back inside myself, dark corners, drowning . . . only this time, it was happening in the air. My chest ached. White spots appeared in my eyes. I staggered and my body threw itself over, like it was acting on its own now. I crashed into the water face-first, sinking beneath the surface, water pouring into my mouth once more—

Suddenly I could breathe again. The feeling of panic instantly began to fade.

It made no sense.

It made sense.

I opened my eyes to see the swirling grit of the sandy bottom. Cool air slid across my back. I was doing a dead man's float in the foot-deep water. My lungs were still;

the constant rise and fall of my diaphragm, present all my life except for ten minutes the day before, had ceased; and yet . . .

This time it was fine.

Everything was fine. Because something new was moving.

My mouth was open, my tongue pushing around against a stream of water pouring in, but not reaching my lungs. My cheeks were expanding and contracting, creating the flow. I could feel the water passing into my throat, then pouring out of me in currents, causing movement on the sides of my neck. Fluttering, like the light waving of fingers. I felt there, felt the wounds. . . .

That weren't wounds at all. They were—

Gills.

Yep, new systems online, the new technician reported proudly. He turned and started shaking hands with everyone in the room. *Thanks for your patience.*

There were a million questions, all starting with, *How.* I had no answers, and yet I didn't feel worried. And even stranger, just like last night in the shower, or even yesterday on the beach, this didn't seem surprising at all. It was almost like this was how things were *supposed* to be, like my body had some plan that it was taking care of, without bothering to tell me. But it felt right, and so I followed a new urge:

Swim.

I kicked, moving away from shore. When I reached the dock, I dove under, slipping into the cooler, deeper layer. I checked for pain in my side, from the weak wall, but there was no tension there, no cramp. Without the strain of breathing, of holding air in my lungs, my whole middle was calm, working like . . . maybe like it was always meant to. That was how it felt. But what did that mean? All I knew was that this seemed right.

Under the lane lines now, I was picking up speed. Waving my arms laterally, kicking up and down, I rolled, looking up at the shimmer of the projected moon. Spinning back, I plunged into the icy depths. Felt pain in my ears, the hollow cavities there, strange human things. I couldn't see very well—my eyes were still the same normal, made-for-air kind—so I arced back up into the warmer layer. It took effort. There was no more giant held-breath balloon pulling me toward the surface. I was a weak creature of air no longer.

I curled back toward the docks. Swimming was so *easy* like this, easier than running, than walking. Nothing had ever felt this obvious. I had a growing feeling like *this* was my world, my domain. *Interlopers beware, or I will drag you under.*

I don't know how much time passed, me looping and darting about in the dark depths, learning how to press against the fluid reality around me. I found faster ways to kick and spin, the best angles to knife up and down, learned water pressures like breezes, thermal layers like rooms in a new home. . . .

Until sharp cracks of sound echoed from above. Groups of concussions. Footsteps on the dock. Then a crash. Something sliced into the water to my right, a trail of bubbles streaming behind it. I saw a long, male body, stabbing deep then sliding up toward the surface. More cracks, and a second breach of my subsurface world. Another male, in a cannonball tuck. Now a third diver, a girl. And another. Each pale body thrust into the depths, but didn't bob up to the surface like some air-breather. They arced and spiraled, then shot off away from the dock, disappearing in the gloom. The last girl took the longest, doing extra somersaults in the underwater free gravity, like she was enjoying it as much as I did, before kicking away.

I watched until they were swallowed by the black, then slipped after them. They were swimming beneath the surface, so I stayed deeper, just below the weak reach of the MoonGlow. As I followed them, I wondered, were they like me? Could they be? How was that possible?

A round, bloated form came into view up on the surface. The bottom of the big trampoline raft. The bodies arced up to it and dragged themselves out. Skin whined against rubber.

I darted away and slowly ascended, peeking out, only my eyes and ears above the surface, gills working safely underwater. I could see the back and shoulders of one of the girls, lounging at the edge of the giant doughnut-shaped balloon. White straps crisscrossed her back. Her hair was long and silver-edged in the moonlight. I couldn't see the second girl.

The two boys were bounding high into the air off the mesh membrane that stretched across the raft's center. One was Evan, obvious by the hourglass top of his shoulders. "Marco! You first!" he said.

The other boy, Marco, launched high, curling into a double somersault before diving into the water.

"Nice," said the girl.

"I got this," said Evan. He bounced and sprang even higher, twisting into a pike, then straightening and grabbing his knee just before he hit the water, bombing Marco's vicinity with a huge splash that mushroomed upward. The waves sloshed against the raft and calmed, but there was no sign of the two boys. Then, they burst from the water, shooting straight up into the air and landing feet-first on the raft.

"So much nicer without the minions around," said Evan, gazing over at the silent dock and empty beach.

I smiled to myself. If only they knew I was here. And I even wondered: maybe I could scare them or—

Something locked around my ankle and yanked me under.

What? I thrashed as the MoonGlow faded away and I was pulled into the frigid dark. The grip was powerful—

Then gone. I looked around wildly. A form appeared right in front of me.

'Boo!'

Tentacles waved, eyes flashed, and I thought of that siren from when I drowned the first time, but then I saw what it was that had attacked me.

'Hey, Owen!' It was Lilly, hovering in the water before me, smiling.

'Hey!' I said back.

'Check it out.' Her fingers wrapped around my wrist and she guided my hand to her neck, above the thin strap of her teal bathing suit top, past the smooth tension of her neck muscles, to where I felt the fluttering.

She had gills, too.

And we were talking underwater. 'How are you doing that?' I asked.

'What?' Her mouth barely moved as she spoke. But I heard it. Or sensed it.

'Talking to me.'

Lilly smiled again. 'Just am. Same way you are.'

As she said it, I noticed that I was hearing something, like clicks or chirps. It was hard to tell in the water. But also, it was almost like I was smelling the words, too, or something.

'Looks like you had those urges,' she said with a smile. Now I noticed that maybe her skin was changing as she spoke too, the color flickering slightly. That was part of it, this fish communication, or whatever we were doing. And like breathing with gills, it was something we just knew how to do without thinking.

All part of the new systems, said the new technician.

'Yeah,' I agreed. So, *this* was what she'd meant by "urges." 'But—'

'Ssshh.' Lilly reached out and touched my lips with her finger.

'Okay,' I said.

'Come on.' She turned to swim off. 'They're going to wonder where I went.' She thrust toward the raft.

'I can't—'

'Of course you can.'

For the first time since I'd entered the water, I felt like my old self, surface Owen, the air breather, the Turtle. I couldn't hang out on a raft with the CITs. But Lilly was leaving. . . .

Just go with it, she'd said this afternoon. I kicked after her.

She reached the raft, and before she broke the surface, she turned back to me. 'When you pull out of the water, push up with your stomach. There's a little air left in your lungs. It will open your epiglottis, and you'll breathe fine.'

'But before, on the beach, I couldn't—'

'Come on. Trust me.' Before I could protest further, she lunged, grabbed the yellow ropes that crisscrossed the side of the blue-and-white raft, and hauled herself up.

I followed. As soon as my head and shoulders were above water, I felt the tightening need for air, my gills fluttering uselessly. I did as Lilly said, pushing inward and up, flexing muscles I barely knew I had. A small gasp of air leaped free, and my lungs kicked back to life, inflating in a huge suck. I felt a wave of nausea, but then it passed.

I checked my neck. My gills were gone. No, not gone, they were still there, but they felt like slits in the skin, and they were getting tighter, smaller, the openings puckering closed. Hidden. Only a slight itching remained. I ran my fingers over the indentations: no more blood.

"NoRad lotion makes the lines invisible," said Lilly, kneeling above me. "Need a hand?"

"Nah," I said, "I got it." I yanked on the side ropes, kicking my feet in the water and struggling to get up onto the smooth rubber, feeling too much like a turtle climbing onto a log. Seconds felt like hours 'cause I couldn't be this pathetic in front of them all . . . but finally I dragged myself up onto my stomach and hopped to my feet.

"Look what I found," Lilly announced.

The CITs peered at me.

"Who's that?" Marco asked. He was shaking water from his shaggy black hair. His shoulders didn't rival Evan's, but they dwarfed mine.

"Owen, from the Hyenas," said Lilly.

"What are you doing here?" Evan asked me. It looked like he was scowling.

"He's one of us," said Lilly.

"One of us?" said the other girl. "He's only been here, like, a minute."

Lilly gathered her hair and squeezed water from it. "Yeah, well, duh, Aliah. He's got 'em." She tapped at her neck.

"That kid?" asked Aliah skeptically. She was smacking on a piece of gum, her face a fine art piece with dark flicking lashes, a little silver nose stud, and tiny eyebrow ring all accenting smooth brown skin. She looked me over. I figured I knew the verdict. But then she just shrugged and said, "Okay."

"Wow," Marco added. He was studying me like I was something foreign, but interesting, at least for the moment.

"You lied yesterday, didn't you?" asked Evan, peering at Lilly. "You told the doctor he was only down on the bottom for, like, three minutes."

Lilly started bouncing in the center of the trampoline. "Yep. It was eleven, actually," she said with a smile. She glanced back at me and added, "But I had my eye on him."

I felt a little surge at hearing that, *She had her eye on me* . . . but tried not to give away that I was thinking about it. I had to seem cool, collected.

Lilly meanwhile shot up into the air, her body long, painted silver by the MoonGlow, then twisted and knifed cleanly into the water.

I was still standing unevenly by the edge of the raft. "You guys all have . . ."

"The gills." Aliah made a motion toward her neck, fluttering her fingers playfully. "Cool, huh? We're a new race."

Marco was still peering at me, an eyebrow wrinkled. "But none of us got them until our second or third *year* here. How did you get them in, like, two days?"

"I don't know," I said. "But what . . . I mean, why—"

Lilly shot out of the water behind me, landing on the raft and making it buck. I staggered, but managed not to fall. "Relax, Owen," she said, and threw a wet arm around me. I felt her skin against my shoulder, the hairs of her forearm briefly against my ear. I tried to stay still, to play it cool. I glanced at Evan. He was watching this. Lilly went on, "We'll explain everything."

"Everything we *know*, anyway," said Aliah.

"Right," said Lilly. "But here's all you need to know tonight. Number one, you're going to be fine."

The trampoline rocked, causing Lilly's hip to lean against mine. Fine . . . right.

"Now that the gills have set, you can use both them and your lungs without a problem," Marco added.

"Okay," I said.

"Number two," said Lilly, "you've got gills because of *this place*." She swept her hand to indicate the lake, the dome.

I wanted to stay quiet, to just be cool with everything, but questions popped out anyway. "What does that mean?"

"Like we even know," muttered Aliah.

"We do know a little," Lilly snapped. "There's something about this place that's caused this reaction in us. Caused us to change, but we don't know what. And number three, you can't tell any of *them* what's happened to you."

"Who, you mean, like, the adults?"

"Especially Paul," said Marco.

As Marco was saying this, Evan got up and started bouncing. He flipped into the air and dove into the black with barely a splash.

"But he knows about my wounds," I admitted.

"Yeah," said Lilly, "he knew we had the wounds too, when they started a couple years ago. There were five of us who got them first. The other was Anna. Her gills set the fastest, and when she showed them to Paul and Dr. Maria, they started doing all these tests on her—"

"Tests that made her sick," added Aliah, sounding bitter, "but the more sick she got, the more tests they wanted to do. They said it was to make her better, but she said it was like Paul was looking for something, trying to figure something out, but he wouldn't tell her what. . . ."

"And then she was gone," Lilly finished.

"What do you mean, gone?" I asked.

"Like one day she just didn't come back to our cabin, and Paul told us that her condition had gotten worse and she'd been sent to the hospital over in the city for advanced care. And we haven't seen her since."

"Can't you ask someone to find out?" I asked. "Like, your parents or something?"

"Ha, parents," said Marco.

"What?" I asked.

Lilly's face softened, like her eyes had increased a size. "None of us have parents. We're all Cryos," she said. "Aren't you?"

"No," I said. "I'm from Yellowstone Hub. I live with my dad."

"He's the first non-Cryo to have the symptoms," Aliah said, looking seriously at the others.

"That we know of," said Evan.

"Anyway," said Lilly, "there's nobody we can ask about Anna. I mean, we tried, but Eden runs Cryo House, just like they run camp. Just like they run the whole city."

"Mama and Papa EdenCorp," added Aliah.

"We've asked people about Anna: our house guardians, hospital directors. Nobody ever knows anything," said Lilly. "Bastards," she muttered to herself. "She was my best friend."

I felt a little tremor of nerves inside me. "So, are you guys being tested, too?"

"Nah," said Aliah. "We never told Paul anything, but as long as we stay like this, he seems to just leave us alone."

"But he's always got his eye on us," said Lilly. "We think he knows."

I thought about the surveillance insects, and the bats,

and checked the sky above. "Probably," I said.

"Which means he'll have his eye on you, too," said Aliah.

"Okay, but how did this even happen?" I asked.

The CITs glanced at one another.

"That," said Lilly, "is the big question. But don't worry, O. The point is: just stick with us, and we'll keep your secret."

What we were talking about was crazy and serious, but at the same time, I had just heard Lilly shorten my name. I tried to keep my expression calm, like the opposite of how that made me feel.

"Cool?" She looked at me expectantly.

I glanced around at the CITs and realized that maybe I had just been invited to join their club, their secret gill-breathing, raft-swimming society.

"Yeah," I said, and I tried to return Lilly's gaze like I had at the dock, saying that yes, I could do this. Only this time, I maybe believed that I could.

"Good." She smiled.

"Can we stop with all the serious talk now, please?" said Marco. "Dawn is going to turn on in, like, two hours."

"Right." Lilly turned to Evan and Marco. "Boys, let's give our newest member a slingshot."

"All right." Evan didn't sound thrilled, but he stepped beside me, towering over me and smelling of some better form of sweat. Then he grabbed me under the arms. "Hang on." He sprang and hurled me straight up into the air.

I tensed, hoping I could keep my feet beneath me when I landed. Below, the other four fish dashed to the corners of the trampoline. "Ready!" Lilly called.

I hurtled down, and the moment I squished into the trampoline center, they all stomped down too. I sank deep, then shot up into the night.

"Nice!" shouted Marco.

I arced through space, losing my balance, cocking sideways. As I plummeted toward the black water, I tried to straighten myself, but I slammed into it in a chin-first belly flop. I dunked deep underwater, my chest compressing, and hung there, for a moment not knowing which way was up or down. My face throbbed. So did my stomach. Then, without even really thinking about it, I made a gulping motion that sealed my throat, and my gills fluttered to life. I sucked in water and relaxed.

A hand closed around my wrist. I looked over, and there was Lilly, cast in moonlight and blue, hair snaking around her, a siren calling to me: 'Come on.'

She pulled me deeper, toward the cold depths. I heard tinny splashes, and soon the other CITs were around me, and we were plunging into the dark.

As we descended into the abyss, I glanced from one outlined figure to the next and wondered how this had happened. Sure, there had been each moment—I remembered those—but it seemed like there had to be something more at work, like a plan or even a God, that had orchestrated this: me, Owen, suddenly something new, a creature of the deep, of mysteries. And I felt like I wanted to be down here forever, in Lilly's grasp, with these others who I almost dared to think of as my own.

PART II

[*GAMMALINK CONNECTION LOADING . . . 100%*—welcome back to the Alliance Free SignalCast—*buffering*—you want to know what EdenCorp is really up to, just look at the locations of the domes. They claimed that their placement was based on climate stability, but the proximity to ancient sites can't be a coincidence. Then there's the secretive EdenNorth complex. No one can confirm its location, but our sources say it's on the coast of Greenland, and is rumored to be some kind of modern-day Area 51. It was the first one they built. So you have to ask yourself: What is Eden hiding up there? And does it connect to what we've heard coming out of Desenna, the former EdenSouth? Rumors of some kind of awakening, or calling, that's only happening to certain rare people? They believe that it's the Gods returning, but what if it's something else? Something ancient, like—*connection fail*]

7

THE MOON PROJECTION SET OVER THE BLACK OUTLINE of the hills to the west, fading into the faint amber glow from the city. Camp Eden was located on a secluded inlet, hills to three sides and Mount Aasgard to the fourth. That distant hazy brightness was the only thing that indicated there was a city in here.

As purple lights imitated predawn on the eastern curve of the dome, we emerged from the water, wading to shore like some kind of invading monster army.

Walking alongside the CITs, I considered that we looked like one of those groups, the kind I always saw from the outside, that seemed so exclusive, such a natural part of the universe, and you wondered how things like that formed, and why they didn't happen to you, and you wanted, just once, to be in one, and to *know* what that secret, sacred thing was that created such an impenetrable unit. Apparently, gills could do it.

I felt the disappointing grit of sand, the pressure of solid ground beneath my feet. Back on land. Dragged down by that persistent tugging of gravity, eliminating possibility, turning me from shark back to turtle. I felt my gills sealing up, tucking themselves away until . . . when? Could this happen again? Tonight? I was already hoping, but would they really want me back?

Distantly, the blowers cycled to life to warm the air. SimClouds began to form along the dome edges. Humidifiers created a hazy effect. I found that my body was staying damp, the moisture not just evaporating right off, like it would have back home in the dryness.

The CITs had thoughtfully brought towels.

"Here," said Lilly, handing me hers after my attempts to use my damp T-shirt only left me with sand streaks on my chest. Her lime-green towel smelled salty from sweat, and there was that strange metallic tinge of NoRad, and it was maybe a little dank too, from lots of uses between washes.

"Thanks."

Birds had begun to chirp and dart around. Off to the north of the beach, a raptor of some kind was circling over the Preserve, a section of forest set apart by nets that reached all the way to the roof. I wondered if the bird was real or a robot.

"Time for bed," said Aliah, starting up the beach. The CIT cabins were straight ahead, in the trees between here and the dining hall.

A clock hanging on the snack shack showed the time was four forty-five. Just over three hours until wake-up. I could already feel that I was going to be exhausted all day.

"See you later, Owen," said Marco.

"Yeah," I said, "Bye, guys." I picked up my sneakers and headed to the right.

There was mumbling behind me, then, "Owen, wait up."

I turned to see Lilly jogging after me, towel around her waist, her damp hair now chaotic. She walked beside me, brushing at the dark tangles with her hand. I could see the faint lines of her hidden gills, like little pencil streaks.

"How are you doing?" she asked.

"Fine, I think."

We left the beach and crossed the grass. The sprinklers were on, so we walked in S curves to avoid the spinning tentacles of spray. "Oooh, water, watch out," I said, trying to be funny. Then I flinched inside because what if Lilly didn't think I was?

But she chuckled. "I know, right?" Then she was quiet.

The sky began to hint at blue. Color was seeping into the trees. A first ray of orange SafeSun lit the top of the flagpole to our left. We would be right back here, in a few hours, just like any other camp day. "It's a lot to absorb," Lilly said quietly.

"I guess," I said. I figured she was right but I wasn't really feeling that way. The gill stuff already felt normal, a part of me like my arms or feet. Okay, maybe not that familiar. But still, it wasn't really on my mind, at least not as much as the fact that here I was, walking beside Lilly. Just a day ago she had seemed so mysterious, a member of another race of beings—which, it turned out, she was. But now so was I.

"Listen, Owen," Lilly began, but she paused, two seconds that I spent wondering if she might say something about us, about me. About this connection we seemed to have now . . . but instead she said, "I just wanted to say I'm sorry for, you know, you drowning."

"Oh." I didn't feel like she needed to be. "That's cool. I mean, you said you had your eye on me."

"But I didn't," Lilly admitted. "Not at first." She stopped, turning to me, but with her eyes focusing somewhere beyond my shoulder. "The truth is, I didn't know you were gone. Not until the test was over. Everybody was back on the dock, and one of your cabin mates asked about you. That kid Beaker, I think. Then I started looking, and dove down and found you, and *that's* when I saw your neck, and knew you'd be fine. But, before then . . ." She shrugged.

"So, you lied back there," I said, "on the raft."

"I just didn't want them to know I'd screwed up."

I didn't know what to make of that. It was maybe a little disappointing. Lilly hadn't had her eye on me, hadn't even noticed me really, until someone else did. So, was this pity? Was she just hanging out with me because she felt guilty about almost letting me die? "Why are you telling me this?" I asked.

"I don't know," she said. "I wanted you to know the truth, I guess."

I thought about that. I wasn't sure if it changed anything. "You still saved my life."

"No, you saved your own life. I made a show of it, when I brought you to the surface, but that was just to help keep your gills a secret."

"Well, but if you hadn't said that stuff to me, I probably would have gone and told Paul and Dr. Maria everything."

"Yeah, I guess I did that part right." Lilly stopped walking. "I should get back."

"Um," I said, like I was going to say something else, but I couldn't think of what.

"I'll see you at breakfast," Lilly said. She reached out and rubbed my forearm. "Thanks for coming swimming. You'll come back tonight, right?"

"Um, sure. Yeah." I nodded and smiled but tried not to do either too much while inside I was thinking, *Yes!*

"Good." She smiled at me and turned, crossing the field. SafeSun warmed her tangled hair and her shoulder blade, sparkled on her toe rings.

I watched her go for a second and then headed into the trees. The wood-chip path poked at my bare feet. Other than in our apartment, I couldn't remember a time when I'd ever been barefoot back home. I thought about slipping my sneakers on now, but didn't. I walked on my toes, enjoying the pine needles clumping between them. I passed sleeping cabins that vibrated with chords of heavy breathing and snores. Even though I was tired, I was kind of hopping along, feeling something like nervous or maybe excited.

I reached our cabin. With the side door shut tight, I'd have to sneak past Todd. I couldn't let him discover that I'd been out, not just because I'd get in trouble, but also because then their eyes would be on me. I needed to stay unknown, easily forgettable, so I could meet my nocturnal friends again.

I was passing the vertical pairs of bunk windows, hearing everyone sawing away inside, when I spied the tangle of Beaker's blanket and sheets, now covered with a day's worth of dirt. He still hadn't come out after them, or hadn't been allowed to by the killer pack.

I stepped over them, then stopped, turned back, and picked them up. I went back around the cabin and walked down into the trees until I figured I was out of earshot, then I shook them out, the blanket then the sheets. I got as much of the dirt off as I could, and folded each up.

It occurred to me that yesterday I wouldn't have done this. Even just helping out Beaker this much was an act of defiance against the pack, and it was going against my plan to stay invisible. But that was with the staff and counselors. When it came to Leech, well . . . maybe if he wanted to harass me about it, I'd introduce him to the monster from the deep, take him on a little ride. *Come on,* I thought. *Try it. I dare you.* It was a new thought for me. A thought with power. I liked it.

I walked back up the rise toward the cabin. I was almost to the little wooden staircase and landing at the side door when I heard creaking footsteps from inside. The door popped open. I froze. Too late to make it back around the corner—I lunged under the stairs, my face meeting spiderwebs.

Someone stepped outside. Probably Todd. He'd noticed I was gone. Caught. Footsteps down the stairs, onto the wood-chip path . . . but then heading away. I watched through the gaps between the warped stairs. The person was walking slowly, with trudging, tired steps. I saw faded sneakers, jeans, the proportions too small to be Todd.

It was Leech. He had a long, black, tube-shaped case over his shoulder. It looked like it was made out of leather. I'd never seen anything like it, except for rifle cases back home, but this was too short, too uniform in shape. What would you put in there? I saw his head cock to the sky as he yawned.

Above, the door was slowly closing. Ahead, Leech was disappearing from view around the next cabin. I ducked out from the steps, put Beaker's bedding on the landing, and jumped up, grabbed the railing, but my knee didn't make it all the way, instead scraping the hard wood, the opposite of fluid water. Stupid surface world, stupid gravity! I hauled myself up, got to my feet, the door almost closed . . . then it paused.

Beaker's head appeared, his hair in a ridiculous black frizz. He squinted at me. "You're not supposed to be out here," he said groggily.

"Yeah, so what?" I whispered back to him, feeling a flash of the annoyance that probably led the other kids to torment him. Little Beaker, always worrying about the rules. As I swung my legs over the railing, I wondered if he was considering turning me in, seeing a chance to earn points with Todd, his only ally. I picked up his sheets and blanket and handed them to him. "Here."

Beaker looked down at them. He looked back at me. His eyes narrowed further, like he was trying to figure out the inevitable joke.

"They were on the ground. I shook them out."

Beaker kept staring, then looked back down at them again and nodded. "I've been using my sweatshirt to sleep," he said. "Thanks."

"Sure."

He turned and went back in. I followed. Everyone else seemed to still be asleep. Except Leech, who was gone. Wouldn't Todd be interested to know that?

But all I wanted right now was sleep. I climbed up into my bunk and rolled over and felt only exhaustion, my muscles relaxing, body melting into a pool, no neck burning, just stillness and peace and thoughts of Lilly, amazing thoughts, but even they couldn't keep me awake.

○ ○ ○

It seemed like only a second had passed when the reveille horn sounded. My eyes blinked open feeling dry. I was groggy, thirsty for hours more of sleep.

Todd came in. "Another beautiful day, girls!" he said, showing us his pit-hair progress.

"Where's Leech?" Jalen asked, looking at his empty bunk.

Todd glanced in that direction, too. "He had to go see the director." I listened for some giveaway in his tone. Was Leech in trouble, or what? But there was nothing. "Owen," Todd said. "Your neck's all better?"

"Oh," I said, remembering that my bandages were gone. "Yup. All good."

"Cool," said Todd like he only cared because it was his job.

We got dressed, passed around the NoRad, and headed for flagpole. Everyone was quieter without Leech around. I noticed Bunsen and Wesley and Xane talking, even Noah joining in, combinations that wouldn't have been allowed otherwise.

The Arctic Foxes were already there. I heard them whispering to one another and I glanced over without really meaning to. I saw Paige and Mina and a couple of the others looking at me. Paige's eyes were narrowed as if she was studying me, and then she put a finger to her lips and nodded, like she was coming to some conclusion.

"Okay," she said, and she must have known it was loud enough for me to hear, "I can go with CP." I couldn't tell if she was being serious or joking and I wondered, did just losing my bandages make the difference? Wasn't I still the same kid otherwise? *I'm not, though,* I thought. *Maybe it shows in some way or—*

Hands shoved me forward. "Sit down already," said Jalen from behind me.

"Knock it off," I snapped over my shoulder, but at the same time I realized that I had been holding up the line, so I didn't push it any further and I moved and took my seat on the bench.

Claudia started leading cabins in cheers. Once they got going, my eyes immediately started to shut, falling half asleep, the world outside my head becoming a distant drone. . . .

"Thanks again for getting my stuff from outside." I opened my eyes to find Beaker right beside me.

"Sure." I glanced around out of instinct to see if anyone was listening, but then remembered that I didn't care. I shouldn't care. I could help Beaker; my cabin could even think we were friends, for all I cared.

A rush of whispers rippled through the Arctic Foxes. I heard someone say, "Here he comes," and saw them huddling their heads together and gazing out at the playing fields.

There was Leech, walking back from the lake beside

Paul, who carried a fishing pole by his side. That must have been what was in Leech's black case. So, he got to go on special morning fishing trips with the director? Was this another perk of being here the longest?

Leech left Paul's side and headed up the aisle between the log benches. He was smirking like he could tell that all eyes were on him.

I glanced at Paul, who was circling around the campers. He was looking at me. I tried not to react. There was his slight smile again, the one that was so hard to read with those glasses on, and it was even weirder now, with everything the CITs had said. What did he really know? Another couple seconds passed and he was still looking at me, and I realized that he probably noticed that my bandages were gone. Maybe that was all it was. But he was still staring, and I felt like ducking or something, just to get out of that spotlight. . . . Then he turned and headed up the hill.

Leech was arriving at our bench, his slopey grin in full effect.

A big squeal of laughter erupted from Paige and her group.

"Foxes," Leech said, looking over at them and taking a little bow. I was amazed again by the amount of confidence that went with the actual physical person who was speaking. Then again, I knew after last night that appearances could be deceiving. Mine included.

Leech had just sat down, when Mike said, "Dude, what happened to your hand?"

Leech's grin tightened. Before he could slip his right hand down beside him, we all saw that there was a thick bandage around the whole thing, making it look like a big white lump. "Nothing, shut up," said Leech. He glared at Mike.

"Sorry," Mike muttered.

We got to breakfast and things were pretty normal. The cross-table flirting was more intense, as now Jalen and Noah seemed to have found girlfriends, though I didn't even understand what that could mean since we only saw the Foxes in the dining hall and during free time after dinner.

The bug juice was called watermelon today and we were eating oatmeal. I sat there with the usual cabin drama happening around me and barely noticed. I focused on getting food in, feeling ravenous from the night of swimming. Once I'd stuffed myself, exhaustion immediately overwhelmed me again. I tried not to fall asleep right there at the table, the whole time swimming with Lilly in the dark water somewhere back in my brain.

"Shut up!" Leech's shout snapped me out of my stupor. He was glaring over at the Arctic Foxes, and for a second it almost looked serious.

Paige and her friends cracked up.

"They asked if he was Paul's little boyfriend," said Beaker, like he was now my personal assistant.

"Huh," I said to him, then turned back to find that Leech had already reassembled his smirk.

"We take the motorboat out," he was saying to the girls. "I know how to pilot it, so, if any of you ladies want to take an early morning ride with me sometime, I know some secluded spots. . . ."

This caused more cracking up and Paige's eyes to go wide, like now she was auditioning for the part of "horrified."

Leech turned back to our table and accepted his high fives from Jalen and Noah and Mike, and ignored Xane's attempt, but I thought about how he'd lost his cool at the mention of Paul. He'd recovered, but that had seemed weird, defensive. Why? Wasn't he proud of being Paul's little favorite?

"Stop gawking, Turtle," Leech sneered at me. "You taking notes on how to talk to girls?"

I didn't say anything, but then I smiled. I didn't mean to. I'd just thought about talking to Lilly underwater, and the smile slipped out.

Leech's eyes narrowed at me. "What?"

"Nothing." I remembered my plan to stay unnoticed, and turned to Todd. "Can I go get more?" I started to stand.

"Sure," said Todd.

"You better leave," Leech muttered as I walked away, and again I had that feeling like, *Yeah? Try it. I dare you.*

I headed back across the dining hall. The CITs were in their still-life positions on the couches. I spotted Lilly but she was reading. I glanced at her for a second, hoping she might look up, then noticed that Evan was nearby, and staring right at me. I turned away quick and tried to find something else to focus on.

Colleen's death made it easy.

I didn't see her fall, just heard the crash of metal tray against concrete floor, the shrill spray of silverware and plates, and the soft thud of skull.

It happened just to my left, and I looked down and there she was, lying fanned out on the floor.

I saw her a second before most of the dining hall. In that one second, all the talking and clinking and clattering continued, a hollow cloud of sound. One of the other cabins was even in the midst of doing a cheer that involved foot-stomping and claps. The morning sun was angling in through the back windows of the giant room, flickering off cutlery and teeth and eyeballs, and arms were moving and waving, heads bobbing, people shuffling . . . and there in the middle of it all was this single tiny form lying completely still. Her spilled cup of bright red juice had created a pool in front of her that was spreading back into her hair and toward her head in a weird reverse scene, like it was blood being sucked back in.

Then heads started to turn, a few, then more, in a water ripple across the room. A little girl screamed, and then counselors were leaping, lunging, running. The Panda counselor was closest and got there first, sliding to her knees in a splash, red juice soaking her jeans.

"Colleen?" she called quietly, almost like she was hoping Colleen was just taking a little nap, like she didn't want to wake her. The counselor pressed fingers to Colleen's neck, looked up, head swiveling wildly. "Someone get Dr. Maria!" She slowly rolled Colleen over onto her back.

We wished later that she hadn't. It turned out, watermelon bug juice was quite a bit different from blood. The stuff that was caked around Colleen's nose and all down over her mouth and chin, like a dam had broken somewhere inside, was much darker, and you could see the stickiness of it, the way it seemed to cling to the lineless skin of her cheeks, collect on stray strands of hair, and stain the collar of the sky-blue T-shirt with the cute, giant-eyed cartoon panda, the words *Camp* above and *Eden* below.

Colleen was still. Her eyes had rolled up into her sockets like she was trying to see what had made this happen, up inside her brain, like she wanted answers from her technicians. I looked around and saw that kids and adults were crying. I thought it was terrible, but it wasn't hitting me on any gut or tear-duct level; I'd never had a sibling and little kids seemed like strange lab experiments, but still, yesterday she'd been throwing up and today . . . this?

A crowd formed and Dr. Maria pushed through, her white lab coat getting pulled half off her shoulder. "Everyone, please stand back!" she barked, her voice finding corners of the high ceiling to echo from in the now utter silence.

She dropped to the floor. Checked the pulse, too. I thought she would start chest compressions, or something like that, but instead she produced that small electronic device with the glass dot in the middle. As she moved it toward Colleen's forehead, it lit up a pale yellow, not green like it had for me when I'd drowned.

It seemed like Dr. Maria swore then, or sighed, her head falling.

"How is she?" Paul had arrived at the edge of the empty space around Colleen.

Dr. Maria just looked up at him, her eyes welling with tears but also like she was saying something silently to him. She maybe looked angry, though with the tears it was hard to tell.

Paul watched, arms folded, eyes hidden. Then he stepped forward, knelt, and slid his arms beneath Colleen's knees and shoulders and lifted the body up off the ground. He turned without a word and headed for the back door, toward the infirmary.

Dr. Maria stood and stared after them. Sobs made her notice the counselor, still kneeling beside her, face in her hands. Dr. Maria reached down and rubbed her shoulder. "It's not your fault," she said, then again, her voice thicker. "It's not your fault."

The hall was beginning to fill with murmuring voices, kids asking, "Will she be okay?" and "What happened?" Everyone was looking around with wide, scared eyes, their mouths slightly open as the scene they'd just witnessed burned a permanent scar in their minds. . . .

Except for the CITs. I found Lilly standing with Marco and Aliah, watching from the Ping-Pong table, all with their arms crossed. Their eyes were narrowed, like they knew all about this.

"It's okay, everyone," Dr. Maria called. "We'll find out what happened. It's—" She paused and put out her hands. "No one needs to worry."

She nodded to herself after saying this and started walking again. She was gazing blankly ahead, and I thought she wouldn't notice me, but then she did.

"Owen." She paused and rubbed my shoulder. "It's okay," she repeated vacantly. Then she seemed to peer at my neck, her brow furrowing. "Your bandages . . ." Her voice lowered. "The wounds . . ." She sounded confused.

"Oh, yeah, all better." I shrugged like things were totally fine, nothing to see here.

This only made Dr. Maria frown. "Okay, um . . . listen, you'd better not come today, with . . . this." She motioned to the door. "But tomorrow, come see me first thing in the morning?"

"Sure, okay."

"Good." Her eyes flashed to my neck again. I'd put the NoRad on thick like Lilly had suggested, but I still felt a surge of unease. Dr. Maria was distracted, though, and in this light there was probably no way she could see the faint gill lines. She hurried off.

Sound was slowly creeping back into the dining hall, but the volume never returned to its original level.

I walked back to our table. Kids were mostly quiet, eating. After a while, Jalen started whispering with Paige, and then turned and tapped Leech on the shoulder. "Dude, Paige says it's your first move."

Leech seemed to snap out of some kind of trance. He'd been bent over the table, and now I saw that he'd been drawing in a little notebook with a black pen. It looked like he'd been into it, because Jalen's tap made him kind of jump. He looked up, but instead of his usual, mischievous smile, his face curled downward. "Shut up," he muttered, like Jalen, Paige, all of it, was annoying and beneath him. He hunched back down over the notebook and returned to whatever he was doing.

"What's with you?" Jalen asked.

Leech didn't reply.

Jalen muttered something to himself and turned away. I wondered what was up with Leech, but soon my thoughts returned to Colleen, to the blood. It all played over and over in my mind. It seemed so weird that a little human could just drop dead like that—could stop being, right in the middle of everything.

Dr. Maria's words played through my mind again: *It's okay, everyone. . . . No one needs to worry.*

And I realized that was weird too, because why *would*

we need to worry? It had been such a random thing, why would any of us ever think that it could happen to us? Unless . . .

Unless *she* thought it could.

It's because of this place, Lilly had said.

My fingers brushed at my neck, feeling the subtle indentations of what this place had already done to me. What else was it capable of?

8

SOMEHOW, DESPITE THE DEATH ON OUR MINDS, we were expected to keep the camp spirit burning bright throughout another perfect day of friendly sunshine. I felt like there ought to be some more discussion about Colleen, some more worry, and I thought maybe I saw some on Todd's face, but he just took us to the archery range over on the back side of the playing fields like everything was normal.

Ten round targets were lined up against the trees. A rope was laid out on the ground, indicating where we were supposed to stand. We walked over to a small wooden shed.

Evan emerged, a black guard strapped to his arm, a bow in his hand. "Hey," he said to us all.

"Evan's here to give us some pointers on shooting," said Todd.

Evan looked over us all like he barely knew what we were, and barely cared. When his eyes swept past me, I nodded a little to him, but he didn't seem to notice. I hoped that was because he didn't want to reveal our secret connection, but I worried it was because he didn't approve of me being part of that connection in the first place.

We all got bows and quivers of beat-up plastic arrows. Evan had a nicer set, a polished bow and wooden arrows with tricolor feathers on the back. He fired a few with lethal accuracy, spearing the yellow center of the target each time. "Like that," he said. "It's all about the power when you draw the bow, and the discipline. You have to keep everything still."

He walked up and down the line giving advice, but right by me without a word. I got one arrow into the red target area, a couple into the blue, and the others ended up flying past the target or landing in the grass in front of it.

After archery, there was some court time playing tetherball, which I did a little better at, then lunch, where no one died, and then the awkward electives hour, when Beaker and I joined the Lemurs at Craft House (Beaker had also failed the swim test, though without drowning). We made leather bracelets, stamping in designs and then putting snaps on their ends. The little kids were doing basic shapes and nicknames and code words from their cabin. I stamped DAD into mine, thinking maybe it would be a good gift for him. Not that he'd ever wear a bracelet. But still. I'd have to hide it though, 'cause it was kind of childish to make a present for your dad.

"Check it out," said Beaker, who was right there across

the table from me again, like we were connected by a magnet. He was holding out his own bracelet. Awkwardly spaced letters spelled out AASGARD. When I didn't really react to it, he pointed up behind me. "Like that."

I turned to see an old wooden sign hanging in the rafters, CAMP AASGARD whittled into it in big blocky letters that had once been painted bright red, but only a few chips of that color remained on the gray board. There was a date in the corner: 1993.

"I tried to do that cool logo, but it was hard," Beaker added.

I saw what he was talking about. To the right of the name was a symbol of triangles and concentric circles:

I wondered if it was Viking, or just something that kids a century ago had come up with. It could have meant anything. But it was kinda cool, so I grabbed a little paring knife and tried to reproduce it, too. It came out okay. When it was finished, I put the bracelet on. I wondered if it was a silly thing to wear but then decided I didn't care.

When we were done, we walked down to the lake and had to wait while the rest of our cabin came in from sailing. Lilly was out on the main dock, watching free swim. If she saw me arrive, she didn't show it.

Beaker and I walked over to the boathouse, beyond

the swim area. It was an old red building with two docks sticking out from it. There were kayaks and rowboats tied up here, as well as the camp motorboat. Our cabin had the sailboats out. We sat at the end of a dock and watched them tacking back and forth, shooting ahead whenever they caught the wind. At one point, a boat capsized. They were close enough for us to hear the laughing from Mike and Noah, who'd done it on purpose. The other boats circled around until they were righted, then finally everyone heeded Todd's calling from a nearby boat to come in. On the way back to our cabin, they all laughed and joked about their sailing adventures while Beaker and I walked a few paces behind.

Paul was at flagpole before dinner, and began by addressing us all. "I know everyone has been worried about what happened this morning," he said. He didn't sound particularly worried. It was more like he was fulfilling a duty. "So I just wanted to let you all know that little Colleen from the Pandas is doing okay. We sent her over to the city medical facility, and the doctors there say she is recovering. She had a severe allergic reaction. Extremely rare. Naturally, we're going over our food protocols and cross-referencing your files to be sure we have your safety first in our minds. But nobody needs to worry."

"Yeah, right," muttered Marco late that night as he bounded into the dark, flipping and slicing into the black lake.

I had just told them about Paul's speech.

"He's full of it," Aliah added. "It was probably those stupid syntheggs that got her."

"Dude, they're better than real eggs. Did you ever have one, b-freeze?" said Evan. I'd learned by now that, among the CITs, *b-freeze* meant before they'd all been Cryoed.

"I liked eggs," said Marco, hauling himself back onto the raft. "I heard they still have them, in Indo-Australia."

"That was the only chicken population that didn't have to be slaughtered because of the strain-three avian flu," said Lilly. I was also learning that she was bursting with facts like these. "EdenWest claimed that their chickens were immune, but that was another lie. I heard they took them out a few kilometers from here and gassed and burned them."

"Come on!" Evan groaned.

"What were the real ones like?" I asked. "Eggs, I mean."

"Mushy," said Aliah with a frown, "you know, like eating any unfertilized embryonic tissue." And I'd learned that Aliah tended to have opinions like this.

"Ugh! What is with you and saying things like that all the time?" Marco moaned. "It's gross."

"They were good with salt," Lilly added. "And with real pancakes—like, made of wheat, not that millet stuff."

"I thought that the Edens were supposed to have all the pre-Rise ingredients," I said. "I can get millet pancakes at home." We hadn't seen wheat again since the first night, though there had still been some vegetables: tough string beans and some thick greens, and also some fruit, which apparently grew okay in the hydroponics towers over in the city.

"Yeah, they did, but not anymore 'cause things are going to hell," said Lilly. "And there's a reason why all the fruit is peeled and cut up all nice. If you go back in the kitchen, you'll see those things do *not* look as good as you remember. It's the increasing radiation, and I've heard it's toxins in the water, too. And all that's just the tip of the iceberg for this place. But back to the dead girl . . ."

"Paul said she's alive," I reminded them. The CITs just looked at me. "What? You don't think she is?"

"Doesn't matter if she is or not," said Aliah. "You saw her. She didn't look like she was going to 'recover.' And why believe *that* when everything else Paul says is so ridiculous?"

"Well, yeah." I agreed that it seemed crazy that Camp Eden had been so careless with us, first with my drowning, then Colleen's allergies, but it still seemed kind of hard to believe that Paul and the camp were actually behind these things, or even *making* them happen.

We were sitting around the edge of the trampoline, legs extended toward the middle, like spokes of a wheel. Little waves slapped against the thick rubber of the raft, making hollow, smacking sounds. Lilly sat to my left, then Evan, and around to Marco, then Aliah. The breeze had been turned up tonight, making the hairs on my arms and legs stand up among fields of goose bumps. The CITs were all wearing rash-guard long-sleeve tops, looking like a team of high-tech warriors, and I felt like the rookie. Lilly's was all black with thin white seams.

Going to bed hours ago with the rest of my cabin, after another chapter of *Pym* from Todd, I had wondered how I'd wake up, but then I just did, my gills burning softly, gently nudging me out of sleep. *Time for care and feeding of your new parts,* the new technician pleasantly reminded me.

This time, as I'd sneaked out of the cabin, I left one of my socks wedged in the door to keep it from latching. Walking down to the lake, I'd been nervous. Sure, Lilly had invited me back, but would the rest of the group really want me there? Then, when I arrived they were already out there and Lilly was like, "Hey, O!" and my name was still a single syllable and now here I was, among them again, one of them, the nocturnal sea monster clan.

"Besides," said Lilly, "Colleen wasn't the first, just the first that happened in public."

"Other kids have died?" I asked.

"Three or four over the last couple summers," Marco reported. "We'd just heard the secondhand stories, though. A boy that didn't wake up one morning—"

"Or probably ever," Aliah added.

"Right," Marco went on, getting up and starting to

bounce in the center of the raft. "But Paul said that kid got better over at the city hospital." He vaulted out into the water, sending a big splash back over us.

"Uh," Aliah groaned.

"Then there was that girl who attacked her cabin with a tennis racket," said Lilly. "She went completely insane."

"The kid who jumped off the Aasgard cliffs, too," said Aliah.

"Wow," I said.

"We don't know that any of those kids actually died," said Evan. It was the first time he'd spoken in a while. I noticed he was staring into the center of the raft, a scowl on his face.

"And we don't know that they didn't," said Lilly, sounding annoyed with him. "But we know what we *saw* today."

"I think that girl Colleen was from Cryo House," said Aliah. "Can't be sure, though—all those little sprouts look the same."

"It would make sense," said Lilly, "if it's connected to what's happened to us. Colleen's body was probably too young to deal with the changes."

"Maybe they gave her a stronger dose," said Marco, pulling himself back onto the raft then intentionally shaking his hair right by Aliah, spraying her with droplets.

She spun to her knees. "Knock it off, butt blister!" She shoved him, but Marco grabbed her wrist and they both tumbled into the water in a tangle of appendages. They didn't emerge right away.

"Dorks," said Lilly, as if such flirting was beneath her. I wondered how one went about flirting with her. I'd have to watch carefully. She was so pretty, but the more I hung around her, it didn't seem like being pretty had anything to do with who she was. Instead, it was more like that beautiful exterior just happened to be there, and she was all about her big ideas.

"Stronger dose?" I asked.

"Yeah, makes sense, right?" said Lilly. "Paul and his minions have got to be dosing us all, like, with a drug or something, that's mucking with our genes. You know, causing mutations."

Evan sighed. "That's so carbon-dated. Nobody's been doing research like that for fifty years."

"Shut up," Lilly snapped at him. "You remember all that stuff with the cloning in Asia, don't you?" Lilly's voice was rising, picking up speed. "How about the pigs with human arms and legs and organs?"

"Sure, b-freeze, when there were universities and people with time on their hands and money to waste on stupid stuff like that," said Evan, "but that's all gone. Young Owen here probably doesn't even know what the hell you're talking about."

I didn't. I also didn't like being referred to as "young." Evan was another king, like Leech, making sure I knew he was above me. "Pigs?" I asked. "With human limbs?"

"Mice with human ears growing out of their backs," said Lilly, "and that was only the stuff that people *knew* about." She turned back to Evan. "Remember those stories about that guy, I forget what he was CEO of, who made, like, six clones of his favorite girlfriend and all that?"

"Oh yeah, didn't the clones gang up and kill him, then, themselves?" said Marco.

"I think so," said Lilly. "And there was the whole thing with people storing DNA to make copies of their pets. You think that science is gone? It's not like there's *nobody* with money anymore. Look around: Who would have the money to run experiments like that?"

"Here we go," said Evan, standing up and shrugging his soccer-ball shoulders against the cool breeze. "Welcome to Dr. Lilly Ishani's Big Theory Spectacular." He stepped to the center of the trampoline and started bouncing, gaining height.

"Screw you," said Lilly.

"Maybe later," Evan scoffed, and flew through the air.

As he disappeared into the water, Lilly turned to me. I was busy wondering: Had they screwed? Or dated? Was that what had just been revealed? But I had to focus, because I was the only one left to listen to Lilly's ideas. And I think I was starting to understand that what she wanted, maybe more than meaty shoulders, was to spin her ideas and have someone listen and get it.

"What's your big theory?" I asked her.

"Well . . ." Lilly looked away and started picking at a fingernail with the thumb and index finger of her other hand, like this was important stuff and she wanted to say it just right. "So, here we are, right," she began, "in EdenWest. Outside, things are a mess, and eventually, this dome is going to fail. And all the other Edens are in the same boat."

"Except for EdenSouth," I added. "That place got destroyed by the Heliad-7 cult."

"Yeah," said Lilly. "Have you guys heard much about Desenna?" she asked with interest.

"Not really," I said.

"Oh," said Lilly, sounding disappointed. "Well, anyway, each dome has a couple hundred thousand people inside. So, ask yourself this: What's going to happen when the domes fail? Where are all those people going to go?"

"But I heard yesterday that the dome is at, like, eighty-six-percent safe or something," I said. "Well, but then we also saw that panel catch on fire."

"Exactly. And that whole dome integrity business is a complete lie," said Lilly. "They fudge those numbers. We've heard it's more like seventy-five percent, at best."

"Not *we*," said Evan, dragging himself out of the water. "*You* heard that from the Nomad Alliance. How do you know any of what they say is reliable?"

Lilly glared at Evan.

"You've talked to the Nomads?" I asked. I'd seen Nomads now and then. Sometimes a pod of them would come to Hub for emergency care, or to trade some valuable item they'd dug up out in the wastelands, but mostly they kept out of sight. "How?"

"They broadcast on the gamma link," said Lilly. "It's called the Alliance Free SignalCast, and"—she narrowed her eyes at Evan—"*informed* people should get the other side of the story sometimes. This little bubble here isn't the entire universe."

"It's all a lie. Those people just want to get in here," said Evan.

"Actually, that's where you're woefully incorrect, *professor*," said Lilly. "The Nomads don't want in anymore. They know this place is halfway to being a microwave oven, and how would *you* know, anyway?"

"Whatever," said Evan. He started bouncing again.

"You just don't want to face facts," said Lilly. "You want to mess around like this really is just good ol' summer camp, like it's, well, Eden."

"Hey, that's what they promised me." Evan bounded higher, and there was an edge to his voice now, like he was really getting mad. "This is what my family *wanted*, why they ice-cubed me and stuck me in here. So I could have a better life than those sorry bastards out there. We're lucky to be here. So what's wrong with enjoying ourselves?"

Lilly slapped at her neck. "What about these, you idiot?"

"As far as I'm concerned? Just another bonus of the good life."

"You're just afraid," said Lilly. "You just don't want to worry."

"Or," Evan was nearly shouting now, "maybe instead of sitting around every night talking about everything that stinks, I'd just like to enjoy life for five minutes!" He shot into the sky and dove back into the water.

"Tell that to Anna, you ass," Lilly muttered after him.

I thought about saying something to show that I agreed with her, that this was serious. And also that I thought Evan was wrong, but Evan was already fired up, and I didn't need him overhearing me and turning his anger in my direction. I needed to get back to Lilly's story. "Okay," I said, "so, the dome is failing, and you think EdenCorp is doing . . . what?"

Lilly's one hand began skinning the other again, fingers digging up white cuticle edges and tearing. "Well, what if they're trying to create a new race?"

"A new race?"

"Or more like a new species," said Lilly. "Look, you know about evolution and survival of the fittest and all that? They probably teach you that stuff out at Hub."

"Yeah."

"And how, like, it's genetic mutations that make animals adapt to survive."

"Sure," I said, "but it takes millions of years."

"Right," said Lilly. The furrow had left her brow now, her eyes lighting up with excitement at this topic. "But," Lilly continued, "sometimes, when conditions get dire, mutations happen faster. It's called . . . oh, right: selective pressure. But even that's too slow for right now. So I think Eden is forcing it: trying to create a human species that can survive out there when the domes fail."

I pictured the landscape outside the dome. "How are gills going to help us in the desert?"

"Not right outside," said Lilly, "and not up north either. The HZ is already full, and the border area is a mess. Plus"—she waved her hand toward the city—"none of those people up there are going to want a bunch of spoiled rich folks who spent the last fifty years living the good life in here showing up on their doorstep. There's a lot of resentment, isn't there?"

"Kinda, yeah," I said.

"And probably even more for the Cryo kids whose mommies and daddies could afford to reserve them slots." It sounded like this concept bothered her, even though she was one of them.

"It's about the same."

"Okay, well, anyway," said Lilly, "Eden's got to figure out where else we can all go where we can actually survive. Maybe the only way to do that is to change ourselves. What if humans could live in the New Everglades down in Virginia? Water blocks a lot of the harmful solar radiation."

"The mosquito strains down there are lethal," I said.

"So, maybe they'll try to have us grow fur or something. I mean, who knows? Gills are probably only the start."

A weird thought crossed my mind. *This is only the beginning.* Who had said that? Lilly, but also that vision I'd had underwater. That siren thing. That had been a few days ago now. She'd probably just been a dream, or a hallucination while I was drowning.

"So," I asked, "how do you think Eden is doing this?"

"I don't know," said Lilly.

"It's definitely the bug juice," said Marco. He and Aliah were pulling themselves back up onto the raft.

"Uh-oh," Aliah huffed. "Are you talking theories again?"

"Yes, and who cares *how*?" said Lilly.

"I do," Marco said proudly. "I haven't had a sip of bug juice yet this session."

"The point is," said Lilly, "Eden needs to experiment on someone. Who better to do their tests on than a bunch of clueless camp kids, especially Cryos who have no parents to complain to?"

"That doesn't explain Owen," said Marco.

"It doesn't explain a *lot* of things," added Aliah.

"Well then, please speak up with all your better ideas," said Lilly. She turned back to me with a look like, *What do you think?*

"It makes sense," I said right away. I wasn't really

sure that it did, but I wanted to agree with her, and there definitely had to be something going on to cause the gills. But that also meant that our secret club was actually a collection of lab rats.

"Woo!" Evan burst out of the water back by the dock, spiking high into the air and doing two somersaults before landing.

Lilly rolled her eyes and shouted to him. "You're like a trained seal!"

"Arf!" Evan called back.

"Can we *pleeease* stop talking about all this heavy stuff for tonight?" Aliah asked.

Lilly sighed. "Fine." She looked at me. "Tandem?"

"What?" I said.

She stood up and offered her hand. "Tandem jump, dummy."

"Oh, sure." I got up and moved to the center of the raft, trying to have good balance, to seem sturdy, but then I stumbled. Lilly grabbed my shoulder and held me up.

"All right, let's do this. On three," she said, starting to bounce.

The worries of our conversation melted away. As we bounced higher, I stopped thinking about whether we were test subjects, whether this place really was some kind of giant, deadly lab. Those questions could wait. For tonight, I just wanted to ignore them, and instead focus on air, and height, and who was beside me.

"One!" Somehow, over the course of two nights, I had become Lilly's tandem partner, her confidant of secret theories.

"Two!" No longer the earthbound, cramp-twisted cabin turtle. No longer the quiet kid in outer orbit, who was never quite part of the group.

"Three!" We arced high over the water, and as we did, I realized that I was also no longer the forgettable, unnoticed one, because I saw that, far over on the dock, Evan stood with his arms crossed, watching us closely.

9

AT BREAKFAST THE NEXT MORNING, I WAS REALLY
feeling it. Tired. Sluggish. These nights with only three
hours of sleep were really starting to catch up to me. And
yet, despite the way my eyes felt brittle and dry, my brain
fuzzy, and how I could barely taste my pancakes, it was
something like amazing to be sitting there while my cabin
played their roles in the never-ending little drama of hurting
one another and trying to look good for the Arctic Foxes,
and to feel separate from it, above it, or maybe beneath, the
sea creature watching the hapless surface swimmers with
their flailing and splashing.

Things were a little more tame this morning, though,
because Leech hadn't shown up yet. He'd been gone again
when I got back to the cabin at dawn. By the time flagpole
was over, his minions were wondering where he was and
looking lost.

When the bug juice came around to me, I thought
of Marco and his theory, and passed along today's

neon-green variety without taking any.

While the cabin headed down to Craft House, I walked over to the infirmary. After last night's conversation, I felt a little paranoid going in there, a fish swimming too close to the net. But I also had to do this, had to keep playing my role as normal Owen, so I didn't arouse any suspicion.

The waiting area was empty, all the doors closed. I was almost across the room when I heard a raised voice from Paul's office. He sounded angry. I moved closer to his door, leaned my ear against the frosted glass, and listened.

"I know the readings, I saw the report! Don't worry, we're covering that."

A voice replied, monotone and tinny, like it was coming over a connection, but it was too low for me to hear.

"That's . . . Yes, we're still on schedule. Everything— Of course, but these things have to be handled a certain w—"

The monotone voice seemed to have cut Paul off. I wondered if it might be his boss. I hadn't thought of him as having one.

"No . . . yes, I'll get it done."

The voice replied.

"Okay, then."

There was a final syllable from the monotone voice, then a short silence. Something smashed against the wall. An object thrown. There was a sound of shards raining down to the floor. Now footsteps, coming toward me.

I turned and hurried toward the infirmary, slipping

through the door and closing it behind me. I listened, heard Paul's door open, more footsteps, but then the front door slapping open and closed.

I walked up the hall, trying to relax, and wondering: What report had Paul been referring to? And who had the authority to make him furious like that?

There was a young boy in the first exam room I passed, a brace on his wrist. That seemed to be all that was wrong with him. No vomit, no blood. The rest of the rooms were empty. I had just reached the end of the hall when I heard muted electronic sounds, like beeps, followed by a series of clicks, like sliding metal. The red door began to swing slowly inward, a green light gleaming on its keypad.

"Hey, Owen." Dr. Maria came out. "I saw you on the security cameras." She walked swiftly, like she was in a hurry, the door swinging shut on its own behind her. I glanced up at the ceiling corners, but didn't see any cameras. And I didn't remember seeing any around camp, either. But, given the butterflies, I realized Eden could have cameras hidden anywhere, everywhere.

"I'm glad you came," she said to me. "Let's go in here." She motioned me into a room, but I was trying to get a look behind her. The hall beyond the red door gleamed in sharp light, like the walls were metal, and yet cloudy, maybe draped with plastic. I caught a glimpse of electronic screens and banks of blinking machinery, but then the door was clicking closed, accompanied by a hissing, like it was sealing tight. It reminded me of the Eye, the high-tech behind the scenes, but why would they need that kind of equipment down here?

"Okay." I walked in and sat on the edge of the bed. The EdenNet was on. Teresa Alamos was reporting about a new violent uprising in the Amazon Archipelago.

"So," said Dr. Maria, "how are you?" I saw her glance at my neck as she moved to the counter. She put down a set of video sheets she was holding. They each showed a similar striped design. They looked almost like X-rays, but maybe weren't, since the shapes on them looked more like lines of dots.

"I'm fine," I said, fighting to hold back a yawn. "Hey," I thought to say, "I heard Paul out there. He sounded pretty mad."

Dr. Maria glanced toward the door. "Oh, well, I think he had a chat link scheduled with the board of directors this morning. Those never put him in a good mood."

"Ah." So that was Paul's boss. "Bad news, or something?"

I hoped that might get Dr. Maria to reveal more, but she just said, "I guess," and turned around with an instrument that had a claw at the end. She held it near my arm and when she pressed a trigger, the claw wrapped around my biceps. Its sides ballooned and it began to squeeze, cutting off circulation. She pressed another button and it deflated slowly. I could feel my blood slipping, then pulsing back through.

"Blood pressure's normal," she announced, and traded the claw for a little exam light. She stepped to my side and gently pushed my chin up with her fingers to get a good look at my neck. "I still can't believe how fast those wounds healed," she said. "Any strange symptoms?"

"Nope," I said, hoping the smear of NoRad I'd coated my gills with would be enough. Dr. Maria took a quick look and let go of my chin, so quick that I worried, *She doesn't need to look because she already knows.*

"Let me take a quick peek in your mouth and ears," she said, and pointed the light into each spot. When she was finished, she stepped over to the counter and tapped the computer pad there. "Well, Owen, you seem to be the picture of health."

She looked at me and smiled. Something about her smile seemed real, and like last time, I got that feeling like she cared, and it made last night's talk of lab experiments seem silly. She couldn't really be part of some plot to change us all into sea creatures, could she?

"So, is that it?" I asked.

"Um." Dr. Maria was back at the table, scrolling on the pad. It seemed like she was reading something. "Actually, just let me get another quick blood sample before you go."

She picked up the syringe gun. I held out my arm and felt the pinprick, followed by the dark, thick fluid jumping into the vial. It was the usual red, not green or purple or any other mutated-creature color.

Still it felt weird, watching my blood leave, my secrets exposed. It couldn't lie like I could, couldn't hide what it was with NoRad lotion. I noticed the yellow-and-white label stuck to the vial. There was a code there: YH4-32.1. I wondered if the *YH* stood for *Yellowstone Hub*. "What do you need the blood for?" I asked.

"Well, you had those wounds," said Dr. Maria, "and there can be bacteria on the lake floor. I just want to make sure you're in the clear." She pulled the needle out.

I thought about that answer, and I found that I didn't totally buy it. It seemed vague. So I asked the other question that had been on my mind: "How is Colleen?"

Dr. Maria had moved back to the counter. She pulled a square machine over and slid the vial of my blood into the top. There was a whirring sound. I wondered if she'd heard me, but then she said, "Oh, she's doing okay. I heard her prognosis is improving."

I thought I heard a shudder in her voice, and she blinked a few times in a row as she tapped at the screen. I watched her face carefully. Were there tears? It would make sense if the event had bothered her. She'd looked pretty shaken up yesterday. She might even feel guilty, since Paul had said it was allergies and it was probably her job to be aware of that kind of thing. Or she might be feeling guilty because whatever had happened to Colleen also had to do with me and the CITs. But I didn't actually see any tears form. I tried to think of something else to ask, but couldn't.

The EdenNet bled into our silence, Aaron reporting:

Thanks, Teresa. We're feeling the effects of some increased solar flare activity today. Rad levels have elevated externally, but the good news is that those OzoneSim panels that RadDefense added have actually raised our current DI reading to 87.5-percent integrity. That said, don't forget your NoRad lotion during midday today.

"You can go," said Dr. Maria absently. The blood machine had stopped spinning. She was looking at the computer.

"Okay." I left, feeling like I was no closer to knowing if I was Dr. Maria's lab rat or not. I felt a fresh wave of exhaustion, and wondered if some of it was from this game of keeping secrets. I'd never had much experience with it.

I headed around the dining hall and down the hill. I reached the flagpole and was starting down the trail toward Craft House when I saw my cabin standing in a ring with a bunch of Spider Monkey boys out on the courts. I walked over. As I got close, I heard the whimpering voice.

I reached the edge of the group and saw that Todd was kneeling beside another counselor, I think his name was Blake. One of the Spider Monkeys was leaning back against him, his eyes mostly closed, a little moan escaping his lips.

"I think those are Rad burns," Todd was saying.

Blake was red-faced, his voice panicky. "But . . . it's only ten a.m. I thought we'd be fine. I didn't check their NoRad application, I—"

"You should get him up to the infirmary," said Todd.

Blake pulled the boy to his feet. His face was puffy and covered with yellowish bumps, some of which had burst, letting a pinkish fluid drip free. I'd seen it before: classic early-stage Rad poisoning. I glanced up at the sky, almost expecting to see burned dome panels falling toward us, the inner skin melting off, but there was just idyllic hazy SafeSun and powdery TruSky.

"I thought it was just heat stroke," Blake mumbled to himself as he led his cabin up the hill.

"Come on, guys," said Todd. He glanced warily upward. "The ropes course is in the woods, so we'll be fine. Everybody hit the NoRad this morning, right?"

"Yes," everyone answered, more obediently than usual.

We crossed the fields and walked through the woods past our cabin, then down to a narrow trail that led along the edge of the lake. I couldn't stop thinking about those burns, about how the EdenNet had said the DI was high, but then how Lilly had heard that those reports were a lie. Paul's angry conversation with the board of directors, too: I wondered if that report he'd been mad about had been related to the DI.

My thoughts started to fuzz out into a half-asleep daze. A voice broke me out of it.

"That was scary, huh?"

I looked over to find Beaker beside me. He was swinging his arms far up and back as he walked. "I mean, Rad burns are serious," he said.

"Yeah," I said groggily. "They're cumulative, though, so, I mean, that kid probably forgot to wear his protection all session. Except—"

I was about to say more when I caught a flash from the water. We were rounding a little inlet where the surface of the water was shaded, and I could have sworn I saw that turquoise-blue light again, the light of the siren I thought I'd seen when I drowned. But now I just saw the green-tinted rocks and plants.

"Except what?" Beaker asked.

I blinked. It must have been the lack of sleep. I started walking again. "Oh, well, just, it makes you wonder if the DI is actually lower than they're saying—"

Find me, Owen.

The voice erased my thoughts. I stopped again and stepped over to the edge of the water.

There it was. Hovering beneath the surface, so faint because of the daylight but definitely there . . . the siren. I remembered it looking kind of like a figure, and it definitely did now. The ripples on the water blurred it, but I thought I could see a face and long hair.

"Owen?" Beaker asked, it seemed like from far away.

Find me.

Yes. I would. I had to fight the urge to jump in right now. My gills twitched at the thought.

In the temple beneath—

A hand slammed into my back and I fell forward, spinning my arms and crashing into the water. I plunged beneath the surface. My gills tingled, wondering if they should wake, but no, not now. Still, I glanced around . . . but the siren was nowhere. Like the spell had been broken.

My feet found the bottom, sneakers filling with mud, and I stood. The water was up to my thighs. I spun around to face the shore, and there was Leech. I hadn't even noticed him rejoining our group. He had his black fishing pole case over his shoulder, like he was just returning from another one of his special mornings with Paul, except Paul had been in his office. Was Leech so special that he could just go off on his own if he wanted? Noah and Jalen stood beside him, laughing. Leech glared at me, and before I could even say anything, he said, "Stop spreading rumors."

"What?" I said to him, and I maybe meant it to come out annoyed, but it just sounded confused.

"You'll scare the mice," he added, nodding his chin toward the water beside me. I realized that Beaker was there, staggering to his feet, soaked as well.

Leech made his smirking face, and all I wanted was to lunge and grab him, drag him down into my lair, rub his face into the mud, but I remembered that instead I had to play the part of the soaked, slow turtle. Still, I had to at least say something back, something to let him know that I was not going to be pushed around like this, except what came out was, "Shut up, I can say what I want." I couldn't believe how pathetic I sounded.

But it had an effect, because Leech's grin turned into a scowl. "Actually, no, you can't. You're just a stupid wastelander and I don't care what you *think* you are, you have no idea what's really going on in here, so don't pretend you do." By the time he finished, his scowl had twisted into a vicious glare. What was he talking about? What did I *think* I was? What didn't I know about what was really going on?

He turned and sauntered up the path. Jalen and Noah looked a little surprised, and hurried after him.

Beaker and I trudged out of the water and started after the group.

"Should we tell Todd?" said Beaker.

"No," I said. "That would just make things worse."

I was damp all morning as we put on harnesses and helmets and crossed rope lines from one tree to the next. I stayed away from Leech but I watched him. He couldn't do the ropes because his hand was still bandaged. He seemed back to his normal self, not angry, just grinning annoyingly and even bouncing the rope really hard one time when Todd wasn't looking so that Bunsen fell off.

But the way he'd reacted to me talking about the DI . . . Maybe Leech's being in tight with Paul meant he knew more about that stuff, and other things, too, like about us gill breathers. If there was one thing about Leech, it was that he seemed like he was observant, always looking for the detail that he could use against you later. But he was also cunning enough not to reveal what he knew. Did he know some of my secret? Did he suspect as much as the CITs did about what was going on here, or did he maybe know even more?

10

THE DAY DRAGGED ENDLESSLY UNTIL THAT NIGHT, when I was back on the raft with my people. We'd been swimming for a while, and now a mellow quiet had settled over everyone. We were lying in our arrangement of spokes, feet to the center. I had my head hanging back just a bit off the edge of the raft, so that I could feel the evening breeze on my Adam's apple. I stared up at the foggy projection of the moon, nearing full now. I imagined Aaron up there in the Eye, changing some setting to make it grow. It made me wonder if this moon was synched up to what the actual moon was doing, outside. And if not, if it was just Aaron's whim, what was that doing to the animals in here? Creatures had navigation and cycles linked to the moon. There were theories that people did, too. Was it messing with all of our balance on some deep, primeval level?

I'd been waiting for a good time to ask the CITs if they'd seen anything like that siren. I still wondered if it was just something in my head, though, and I didn't want to sound all weird and crazy. Besides, we'd been busy having fun, and now they were trading stories about their past lives and it was Lilly's turn.

"I remember the last day of water," she said. "I was eight, I think. It was January and, like, a hundred and five degrees. We woke up early 'cause we only had until one p.m. At one, Las Vegas was shutting down for good. They had already drained Lake Mead so low that the pumps were pulling in mostly silt. Just about everyone had left, heading north toward the HZ. My dad worked for the city, so we were part of, like, the last thousand people, there to close the coffin lid.

"We'd been packing for days, but then right before we left, I took a walk around our yard. We had a saguaro cactus in our backyard, but even it was brown and dead. Did you guys ever see those things? They were giant, built for so little water, but now we had even less. We'd had a pool, but it had been dry for a couple years, and the bottom had filled with sand ripples. I remember looking inside and thinking about how, like, in ten thousand years, some new humans, or whatever humans become, were going to come along and they were going to dig down into the new layers of earth and maybe all they would find would be this pool, this curvy cement thing, and, like, what would they think it was? Who would they think we were, or what our culture was, based on that?"

"Gill people," said Marco. "And those were our water houses."

"Ha," said Lilly. "So anyway, the lawn was dried and gone, and it would crunch and disintegrate under my toes. From the back of the yard, I could see what was left of the Strip, you know, all those casinos that used to light up the sky so you couldn't see the stars. They'd had this big closing party, like a festival really, that ended up getting out of control and going on for weeks, with all the Blazers coming in and going on this bender of booze and sex and gambling and everything."

"Who?" I asked.

"Blazers were people, back when the Rise was really starting to hit, who decided that life was doomed, that everything was going to hell, so they just came to Vegas with everything they had left and tried to go out in a blaze of glory. Basically kill themselves. But it got so crazy it led to the Strip Fire, when ten of the casinos burned and people were dancing and throwing themselves into the flames and a lot of other terrible things you'd hear about. We stayed away from the Strip, but I remember being able to see the fire from my window, watching it go for days, and almost thinking it was beautiful. I mean, not actually beautiful but . . . you know how you feel like if the world is going to end, you want to be there to see it? You want to know what comes next?"

"Totally," said Marco.

"It was like that. 'Course what came next was lighting

our own house on fire."

"You had to burn all your stuff?" Aliah asked.

"No, but most of it. You didn't have to burn your house, but there was a citywide initiative not to leave too much fuel for wildfires, or possessions that might encourage vandals. Back then, there were reports of Nomad groups starting to organize, too, and word was they would comb over the abandoned towns, gathering supplies. For some reason, that bothered some people a lot. They didn't want their things being taken by anyone else. But then there were other people who couldn't bear to burn their stuff, like doing that was somehow burning their identity. It was like your things were somehow you. I'm not saying it didn't suck to get rid of my bed, most of my clothes, stuffed animals, and all that, but I'm glad my parents decided to burn it. We'd backed up all our photos and videos and filled the trunk of the car with clothes and camping supplies for the drive north, and so it was kind of poetic, how by burning we were helping the earth recycle itself or something.

"We all stood at the end of the driveway, crowded around the incendiary line. Dad gave my brother, Anton, the match, but he didn't want to do it, so he gave it to me. Then, just before I did, Mom freaked out and ran back inside and she came out with this dumb little lamp that was shaped like a palm tree, that I guess she'd gotten in college or something, and she was crying and was like, 'Please can we just take this too?'

"Dad said okay, and then I lit the line and watched the spark go bounding up the driveway like a little freed animal, and then it hit the dead shrubs, and leaped to the baseboards, the front door, and then the house went up. We watched it burn and Mom cried and Dad kept saying over and over that it would be all right."

"That must have been hard," I said.

Lilly laughed. "I think I kinda liked it. Watching it all burn? I don't know, it was . . . exciting. I mean, it was where I spent my whole life, and then suddenly all of it was being reduced to a thin layer of ash. I guess I should have been sad, but it didn't even feel like we had a right to it anymore, you know? Who were we to get some house with eight rooms and two bathrooms and water and electricity that just magically appeared if you turned a knob or flipped a switch? Already, lots of people were living without that stuff, and we'd watch the news about the fighting and the riots up north and the mass suicides in Lagos, and my dad would say it could be worse."

"You don't miss it?" I asked.

"Nah," said Lilly, like she was certain she didn't. "Well, but it was strange. I mean, I was only eight, so I think I just assumed we'd get to have a new home pretty soon. But then we traveled north, spent a couple years in Calgary living in this one-room apartment where you shared a bathroom with the whole floor, and waiting for the war to calm down and for our ACF immigration papers to get processed. And things were bad there, and getting worse around the world, and then Mom started getting sick, and Anton took off and . . . that was when my parents decided to put me in here. . . ." She paused. Her voice had gotten heavier at that last part. When she continued, she was quieter. "And it was weird to wake up and have everything be perfect, you know? To be in this place. I felt like I'd missed out on the life I was supposed to have, almost like I'd died, and like this was the afterlife. Like I got cheated."

"You were lucky," said Evan. It sounded like he was trying to be sensitive. They seemed to have a truce in place tonight, but I still wondered if this would be the comment to break it.

"Right," she said quietly.

Silence passed over us. I wanted to ask her about what had happened to her brother, what it was like to say good-bye to her parents, but I wasn't sure if she'd want to talk about it, and the CITs probably already knew.

There was a white flash in the sky behind us, and a low rumble, like thunder. "What was that?" I asked, leaning my head back off the trampoline. Another bolt of white lightning appeared, zigzagging from straight above us over toward the hills. Thunder rolled around the dome. I had an urge to head for cover, like I was back home and lightning rains were coming.

"It's particle de . . . ," said Marco. "De-um . . ."

"Deionization," finished Lilly.

"Nerd," said Aliah.

I stretched my neck to look over at Lilly. "What's that?"

"The solar radiation hitting the dome all day causes charged particles to build up," she said. "The lightning burns it off. There's that big antenna hanging below the Eye, and then a tower over behind Mount Aasgard."

Another bolt flashed.

"It's cool," I said. "Safe lightning."

"Yeah," Lilly agreed.

We all watched and waited. There was one more flash, and that was it.

"Hey, Owen." It was Marco. "Do you guys still have holotech out there in the Hub?"

"Yeah," I said. "Just, like, at the rec center, though. Not in our houses like I heard it used to be."

"I heard they still have full-on holotech communities up north," said Evan. "Even the porn ones."

"Pervert," said Lilly.

"You bet." Evan grinned.

"What's it like?" Aliah asked.

"The porn?"

"No, yuck! I was talking to Owen. What's it like living out there, in the present? Like, the real world, not our little bubble here."

"I don't know," I said. "It probably stinks, I guess, compared to here, or what you guys remember the world being like."

"Eden is way better than what the world was like b-freeze," said Evan. "Everything was going to hell, if it wasn't there already."

"Yeah, but at least it was real," said Lilly.

Evan made a sound like he was maybe laughing to himself, but he didn't say anything.

"Well," I said, "out at Yellowstone, I mean, it's not *that* bad, but we are underground most of the time, and you can't really go anywhere. I feel like I live in a world right after the big party. Like, everything was amazing and alive and people were having the time of their lives way back when, and now when I live is like the next morning, and everything is broken and trashed, technology and ideas just lying around empty, and it's like we missed it."

"Yeah," said Aliah, "and what about how I heard there's a garbage patch out in the Pacific that's so big that people live on it?"

"The Flotilla," said Marco. "It sounds pretty cool, actually. Hey, we'd be rock stars out there, with our gills."

"Come on," said Evan. "They'd probably make us slaves for catching their food. At least here we get to do what we want."

"Yeah, but, should we?" said Lilly.

"What do you mean?" asked Evan.

"I mean: Should we get to do what we want? Isn't that how the whole planet got screwed? Because we thought we should be able to be, like, in holotech with our me-friends in Dubai, and eating sushi at a Mexican chain restaurant at the same time, while clothes we bought from bed were getting delivered to our front door? I mean, you know?"

"So you're saying it's bad to want things?" asked Evan. "It's wrong to try to make things as good as they can be?"

"I don't know, Eden boy," Lilly snapped. The truce was over. "Why don't you ask the six billion dead people?"

"It's human nature," said Evan.

"Part of it," Lilly spat, "but not all of it. Some of it is selfish and reckless."

"Honestly," said Evan, "you're a hypocrite. You live here in Eden. If you think it's so *wrong*, why don't you just leave?"

Lilly bolted up. "It wasn't my choice to be here! It was my parents', and they were just trying to protect me. Believe me, if I could get out of here, I would."

"And do what?" said Evan.

Marco and Aliah giggled quietly to each other and then toppled back into the water. They'd apparently had enough of the argument.

"Something," Lilly said, glaring at Evan. "More than the nothing you're doing."

"Whatever," Evan muttered.

Lilly jumped up to her feet and started bouncing in the center of the raft. She looked at me. "Wanna swim? There's a shipwreck." She held out her hand.

"You're taking him to the wreck?" Evan asked, clearly annoyed.

"Sure," I said. I got up and took her hand and kept my gaze away from Evan as we bounced high and shot off into the deep.

It was a relief to be back in the water. The dark and cold pulled me into an embrace that seemed to make my skin irrelevant, like I was just a concentration of energy within a medium, and one with the world around me. I shoved air out of my lungs, a rebellion in bubbles, then flexed my throat and felt it seal off, felt my gills opening like windows slipping up, fresh breezes fluttering curtains.

Sinking through layers of deepening cold, losing sight. I arced back up to midlevel, the world of silhouettes where the MoonGlow died. I saw Lilly do the same. This was the depth, about five meters below the surface, where the primitive sinuses in our ears barely ached. I was dolphin kicking, just like in the butterfly stroke that drowned me, except not awkward at all when you were subsurface. It actually made my body a smooth wave within the fluid. It was the opposite of what you thought: muscles not taut and rigid, but loose, not fighting.

I swam toward Lilly and she darted left and spun a ring around me, a blur of trailing hair. I threw myself in a wild spin, trying to keep up with her, heard the chirps and vibrations of her strange fish laughter.

Then she was gone.

I looked around. Strained to see further in the dark. Behind me, I spied Marco and Aliah, floating in a tangle of each other beneath the raft.

Arms around my abdomen. Yanking me back. 'Gotcha!' My body pressing against Lilly's. I felt an electric charge burn through me. Just as fast, she shoved me away, then swam around in front of me again. 'The wreck is this way,' she said.

I nodded. She took off ahead and I followed, working hard to keep up. She was fast, but I had been getting faster too, hour by hour, night by night.

Leaving the raft, we lost all contact with the earthly world. There was only black in all directions, and the fluid form of Lilly. As we swam, I spun onto my back, looking up through the shimmering glass surface at the projection of the moon and stars, here and there fractured by the geodesic superstructure of the dome.

I thought about what Lilly had said, how if we were something new, a new species, then there were thousands of miles of ocean where we could swim. Sure, there were the dead zones, the garbage gyres, the algae tides, and the gel-oil-plastics slick that made most of the coastlines useless. . . . But the ocean was massive. We could swim beneath the destruction until we found clean water, search the seas until we discovered the one archipelago where the surface was clear, the water blue, the coral still multicolored and the fish still the work of a fanciful God, not the gloom-and-doom Gods that seemed to be in charge now. Lilly and I could find that place and start over. Maybe even raise a gill family.

'Hey, daydreamer, over here.' Lilly was back behind me. She'd taken a sharp turn in a different direction.

I caught up and saw the lake bottom rising beneath us. Ahead, Lilly stood. I joined her, emerging from the embrace of the water into the harsh night breeze. I shivered in the cool as I pressed my lungs back open.

"Where's the shipwreck?" I asked as she waded ashore, toward a solid black wall of pine trees.

"It's close, but we need light."

I followed her into the trees, feet wincing at the unwelcoming textures: pine needles, roots, rock spines.

"Here," she said. "We stashed some stuff for when we go on longer swims." Ahead was a fallen tree, its roots having pulled up the forest floor like a flap of skin. She crouched and ducked under the thick base of the trunk. With a grunt, she pulled out a red bag made of smooth, waterproof fabric. She unclipped big metal buckles and pulled out a bulky yellow flashlight. She flicked a switch, igniting a beam of white light. "Waterproof."

"Cool."

She stashed the bag. "Come on."

We walked back to the water's edge and had waded in knee deep when I paused. We were far enough from camp that we'd reached the edge of the inlet. The wide center of the lake spread away from us, and on its far shore, a couple kilometers away, was the EdenWest city. It twinkled in vertical stacks of amber-and-emerald lights. I'd seen photos of the old technopolises, with their miles of skyscrapers, and of the new, more modest ones up north, like Baffin City, Yellowknife, Helsinki Island, and New Murmansk. EdenWest was probably not even close to that scale, but still, for someone who had spent his life in a flat, hunched world beneath rock ceilings, there was something amazing to me about the straight, reaching towers, the idea that people might have existed, once upon a time, making free use of the sky.

"There's Neverland," said Lilly.

"Huh?" I didn't know the reference. When she didn't add more, I asked, "Is it cool there?"

"I guess. If you're like Evan and you just want to live your little life pretending everything's fine, while the world outside goes to hell."

I laughed, but cut it off when I saw that Lilly wasn't smiling.

"It's not all bad," she said. "There are museums and stuff, entertainment, sports, shows and games that travel from one Eden to the next, and you know, lots of boutiques with the styles from up north, SensaStreets made of hyperbricks that synch with your me-self and advertise to you and play your own sound track as you walk, but . . . I'm mainly at Cryo House." Her voice quieted. "You don't get out much when you don't have parents to take you anywhere."

She hugged herself, like she might be cold. I thought

about putting my arm around her, but wasn't sure if that would be okay. And how did you find out if it was? Did you ask? It seemed like you were supposed to just *know*.

But then Lilly said, "Come on," and I'd missed my chance.

We plunged back under, descending with the lake bottom until we were in new depths, maybe ten meters down, ears aching. Lilly switched on her light and we leveled out, losing the bottom and moving into the black, the light beam waving back and forth. You couldn't tell up and down by sight, but there were other clues, variations in temperature and pressure, things your body could sense if you listened in new ways.

Lilly's beam caught something white in the water. She paused and aimed the light as I swam up beside her. I looked down and flinched. There were eyes down there, large and black . . . a fish. An enormous fish, barely moving, just hovering lazily in the dark. Its body was a sickly peach color like dead flesh, with a pattern of dull coal-colored blotches like incomplete stripes. It had a square head and a fat body. Its fins flicked slowly.

'What's that?' I asked.

'Zombie koi. That's what we call them, anyway.'

'It's gross.'

'Yeah. I guess back when they opened this place, they thought it would be cute if the lake had pretty fish like some Asian garden, so they put koi in with everything else, but then the koi ended up outcompeting the other fish, either by eating them or killing the plant life in the lake.'

'I saw fake plants on the bottom,' I said.

'Yeah, and then this lake never gets cold, like winter, so the koi just kept eating and growing all the time. And then, get this: Eden even put in these fish called walleyes that used to be here, to eat the baby koi, but then the koi and the walleyes just got it on, and that's how you got these mutant zombie freaks. Oh, and the koi eat those walleyes now.' Lilly turned to me and smiled. 'This lake is full of weird creatures.'

'Ha.'

'Don't worry, though; they might look creepy, but they're just big dopes.'

The fish kept floating there, shimmering in the light beam. It rotated to aim its other eye at us, then must have decided we weren't food, and slithered off into the darkness.

We kept swimming, every once in a while seeing another zombie koi floating along in the murky depths. The story made me feel a little bad for the creature. I thought again about how this lake, this whole place, seemed like a giant lab, a weird mad scientist's chamber of robot butterflies, creepy fish, and mutant gill people.

Now Lilly's flashlight reflected off metal. The side of the wreck. It appeared to us as a long wall looming out of the dark, rusty and twenty feet tall, red paint remaining here and there. It hung cockeyed, impaled on a spear of rock rising up from the unseen bottom. A flat deck in front, then a square cabin, and in back a bunch of cranes and ropes like maybe it had been a fishing boat.

Lilly swam to the side railing and into the cabin through a door that hung open. I followed. Inside was a little room with a dining table and benches. Everything was coated in furry green slime. I found her pretending to sit there at the table, despite the steep angle of the ship, her hands folded. 'What's for dinner, captain?'

I laughed and swam toward the door to the next room. 'This is cool.'

She slid beside me in the doorway. I felt her arm against mine. 'We thought there might be bodies, but no luck.'

We slipped into the next room, and the flashlight beam illuminated buckled counters, the gnawed remnants of rolled papers, an ancient computer floating upside down in the corner. The floor was littered with a mess of rotted books, plates and cups, electronic debris. Schools of small silver fish scattered around my feet. I wondered if they hid in here from the zombie koi outside.

'What would you like?' Lilly asked.

I turned to see her near a stove, holding a rusted frying pan. She was smiling.

I was supposed to say something witty, I knew that. But what? 'Um . . . ,' I said.

Lilly drifted over to me, the pan in front of her, the flashlight pointed straight at my face. 'Jeez, it's not a test.'

'No?' I said, wincing against the beam.

'You're funny,' said Lilly.

'Me?' I felt my insides spinning into overdrive. Funny? Where did she get that idea? 'I'm never funny.'

'Yes, you are. Your whole awkward thing.' Maybe it was just the currents in this room, but Lilly seemed to be inching closer. 'The way you get so flustered.'

'I don't get . . . I . . .' I had no idea what to say.

'Exactly what I'm talking about. You never try to act all cool around me. You never try to put on a show.' The frying pan bounced against my abdomen. She lowered it and let it sink to the floor. The flashlight beam pointed up, giving us sinister faces.

'I—show? I wouldn't even—'

'That's what I like.' Lilly smiled, and her eyes seemed to get bigger. 'The Owen Show isn't a show, it's real. It's just what you are.'

Closer. A shocking thing suddenly crossed my mind. Was Lilly flirting with me? Like, real flirting? The actual *I like you* flirting? I felt frozen. How could this be possible? And what was I supposed to do? I felt like I should say something witty, something smooth, but there was no time and so I just replied, 'Sorry,' and then I thought, *Why did you say that? YOU ARE AN IDIOT!* Why would I say sorry? I—

Lilly laughed. Moved even closer. 'Owen, it's not a bad thing.'

Our bodies were only centimeters apart. Now what?

'I fluster you,' Lilly said, her face like some kind of black hole, sucking me in, bending time. Could this really be . . . that? Could we really—

Owen.

A blue glow caught the corner of my vision.

Lilly was right there, our eyes locked—

I turned away. Now, of all times, but I had to, because it was *that* blue glow.

Find me.

It flickered from the porthole window behind me. 'It's back,' I said.

'Wait, what?' Lilly asked.

I was ruining the moment, but I couldn't help it. I slid over and pressed my cheek to the glass, realizing with a tight twist of nerves that I had just missed a gigantic chance, though I was maybe relieved more than anything else, my head still spinning from the possibilities.

The glow was to the right, faint blue, but unmistakable. 'Come on,' I said to Lilly, and shot back into the first room and out the door.

'Where are you going?' Lilly asked, following me out. Did she sound annoyed?

Maybe. But . . . the siren . . . It was real. I felt sure of it now, and I *had* to see it. I arced up and over the top of the ship, getting a view down the other side of the hull.

Only black.

Lilly arrived beside me. 'Owen, what is it?'

'I saw something,' I said, but now I felt like an idiot. There was nothing. I'd been making things up because I was too scared to—

Wait, there. The faint blue light again, this time out away from the ship, almost swallowed by the murk. I pointed. 'See it?'

Lilly followed my finger. 'See *what*?'

'The . . . the thing.' It was hard to see, but it was definitely the siren's ghostly human form, flickering blue, swimming away. 'You see her?' I said, kicking in that direction.

'Her?' Lilly definitely sounded annoyed. 'Okay, I have no idea what you're talking about. Where are you going?'

I squinted. The image—because it almost seemed like a picture rather than a solid object— was getting smaller, distant. We had to hurry if we were going to catch it.

What is oldest will be new, what was lost shall be found.

I spun back to Lilly. 'That! Did you hear that?'

Her eyebrow cocked. Arms crossed. 'You're not making any sense.'

I looked back. The siren was almost gone.

Find me.

'Come on, we have to catch it.' I started to swim.

'Owen! Catch *what*?'

'The—the thing, the siren, I mean, that's what I call her, it . . . whatever! Just come on.' I thrust ahead, attacking the water, swimming as fast as I could. When I turned back, Lilly was still at the ship, already distant. 'Come on!' I called to her.

No answer. I spun around. The siren was maybe a little closer, but still dim. I'd lose her if I stopped.

In the temple.

Okay, fine. I couldn't believe I was doing this, couldn't believe I was leaving the moment I'd just left, and possibly ruining any chance of future moments, but . . . Lilly would catch up if she wanted to. 'I'll be right back!' I called to her, and took off as fast as I could.

I hurtled through the water. The siren was still far ahead. Glanced back: Lilly had been swallowed by the dark.

Kicking. Reaching. A knife through the liquid. I gained some ground, and started to see the siren's shape again, and though the blue light was muted and impermanent, I thought I could see legs kicking in smooth dolphin style, arms moving, hair maybe flowing out behind her.

My muscles were starting to burn. I was even getting a dull pain in my abdomen. And yet there she was in front of me, that flickering, ghostlike figure, and I felt a certainty: *Keep going.* Even if I was leaving Lilly behind . . . This meant something. It knew me. It had something to share. Something about . . . everything. I felt certain of that.

Minutes passed, maybe a half hour. I couldn't tell. All I knew was that slowly I was catching her.

'What are you?' I called.

There was a humming sound in the water now, and a distant din like moving parts. I could feel it saturating my ears, and yet the siren's voice seemed to be somehow inside my head again. It was warm-sounding, maybe even electric. *What is oldest will be new. What was hidden shall be unlocked. The secrets remembered by the true.*

I swam harder, trying to close the gap, and saw that now shapes were beginning to draw themselves into existence in front of us. I was maybe ten meters behind the siren, and maybe another twenty meters in front of her was something solid, vertical—a wall. Closer, and I could see that it was made of concrete. The edge of the dome?

Rocks had appeared from below, the rising lake bottom. Ahead on the wall, halfway from the surface of the lake to the floor, were two horizontal lines of large cylindrical holes. There were yellow lights glowing in rings around them. I was parallel with the top line, and I could feel the push of water coming through them. Looking up, I saw the wavy outline of a tall, triangular building above the surface. This must have been the Aquinara, where the water of Lake Eden was filtered and continually recycled. It also created the water vapor necessary for clouds and rain in the dome.

This way.

I looked down and spied the siren flickering among the black boulders at the base of the wall. She circled and vanished into what looked like an opening in the rock.

I started down, but I was exhausted. The pressure

seemed to close in tighter than before. My side ached. My legs were burning, feet cramping.

I grabbed at the fluid, pulling myself deeper, pushing through the current of incoming water, down toward the fissure. I could see the blue of the siren glowing from inside, almost like she was waiting for me. . . .

Come home, Lük.

'What—?' I started to ask.

But suddenly my vision exploded with light and it was like the inky dark of the lake had been washed away by white. I lost track of everything, and was greeted by a vision that I couldn't explain and yet felt like I knew, almost like it was a memory:

There was a massive city built of stone, copper, and gold. It sat high in a steep-sided valley, with a great curving wall at its end, meeting the sea. Sailing ships moved to and from giant stone docks. More ships in the air, too, somehow. Mountains rose behind the city, jagged peaks topped with snow and cradling glaciers. The sky was dark gray, red sunlight edging the horizon.

At the center of the city was a giant structure, a pyramid like something out of ancient Egypt but with a flat top that was bordered by strange round globes, glowing like fire, but with white intensity.

Atop the pyramid stood a cluster of people, adults in crimson robes adorned with turquoise, and in the center, three teens, dressed in virgin white, on their knees on soft pillows, staring straight ahead. Things blurred. . . .

And I was one of the three. Before me was an object of brilliant crystal, sparkling translucent white. There was one in front of each of us. They glowed brighter than they should have, given the dim, smoky sky. I now noticed the weightless snow that was falling on me—gray snow, dead, leaving streaks on my white robe. I glanced to my right. Beside me was a girl: black hair, a round face, coal-black eyes. She looked back at me. I didn't know her, or did I? Tears were leaking slowly down her cheeks. Beyond her was another boy, but his face was obscured in shaggy hair. But this girl . . . who was she?

She nodded slightly then turned back to face the giant crystal before her. I did too, and I looked into the pale light, the crystal object the size of my head. On its surface I saw a distorted reflection of a face that wasn't quite my own, yet the features were similar, almost like we were related.

Behind the crystals, the priests and priestesses moved their hands in slow circles, performing final rites. One of them cried, but we all knew this was what had to be done.

I watched that one woman's gaze flick over my shoulder, and, though I could not see them, I understood that behind us stood men, men with daggers, men who were stepping forward and placing those perfect blades to our necks.

And then the crystal's glow increased, overwhelming everything and blinding me of every other thought. The blade pressed in and I felt searing pain and my eyes widened and I saw that the crystal before me had been perfectly carved into the shape of a human skull.

Its hollow eye sockets gleamed at me and I stared at it and I was so afraid but sure this was right, that all would be right. The giant skull, smiling a skinless grin of perfectly etched teeth. I believed. I believed. . . .

The pain of the blade was like the burning of forming gills only worse, and deeper, until there was nothing but the mineral light of the crystal skull, growing brighter, and I was gone within it, of it, in an oblivion of pure white.

11

GREEN.

My eyes blinked open to a view down into sun-streaked water. A few feet below me, among the angling sunbeams, a giant puke-colored zombie koi hovered, watching me like it was waiting to be sure I was dead. Its gills billowed slowly in and out. Its eyes flicked around almost as if it was embarrassed that I'd noticed it.

I waved my arms, and the movement made the big, bloated fish turn and wander off.

My head hurt—dull, throbbing pain—and my back felt hot, exposed. Everything sore. Only my gills were humming along at normal speed. I rolled over. The lake surface was a couple feet above me, the TrueSky pale blue, with the occasional puffy SimCloud floating by. I righted myself and swam up, sticking my head out of the water and opening my throat to gulp in air.

The Aquinara was to my right. The city was another half mile up the shore, humming with activity. A couple sailboats and yachts were cruising nearby. And there was another buzzing sound, closer: a motor.

"Owen!"

I looked toward the Aquinara and saw a small boat headed right for me. The camp motorboat. Paul was standing at the wheel. Leech was with him.

I thought about diving under, but I felt too exhausted. And they were already pulling up, Paul turning off the motor, the boat drifting close to me, bringing a tingling electrostatic smell from its hydrogen-cell engine.

He gazed down at me from the shade of his black hat and sunglasses. He had on a short-sleeved button-down shirt, but still wore a tie tight against his neck. "Well, look what we found."

"Hey," I mumbled, not knowing what else to say. My thoughts were racing, trying to figure out how I was going to explain what I was doing out here. . . .

"Looks like someone got up early for the polar bear swim," said Paul.

"Oh," I said, "yeah."

"I think, technically, the rules are that you stay in the camp swimming area." Paul looked around as if to point out how far away that was. "You needed a little more exercise, I take it." He looked back down at me.

"I guess," I said.

He knew something, I felt sure of it, except, as usual, I couldn't make out his expression.

"Well," said Paul, "why don't you climb in." It didn't

sound like a question.

I grabbed the edge of the boat and dragged myself over the side. I thought it would be hard, but maybe the last couple nights of swimming had given me some added strength. I slid onto the floor and then sat up on one of the bench seats, on a slippery white vinyl cushion.

Leech sat across from me, silent. His short hair was this-way-and-that, like he'd rolled out of bed early again. He had his black pole case beside him, and that little black notebook in his lap, closed, but he had a pen in his hand like he'd been sketching before I showed up. The bandage was off his other hand.

Paul keyed the engine to life and the boat lurched forward, accelerating across the lake.

"Guess your neck really is feeling better," said Paul.

"Oh, yeah," I said.

"The cramps too, I take it." This didn't sound like a question either, but more like he was checking off things in his mind. "Did you realize you'd gone over two kilometers from camp?"

"Nah, not really, I was just going along," I said, gazing at my puffy, waterlogged hands. "And I, um, lost track of where I was."

Leech made a slight coughing sound at this, but when I looked over he was squinting out at the water.

I glanced up at Paul, wondering what question would come next, but he just looked ahead, guiding the boat along.

He doesn't need to ask anything else because he knows, Lilly would probably say. *He knows what's happening.* Then I wondered: *Does he know about the siren?* How could he?

"You guys been fishing again?" I asked Paul.

"Yes indeed," said Paul, his glasses reflecting the water. "Some of the deepest water in the lake is down here by the Aquinara, right, Carey?"

Leech didn't respond.

"This is where all the gill breathers like it best," said Paul. No smile. No head movement. But that comment . . .

I tried to act like everything was normal. "Did you catch anything?" I asked, looking around the boat for a bucket of fish or something, but other than Paul's fishing pole, there was nothing. Not even, like, a box for bait or whatever they'd need.

"They weren't biting today," said Paul. "You know how fickle fish can be."

"I saw some big koi down there," I said.

"Did you?" Paul looked at me. "Well, do me a favor, Owen, and let's just keep that between us. People over in town get all worked up about the *environment*, as if they have anything to complain about. We keep the koi contained, just like everything else, so they can enjoy their day." Paul waved a hand toward a sailboat in the distance.

It surprised me to hear that note of disdain, as if Paul looked down on the people in EdenWest.

"Heads up," he said, and I looked up to see him tossing me a dark-green towel. "You look cold."

"Thanks." I wrapped it around my shivering shoulders, and squinted through the glare of sun and water, watching the leafy coastline slide by. The motor and the wind created a drone that made it easy to just sit there and get lost in your thoughts.

I remembered the dream. . . . What had that been? It was already fuzzy in my memory. Lük, the siren had said. Was that the name of the boy in that scene, the boy I had become? And what was that skull made of crystal? It seemed like, in the vision, I'd known what was happening to me, like I was expecting to die, maybe even thought it was necessary, and now I sort of felt like it was something that had really happened to me, almost like it was a memory, but . . . None of that made sense. Then again, neither did the siren. And were these things connected to my gills?

Maybe I had just gotten so tired that I passed out, and it had all been a dream or something. Except the whole thing had felt real, and big, too. Like I hadn't just been seeing that vision, I'd also been in it, and connected to something huge.

We started to turn, and I saw the little beach at the edge of the inlet, where Lilly and I had come ashore for the flashlight. It had only been a few hours ago, but it seemed like days. We passed the blue trampoline raft, the swimming dock. I looked at the raft—empty, no sign of its nighttime occupants—and then I wondered if Lilly had been mad that I left her. I couldn't believe I had, especially in that moment. All that was almost as unbelievable as the vision. . . . Lilly had actually been hitting on me, and I left! What had I been thinking? But at the time it had seemed like something I had to do. I wondered why she hadn't caught up, but maybe she hadn't understood what she was seeing. Or hadn't seen it at all.

I had that feeling again, and found Leech looking at me. His eyes were narrowed, studying me in that king-of-the-lion-pride kind of way. Or maybe it was just the brightness of the sun. Either way, it reminded me of the day before, of being pushed into the lake.

"Problem?" The word had popped out of my mouth before I even knew I was thinking it.

Now Leech definitely sneered. "Yeah. You."

"Now, now, gentlemen," said Paul.

I turned away from Leech, drying off my hair.

Paul eased the motorboat up to one of the boathouse docks. Leech hopped out, grabbing a rope to tie the bow. I went to do the same with a rope at the stern, but had to watch him out of the corner of my eye to see how to loop the thick, scratchy rope through the cleat, and hated how I needed him for things like that.

I stood up and started folding the towel, gazing at the tied-up sailboats as I did. I felt the light breeze that was always on in the morning. I turned, looking back at the narrow bay. *Wind from the southeast . . . maybe five knots. . . .* More thoughts followed along. *You'd have to tack east-west to get to the bay mouth; from there, a northwesterly course unless the wind shifted with the open water—*

"You'd better hurry back to your cabin, Owen." The words snapped me out of a trance. I turned to find Paul already on shore. Leech was nowhere to be seen. "Flagpole is in thirty minutes." said Paul. "I could walk you back—"

His watch started beeping. Paul looked down at it. "Well, rain check on that."

"What is it?" I thought to ask, not figuring he'd tell me.

"Looks like the board of directors is requesting a chat link. Well, that's unexpected, but we wouldn't want to keep them waiting."

Again I looked for some sign of emotion on Paul's face: given yesterday's shouting chat, had the comment just now been sarcastic or sincere? But there was nothing, until he saw me studying him. Then, he seemed to lean forward with interest. "Unless you have anything pressing you want to get off your chest? I could tell the board to wait. . . ."

I turned and started off the dock, desperate to get away from that gaze. "No, I'm good. Thanks for picking me up. Sorry I was out there."

"Like I said before, I'm here for you." I could feel him watching me as I hurried across the sand, away from the boathouse and toward the swimming dock. My clothes weren't there. They'd probably been found by the polar bear swimmers, ended up in Lost and Found or something.

Crossing the beach, I found myself looking at the water again. What had I been thinking back on the dock? Something about wind direction and sailing. But I'd never sailed before, never even been out in a boat until just now. I noticed the ripples on the water. *Yeah, southeasterly.* There was that thought again. Where was it coming from? And I felt weird, too, maybe had been feeling weird since I'd woken up in the lake, now that I thought about it. Not good or bad, just . . . different, like my insides were working fine except with new software, like they'd been reorganized. *Wind gusts up to about eight knots . . .*

The sound of giggles snapped me out of it. I'd stopped walking without noticing, at the edge of the playing field grass. Turning, I found the Arctic Foxes emerging from the trees, on their way to flagpole, an army of ponytails and sweatshirts and flip-flops, and I remembered that I was standing there in my bathing suit, my skinny self on display for everyone. Except then I glanced down and realized that maybe I wasn't quite as skinny as I'd been. Maybe there were curves now on my shoulders, some actual muscle on my chest. Nights of swimming, all the big camp meals, maybe it was having an effect. Though probably that was only visible to me—

"Hey, Owen." Or maybe not. I looked back and saw that Mina and another girl were lagging behind the others, looking in my direction.

"Hi," I said. I figured I was supposed to say something else, something more, but I didn't know what. Mina had stopped and was now standing there shifting from one foot to the other. Wait, was she nervous about talking to *me*?

"Did you do polar bear?" Mina asked.

"Oh, yeah," I said, and then I didn't know what else to say so I added, "It was cold."

"Um, you going tomorrow morning?" she asked. Her friend cracked up. Mina bit her lip.

"Maybe?" I said.

"Well, then maybe I'll see you there?"

"Okay . . . ," I said, meanwhile thinking, *What is happening to me?* As if gills and sirens and Lilly and thoughts about wind direction weren't enough . . . Now I seemed to be getting asked to dawn swims by Arctic Foxes. "I gotta go and, um, put on clothes."

"Mina doesn't think so!" Paige shouted from the group of Foxes who were waiting halfway across the field. How did she even hear me?

Mina blushed. "Okay, see you at flagpole?"

"I'll be there," I said, and felt like there was no way I was going to be able to handle all this.

Mina and her friend turned and started after the rest of the Arctic Foxes and as they walked they leaned into each other's shoulders and started whispering and laughing. I realized as I turned away that this time I did *not* assume that they were making fun of me. Instead, I considered that maybe I was someone worth waking up early for polar bear swim for. And even though it seemed crazy, I also smiled about it for a second, and then thought of Lilly, and smiled more, until I remembered that I'd left her last night.

Idiot! What was I thinking? But the siren. That vision . . .

And now the wind.

What did it all mean?

I walked back to the cabin in a daze, all these thoughts jumbling around. I was just nearing the side door when it popped open.

"Owen." It was Todd. He looked at me expectantly.

"I just went to the polar bear swim."

Todd looked me over. "Okay, but you're supposed to let me know the night before."

"Sorry."

He held the door for me. Inside, everybody was up and getting dressed, and Jalen greeted me with "Turtle!" but that was about it.

I threw on clothes and turned around. Beaker was a foot from me again.

"Dude, can you stop doing that?" I said.

He looked at me almost like he was expecting something. "What?"

He glanced around, then leaned close. "I saw you leave in the night."

I looked around, too. "Did you tell anyone?"

"No."

"Well, don't, okay?"

"Where were you?"

"Just . . . out. I needed to take a walk."

"All night?"

"Yeah."

"Can I come next time?"

"Probably not."

Beaker was going to say something else, but Mike passed and shoved him down onto his bunk. "Don't block the door, scrub."

As he got up, wincing, I said, "Just forget you saw me, okay?"

"But . . ." He sighed. "All right," he said, sounding disappointed.

We headed down to flagpole. I stumbled along, feeling like I was going to fall asleep on my feet. As we sat down, Mina waved hi to me and I waved back and then slumped in my seat and closed my eyes as Claudia began her announcements. "For everyone's safety, we'd like all cabins to continue using NoRad on the two-hour cycle from now on. Now, we have lots of things on the schedule today. . . ."

I faded out again, into the half sleep I was getting good at during the day. I saw that place again, that city and the pyramid, or temple. . . . The siren had said something about a temple . . . and then I remembered that girl, too, one of the other sacrificial ones, like me—no, not me, but . . . me? But then who was that siren anyway? Was any of it even real?

Could be leftover trauma from your drowning, a technician suggested.

Maybe we have a faulty block in the memory drives, said another, looking over a map of my brain. *Hard to say.*

Well, figure it out, already! I said to them. They seemed surprised to be getting an order from me, and grumbled as they hurried around.

I needed to talk to Lilly about all this. Were the CITs seeing sirens or having visions or thinking about wind speeds?

". . . for tomorrow's predator-prey competition," Claudia was saying. Now there was the usual giggle from the Arctic Foxes as Leech and Paul arrived and Leech did his grand entrance thing. Where had they been since I'd left the dock? Did Leech get to sit in on the board of directors meeting? I avoided looking at Paul as he headed up the hill.

Back into my thoughts . . . what had the siren said? *What is oldest will be new. What was hidden shall be unlocked. The secrets remembered by the true.* The *oldest* part made sense with the vision. Whatever that had been, it looked like it had happened a long time ago, but it hadn't looked like any history I remembered hearing about. Where had there been pyramids with some kind of electric light, in snowy mountains by the ocean?

Claudia's speech filtered back to my ears. "We'll be using the Preserve for the game—"

And then she was cut off by a huge, thundering sound, immediate and sudden, and a wall of air slammed into our backs and pushed everyone off their benches. The older kids stumbled and staggered to our feet. Little ones were thrown to the ground, hitting their knees and chins.

Everyone spun to see a huge plume of black smoke rising from behind the dining hall like a thrust fist. It billowed up until it hit the side of the dome ceiling and then began to roll and spread, dimming a bank of the SafeSun lights. For a moment, I saw the entire wall of the dome shudder, almost like it was made of rubber.

Echoes of the explosion rolled away across the lake. An alarm began to sound.

"Everyone meet up with your cabin!" Claudia shouted.

"Over here!" Todd was calling. All the campers clustered.

"Nomads," Leech said knowingly. "Probably mounting another attack." Everybody tensed at this. One of the younger kids standing nearby overheard Leech, turned, and whispered frantically to his cabin. The panic spread, some children starting to cry.

"Hey, Carey!" Todd snapped at Leech. "We don't know what happened."

Leech looked at the rest of us and rolled his eyes.

"All right, everyone!" We looked back to Claudia, who was holding a subnet phone to her ear. "Everything is secured, nothing to worry about. We're to proceed to breakfast as usual."

We headed up the hill, everyone mumbling nervously.

"They tried one time back in the spring," Leech was saying. Everyone in our cabin, even Beaker and Bunsen, stayed within earshot of him like he was our wise sage. I couldn't help listening, too. "Blowing a hole in one of the supply entrances. There was another time when they tried to get in through the observatory roof. But the Security Forces took them out. Stupid savages."

"Sometimes they show up in Dallas Beach looking for supplies," said Noah. "They're always dressed weird. My brother says they wear skulls around their necks."

"I heard they practice human sacrifice, and worship, like, sun gods and stuff," said Jalen.

I was pretty sure Jalen was wrong about that. The sun god stuff was down in Desenna, the human sacrifice too, but that was only rumors. In fact, I was pretty sure I'd heard that the Nomads were the victims of these sacrifices, but I didn't feel like getting into the conversation.

"I heard that they're just kinda normal," said Beaker.

"Yes, but you're an idiot," said Leech.

We reached the dining hall doors and waited to file in. A trail of smoke was still rising from behind the camp office buildings. While we stood there, a little cart rushed by, carrying five of Eden's black-suited Security Forces, four guards sitting on the sideways benches behind the driver. There were three men and two women, all wearing helmets and high-laced boots, with rifles over their shoulders. I knew the Edens had security, but it surprised me how much these officers looked like an army.

"Man, I'd like to suit up with those guys and go kick some Nomad ass," said Jalen wistfully.

We filed in and headed to our table. Everyone was quieter than usual. You could hear the words *nomads* and *attack* being muttered everywhere. Todd started filling everyone's cups with bug juice. Today's color was neon pink and, again, I waved it off.

When it was our turn to get food, I looked for Lilly in the CIT area. There were six of them sitting over there eating, but none of my gill breathers were with them.

I went into the kitchen and got a tray. I took some gray waffles, some fried syntheggs, then I grabbed a cup of the fruit salad and turned—

Lilly was standing right in front of me. She took my tray and put it down beside the fruit cups. "Come on," she said, and pulled me by the wrist. Instead of heading out the kitchen door into the main dining room, we left through a side door that led into a hallway.

"Where are we going?"

"To see what happened before the official story gets written."

"Story?"

"History is always written to serve the powerful," Lilly said over her shoulder. "Whatever just happened, Paul will change the story so that none of us are afraid."

"You think we should be afraid?" I asked, not really understanding what she was getting at.

"Not of the Nomads," said Lilly.

She led me out double doors. We were on the dirt road that led between the dining hall and the administrative buildings. Evan, Marco, and Aliah were standing there.

"Okay, *now* can we go?" asked Evan.

"Everybody needs to see these things together," Lilly snapped at him. Then she glanced sharply at me. "If somebody runs off on their own, we can't defend each other. Remember Anna?"

I figured she also meant me, last night. "Sorry about that," I said quickly.

"Yeah, dude, what happened to you?" Marco asked.

"Later," said Lilly. "Let's go."

"Roger that, commander," said Evan sarcastically. Lilly huffed and brushed past, her shoulder bumping him.

I followed after them, wondering if Todd had noticed yet that I was gone. But whatever, it felt good to be back with my people.

Lilly led the way, ducking off the road into the trees between a staff office building and the infirmary. She turned around and held a finger to her lips, then tiptoed ahead.

We got to the edge of the building and peered through the underbrush. Ahead was the wide paved area and the tall metal double doors. The elevator shaft was off to the left. Before the doors there was a trench, like a dry moat, separating the ground and the wall. A steel bridge stretched over it.

Between us and this bridge was an overturned supply truck. Its squat, square frame was charred and smoking, twisted like it was made of clay. Same for the bridge, which had buckled and half given way. The little security checkpoint house had been flattened. A small fire flickered in its black remains, and one of the Security Forces was spraying it with an extinguisher.

"The bomb must have been in that truck," said Lilly.

The dome doors were cockeyed, creating an awkward triangular gap. Everything was smeared with the black of the blast. A few inner panels of the dome had fallen from points above, wide triangular sections that had what looked like frosted glass on the front and then a feathery layer of radiation insulators on the back. The glass had mostly smashed all over the blast site, like someone had scattered diamonds. The air was sour with a smell like burned sugar and melting crayons.

But it was that tiny view out the cockeyed doors that caught my eye. I could see the dry steps of rock, a distant leaning water tower gleaming in white hot sun.

Lilly caught my eye. "Almost makes you want to make a break for it."

"Yeah, an express run to death," said Evan.

"There's Paul," said Aliah.

He was jogging toward the bridge. Shouts were coming from outside the doors. Three security guards appeared, ducking through with a fourth figure, whose hands were bound behind his back.

"Whoa, they got one," said Marco.

The prisoner wore dirty jeans and a long, thickly padded coat with a silver reflective surface. He had tinted goggles pulled up onto his forehead, and a black triangle of plastic stuck onto the bridge of his nose. I'd seen these clothes before: all of it was to protect from exposure. He walked tall as they crossed the bridge, a defiant smile on his face.

Paul was calling someone on his phone as the security team edged its way across the twisted bridge. When they reached the other side, Dr. Maria appeared.

Paul motioned to the captive. "Take him to medical," he barked, his normal mellow demeanor gone. "And we'll want him to talk."

"You know why we're here!" the prisoner suddenly shouted, clearly trying to get as many of the personnel to hear him as possible.

"Shut him up," Paul growled to Dr. Maria. He turned to the Security Forces. "Cartier, is this under control?" he called.

One of the officers, a short, burly man who wasn't wearing a helmet, turned around. He had rough features and short hair. There was a silver bar pinned on his shirt. "Yes sir."

"Good." Paul spun and started back toward his office, like this was just one of many crises he was dealing with.

Dr. Maria had produced a syringe from her coat pocket. Her face was set seriously, but she also looked almost fearful as she approached the Nomad.

"This is all a lie!" the Nomad shouted. "You'll all be left behind! You've got to bring down Project Elysium!"

I saw Paul pause at the door and turn back toward him.

"Hold him," said Dr. Maria. I saw the syringe shaking in her hand.

Cartier put the Nomad in a headlock, pulling him sideways by the hair and exposing his neck. The prisoner saw Dr. Maria's needle and stopped struggling, instead just glaring at her coldly. She pressed the needle into his neck and he slumped into the guards' arms. They dragged him toward the infirmary. Paul disappeared inside.

"We should get back," whispered Evan, checking his watch. "We're supposed to be at the dock in ten minutes for morning lessons."

For once, Lilly just agreed. "Right."

We crept back through the trees to the road. "What did he mean?" I asked.

"Project Elysium?" said Marco. "No idea."

"Not *no* idea," said Lilly. "I've heard about it on the Free Signal." She looked around suspiciously. "We shouldn't talk here." She glanced at me. "Tonight?"

"Yeah," I said.

Lilly nodded, and the CITs headed up the road.

Back inside, I got a new tray of food and returned to my table. Everybody was finished eating.

"There he is," said Todd. "Owen, Pedro tells me you were talking to a lady friend in there."

I glanced over at Beaker and tried to say thanks with my eyes. "Yeah," I said to Todd.

"All right then," he said with a smile. "Eat up."

I sat and started shoveling food. When I finished, I found Leech staring at me. That weird look again, from the boat, from the other day, too. Like he was studying me. Like nothing about me convinced him. Or . . . *like he knows something is up.* It seemed more certain than ever.

"Hello, everyone," Paul's voice echoed over the speaker system in the dining hall. I looked around, but he wasn't anywhere in the room. "I just wanted to give you an update on this morning's accident. It turns out one of our supply trucks had a faulty battery cell, which caused the explosion. The driver has some minor injuries, but otherwise everyone is all right. I know many of you have been worried that this event had something to do with the Nomad Alliance and so I just wanted to end those rumors. Everything is fine, and no one is in any danger. So, have a pleasant day."

I heard Leech murmuring and glanced over. "Yeah, guess that's all it was," he was saying seriously, like he was Paul's special agent to the Spotted Hyenas.

History is always written to serve the powerful, Lilly had said, and here was proof: Paul rewriting what was only moments old. Had he done the same for Colleen? What about the DI? All of it was in question now, and I had to wonder, what about EdenWest *was* what it seemed?

12

WE SPENT THE MORNING PLAYING DODGEBALL
and tetherball on the paved courts. Having gills did me no
good at surviving the screaming red rubber balls. If anything,
trying to move my legs on land felt more inefficient and
useless than ever. Every time I tried to twist or duck and
the ball went *puunk!* on my head or back, I would look up
and wish I could take that grinning face off Jalen or Mike,
Noah or Leech, and show them the depths of the lake,
drag them deep until their lungs felt like balloons trapped
against a ceiling. I would imagine their eyes bugging out
and their pupils saying, *Don't do this!* Their arms flailing.
I would see the bubble pressing out against their squeezed
lips and—

Puunk!

"Ha, Turtle!" shouted Jalen.

I spent most of the game on the sideline, waiting for
dark, for my time.

Lying in our bunks that night, Todd reading to us, I

got a turn on the computer pad. I was surprised to find my camp mailbox empty. I thought I'd hear from Dad. It was strange, though, how little I'd thought about him the last couple days. I'd been so caught up in Lilly and everything else. I almost felt guilty now.

I started a new letter:

Hey Dad,

It's Saturday now. Things are okay here. I think you'd be proud of me. I've made some friends. Older kids that I actually have some things in common with. They're better than the kids in my cabin.

Also, you maybe heard about that explosion here today. I don't know if that would make the news or not. Well, I'm not sure what you heard, but

I stopped there and wondered: What should I tell him? What I'd seen, or what Paul and Eden would have said? Then I thought about how much I already *hadn't* told him in the letter. My gills, the siren, all of that. How exactly was I going to explain that stuff to him, anyway? He might freak out if I told him, and pull me out of camp early. Did I want to leave early? Things didn't seem safe here, but if I left I'd lose Lilly, and I'd never know what was really going on with me, with this place. And that didn't even factor in that I'd be the only kid at Hub with gills.

I deleted the message.

Soon, Todd left us, and after the usual joke-filled conversations about the attractiveness levels of various Arctic Foxes, the cabin descended into snores and breathing. I closed my eyes and fell asleep too. . . .

Until my gills woke me up, like clockwork. I got out of my bunk quietly, double-checking to be sure that Beaker was asleep. I had already put on my bathing suit before bed, so I slipped on my sneakers, grabbed my towel, and headed out.

I heard the light murmur of voices as I crossed the beach. Saw the silhouettes of heads and shoulders sitting out on the raft. I walked out to the edge of the dock, my gills sensing their home and flicking open. I blocked my throat and dove in, all the sensations of water a relief. I did a few circles before heading out to the raft. As I got close, I decided to try the shooting hands-free jump that the others always did. I swam straight down, launched up into the air, landed, and managed not to fall over. "Hey!" I said, but I immediately tensed.

Lilly wasn't there.

"She took off," said Evan, noticing me looking around. "She was pissed."

"Oh," I said. I felt exposed standing there, and almost like, without Lilly around, I wasn't actually welcome. "What's she mad about?"

"Him," Aliah said, sitting with Marco's arm over her shoulders, and I saw that she was glaring at Evan.

"Oh, come on," Evan said. "It's not my fault she was being ridiculous."

"It wasn't ridiculous!" Aliah shot back. "I think she might be right."

"About what?" I asked.

"She wants to bust out of here," said Marco.

"Which is a stupid idea," said Evan, "be—"

"It's not a stupid idea!" said Aliah.

Marco looked at me. "Lilly thinks that we might be part of what the Nomad said, that Project Elysium thing. Like maybe that's what's been giving us our gills and stuff."

"Making a new species," I said, filling in Lilly's theory.

"Right," said Aliah, "except, it could be worse than that. What if we're not the new race? What if we're just the test subjects? You know, like the animals in cages that they test the NoRad lotions on, when the results are actually for someone else."

"For *them*." Marco waved his hand dismissively toward the glow of the city.

"The privileged few," said Aliah. "So Lilly thinks we should try to get out, find the Nomads, to expose what Eden is really up to."

"We don't know if we're part of the project or what," said Evan, "but it would be stupid to try to break out because, *A*, the Nomads are savages—"

I was about to say something to refute that when Aliah jumped in.

"Oh whatever, that's just what you've heard on the EdenNet news, and who makes that news? EdenCorp does. Lilly says the Free Signal isn't like that at all—"

"*And,*" Evan said over her, "*B*, there's no way out of here anyway! That's my point! Even if we wanted to, how are you going to get out? The main entrances are completely guarded. That's why I keep saying we should just go to Paul and ask him. What reason would he have to lie to us? People are going to find out about our little fish club here eventually. We could work together."

"And end up like Anna?" said Aliah.

"We don't know what happened to Anna!" Evan was shouting now. "Why do we have to assume that something terrible happened to her? What if it's true that she really is at the hospital over in the city? Maybe they're trying to figure out why she has gills. Maybe it would help them figure it out if they could study more of us."

Aliah glanced over at me. "This is why Lilly took off."

"Which is fine, because I'm getting tired of her whole crusader thing anyway. She's going to go getting us killed by savages over things she doesn't even understand."

"Like you do," said Aliah.

"This isn't good," Marco muttered. "We should be sticking together."

"Do you know where she went?" I asked.

"Oh, what are you gonna do, go find her?" Evan was peering at me. "You gonna try to make your move now,

Owen? Little scrub gonna try to score with the CIT?"

"Evan . . ." Aliah rolled her eyes.

I felt like turning and diving in, getting out of there, but I stayed. "No, that's not it."

"Nobody even wants you here!" Evan stood up. "And Lilly's still mad at you about whatever you pulled last night, anyway, so why don't you just go back to your baby cabin?"

"Evan, that's enough, buddy," said Marco.

Evan walked out into the middle of the raft. I felt another urge to run, but instead I stayed where I was. I thought I might fall over but somehow I held my balance as he loomed over me. I was shaking and it wasn't from the cold, but I was not running from this. If I had to stand here and get slammed by Evan for Lilly's sake, then fine.

Evan glared down at me. This was going to hurt. So, let it hurt. Enough from these kings, Evan, Leech . . .

"Not cool, Ev," said Marco.

Still staring at me . . . then Evan looked over at Marco and Aliah. "All right, fine, screw you guys." He turned and dove into the water. A minute later he emerged on shore.

"Sorry about him," said Aliah.

I shrugged. "It's okay." I looked around. "So, where did Lilly go?"

"To her special place," said Marco.

"Her—"

"Sometimes she just takes off on her own." Aliah pointed out toward the mouth of the inlet. "That way."

"Oh."

"Go ahead," said Marco as Aliah snuggled into his shoulder.

"What?"

"We usually let her come back on her own. But go ahead and find her if you want."

"Yeah? Um, I'm gonna go do that."

"Have fun," said Aliah.

I nodded, not knowing what else to say, and dove off the raft.

I headed out of the inlet, breaking the surface now and then to check my bearings. I waded ashore at the flashlight point but Lilly wasn't there, so I swam out into the wide, main lake. To the right, the city and the Aquinara glowed, their lights reflecting on the water. A few lights blinked closer, people out on their yachts. To the left, the water stretched into a wooded bay where the lake ended, Mount Aasgard a dark silhouette above it.

I headed toward that bay first. As I swam, I watched for the blue light of the siren, but didn't see it. If I didn't find Lilly, maybe I'd head back to the Aquinara and try to check out that fissure again.

I swam into the middle of the wide bowl of water and poked my eyes above the surface. The forest was dark. The moon wasn't up yet, but the MoonGlow lights were on, frosting the tips of the pines. There was nothing over here.

The water undulated with swells, increasing down the

long channel of lake from the city. *Northeasterly winds. Almost ten knots tonight,* I thought, and again wondered where a thought like that was coming from. Now I noticed a shadow. Above, some disk-shaped clouds were cruising overhead, blotting out the SimStars. They seemed thicker than normal.

I took one last look around, about to head up the lake, when I saw a small flicker of light. If it hadn't been for those cloud shadows, I might not even have noticed it. It was to my right, near the far side of the lake.

I ducked under and swam close. The bottom rose to meet me, and I surfaced to find that the light was flickering through the trees of a tiny sliver island, a little way from shore. The island was narrow, maybe seven meters wide and like twenty long. It was covered by a grove of wispy birch trees, the MoonGlow flickering through their small leaves, which rustled in the night breeze.

I stepped out of the shallow water onto soft, spongy dirt, crisscrossed by thick roots. I slipped between the slender trees, getting closer to the little light, and stopped at the edge of a tiny clearing.

A large birch trunk had snapped off a meter from the ground. Above, a hole was open to the sky. A tiny circle of grass had taken advantage of this. Near the center was a flat slab of rock, and on it flickered three candles set in old aluminum food cans. The upper halves of the cans had holes punched in them in geometric designs. There was a station for making those at Craft House.

Lilly sat beside the rock, wearing a baggy hooded sweatshirt, a blanket over her shoulders, her wet hair falling down her back in thick strands. She seemed to be checking out something in her lap. I watched her, heard her breathing.

She lifted her head. "It's okay to come out. I know you're there."

"Oh, sorry," I said. I stepped out, crossing my arms. "Um, hey."

She didn't turn around. I walked over to her. She held a small device in her hands. A mini computer pad. There was a window open on it, showing a connection bar and a tiny graphic of a satellite. Soft static hummed from the pad and a message blinked:

SCANNING FOR SIGNAL . . .

I thought about what to say. Maybe I should just start by apologizing for last night and trying to explain all that, but it didn't seem right. Besides, Lilly seemed busy. "What are you doing?" I asked.

"Trying to find the Nomad signal," she said. "My parents left me this. You only get one storage box when you're a Cryo. They mostly filled it with mementos I'd kept, stupid stuff like dolls and knickknacks, and some photos. But my dad put this in there, too. It's an old model but it has the gamma link for satellite connections. You can't get these in here—only the ones that work on the EdenNet.

It's like he knew I might want to get more sides of the story than just Eden's. Problem is, not many of the satellites work anymore. And most of the ones that do are encrypted. The Nomads hack one now and then to send their signalcast, then they pass the code around to their sympathizers. I have a friend over in the city who gave me a code before camp started. I think it might have changed, though. I haven't heard anything for a few nights."

"My dad said that most of the shooting stars we see these days are dead satellites," I said.

Lilly glanced up. "Can't see 'em from in here. I've never seen a real shooting star. They're probably beautiful."

"Yeah, they're pretty cool."

"Kinda poetic too, our trash raining down on us."

"Yeah." I wondered what to say next. "I'm glad I found you. Evan was just going on again about how he thinks the Nomads are savages."

"Evan is full of roach shit."

I laughed, but only a little, trying not to show how much I enjoyed hearing her say that. "What do they talk about on the signal?"

"Lots of things," said Lilly. "Trade, where to find supplies or spots where agriculture or fisheries are working. The Alliance works co-op. They talk, too, about the insurgency against the ACF, about getting into the Eden Domes, though mostly they don't want any part of these places anymore. They know the domes are failing. They say the DI is way lower than Eden will admit. And they're worried about this Project Elysium. They say, too, that the ACF, the People's Corporation of China, even the Russian Kingdom are all pressuring Eden to reveal what they're up to, but they won't."

"Do the Nomads have any theories on what Project Elysium is?" I asked.

"They don't really know, but they say the domes are placed in specific locations for a reason, and that EdenCorp is looking for some kind of technology or something. But their specifics are sketchy. One broadcaster thinks they're looking for a spaceship, another thinks it's some secret lab or something. Nobody really knows. All they know is there's something."

"A couple of the other domes are near landmarks, like the Pyramids and Stonehenge."

"Ancient sites," said Lilly. "Yeah, the Nomads think that's intentional."

I thought about the vision of the pyramid and the skull. "Maybe they're looking for something old?"

"Maybe." Lilly swiped her finger over a bar graphic, scanning satellite frequencies, but there was only the whispering static of dead air and space junk. She sighed and flicked off the pad.

She put it on the rock by the candles, and I noticed a photo frame there. It showed Lilly standing in front of two adults, a man and a woman. The man in a suit, the woman in a sari. There was a tall, older-looking boy beside them.

"That's your family?" I asked.

"Yeah," she said softly. "Mom, Dad, and Anton. All dead now."

"What happened to them?" I asked.

"Life," said Lilly with a shrug. "Anton died in Bangladesh. My parents had tried to get him in here, too, but he didn't want it. He was sixteen, old enough to say no. He said, with the world in such bad shape, it was wrong to just hide away when we could be helping. And then he ran off and joined a relief group to help climate refugees. I was only ten at the time, stuck doing what my parents said. Then, six years after I was Cryo'd, Anton drowned in a ferry accident.

"And my parents, I guess after they froze me, they kept trying to get into the ACF, but they never could. The HZ had filled up. They ended up staying in Calgary in the Borderlands. It wasn't as bad there back then, but it was still bad. Mom died of the plastics cancer. One of the super-pneumonia epidemics got Dad."

"I'm sorry," I said, not knowing what else to say. "Those got my grandparents, too."

Lilly went on like she hadn't heard me. "You know what's creepy is that there are vid chats, from my parents, that they made me throughout their lives. I guess they made one each year so I'd know them. There's a few from Anton, too. . . ."

She sniffed. "They called me Tiger Lilly, their little

princess-warrior. I have the files here with me, but I've never watched them. I started the first one once, but . . . it was too hard. I know they wanted the best for me, to save me from the chaos. Now I'm here, and I don't want their big sacrifice to be just so that I end up as some experiment."

She glanced up at me. I saw rims of tears beneath her eyes. "Have a seat."

I moved to sit across from her, but she raised her blanketed arm like I should sit beside her.

I sat down in the grass and was careful not to touch her, in case that would seem too forward or weird, but then she scooted over and tossed the blanket over my shoulder. Her smooth bare thigh touched mine, her sleeve against my arm.

I saw she was looking up at the stars, so I looked up, too. "My mom left when I was seven," I said.

"Where'd she go?" Lilly asked.

"She didn't say. She left a note, but all it said was that she had to find her place, and that she was sorry she couldn't be happy with us. She left with a medical caravan and we could never track her down after that."

"That stinks."

"Yeah. Mostly 'cause I would've liked to go with her. She got to go off to find herself, and Dad and I were stuck at Hub, living like moles."

"You could have gone after her."

It didn't surprise me that this was Lilly's first thought, and it made me feel lame for never really considering it.

Well, I'd thought of it, but not in any real way. "I didn't want to leave my dad," I said. "He's kinda sick. And he likes having me around."

Lilly shook her head. "Parents." I thought she'd say something else, but she didn't.

"How'd you get this stuff out here?" I asked, nodding to the candles and radio.

She pointed behind us with her head. I saw that there was another red waterproof bag lying against the tree trunk. "I brought it out awhile ago," she said. "That way I can come here whenever. Have some space to think."

"Tiger Lilly Island," I said, trying out a smile as I said it.

Lilly cocked her eyebrow at me. "Corny," she said. Then she punched my shoulder, "Just kidding, O. I like it."

She liked it. That was all I thought about for a few seconds.

An owl called in the distance, lonely, searching. There was no answer. I pictured it out there somewhere, looking for another of its kind, except then I remembered that it might not even be real.

"They told me you want to try to break out," I said.

"Tsh," Lilly chuckled. "You probably heard how that went over."

"Yeah. Do you really think we're part of Project Elysium? Or in danger from it, or whatever?"

Lilly turned and gazed at me. It was too dark to tell what she was thinking. "First, you tell me why you ran away from me last night. Then I'll tell you what I think."

"Oh, yeah," I stumbled, not knowing where to start. "You mean . . . the siren?"

"That's what you said last night." Lilly's eyes narrowed. "You mean like the sexy mermaids that drown sailors?"

"Well, no, but—I don't know what else to call it. And it looks like a girl. Well, sort of, it—"

"It's okay. I know," said Lilly, rubbing my arm. "I saw it."

"You did?"

She nodded. "Yeah, just, not at first, not when you started talking all crazy and took off. But as you were swimming away, I saw it. I tried to follow you, but you had too much of a head start. You've gotten fast, by the way."

"Oh, thanks."

"Anyway, I swam for a while, but then I figured you must have headed back and I'd missed you."

"Okay, good," I said, feeling a wave of relief wash over me. "I'm glad you saw it, too. I was starting to think the whole thing was in my head."

"Yeah, well, I'm not saying it's *not* in your, or, our heads. I mean, I saw it, but you acted like you knew it. You asked me if I *heard* it. And I didn't hear anything. What did you hear?"

"It says stuff to me." I explained mainly what the siren's messages had been.

Lilly frowned and didn't respond.

"What?" I asked.

"Well . . ." Lilly started picking at her fingers. "A lot of things. I mean, that's weird, don't you think? Seeing this siren thing, when the others haven't?"

"They haven't ever seen it?" I asked.

"No, nobody's ever talked about anything like that. What do you think she means by all that stuff she said to you?"

"No idea."

Lilly shook her head. "Also, your siren doesn't really sound like it has anything to do with Eden. I mean, spiking the bug juice is one thing, but I don't think Paul is making some ghostly chick appear in the water to lure you away."

"Yeah. I know," I said. I thought about the vision, the pyramid, the skull. Maybe I'd save that part—I looked over and found Lilly staring at me, one eyebrow raised. "What?"

She kind of half laughed, a little hitched noise. "You have a look like either you have to pee, or there's something you're not telling me."

"Well, okay, yeah, there's one other thing." I told her about the vision, about how it felt like my throat was being slit. When I was done, she just looked at me. "It felt real," I added.

"Whoa, okay, that's . . . I don't know what that is." Lilly seemed to make up her mind then. "We should check out that area again, over by the Aquinara. Maybe we can find the siren, or this temple thing, whatever that means. It's *got* to be part of what's going on here, somehow."

"Yeah?" I said. "Should we go now?"

Lilly thought for a moment. "Nah. Tomorrow night. I've gotta be in the Preserve early in the morning to set up for predator-prey, and we have to keep up appearances, you know? We can't let Paul get an idea that this is going on."

I glanced around into the darkness. "He might be watching us right now, with bats, or even cameras in the trees. Who knows?"

Lilly just shrugged. "Maybe. Still, even though most things here are completely lame, predator-prey is actually fun. We CITs get to be the top predators." She smiled at me. "You guys are *so* dead."

I didn't really know what she was talking about. "No chance," I said anyway, "you'll never catch me."

"Will too." She nudged me with her shoulder. Our eyes met—stayed meeting. . . . I felt myself freezing in place.

Then Lilly twisted around. "Ooh, I have something."

She rummaged around behind us. "Here," she said. She had a soaking-wet plastic bag. Inside were two brownies. "Felix in the kitchen gives me anything I want."

"Of course he does," I joked.

Lilly narrowed her eyes at me. "Hey, watch it. You want one or not? I don't usually share when it comes to chocolate."

She gave me a brownie and then lay back on the grass.

Her movement pulled the blanket down, and me with it, so that we were shoulder-to-shoulder, staring up at the SimStars.

"They're so much brighter here than they were in Las Vegas," said Lilly. "There was a ton of city light there, until the end."

"That's funny," I said. "Out at Yellowstone, the stars are way brighter than this. You can barely make out constellations, there are so many."

Just as I said it, a cloud passed over. Then more . . .

Something cold hit my eye. "Ah!" I grabbed my face. Another hit my foot. Tiny cold splashes. "What—?"

"Are you serious?" I glanced over and Lilly was staring at me. "Owen, it's rain."

"I've never seen rain," I admitted. "Or felt it."

"Never? Really? I mean, we didn't get it much in Vegas either, but . . ."

I thought back to Hub. "Every now and then you hear rumors that it's rained on the surface, overnight. One time I sneaked up top with some friends to look for puddles, 'cause people said that cougars or wild dogs would come to them, but we didn't find anything."

"They turn on the rain once a week here in the summer. EdenWest," Lilly said mockingly, "fulfilling wet dreams since 2056."

We laughed. The rain got heavier. I was blinking nonstop. "It's cold," I said, but then hated how wimpy it sounded 'cause I didn't mean it that way.

"Oh yeah?" Lilly suddenly pulled the blanket away. More icy fingers pricked me, all over: face, chest, thighs.

"Agh!" I cringed as each one set off shivering tremors, and yet, they felt like little jolts of energy, too, and I had a grin so wide it almost hurt.

"We should celebrate," said Lilly. "Owen's first rainstorm."

I felt her moving. Wait . . . Her leg brushed against mine, the side of her body moving against me. She appeared above me, her hair creating an umbrella, her body half on top of mine. Her smile had shortened, her mouth slightly parted, her lips right . . . there. . . . And I thought oh yes oh no oh God, could this possibly be the moment? Was this really going to happen?

I'd only kissed once before, a one-second thing with a girl named Sierra that had started our one week of dating. We only really went out because our mutual friends were, and the kiss had tasted like the canned salsa we'd just had at lunch, and our teeth had collided and it was so . . . not . . . this.

There were electric tremors running through me. I had no idea what to do, and yet I did, I could. . . . I started to crane my neck upward, toward Lilly, her giant eyes sharklike and black in the shadows and flickering candlelight—

She shoved her brownie into my mouth. "Double

brownies for the rain virgin!" She rolled away, her warm body leaving me to the freezing water once more.

I fell back, awash in the drops, glad right then for how cold that water was. "Ganks," I said around the mouthful of mushy chocolate.

Lilly didn't reply, but she curled herself into a half moon, her head on my shoulder, and pulled the blanket over us both.

The rain picked up in intensity. My gills fluttered at the rivulets dripping down my neck.

"Why do you like me?" I asked quietly, beneath the hissing of water through leaves.

"Because you're Owen," said Lilly.

"Yeah, but really . . ."

Lilly didn't answer.

I wondered for a second if I'd blown it somehow . . . but then she said, "You know how there's all that stuff, between boys and girls, like how you're supposed to act? And what you're supposed to say?"

I thought of my cabin and the Foxes, and of my own meager dating experience. "Yeah."

"Well, it's weird, but like, with you, it was like we were already past all that. Like I already knew you, almost as if I always had. Does that sound crazy?"

What sounded crazy was the way my heart was pounding as I listened to Lilly's words. "No," I managed to say. "Not crazy."

"I mean," Lilly went on, "it's not like I understood all that right from the start."

"I thought you were just taking pity on me," I said.

Lilly rubbed my head. "Well, you were all cute and pathetic. But it wasn't pity. I was caring about you."

"Okay," I said. "Even though I don't have, you know, like, killer shoulders and stuff?"

"Oh stop it," said Lilly. She was smiling. "Your Owen muscles suit you, and they look good to me."

"Huh," I said, smiling too and thinking, *Whoa.*

Lilly's grin turned devilish. "And I *heard* about how all those little Arctic Fox girls are all worked up about the new hot boy."

"What?" I said, "No, come on. . . ."

"Mina."

"Okay, maybe one."

"Told you," said Lilly.

Her lips touched my cheek, pulling away and leaving an echo of heat. She laid her head back down on my shoulder. I thought about what to say next, found nothing, and so I didn't.

Time passed, unknowable amounts and I had no sense for it. There was just the blanket and grass, the cold of rain and the heat of Lilly like a small sun beside me, and we lay there until the clouds left and the SimStars reappeared. Later, the burn-off lightning started to jump from the array high above, its gentle thunder rolling around.

When the first purple lights of dawn turned on, Lilly said, "We should head back."

"Okay." I wanted to say something about what I'd been thinking of again, about us swimming the earth over, finding our own archipelago of clear water, of endless nights of rainstorms and candles, just like this. But I saved it.

I helped her stash the gear. We swam back through the depths, emerging at the empty raft.

We trudged onto shore. The dome was turning pink. The CITs were gone. I wondered what to do—give her a hug, say something—but when I turned, she had already started across the sand in the other direction, our spell broken. "See you in the Preserve," she said. "I'm going to catch you and eat you up."

"You can try," I said back. I still had no idea what this predator-prey game was, but now wasn't the time.

"Good night, Owen."

"Good night, Lilly."

I headed for my cabin, my steps getting heavy, bare feet swishing in the dew-soaked grass. I was so shot from these nights. I needed my three hours of sleep desperately, or more like three days of sleep, but I ended up walking slow, taking my time, through a dawn southeasterly wind that felt like four knots and rising steadily. My mind had put aside thoughts of gills, secret projects, and sirens. All seemed less important, less real than Tiger Lilly and her secret island. The night felt like it had gone by so fast, yet every second of it was bright and burned into my mind, and I felt sure I would never forget any of it, almost like I'd left some part of me back there on that island, a piece carved out that wouldn't travel into whatever came next. It would just stay behind, living that night over and over.

13

"THERE ARE THREE GROUPS IN THIS GAME OF predator-prey."

Sleep was too short. The sun seemed too bright, the air too humid.

"The following cabins will be the herbivores: Spider Monkeys, Lemurs, Koalas, and Tree Frogs."

I had stumbled through breakfast, mostly head down. The bug juice, aqua-blue today, tasted like mint and the edges of plastic cups. I forgot to turn it down. There was a light fuzz to all of my movements. My shoulders were finally starting to ache with soreness from the hours of swimming.

"Spotted Hyenas and Arctic Foxes will be the omnivores. In the food web, you are the equivalent of skunks or raccoons."

"You're the skunks!" Paige shouted at us, her face painted with stripes of green and black. The Arctic Foxes cheered.

I glanced back to where the Foxes were sitting, and pairs of eyes immediately sharpened into glares at me. Mina had thought I was going to show up for polar bear swim. After the night with Lilly, it had never even crossed my mind. Now, I had jerk status with the whole Fox cabin. Mina leaned over to another girl, and they whispered and laughed and glared some more. Vaguely, my foggy brain considered that I'd never been at this level before, from unnoticed up to noticed and now to hated, but I was too tired to care.

"The CITs will be the carnivores, top predators. They are already inside the Preserve."

Everyone buzzed around me. We were gathered on the far side of the boathouse, on a slope of ground with log-bench seats, like a little amphitheater. Behind the small stage where Claudia stood, the steel mesh net rose to the ceiling, enclosing the Preserve, a relic forest from before the Rise, its trees thicker and darker than in the rest of Eden, mysterious.

Inside were species of birds, mammals, and reptiles that existed nowhere else in this area anymore. There were some enclosures inside that were more like a zoo: with cougars, black bears, and coyotes. The large bird I'd seen the other morning had been confirmed as a robot. Apparently, years ago there had been a bald eagle, but it had been too sensitive even to the inside rad levels.

The Preserve was off-limits to the campers except for

naturalist walks now and then, and for this: the two-hour game of predator-prey.

"In order to win," said Claudia, "you have to survive and increase your population. At the end of the game, the teams in each category with the largest viable populations are the winners. Herbivores, you have your teams of ten."

The younger cabins all erupted in cheers. All the teams had painted their faces like their cabin animal: little gaggles of whiskered creatures. Even though the youngest cabins, the Pandas and the Ocelots, didn't get to play, these midlevel kids still looked young, like fresh meat.

Our cabin was split into two teams of five. I'd opened my eyes to everyone already up and working silently on face painting, but unlike the little kids', ours didn't look like animal designs so much as camouflage war paint: blotches of greens, smears of black, browns, grays. I hadn't had time to put any on.

"Herbivores," Claudia continued, "let's see. . . ." She glanced back at the pad in her hand, flicking through instructions. Apparently Paul would usually do this, but Claudia said he was tied up in another meeting this morning. "Your goal is to collect the food tokens that are hidden throughout the Preserve, and to avoid being eaten by the omnivores and carnivores. Every twenty food coins you collect equals one new population member. At the end of the game, the herbivore team with the largest population wins. You will be hunted by the omnivores and carnivores.

There are three safe zones within the Preserve, but if your team gets caught, you must hand over the appropriate food and armbands, and return to the gate. After ten minutes, you'll then be allowed to reenter to start again. Remember, stay with your counselors at all times. Listen for the horn at the two-hour mark. That ends the game. Ready?"

The younger kids all cheered again, then moved toward the entrance, chattering excitedly in their little herbivore clusters. Their counselors had painted faces, too.

"Enter!" said Claudia.

A counselor pulled open the squeaky metal-framed door, and the teams entered one at a time. As they stepped into the shadows, their cheers quieted, their necks craning to look up at the high trees.

"See you soon, snackies!" Leech called after them. A few girls in the last group looked back with wide, prey-like eyes.

"Okay, omnivores," said Claudia, turning to us and the Arctic Foxes. "Your goal is to gather food by collecting food tokens and hunting the herbivores. Each time you catch an herbivore team, you can take thirty food—"

"I thought it was forty?" Leech interrupted.

Claudia looked flustered as she checked her notes. "Yes, okay, yes, that's right . . . forty food credits per member of your group. If the herbivores don't have enough food, you take their armbands instead. Armbands are worth twenty. For each hundred credits you collect as a team, that equals a new omnivore. The team with the largest population at game's end wins."

"That will be us," Leech announced loudly. Todd had drawn names from a hat to make the teams. I was on Leech's.

"But remember," Claudia continued, "the carnivores will be after you."

As Claudia said this, I pictured Lilly somewhere in those dark woods, hunting me, and felt a twist of excitement that made it hard to keep still in my seat.

"And there are no safe zones for omnivores. If they catch you, you must give them one hundred credits each in the form of your food supply or armbands, then return to the entrance and wait twenty minutes before entering again. Obviously if you are captured after the one-hour-and-forty-minute mark, you're out. Your counselors will be patrolling the Preserve to assist with questions and in case there are any injuries. Remember, as senior campers, you have earned the privilege of acting as your own leaders during the game. Please don't abuse that tradition.

"And one last thing," said Claudia. "Teams should not leave the trail system except to hide, and then hiding is only permitted within ten meters of a trail. Any team spotted cutting between trails will be sent out to restart. Omnivores, are you ready?"

We shouted snarling cheers, and of course we were drowned out by the Arctic Foxes.

"Survival of the fittest, of the strongest and most cunning," said Claudia, reading from the pad. Paul probably would have been excited about that line. "Okay, let the contest begin." She waved us toward the door.

We passed through the entrance. Three paths branched out into the dark woods.

"Have fun getting chomped, everybody!" Leech shouted. Our team also had Noah, Xane, and Beaker.

"You're going down, skunks!" called Paige as her group split off to the right.

"We're heading left," Leech announced. "Nobody follow us."

"Who'd want to when you have *him* on your team?" Paige pointed at me with her chin.

We turned, and the other groups headed off in separate directions.

"Dude, that's aMAZing!" said Xane, punching my shoulder. "They HATE you!" He seemed impressed.

"Yeah," I muttered.

"Way to blow your chance, Turtle," said Leech.

I was about to respond when, behind us, an air horn sounded.

"Showtime," said Leech.

Quiet closed in on us. We walked in a cluster up the wide dirt path, peering left and right into the muted world between the trees.

"Shut *up*, Beaker!" Noah hissed.

"What, I didn't do anything!" Beaker replied, pulling his fingers away from his mouth, where he'd been chewing his nails.

The trail crested a small rise. At the top, Leech immediately turned and left the trail, darting between the trees along the ridgeline. Noah followed.

"Where are you going?" Beaker called. He stood beside me on the trail's edge.

"We're going this way," Leech said like it was obvious.

"But we're not supposed to leave the trails," said Beaker, and I hated how he sounded like such a wimp, even though I felt the same way.

"Hey!" Leech snapped. "Who's played this game three times before and won twice? This was the plan we made this morning."

"Take the high ground to gain surprise," Noah added, as if this cleared anything up.

"What plan?" I asked.

"You wouldn't know," said Leech, "would you, freak boy?"

"What's that supposed to mean?"

"You know what it means." Leech turned and kept going.

"They didn't tell me the *plan* either," said Beaker.

But I was busy trying to contain the squeeze of adrenaline spreading in my gut. Leech knew about me. Freak boy. What else could that mean but gills?

"I'm going," said Xane, almost like he was apologizing, and followed after Leech.

"What should we do?" Beaker asked me.

I looked up and down the path we were on, then at Leech's, Noah's, and Xane's silhouettes, then at Beaker, who was apparently going to do whatever I did. Great. "Let's stay with them," I finally said. We started into the woods.

We walked through the shadows, our feet making light scuffs in the pine needles as we followed the line of crumbled rock along the ridge. The tree canopy was thick above us. Things scurried in the foliage, and I saw flashes of birds and little creatures. The air was still, heavy, and smelled like baked goods and soil. I felt a slick coating of sweat forming on my skin.

We heard distant squealing, hollow foot crashes echoing in the underbrush, then a high-pitched wail, a battle cry by one of the Arctic Foxes as they pursued their first prey. I peered through the gloomy labyrinth of trees, wondering where Lilly might be.

Beaker and I caught up as the others descended into a little gully that held a pocket of cooler air. A stream gurgled down the center, cascading over smooth rocks. There was a path running alongside it. The flats on either side were coated with furry moss.

"See anything?" Noah whispered.

Leech peered up and downstream.

"What are you looking for?" I asked.

"Food tokens, obviously," Leech muttered. "There's always some hidden around this spot."

"Here they are!" Beaker called. He was crouched by a boulder, pointing underneath.

"Sweet!" Leech ran over and elbowed Beaker out of the way. He picked up the palm-sized stack of wooden coins. There were five disks, four painted blue and one black. They were each marked with the number twenty.

"Why is one black?" asked Beaker.

"That's the food carrying toxic chemicals," said Leech. "We don't have to worry about those, but if the carnivores get too many, it kills them off. Here, you can have the toxic one, Beaky." He handed a blue each to Noah and Xane, and stuck the other two in his pocket.

I watched this, and almost thought about not saying anything, but then I did. "Hey, what about mine?"

"No food for you at this stop, mutant Turtle." He smiled at me like it was a challenge. "Okay, let's keep moving up the hill—"

But no. I felt my nerves and anger twisting together. As he passed me, I pushed his shoulder. "Give me one of the tokens."

He glanced at me but kept walking. Just smirked.

Lack of sleep, I would think later, lack of sleep clouding my judgment was the reason for what I did, because I just ran at him. Slammed both hands against his back. The blow was harder than I'd meant, or maybe not. Leech's head whiplashed and he toppled over, hitting the ground with his face first. He rolled over holding his nose. "Guh!" He pulled his hand away and there was a smear of blood.

"Dude!" Xane shouted.

"Whoa," said Beaker softly, like I had just performed some kind of sorcery.

"Sorry," I mumbled, but then I hated that I'd said that, almost like some little unconscious betrayal. I didn't need to be sorry. I wasn't. Though I hadn't meant for there to be blood.

Noah glared at me. "What's your problem?" He watched Leech like he was waiting for instructions.

Leech surveyed the blood on his hand. Looked up at me. "You want to die, huh? That's what this is?"

"Give me a food token," I said, trying to keep the shaking out of my voice, the pathetic fear of this little kid, but I had changed the game just now. It was something I'd never done before. My heart was slamming against my ribs. My fingers tingled as adrenaline coursed through my body.

And then Leech was up, springing to his feet and coming at me, and I had no idea what to do, how to move or defend myself. All I did was put out my arms, but he barreled through them and crushed against my chest. I staggered back. One arm was around me but the other clawed at my neck, his long nails scratching. Was he going for my gills? His fingers slipped on the slick of NoRad I had there. I grabbed his T-shirt and whipped him to my side, spinning away, his shirt tearing at the collar.

He turned toward me again. His face was beet red. Blood had streaked from his nose down over his mouth and it splattered when he spoke. "So this is it, huh?" Drops rained down onto his shirt. "This is where you think you make your big move?"

I could feel my face burning too, my chest and neck aching, but at the same time, what he'd said had thrown me off. What big move was I making? I wondered if this had something to do with Paul. Was Leech jealous because Paul seemed so interested in me? He almost sounded like Evan had the night before.

Leech stepped toward me. "I'm gonna take you out, Turtle." His eyes narrowed. We were about to become savages, and it sounded fine to me. I'd had enough.

"Try it," I said.

"Whoa, someone's coming!" Xane hissed.

Then we all heard it. The top pitches of a group of voices, carrying over the sound of the stream.

Leech looked over his shoulder. "From down there," he whispered. "Hide." And just like that, our battle was suspended.

We all scattered to different rocks and dropped to the moss. I lay on the cool carpet, springy and soft and sweet-smelling. Dampness on my bare knees and elbows. I was still breathing out of control. My side ached, my shoulder too, but I was glad to have the confrontation over, glad to just be back in the game.

A group of herbivores appeared, girls from the Koala cabin, their faces painted with cute whiskers and black noses. They were silent, nervously glancing up at the ridges on either side, a few clutching food tokens to their chests.

They had nearly reached us when Leech cupped his hands to his mouth and called, *"Whoop-oop-oop!"* A battle cry, and though I hated him, it was also the right thing to do, because the girls jumped and screeched, terrified, and we all leaped up from our hiding places.

They spun and ran, bumping into one another. "This way!" shouted their counselor, and they fled back down the hill. We took off, a pack in pursuit, the gravity of the hill spinning our legs. We were all making the whooping animal call now. I hadn't even realized I was doing it at first, but it felt good, and combined with all the adrenaline and nerves left over from the fight, I felt myself in the grip of a bloodlust, a predator, running full speed after the meek beings below, mine for the kill.

We caught them as the trail flattened out. Noah and Xane tagged the last girls in the pack and both shouted, "Caught!" and then I was reaching a little girl in pigtails who saw me and squealed in terror. Nearby, a girl tripped and fell and skinned her knee just as Beaker was about to grab her.

"Ooh, sorry!" said Beaker, the least predatory of us all.

"Okay, that's enough!" the counselor called. "You got us."

They had only found one stash of food so far, so we got all one hundred credits of that, plus five of their armbands. The counselor collected the loot from the girls and then turned toward us. "Here."

Leech stepped up and took it.

As the girls headed back to the entrance to get new armbands and wait to reenter, Leech turned with the spoils. "Everybody gets their forty," he said, and handed things around. He gave me a token and an armband without looking at me.

I tensed, ready to pick up where we'd left off, but Leech just said, "Come on." He wiped at the still-trickling blood beneath his nose and started up the other side of the gully, off the trail again. I figured our fight wasn't over, but maybe it was suspended for the rest of the competition.

Noah and Xane followed Leech. Beaker was watching me again, to see what I'd do. I thought about taking off on my own, but I kept following them. They knew these woods from the previous games, and I didn't.

We continued cutting our own trail. At one point we had a silent run-in with an Arctic Fox team. Now and then, we heard the ghostly sounds of other kills happening in the distance. I walked behind Leech and Noah. Each time they leaned close to whisper, I tensed for the retaliation, but then they'd just change direction. Noah would turn back to me and Beaker and Xane and make a pointing motion in our new direction, like we were a military unit.

"Where do you think the carnivores are?" Beaker asked quietly.

"I don't know," I said. In terms of winning the game, I wasn't supposed to want to run into them, but the thought of that encounter, of Lilly and the chase, was starting to dominate my thoughts.

We crossed another stream and passed a high-fenced pen where two black bears were sleeping in a rock enclosure. They didn't move. I wondered if they were real. A sour stench seemed to indicate that they were.

In the distance, the air horn sounded twice.

"What was that?" Beaker asked.

"Halfway point," said Leech, "but it also means that half the food in the game has been taken away, to symbolize it being lost to the Great Rise. Resources are scarce now, so we have to be extra careful."

We twisted through the trees, peering in all directions. Heard more screeches of a distant attack in progress.

"Wait," Leech suddenly hissed. "Did you hear that?"

"What?" I asked.

"Listen." He pointed toward a huge boulder, maybe three meters tall and wide, just off the trail. We were silent for a few seconds, and then we heard someone snicker, then a shushing and a young giggle.

"*Whoop-oop-oop!*" Leech shouted again, and we rushed the stone. Herbivores sprinted from behind it, a herd of squealing little boys all with black-and-white stripes on their faces. They headed straight back through the thick forest, dodging and twisting through the underbrush.

We tore after them, screaming our banshee wails and closing fast. The boys answered with their own screams of terror.

"Over here!" Their counselor had found a path. The herbivores veered after him. Ahead, a dirt clearing opened up, ringed by trees. There was another animal pen, with a little rock mountain in it. A cougar lounged atop it, basking in the SafeSun, watching us mildly.

We broke out into the space right on the heels of the herbivores, our fingertips almost to their shirts, when more cries and shouts sounded.

Our cabin's other team suddenly swept out of the trees on the far side of the clearing, Jalen leading the charge, fangs bared. The little ones screamed even louder.

"Get there first!" Leech shouted.

We sprinted. The kids were heading straight toward the fence of the cougar pen. Nowhere left to run. But then as soon as they hit the fence, they all turned and started shouting, "Safety Zone! Safety Zone!"

I saw it now, the yellow signs hung on the fence.

"Damn!" said Leech.

The little kids huddled against the fence, looking at us, relieved and yet still wide-eyed. We'd all arrived at the same time, and now both teams stood in a semicircle around them, panting, like animals leering at the edge of the firelight.

"We can wait all day, meat," said Leech.

"We get five minutes here," said the herbivores' counselor. "Then you have to give us a head start."

Leech began to say, "No probl—"

But he was cut off by a sound from the trees. A call, starting in a low pitch and rising steeply to a high screech at its end. *"Ooouup!"*

We looked around wildly.

Now an answering call, from nearby: *"Ooouup!"*

Everybody peered into the trees.

"Ooouup!"

"CITs?" Xane whispered.

The calls seemed to be coming from so close that someone should have been able to see them. Unless . . .

I looked up. Thick branches, fans of needles . . . And then I saw a shadow, high up against one of the trunks.

"They're in the trees!" I shouted, and even by the time I had turned to run, they were swooping down on us, on ropes they'd tied in the branches. I saw that they weren't my CITs; this was a team of others. Five of them, coming from all sides.

"Ooouup!"

"Ooouup!"

"Run!" Leech screamed.

Our group had two steps on the other half of our cabin,

and that turned out to be the difference. We careened around the side of the cougar pen and blasted down a path that sloped steeply downhill through the trees. Behind us, I heard Jalen cursing as his team was caught.

"That way!" one of the carnivores shouted. Footsteps pounded after us.

Our legs wheeled beneath us. The path dropped steeply and then flattened out and opened up at a tiny pond bordered by tall grass and weeds. We broke out into the sun again, all turning around to look for our pursuers.

"See anyone?" Leech asked, breathless.

"Nothing," I said, and the others agreed. The forest behind us had become eerily silent.

"Why would they let us go?" said Beaker.

"They're probably collecting tokens from the other group," said Leech. "I think we're safe."

I turned, hands on my knees, catching my breath. My eyes fell on the little pond, its surface reflecting the sky.

But beneath that, something moved.

"No, we're not," I said, scrambling backward to my feet.

"What?" asked Leech.

But the tan water was already starting to bubble and roil. As I stumbled back, my fellow monsters burst out of the pond.

"It's a trap!" Noah shouted.

They surged out of the frothing water, Evan, Marco,

Aliah, and Lilly, skin and bathing suits glistening, and, only apparent to me, gills tucking themselves away.

Or maybe Leech noticed them, too. "Fish monsters!" he shouted.

In the second before I ran, I caught Lilly's eye. She was smiling wickedly at me, and I knew our game was on.

My team scattered. I sprinted into the trees, the crashing of footsteps seeming to come from everywhere.

"*Ooouup!*" The call came from up the hill. Silhouettes hurtled down toward us. The other CITs were joining in the pursuit. Now they had us pinned from both directions.

I ran to my right, figures flying on both sides of me, everyone darting and flicking among the trunks.

Behind me I heard a scream like someone had been grabbed. Technically, the rules were that if someone in your group was caught, that was it, but I saw Leech still sprinting, and I kept going too, sure that Lilly would be doing the same.

Someone came flying down from my left. A CIT I didn't know. I angled down the hill, vaulted a fallen log, amazed I even landed the jump, heard a scraping of dirt, and looked behind me to see the CIT girl tackling Xane in a spray of pine needles.

I raced on, glancing back over my shoulders. Bodies still moving back there. Where was Lilly?

I wove through the trees and emerged into another patch of sun. I was at the far edge of the little pond. A stream burbled out of it, through tall grass and then down a cascade of rocks, disappearing into the dark woods in the direction of the lake. A narrow trail ran beside the stream. I started that way.

A butterfly dropped down, bouncing on the air nearby. It had teal wings with jewel-green dots, and seemed to hover, facing me, and I wondered if, up in the Eye, someone was monitoring our locations in the Preserve.

Then footsteps, pounding, close behind me. The sound of the stream had masked their approach.

I glanced over my shoulder, smiling, ready for the chase—

But it wasn't Lilly. The figure was too big, still-wet shoulders working. Eyes peering at me coldly.

Evan.

I turned and sprinted down the little trail, pressing as hard as I could with each step, telling my legs to do all of this faster, this moving up and down and still avoiding rocks and roots, things they were not good at.

I could hear him closing.

The stream and the trail leveled out and left the trees again to meander through a flat area of high bushes. I could barely see over them. Their branches scraped my arms and thighs.

The trail made a sharp turn. Ahead was a tiny wooden bridge over the stream—

"Gotcha!" Arms wrapped around me and shoulders

slammed into me and I was falling forward, to the side of the bridge, into the tearing fingers of the bushes then out and down a dirt bank, weight crushing on top of me, down to the stream's edge, my hands smashing against rocks, my face ending up right by the water.

Hands flipped me over.

"What's up, flavor of the moment?" Evan leered down at me, his princely face twisted with malice, and now I knew that Leech wasn't the most dangerous predator in these woods.

I didn't answer him.

He punched me in the face.

The fist hit jaw, nose, temple, and the world went out of balance and the sun got brighter in my eyes and there was a second where it hurt so much it didn't even hurt.

Then the pain spread in white-hot waves all across my face. I tried to struggle to get free, but my movements were little more than loose flopping.

"Whatever," Evan spat at me. "You're all head over heels, but do you think she loves you or something? You're just the next distraction. Which I guess makes me an idiot for being the last one. But at least I was smart enough to push back against her crazy ideas. With you being her little yes-boy, she's going to ruin everything here!"

I stared up at him, realizing that at least part of this fury was meant for Lilly. I was getting punishment for two. But I had no comeback, my face useless, my body pinned tight.

He raised his fist again.

I watched it. My cheek tingled in preparation. I tried not to wince.

Then I noticed the curious green light that appeared on Evan's chest. It moved to his neck. His fist began its descent.

But before it could reach me, the dart *thwipp*ed into his neck, a silver needle with shimmery blue feathers, nearly five centimeters long.

"Tch—," Evan coughed. He thrashed backward and slapped at his neck. The dart popped free in a little splash of blood.

Its work was done, though. Evan's eyes bugged wide and he pitched forward, his sweat-smelling torso meat crushing down onto me.

I struggled to push him off, which dumped his body facedown at the water's edge.

I rolled over, dug my elbows into the slick dirt and got a few feet away, then collapsed on my back. My whole face was pounding.

What had happened?

In the bright slice of sky above me, the teal butterfly appeared, bouncing to its wingbeats. It hovered over me, and for once I was almost glad that someone had an eye on me.

There was a pop of air, and the butterfly jerked back and disintegrated in a burst of sparks, a little rain of electric debris falling on and around me.

Footsteps clomped onto the little bridge. Those feet landed, burly high-laced boots beside me, half in the water. The figure above was a shadow, backlit by the bright sky.

A whistling sound. This person whistling. Now a response from nearby. Sounds in the underbrush. Bodies emerging. More predators, but these weren't CITs.

14

"YOU'RE SURE THAT'S HIM?" ONE OF THEM whispered.

Three people standing in front of me now. Three adults in ragged clothes, denim and flannel and LoRad fleece jackets. All the clothes were originally other colors but had been dyed in a camouflage of dark greens and grays and blacks. Their faces were painted, but not with lively designs. Mud brown. Simple. And the paint didn't hide all the purple lesions or crimson boils. The effects of exposure, of a life spent on the naked surface of the earth. They held rifles.

"Definitely. Check the photo." The Nomad woman held out her subnet phone, showing the others the screen.

"That's him," one of the men replied.

"Okay." The woman had short, spiky black hair and a chiseled face. She spoke into her phone. "Robard, this is Beta Team. We have our target. Any word from the others?"

"None yet," the voice of Robard replied. "You guys get out of there, pronto."

"Who areeyyou?" I asked, the words slurred by Evan's fist. I knew, though, despite the cloud from my now swollen eye, that they were Nomads.

"Relax, Owen," said one of the men. "We're your rescue team. We're going to get you out of here."

"Out of here?" I mumbled.

"It's okay." The woman knelt down. Her brown irises swam in whites that had been irradiated to pink, the blood vessels singed to near black. "I'm Pyra, and this is Barnes and Tiernan. We know who you are, Owen. We know *what* you are. Our contact here alerted us to you."

"What I—"

"Sshh. Don't talk." Pyra was fiddling with something in her hands. She held up a circular piece of fabric between her fingers. She reached to my neck, pressed it there, and a white wave of unfeeling spread through my body.

My words came out as whispers. "What did you do?"

"Neuro dampener," said Pyra. "To ease the pain. Don't worry, you'll still be able to move."

Barnes and Tiernan lifted me up and slung my arms over their shoulders. They were both lean and strong, Barnes with a wiry brown beard, Tiernan with thick glasses and one of those false ears made of pale-pink plastic. I could distantly feel my feet on the ground, but they seemed far away. Pyra was right, I could still move, but not enough to try to escape.

"We're going to take you out of here," said Tiernan.

"Get you away from Project Elysium before it's too late. And once we're out, we'll explain everything. Promise."

"But right now we've got to move," said Pyra. "Fast."

They dragged me back up to the trail and we crossed the bridge. I heard some commotion of the game back toward the pond, maybe even the shouting of names, but we were headed in the other direction. Were they looking for me? Would they even notice I was gone?

Up a hill, and then we turned off the trail, weaving through the trees.

I could barely control my movements. My feet were stumbling along almost on their own. At least the pain in my face had been numbed.

I heard Pyra talking into her phone. "We're en route to the extraction point, copy."

"Good," Robard replied. "Alpha Team?"

"We are holding position," another voice replied, "and looking for an opening to acquire our target."

A woman's voice spoke on the phone. "This is Skull Team, over. We're almost to the temple. Disabling the alarms and cameras took time, but we're at the nav room now and are about to try—"

A sharp crack cut her off, then an electric shriek tore out of the phone.

"Agh!" Pyra jerked it away from her head. "Robard? Come in, do you copy?" No one replied.

"They could be jamming us," said Barnes.

"Sounded like rifle bursts," said Tiernan.

Pyra tried again. "Robard? Alpha Team? Anyone copy?" The only reply was a hiss of dead air.

We jogged through the forest, moving up a series of undulations. I thought we were maybe parallel with the pond, and then likely past it. I couldn't tell how long we'd been going. Maybe ten minutes. Maybe more.

"Robard," Pyra whispered. "Skull Team . . . Someone answer!" Nothing.

Ahead it was brighter, and we reached an abrupt end to the trees. In front of us was the high fence, the dry moat, and then the dome wall. We turned left and followed the fence. At the bottom of a hill, we reached a gate. It hung open, a blackened hole where its lock had been. Beyond the gate, a narrow metal bridge with wire railings crossed the moat. At the other end, a thick hatch-like door hung ajar, its handle similarly blown out. Beyond that door, brilliant sunlight baked barren rock.

We stopped at the broken gate.

"Robard, anyone, come in," Pyra repeated. When no one replied again, she glanced wildly in all directions.

"Now what?" said Barnes.

"Not sure," said Pyra, her voice tense. "We were supposed to meet back here."

"We should just get out," said Tiernan. "The other teams may have been compromised. If we've got the boy, we don't need the skull anyway."

"Yes, we do!" Pyra snapped. "He'll be useless without its information."

"But there's the other one, down south. And the girl."

"That's not how it works!" said Pyra. "At least, not according to Dr. Keller's studies." She tried the phone again. "Robard, do you copy?"

As she listened to the static, I wondered, What was this? They were talking about a skull, a temple, and a girl. The skull from my vision? And the girl they mentioned, was that Lilly? Were they after her, too? Either way, what it definitely meant was that these Nomads were related to what was happening to me, and to that vision, even the siren. Somehow, all of it was connected.

"Okay, you're right," said Pyra. "We'll make for the rendezvous and hope for the best."

The men angled me through the fence and out onto the narrow bridge. Pyra followed behind us. Tiernan let go of me and started toward the door, gun raised. Barnes guided me from behind. I glanced over the meager wire railing at the ten-meter drop to the concrete floor of the moat.

Then, I looked ahead at the approaching brightness of the outside world. I was being taken from EdenWest. And I couldn't move to do anything about it.

"Robard, this is Pyra, we are exiti— *Gluh!*"

The bridge shuddered, the wires to my side springing like they'd been plucked.

"Pyra!" Barnes shouted. He let go of me, his shoulder

brushing my back as he spun around.

There was a hissing of air.

"Agh!"

I was turning around, trying to control my balance, when Barnes jerked backward into me. In the blurry sweep of my vision I saw that Pyra had vanished from the bridge. And something was wrong with the back of Barnes's head. The shape wasn't right.

Something hot on my face.

Hands grabbed me by the armpits, dragging me back toward the door. "Come on, kid!" Tiernan shouted.

I watched Barnes slump to the ground, saw the movement back in the trees. Black figures emerging from the shadows, helmets on, amber visors down, rifles raised.

"Put the boy down!" one of the soldiers shouted.

Something cold pressed against my neck. A knife. The dream, on the pyramid . . . no, this was now. "Don't come any closer or he dies!" said Tiernan. I saw our shadows cast in front of us by the daylight. We were almost to the door.

A pop. Another hissing of air. The feel of more hot liquid, this time spraying onto the back of my neck.

I was tossed forward. The knife clattered off the side of the bridge. I couldn't stop myself from careening over face-first. I got my arms out, but they didn't do much good. My forehead slammed against metal.

Tiernan fell on top of me. Drops of warm fluid falling onto my cheek. Streaming to my nose and falling free. I watched Tiernan's blood as it plinked on the grated metal floor of the bridge. Some drops slipped through and fell all the way to the concrete below, to where Pyra's body lay in a twisted S shape, a pool of blood spreading from her head.

Footsteps banged on the bridge. The body was pushed off me. Gloved hands under my armpits. They pulled me up.

"I have him," the officer said. He set me on my feet. "Can you walk?"

I glanced at his amber visor, reflecting the bright real sun and the open door behind me, and tried to answer, but no words actually came out.

"Okay, just hang on to me." He slung my arm over his shoulder and led me back toward the gate. We stepped over Barnes, over his contorted face and misshaped head, some important piece of it missing now. I saw red among the hair, insides now exposed.

It all passed over me. Images. Things. None of this was real. Couldn't be.

Back through the gate, and there were many officers now. They sat me against a tree. I watched them use ropes to get into the moat. I looked down and saw blood splattered on my shirt, my arms and legs. Other people's blood.

"Owen!" I looked up to see Dr. Maria running over. She dropped to one knee in front of me. "You're okay," she said. "Don't worry." She yanked the patch from my neck.

"Better than them," I whispered.

Dr. Maria glanced toward the bridge. An officer was climbing up out of the moat, Pyra over his shoulder. He carried her off the bridge and dumped the body to the pine-needle ground with a hollow thump.

When Dr. Maria looked back, there were wet edges beneath her eyes. She sniffed, like the sight of the bodies had gotten to her. Then she saw me noticing. "Sorry," she said, wiping at the tears.

"It's okay," I said.

Dr. Maria opened her black backpack and pulled out a red medical kit. She checked my eyes with a penlight. Took my wrist and checked my pulse. "Anything hurt besides this?" She touched my swollen cheek lightly.

"Nah," I said.

She pulled an ice pack from her backpack, shook it, and put it in my hand. I noticed that her hand was shuddering. "That's for your cheek," she said. "The neuro dampener should wear off in a few minutes. You'll get your feeling back."

"Okay." I could already feel prickling in my toes and fingers.

She rummaged in the kit. "Just one more thing . . ." She pulled out that square box with the glass dot. She held it toward my forehead. The light blinked green again. "Good."

"What's that mean?" I asked.

"It's—"

"Owen." Paul was striding toward us. Beside him was Cartier, the head of security. Paul introduced him, then glanced over his shoulder. "This is very unfortunate," he said, as if what had happened here was just a bad-tasting meal rather than the deaths of three people. "Owen, listen: we're going to need to know everything they may have said to you. I'm sure most of it was lies—the Nomads are experts at misinformation—but still . . . it might give us a clue as to what they're up to."

I almost laughed at this. Lies . . . As if he was one to talk.

Dr. Maria sniffed. I saw her scowling as she busied herself with her pack, like she felt the same way.

"How is he holding up?" Paul asked her.

"Seems fine so far," Dr. Maria mumbled.

Paul knelt down. I saw my face in his glasses. There was a streak of blood across my cheek, like someone had been careless with a paintbrush. "It's important for you to understand me right now. It turns out we were wrong about yesterday's bombing. It was actually designed to draw our attention away while this Nomad team got inside. They had help, too. Someone on the inside hit our detection systems with a virus. Whoever was behind this, they knew our schedule, knew you'd be in the Preserve unsupervised. They probably figured this was the perfect time to make their move."

"Did they get anybody else?" I asked.

"No," said Paul, but my question seemed to interest him. "Why do you ask?"

"They were talking," I started to say, then thought I should hide what I knew. "I couldn't make out much of it."

Paul nodded. "Do you remember anything else?"

"No," I said. "They just grabbed me, told me to keep quiet."

"I think he's in some shock." I looked over at Dr. Maria and found her gazing at me seriously, and when our eyes met, her head seemed to hitch slightly. Had she just nodded to me?

"Maria," said Paul.

"Yeah?" Her head snapped away, up to Paul, and I thought her eyes looked wide, like she'd been caught.

But Paul was looking across the clearing. Two officers were carrying Evan out of the trees. He was still unconscious. "Go see to him, would you?"

"Okay." Dr. Maria grabbed her bag and hurried away.

Paul turned to Cartier. "Go check the bodies for information," he said. "I'll meet you over there."

Cartier left, and now it was just me and Paul.

He leaned closer to me, lowering his voice. "Look, Owen: it's time we talked more frankly about what is going on here in EdenWest." He reached out and rested a hand on my shoulder. "About what's going on with *you*." I wanted to slide away from his touch, but my body was still foggy from the dampener. "I thought we could take our time,"

Paul went on, a slight smile forming and fading, "let things develop in their own way, but I'm afraid this little incident illustrates that we're going to have to get right to the point. Do you understand me?"

I didn't answer.

"I think you do, Owen," Paul said like I was a child, "but this is my fault. You deserve to know what's really going on here, and I, I need to know everything that you know." He glanced to the bodies, then back at me. "It's the only way I can keep you safe."

For a moment, I almost had an urge to tell him. After the bullets, the deaths . . . Paul was the most powerful person here. If I had just gone to him about my gills, told him about the siren and the vision, he might never have let me out here, and none of this would have happened. Maybe it was time to stop playing games, to stop keeping secrets, before there were more bodies.

Except, who was really the one playing games? Paul had lied to the camp multiple times. I'd seen it. And what he'd just said: it sounded more than ever like he knew way more about what was happening to us than he was letting on, and he was just sitting back and letting things *develop*? So, if I told him everything, what would he do then? Was that when the experiments would begin like he did with Anna?

And I reminded myself that these Nomads weren't the only victims of this place, of Paul's Eden. There was little Colleen, and the other kids the CITs had talked about. Paul hadn't kept them safe. And it was more than just me who was in danger now. There was Lilly. The Nomads mentioned a girl. Lilly was the only one who'd seen the siren, like me. I wished I could find her right now. She was the only one I could talk to about all this. The only one I could trust.

Paul's hand lifted off my shoulder. "Listen, I have to clean things up here. In the meantime, I'm going to have you brought to my office. We'll have a talk. It's long overdue. That sounds good, doesn't it?"

I looked into his black lenses and wondered what to say, but there was really only one answer. "Sure."

"Good." He patted my knee. "Just sit tight. I'll have some officers take you back." He stood and left.

As soon as he was gone, I tried moving my legs. They were still a little like jelly, but I got my knees to my chest and wrapped my arms around them. I started to shake. From everything.

I watched Paul return to where the three bodies were now lined up. An officer handed him Pyra's phone. I looked over to where Dr. Maria was tending to Evan. She kept glancing over at the bodies. Paul the liar. And Dr. Maria, the . . . what? What had that nod been before? And her tears about the Nomad . . . Maybe it had just been the sight of death, or was it something more?

I pushed up harder with my legs, my back scraping against tree bark as I stood. It took a second to center my balance.

Paul had moved out to the bridge. He and Cartier were

inspecting the broken lock on the hatch door.

Sit tight, he'd said. Right. Sit back and wait for the next thing to happen. For the next drowning, strange vision, veiled comment, for the next attempted abduction, the next death. All of these things that kept happening to me, with no explanation for why. And really, wasn't it my fault, too? I'd been ignoring the dark questions about what was going on here, about my gills, all of it, focusing instead on nights with Lilly, on finally belonging to something. But I couldn't avoid it anymore, not after this.

There was a tingling in my fingertips. I could feel my heart rate increasing, and my body shuddering more.

Ten meters away from me lay three bodies, dead because of me. And not far away was another body, Evan. He'd been trying to ignore the questions, too. And while any other day I would have been happy to see him flat on his back, not today. Would he be okay, or was he another casualty of me? And what if that had been Lilly back there in the game? What if they'd gotten her too? There could have been a stray bullet, a fall off the catwalk, she could be a still body on the pine needles now, too. . . .

I wanted to talk to her so bad. She'd know what to do. But, no, talking to her wasn't an option right now. *I* needed to know what to do.

I leaned on one foot, then the other. Flexed my toes. Swung my arms. *All systems back online?* I asked the technicians.

Yessir, looking good, they reported.

Then hang on, I told them.

Paul and Cartier were still checking the hatch. Dr. Maria was bent over Evan with her penlight.

Everyone had their back to me.

I turned and ran.

Full on. Not looking back. Straight into the trees, tearing down the slope, my feet slipping in the orange needles. Once I'd covered some ground, I dared a glance back. No one was following. How long before they noticed? Probably just a few more seconds.

I cut left. Trying to retrace the path my captors had taken. Heading for that stream, heading for the lake. I wished Lilly was with me, but I had to fight the urge to go and try to find her. There was no time now. This was my only chance.

No more sitting around waiting. I wasn't going to Paul's office. I wasn't letting anyone take me anywhere, anymore, unless they were ghostly blue and deep in my world only.

I was going to the temple.

15

I CAREENED DOWN THE HILLSIDE THROUGH THE dark pine gloom, heard a familiar gurgling sound, and reached the tiny bridge where, some blurry stretch of time ago, there had been fists and darts and abductions. Remnants of the butterfly sparkled on the mud bank.

I jumped down off the bridge, landing in the shallow water. My ankle twisted. My hip cracked against a tall boulder. Already out of breath. Already feeling the screwtop twist of the cramp in my side. My lungs felt like metal cans that wouldn't expand enough.

Behind me, something crashed in the woods. Were those voices?

Keep moving.

And now I was in water, the cold seeping through my socks and shoes, causing tremors up my calves and tingles in my gills. Water would be my savior, I just had to follow it. This stream babbled downward; it would lead to the lake. There were shallow slopes to either side but no trails, so maybe they wouldn't think I'd gone this way.

I splashed rock to rock, fallen log to wet sand, slipping, hands out to steady myself.

The incline increased and the stream began to blur with bubbles, the water channeling through more narrow gaps, sometimes plunging under boulders. My run became more of a hop downward, palms bracing against rough stones. A knife edge of rock tore the pocket off my shorts.

The stream fanned out over steps of sandstone. I scrambled down them, but my feet slipped on the smooth rock. I started to fall to the right, threw myself back the other way, lost my footing, and toppled face-first into the pool at the bottom. I popped up, but now my throat was stuck. My gills, confused, had opened. I staggered, telling them to close, coughing at the same time, cramp knotting tight.

Then, ahead through the trees I saw the sun streaks on the lake. Almost there. Stumbling, just had to make it. My shoulder slammed into a tree, half spinning me, spots in my eyes, nothing working.

I staggered forward and reached a ledge of rocks, the lake lapping a few feet below, and I threw myself in.

My body slapped against the surface and I sank, emptying my lungs, letting go of everything. I felt the cramp ease, felt my gills begin to flutter, water through my mouth. The coolness relaxed all my burning muscles. My stomach gently brushed against the algae-slick rocks of the bottom. I spread my arms and pulled myself out a few meters to deeper water. There, I peeled off my shirt, shoes and socks. I pinned them beneath a rock on the bottom, so there would be no evidence of my escape. Then, I rose to the surface and peered around to get my bearings.

I was at the far side of the camp inlet. The boathouse was to my left, the trampoline raft straight ahead, the empty dock beyond that.

"So, now you're trying to ditch me?"

I whirled to see Lilly standing on the rocks, hands on her hips, in her teal bathing suit top and red shorts, breathing hard. Marco and Aliah stood just behind her. Lilly's gaze was stony, and I couldn't tell if she was really mad or not.

I pushed my throat open. "I—"

She rolled her eyes. "Kidding." She smiled, but then her face got serious again. "What happened to your face?"

I felt the swelling by my jaw. "Evan."

"That—" She scowled, but didn't finish. "And those were Nomads, weren't they?"

"Yeah."

"We saw the aftermath up there. Are you okay?"

"Yeah, but"—I glanced past her into the woods—"I've gotta go, before they find me."

"I thought they were all dead," said Marco.

"Not the Nomads. Paul and the Security Forces."

"You're going to the temple, aren't you?" Lilly asked.

I nodded. "The Nomads were talking about it. They

sent a team there, to—" I stopped, looking at Marco and Aliah.

"I told them," said Lilly, "About the siren that we saw, and how you had that vision."

"Crazy stuff," said Marco.

"I don't get it," said Aliah. "How come *we* never saw this thing?"

Lilly looked back at me. "There's something different about Owen," she said.

"About us," I added. "The Nomads were after you, too."

"Me?" Lilly's eyebrows bunched up like she didn't believe it. "How do you know that?"

"They said they were after a girl, too, and you're the only other one who's seen the siren."

Lilly nodded slowly. "Oh." She sounded unsure, or maybe overwhelmed.

"We have to find out what's going on," I said, "before more people die." I looked at her as seriously as I could. "Come with me."

Lilly's eyes stayed on mine. She bit her lip. "Yeah," she said. She turned to Marco and Aliah. "Can you guys cover for us? And see about that bastard Evan."

"What should we say?" Aliah asked.

"I don't know," said Lilly, "tell them Owen and I sneaked off to hook up or something, that we can't keep our hands off each other." She shot me a slight smile.

I tried not to melt into the water. Of all the times for a girl to say something like that in relation to me, why did it have to be now?

Aliah laughed. "I think Owen liked that idea."

I felt my face burn. "We should go."

"All right, but where to meet up?" said Marco. "The raft?"

"Too obvious," said Lilly. She tore at her fingers, thinking. "How about the ledges?"

I'd heard them talk about this place, up at the top of Mount Aasgard.

"Sounds good," said Marco. "We'll head up there after lunch."

"Be careful," Lilly said to them, then she turned and dove in.

"Thanks," I said to Marco and Aliah.

Marco nodded and Aliah raised an eyebrow, but neither said anything. They were looking at me like this was all my fault. It gave me a heavy feeling. I hadn't done anything wrong, and yet, they were right. This was about *me*, weird as that was to get used to.

I ducked under, sucked in water, and thrust out to where Lilly was waiting, gently drifting beneath the surface. As I neared her, I wished this was the moment where we were leaving, off to find our own ocean somewhere, with no danger of Nomads, where the only mysteries were what strange fruits and flowers we'd eat, and where we'd sleep.

'Ready?' I said to her.

'Yeah.' She reached out and touched my swollen cheek. 'He had no right, Owen. . . .'

'It's okay.' And then I felt a rush of nerves about what I'd just thought to say next, and somehow I actually said it. 'It was because of you.' I started to swim past her and added, in my fish clicks, 'And it was worth it.'

Her hand clamped on my ankle and pulled me back, spinning me over so that I was facing the surface. She slid over me, silhouetted by green-tinted beams of SafeSun, her face in shadow, hair like a corona, and she drifted down until our bodies were touching, cold skin, contact from the tops of our feet to our chests.

She kissed me.

Somehow I was ready. Waving my hands to keep myself steady in the weightless water, craning my neck up as her face neared and our cool lips met. The strange gill currents made extra suction in from the corners of our mouths, and I tried to feel how her soft lips were moving and do the same thing she was.

I realized my eyes were shut tight. I opened them to find Lilly's eyes open too, the backlight making them dark and almost predator-like again.

Then it was over. She pulled away. 'Come on,' she said with a gentle smile, and shot off ahead. How long had that been? A second? An hour? I felt like I had no idea. For a moment I just stared up at the blur of sunny sky. My first real kiss. With a girl I still could barely believe I got to be around. In spite of all that was happening, in spite of the way my nerves were ringing, I felt a sadness that it was already over. Would we ever have another chance? Why couldn't this just last?

Owen. Find me.

The siren was one reason why. The dead bodies, the siren, the gills . . . I flipped around and swam after Lilly. As I caught up to her, I scanned the depths. 'Do you see her?'

'Not yet . . . ,' said Lilly.

'There.' I pointed out to our right. There was the slithering, flickering form.

'Oh . . . yeah, I see it,' said Lilly. 'Lead on, O.'

I kicked hard and we were off, skimming the lower edge of the sunbeams, out over the shipwreck and then across the open lake.

What is oldest will be new. What was hidden shall be unlocked. The secrets remembered by the true. She stayed out ahead of us, always distant, and yet always in view, until we reached the Aquinara, where the rocky bottom rose up to the concrete wall, the intake and outflow tunnels doing their cyclical work.

The siren slipped down among the black rocks at the lake bottom.

We followed, diving deep.

Come home, Lük.

White light started to creep into my vision again, almost

as if that vision of the city, and the crystal skull, had to do with proximity to whatever was down here. I saw the image forming again, like it was downloading into my mind—the pyramid, the ash sky, the kids kneeling on pillows, knives at their throats—but this time I concentrated on the water and rocks around me, on Lilly, the blue of the siren, and tried to keep that vision from overwhelming me.

There was a moment of stretching, almost like new spaces were opening in my head, and then I could see both things at once. It was like there were two screens in my mind's eye, like at different depths, and I could slide back and forth between the two. Out in front, at the surface of my mind was the lake. Back deeper in my head was the boy Lük, skull before him, about to die.

Not to die, the siren added, as if it could see this vision too. *To transform. To evolve.*

As we swam down, the water pressure strengthened. I felt my sinuses compressing, my ears popping. I pulled deeper, kicked harder, first battered by the outflow water, then resisting the sucking of the intake.

And then we were beneath the currents and among the shadows and the brown-slicked rocks at the lake bottom. Ahead was the dark opening. The siren's pale light flickered from inside. Lilly was off to my left, peering around like she'd lost sight of the light. 'Over here,' I called.

I swam toward the opening. It had looked like a random gap in the rocks from up above, but from down here I could see that it was actually more of a rounded hole, kind of like a tunnel. The edges were rough, like it had been hand-carved. The siren's light flickered from a few meters in, and around a bend.

'We're going in there?' Lilly asked.

I peered inside, where the ghostly light beckoned.

Come home, Lük.

I pulled back inside my head, saw the boy having his throat slit, his world becoming white. Then I pushed back out to the world of water.

'Yeah,' I said. 'We're going in.'

16

I SWAM INTO THE TUNNEL. IT WAS DARK EXCEPT for the siren's light. Reflected in the blue were the heavy, oblong figures of zombie koi, a pack of them, hovering in here, almost like guardians. We had to angle ourselves to pass between their fat, fleshy bodies, brushing against their clammy scales, and I almost wondered if they would turn on us, converge and devour us to protect this place's secrets. But they just stared dumbly as we passed.

'I hate these things,' I said to Lilly.

'They couldn't be grosser.'

We rounded a bend. The siren was floating far ahead, at the end of a long passage. As we swam forward, she rose up out of sight.

'Mine shaft,' said Lilly.

I turned to her blue-tinted face. 'What?'

'I heard on the Free Signal that EdenWest is right near the site of ancient copper mines.'

'Oh yeah, Paul said something about that. People that

came here before the Vikings.'

The tunnel ended at a solid wall where the siren had been. A round shaft opened up above us. I pushed off the rock floor and rose through it. There were notches like ladder rungs carved in the wall. After a few meters the tunnel turned and continued upward at an angle. As I swam, I felt the pressure lightening. Above, the blue light seemed to ripple and separate in glassy diamonds. We were nearing the water's surface.

I stopped just below and then slowly lifted my head and eyes. The tunnel angled up out of the water and, a few meters ahead of us, opened up into a large chamber.

Lilly's eyes rose beside me. I nodded to her and we slowly crept ashore, gills tucking away, pulling in breaths of cool, damp cave air. As we stepped onto solid ground, her hand slipped into mine.

We entered the chamber. In the flickering blue, I saw circular walls and a curved ceiling. And there, hovering in the center of the space, was the siren.

I'd never had such a clear look at her, and now I saw that she was lovely, and yet, different. She had long, dark hair flowing down to her waist, the hair pushed back off her forehead with a band made of gleaming stones. She was all monochrome, shades of blue light, and yet I felt like, in my deeper mind, she had color. The simple dress she wore, sleeveless and down to her knees, was that crimson fabric of the priests on the pyramid, the belt tied loosely around her waist of hammered copper disks with turquoise crystal centers. The band above her forehead that held her hair back was ruby and jade. She wore a pendant around her neck, a leather strap holding a soapstone carving of some fearsome animal, a tiger maybe, only it looked larger, more fierce, but it was hard to tell because her light was brightest around her heart.

And the structure of her face, deeper-set eyes and a more pronounced forehead, high cheeks, her dark-toned skin—everything was so similar and yet so different. It was as if we were connected, and yet by such a distance of time, by so many thousands of generations, that we were almost different models of the human form.

"Hello?" I said to her. My voice echoed in the chamber.

She floated, not replying, gazing at me almost like she was sizing me up, deciding if I was worthy.

"What now?" asked Lilly.

"No idea," I said, and yet I felt like that wasn't true. I didn't know what to do next, what was about to happen, but I had a strange certainty that something would. Like I'd boarded a train that was now in motion.

Then the siren spoke, its voice louder, harsher than I remembered it. *The key is inside you.*

"What?" I asked.

The siren winked out. The world went black.

But not silent.

"What's that?" Lilly whispered.

There was a humming, faint, but electric-sounding. Ahead, I saw a sliver of white light in the black. I gripped Lilly's hand and headed for it.

As we neared, we saw that the light source was larger, but farther than it had seemed. My shoulder cracked against a rock wall.

"You okay?" Lilly asked.

"Fine," I muttered. We rounded the little wall and found ourselves in another curving passage. The light was coming from its end. Electric light, spilling down this tunnel from a round opening.

We crept up to it and ducked in the last triangle of shadow. Ahead was a wide passage. It was also rounded, carved out of the rock, but its floor had been covered in smooth concrete, and a line of naked lightbulbs had been strung along the ceiling. I leaned out. To the right, the lights ended at a steel ladder that led up through a hole in the rock, toward more bright light above. The tunnel continued into darkness past that. To the left, the lights stretched away as the tunnel sloped steadily downward.

"Which way?" Lilly asked.

I looked for the siren's light, but couldn't see it. And yet, I could feel a steady tug inside, seeming to lead me in the right direction. "Down," I said, and headed left.

We half ran down the tunnel, our bare feet slapping on the concrete. It went and went, other tunnels, unlit, branching off to either side. The rock walls were red.

"Look," said Lilly as we started down a new passage. She was pointing to the wall. There was a shape carved in it.

"I've seen that before," she said.

"Me too. On the Aasgard sign at Craft House."

"Is it water?" Lilly asked. "Mountains?"

"Not sure." I turned and kept moving. I had a feeling we were going to find out.

We'd been going a few minutes when we heard footsteps coming toward us. I squeezed Lilly's hand and pulled her into a dark side tunnel. We retreated into the shadows and crouched, her slightly behind me, and I thought for a second about the fact that suddenly I was leading the way on this adventure. Owen Parker, first a turtle, then a fish, now some kind of action hero, like Tech Raider from those films we got from the ACF, the guy who always went into the flooded technopolises in search of treasure. He'd battle radiomutants and chem-zombies and always find some unbelievably attractive girl who'd been hiding out there with the bones of her dead parents, and then she'd join him and he'd take her by the hand and lead her to safety, and along the way it would turn out that she was good with a pulse rifle, too.

The footsteps were getting closer, two sets, and a dragging sound. Now voices:

"Don't know why these fry-brains would want any of that junk down there," said one. "Taking hostages, I get. But a bunch of Viking junk? What kind of sense does that make?"

"Can't very well ask 'em now, can we?" said the other.

"Shoot-to-kill orders were a little odd, don't you think?"

"Cartier said that Mr. Jacobsen was pissed about them knocking out the cameras down here. Apparently it's going to take a while to fix all the wiring. Anyway, it was fun, right? Poppin' some fry-brains. To do what we were trained for."

"Yeah. Fun enough. And word is, once this Elysium thing is ready, we'll be doing that a lot more." I wondered what he was talking about. It sounded like shooting more people.

"Sounds good to me," said the other. "Finally, some of the action they promised us."

The two officers passed our tunnel, dragging a body. It had the dyed brown Nomad clothing. I wondered if this was a member of the Skull Team.

We waited until their footsteps had faded away and then kept going. The hallway continued angling downward, the air getting cooler and more moist.

As we walked, I felt like I was getting heavy, my legs slow. All my muscles felt like they were being buzzed somehow, like I was walking through an electrical field. I had a feeling like I was close to something, something big, calling to me, drawing me in like a magnet. And it felt like I couldn't *not* go to it.

We used the string of lights as a guide, following a tunnel to the right, then left, and right again. It ended at a hole in the floor that had been braced with a metal ring. A steel ladder led through it. We climbed down, followed another passage to another ladder, down again, a passage, another ladder hole, all the while the magnet pull in my chest increasing. The fourth ladder hole was different. The light glowing out of it was brighter. I lay on the floor and inched forward, peering down.

"It's a room," I said, pulling myself back up. We climbed down, and as soon as we cleared the ceiling, the humming of energy became a low whine in my head. My foot slipped off a railing. My palms had gotten slick with cold sweat. I reached the floor and bent over, panting. The air smelled old, dry and sweet, and I felt like I couldn't quite breathe in all the way.

"You okay?" Lilly asked, arriving beside me.

"I don't know. Yeah, I guess."

"Look at this place," Lilly said quietly.

I slowly stood up. The walls made a perfect circle. More lights had been strung around the perimeter, but it was almost like they weren't needed. The place seemed to light itself, as if all of its smooth surfaces were luminous. It had a domed ceiling, but unlike the caverns above, this time there were mathematically perfect arches built out of stone blocks, reaching from the edge of the wall up to the center of the ceiling, where a huge round stone, a ball of rose-and-white marble maybe two meters across, was lodged in what looked like it had once been an opening.

Directly beneath that ball, on the floor was a narrow, chest-high hexagonal pedestal made of tan stone, lighter than the color of the caves we'd come through above. Balanced on the pedestal's flat top was a perfect sphere of black crystal.

"Obsidian," I said, nodding at it. "Volcanic glass."

"Check out these floors," said Lilly, gazing down by her feet. We were standing on smooth, polished tiles. There was a design on them, something in blue-and-white blotches with gold borders. It looked like a giant map of landforms and oceans, but I didn't recognize any of the shapes.

"And these walls . . . Owen, what is this place?" Lilly was walking slowly forward. The walls were covered in chipped and fragmented mosaics, their colors faded and in most places gone, though in what remained there seemed to be cities, stone pyramids and obelisks, coliseums and spiraling towers, arched bridges, and then ships, all similar to what I'd seen in the vision. There were also creatures, things with giant tusks, a striped catlike one with saber teeth that reminded me of the siren's necklace.

I joined Lilly in the center of the room, still looking around. "I don't know," I said, "but I think it's old. Really old." Beside the pedestal was a simple rectangular folding table covered with papers and video sheets, and a lamp that was turned off. I looked up and spied the cameras around the ceiling. I hoped they were still disabled.

"Look," said Lilly, pointing to the wall, at a section where someone had etched letters into the mosaic. They were crude symbols in comparison to the artwork behind them.

"Vandals?" I asked.

"Those symbols are Norse," said Lilly.

"How do you know?" I asked her.

She laughed. "I've been coming to this camp for six summers. That whole Camp Aasgard thing is based on how Vikings came here once. And we learn about it in school over in EdenWest. There are other sites with artifacts around the lakeshore. But, these Viking symbols are on *top* of the mosaics, which means they didn't build this temple. So who did?"

"Paul said these copper mines are over ten thousand years old," I said. "Maybe whoever was mining here back then built this temple, too."

I looked beyond the map-covered table, and that's when I spied the other Nomad body. She was lying over by the wall, her head at a wrong angle, her arm extended out so that it was leaning up on the wall. There was blood on the floor. On her hand too. Her palm was covered in it. I looked around. What had they been after? The skull that the Nomads mentioned? Could that be the same as what I'd seen in the vision?

"So, that would mean that before EdenWest, before America, before the Vikings, someone was coming here, and they built this place," said Lilly, looking around. "Wait." She gazed at me with wide eyes. "What the Free Signal said, about the Eden domes being near ancient sites. Do you think EdenWest was built in this spot because *this* place is here?"

"Maybe," I said. "Maybe that's why the Vikings came here, too. Searching for this place. And now the siren brought us here."

I scanned the piles of papers on the table. They were all large, their edges curled inward like they'd been rolled up. I stepped over and twisted the top one so I could see it, pressing it flat with my hands.

"These are maps," I said. They were skillfully hand-drawn in black ink, but not ancient. "I've seen others like this."

"Where?"

"On the wall in Paul's office. Maybe he drew them." I looked down at the floor. "Like he's trying to decipher this room, or something." The paper had faint blue lines creating a grid. While the floor map looked like it spanned the world, these maps were zoomed in to coastlines and islands. In the large stretches of blank ocean were little sea monster sketches. Things with serpent backs or giant mouths. Paul didn't seem like the type to waste his time doodling. Maybe he had brought in a cartographer or something. Maybe the monsters were because it got boring sitting down here drawing for hours on end.

I flipped through the stack. On some of the ones deeper in the pile, a second set of grid lines seemed to have been drawn atop the first, at an angle to the blue ones. Sometimes there was a word or two scribbled in the bottom corner. I caught: *Matches Malaysian changes?* Another read: *Easter Island?* And also: *Recheck alignment to Hudson Polar.*

A flash of light burst in the corner of my eye.

"Whoa!" I looked over to see that Lilly had placed her hand on the black sphere, and it had come alive, tiny pinpricks of light shooting out of it, hundreds of little beams hitting the walls.

"Stars," said Lilly, gazing around the domed ceiling.

"What did you do?" I asked.

"All I did was put my hand on it."

The lights coming out of the sphere had made the dome above us into a map of the night sky, though it was dimmed by the electric bulbs strung around. It was funny to think that someone had made a dome here, complete with a fake sky, long before Eden. Lilly looked from the stars to the floor, with its land and water shapes. "So, this room is like a giant map."

"Yeah," I said. I let the pile of maps fall to the table and started toward Lilly. There was a clink of glass and then a rolling sound. I looked down to see that I'd kicked something on the floor: a glass cylinder. It rolled in a slow circle, stopping against the outstretched fingers of the Nomad woman.

"What was that?" Lilly asked. She took her hand from the obsidian. The stars went out.

I bent down. It was a vial, missing its top. It had a yellow-and-white label and was mostly empty, except for a few leftover drops of blood. I picked it up and looked at the code printed on it: YH4-32.1 I felt a burst of adrenaline, my head spinning. "Uh-oh," I said.

"What?" Lilly arrived beside me as I stood up. I looked down at the Nomad. Her dead eyes stared up at the ceiling like she'd seen something awe-inspiring up there, or awful. There was a bullet hole in her chest. A pool of blood with crusted edges spread out from beneath her back. I looked at her outstretched arm, leaning on the wall. The palm up, covered in blood. Not a smear, but instead evenly covered, almost like it had been painted on.

Lilly stepped past me and reached down to the body. There was a long, narrow knife in a sheath on the woman's belt. Lilly unsnapped the button and took the knife. She stood up and slipped it into the waist of her shorts. "Just in case," she said.

I nodded, my mind on other things. "The blood," I said vacantly.

Lilly looked down at the body and exhaled slowly. "Yeah, gross."

"No." Things were spinning into webs. Dr. Maria taking my sample the day before yesterday, those looks she'd given me, given the bodies, up in the Preserve. "*My* blood," I said.

"What?"

"The—" I was going to explain what this had to mean. Dr. Maria was working with the Nomads. She'd given them this vial of my blood, but to do what?

I looked around. There. A few feet back up the wall from where the Nomad had fallen was a small recess, a little triangular alcove carved into the wall at chest height. It was just above her feet, like that's where she'd been standing when the bullet hit her.

"Over here." Inside the recess there was a depression carved out in the shape of a hand. It almost looked smooth in the shadows but, peering closer, I saw the spikes. Tiny little pins made of something white, maybe bone. They were polished to perfect points. There were maybe twenty, spaced out around the handprint.

Lilly peered in at it. "Yowch," she said. "That would be like putting your hand on a cactus."

"Yeah," I said. I moved my shaking hand toward it.

"What are you doing? Owen!" She grabbed my wrist.

"It's my blood, on the Nomad's hand," I said. "She covered her hand with my blood to use this. The siren said the key was inside me."

"What?"

"Back in the tunnels," I said.

"Oh," said Lilly. "But, so . . . you think the key is your blood."

I nodded, but it was more like I *knew*. Almost like that

boy Lük was watching me and smiling.

"The key to what, though?" Lilly asked.

I took a deep breath. "Let's find out." I tried to ready myself, to tense all my muscles as I put my hand over the spiked impression. I was shaking, but it seemed more like anticipation of what was about to happen than for the pain. I lowered my hand, the magnet pulling. . . . I pressed down, felt the resistance of my skin, bending against the little spikes. . . . And the popping as needle after needle broke through my armor, pierced me like a piece of fruit. Each stung, the pain a quick jolt, and then my whole hand began to come alive with screaming. My arm shook. I squinted against tears.

"Breathe," Lilly whispered, rubbing my shoulder.

I hadn't realized that I wasn't. I was wincing, gritting my teeth, my body like a stone. I pressed harder. The spikes dug deeper, and around me I began to notice that nothing was happening.

I pulled my hand off. It felt like it was burning from the inside out. The holes were bright red, drops of blood bubbling out of them. They grew fat and then started dripping across my hand, making streaks. I rubbed it on my shorts and looked back at the handprint. The little spikes were coated, the blood dripping down, collecting around the base of each and seeping into narrow spaces around them.

The room started to shake.

"Owen . . . ," said Lilly.

I glanced around. The walls were vibrating, dust falling from seams. A loud crack sounded from behind us and we turned to see the black sphere and its pedestal lowering into the floor. More sharp sounds, a deep rumbling, growing louder, and the floor around the pedestal began to lower too, but in segments, each lower than the next, forming a spiral staircase that led downward.

"Okay . . ." I watched, stunned. My blood had done this—opened a staircase into a floor, deep in an underground temple. "What is this?" I mumbled.

"The table!" Lilly darted forward. The floor was lowering beneath its far legs and it was starting to lean into the hole. Lilly grabbed its edge. I lunged for the papers, somehow remembering to slap my nonbloodied hand down on them. As we pulled the table back, its legs squealing, I considered that if it was positioned over these stairs, then that likely meant that Paul didn't know that the floor opened. That this was a secret he knew nothing about.

The rumbling ceased and the floor stopped moving. A wide ring remained around the edge of the room, and the whole middle had sunk. We peered down. The staircase spiraled two times, narrowing as it went. The black sphere seemed to be suspended about halfway down, and below that, something flickered like metal.

I looked at Lilly. Her eyes were wide, but she waved her hand. "Lead on. Whatever this is, it's for you."

I almost didn't want to. That vibrating inside me had reached a steady hum that made it hard to think. How could this actually be for me? And yet, was there really any doubt?

I started down the stairs. Each was wider at the edge, tapering to the center. We passed below the obsidian star ball, the pedestal, and saw that it was suspended in space by thin copper rods that stretched out from the wall. A dome of copper hung beneath the bottom of the pedestal, like a giant metal umbrella.

Below, we could see down to a stone-block floor. There was something on it, kind of a triangle shape. It looked almost like the hull of one of the little sailboats up at camp.

The stairs ended above this. A catwalk led over to the wall, to a narrow platform that ringed this lower chamber. Everything was carved from stone. We walked slowly across, arms out for balance. In the dim light spilling down from above, I could see that the boatlike object was about five meters below us. A final set of stairs continued down to it from the far side of the platform. The stairs above us kept the walls all in shadows.

I moved around the platform, keeping my back against the wall, until I got to the far staircase. I climbed down. The little craft was lying on a stone floor. It had more geometric sides than a sailboat, and could probably hold about four people. I stepped in. There were flat seats along the sides. It had a copper mast near the front, and a series of little metal poles, like the ones in a tent, that arched from one corner of the craft to the other, outlining a little dome over the front half of the craft.

In the center of the vessel floor was a triangular block of sleek black metal, and sitting on top of that was an oval-shaped clay object, like a pot. There were three more of these pots strapped inside the bow. Closer to me, I spied a tiny metal pole sticking out of the floor and ending at a little gold button. It had a curved depression in it about the size of a fingertip. In the middle of that depression was a little round hole. Its edge stuck up a little. It looked sharp. I wondered if this was another switch for my blood key.

"What is it?" Lilly asked from above.

"Some kind of boat," I said, but I felt like there was more to it than that.

"Are we supposed to do something with it?"

"Don't know." If we were, I had no idea what. It wasn't like there was any water down here to sail it on, and it seemed way too heavy for us to lift. I looked around at the walls.

Blue flickered up on the walkway.

"There," I whispered, pointing.

"What?" Lilly asked. It was too dark for her to see where I was pointing. I got out of the craft and climbed back up the stairs. I was stepping lightly, trying not to make any sound. I had this feeling that something was down here. Something that we might awaken if we weren't careful.

The siren seemed smaller, flickering along the wall,

and then she disappeared as I arrived. I ran my hands over the stone and found a narrow gap, impossible to see in the shadows. It was barely wide enough to fit through. I had to turn sideways.

"You sure this is a good idea?" Lilly asked, behind me.

"No," I said, but I also knew at this point, I was going as far as I could. The magnet pull was undeniable now. I slid into the narrow passage. My shoulder almost immediately hit stone. A flash of blue to my right. I struggled to turn myself and found that the passage continued that way. I slid until I hit another wall. The passage turned again, and again. I smelled the damp, cool stone against my bare skin. My wet shorts caught on the rough surface. The space was tight, I could barely inflate my lungs. I twisted around again, squeezing and sliding in pitch-black, and finally I slipped free into another chamber. This one was small with round walls bathed in brilliant white light.

"Owen?"

I turned back to the narrow, twisting hall. "I'm through. Come on."

I waited, hearing Lilly's arms and shoulders sliding along the rock. I stared into the black of the narrow entryway, waiting for her, and also not wanting to turn around and face what was behind me.

Lilly appeared. The white light washed over her face.

"Whoa," she said, squinting to look over my shoulder. "That's it, isn't it?"

I already knew that it was. I turned around, holding a hand up against the blinding brightness. In the center of this small circular chamber was another pedestal.

On it was the skull.

It gleamed in pure crystal-white, the light seeming to come from inside it, just like in the vision. We walked over to it. I could feel it humming, or myself humming, it was hard to tell, but I felt like this was the source of the magnetic pull, or maybe we both were, and we were being drawn together. I stood over it, looking down into the clear crystal, its sparkles and fractures refracting its own light, making little rainbows. My bones and its stone seemed to be vibrating at the same frequency.

And I knew what to do.

I put my palms on the smooth crystal. It was warm.

"Owen, you're glowing . . . ," Lilly said.

But her voice was already distant. I was leaving. Into the white.

17

"HELLO."

There is no time inside the skull. There is before, and there will be after, but within the crystal electric medium there is only a sense of now and that all things are and have been and will be.

And I feel that this sense is called something. But I don't yet know the word. Or it feels more like I don't remember it yet.

Above are dark clouds. I sit on a stone floor, outside. Tan pyramid peaks and carved spires of the stone city are just visible over a low wall. Soft white, heatless light glows from globes on metal stands around us, on nearby balconies, and in window recesses. The air is flecked with that gray snowfall.

I look down to find myself in a plain white fabric shirt and pants. My feet are bare. As flakes of the dark snow hit my clothes they make soft smudges, and though the flakes are cool, they are not wet.

"It's ash."

Across from me is the boy from the vision, Lük. Between us, the skull glows softly in the twilight, illuminating our faces.

"It's midday, actually," says Lük, hearing my thoughts. "It never gets brighter than this, anymore."

He has a face similar to the siren's—I think, *Primitive*, but that is wrong. That implies less intelligence, and I can feel the intelligence radiating from him like heat from a fire. My dad has photos of fifth-great grandparents from back at the dawn of photography, and even just that many steps back in time you can see how things have changed, like head shapes, nose curves, shoulder slants.

For Lük, the word I am looking for is *ancient*.

And yet he is so familiar that the first thing I ask is, "Are you . . . me? Or, am I . . ."

"No," Lük replies. "You are you, and I am me. But we are related."

"How are we speaking?" I ask. "I mean, you— You probably don't speak English."

"We are communicating beneath language," says Lük, "through the harmony of the Qi-An."

"The what?"

"There have been many names for it before us, and no doubt there have been many since, names that describe the energy that binds the cosmos. . . ." He closes his eyes and in the silence I feel a strange presence in my head, like fingers flipping through pages. "A term for it in your mind is yin-yang. We referred to it as the Qi-An."

"Energy," I say. "You mean like gravity."

"Gravity is one face of the Qi-An. There are many more. The Qi-An gave birth to the living presence in the cosmos. It is called, let me see"—I feel that sensation again, like a breeze over my thoughts—"what you might call the Gaia. We called it the Terra."

"And you're . . . dead."

Lük smiles. He glances over his shoulder. I follow his gaze and see the three pedestals where the skulls were, in the vision. "Yes," he says. "Not in here, though."

I look around. "Where's here?" For a moment, I think to ask if this is heaven or something like that.

"There would be truth to that," says Lük. "But I think, technically, rather than getting into talk of metaphysics and harmonic energy transfer for now, the easiest way to put it is to say that we are inside the skull."

"How is that possible?"

"You are still standing in the temple, obviously, but the skull has"—Lük squints as he checks my mind again—"uploaded," he says. "Your consciousness has uploaded to the skull, where mine is."

"So," I say, "you died, and they put you in here?"

Lük's forehead creases as he thinks. "Close enough."

A flake of ash falls on my eyelashes. I look around. "And where is this?"

Lük stands. "Come see."

We get up and he leads me to the wall. We lean over the edge. He is shorter than me by almost a foot.

The city fills the center of a steep-walled mountain valley. Snow-capped peaks soar on either side. To our left, twisting veins of light trace roads that lead farther up into the valley's tail, where a glacier looms. To our right, the city ends at a massive wall. On the other side is a rough and frothing sea. Huge waves roll into a winding fjord and pound against massive stone docks in explosions of white spray. There are boats tied there, enormous boats with giant sails, their edges and masts gleaming with copper plating and bolts.

"This is our last city," says Lük. "The rest are lost, and soon this one will be, too."

"Who are— Who *were* you people?" I ask.

Lük turns to me. "We have been called by many names: Viracocha in the Inca tradition, Tartessians in southern Spain, and, most commonly, Atlanteans. From the Atlantis of your myths. Not that we called ourselves that. For thousands of years we navigated the world, building our cities, learning from the earth, the ocean, and the stars, creating a great global civilization. But much of what we have known has already been lost. We're dying out. This is the end."

I look over the glowing city. I turn to Lük. "Are you serious?"

This seems to amuse him. "Very."

"And this," I say, "*this* is Atlantis?"

"Part of it," says Lük. "There were once many cities around the world."

As we pause, there is an ominous rumble. I see Lük's fingers tighten on the railing as he tenses in fear. I do too. I feel like I know this fear in my bones, as if some part of me remembers this past, but still I have to ask, "What was that?"

"That," he says, "is what we've done to ourselves. We learned enough about the Terra to think that we could change it. Once, we felt the rhythms of Qi-An, heard nature's whisper and acted as one with it, of it. But as we advanced technologically, we lost our ear for that divine music. We thought we could control the Terra itself. Thought we could shape the world in our image."

I think about the Great Rise and its causes. About how this sounds familiar.

"Yes." Lük agrees with my thought. "As a result we made things worse. Terribly worse. We harnessed power we had no right trying to control. Now, the entire world is falling apart. We've lost the sun, caused a great flood. I believe you know this flood, from your myths."

"You mean like, *the* flood? From the Bible?"

"Yes. Noah and his ark, the story of Manu in the Hindu tradition, Deucalion of the Greek myths, Utnapishtim in the epic of Gilgamesh. All speak of the same event. And it's more than just a flood. Whole continents are moving, sinking, mountains rising, all of it by our hand."

He waves down to the city. "We must leave here, now. The skies have become too unstable, so we will only travel by sea. That is the safest way to ride out the flood. When the cataclysm subsides, we'll disperse, and take up our existence in the stable corners of the world. We'll pass on what we feel is safe, let it change, let it adapt. But some things, we will leave behind, to be lost in time."

I look down into the streets and alleyways of the ancient city. "And this is all happening, or happened, how long ago?"

"About ten thousand years," says Lük. "Give or take."

Below, these Atlantean people make their way in slow moving lines toward the giant docks. I feel grief for them, almost like they are family. It makes a knot inside me.

"That is because they are," says Lük.

"What?" I ask.

"You, Owen, your family. You are an Atlantean. Through the thousands of years from me to you, the human . . . what would you call it . . ."

I feel his fingers sifting through my mind.

"Yes, genetic code . . . has branched and evolved, with certain traits being favored over others, forming vast variations. New areas of the human code have been favored, come alive, while others have fallen dormant and been lost. And through all that change, you contain what is closest to the pure Atlantean version."

"Code, you mean, like DNA?"

Lük sifts through my mind. "Yes, but it is more than how you think of DNA. It's not just eye color and whether you are tall or short. It is also perception and memory. You carry in your genes an understanding of the Atlantean consciousness, a connection to our existence. Our lost civilization lives on inside you."

"Okay," I say, thinking that this is all crazy, unbelievable, and yet I feel like I completely believe it, as if I've always known it. "So you're saying I have, like, Atlantean DNA inside me, and it's been, what, turned on?"

"That is more precise than you know."

"But turned on by what?"

"By proximity to this skull. It is tuned to the Qi-An frequencies of your Atlantean genes, designed to make them function once more."

"So, this thing, and this awakening, that's why I have these?" I point to my gills, but at the same time I am looking at Lük and realizing that he doesn't have the lines on his neck. "Wait, do you—"

"The awakening process involves the activation of parts of your code that have been dormant for thousands of generations," says Lük. "The process of turning on these areas is bound to cause some upheaval on the genetic level, a bit of reshuffling. Any side effects of the awakening should select themselves out in time as the organization progresses."

"Oh," I say. "So you guys aren't gill people."

Lük looks at me and suddenly he laughs. It is an odd sound, short and sharp, again showing the gulf of time between us. "No. Though our babies have gills, sometimes, but they fade. And we have legends of gill people, in the past. We did all come from the sea, after all, if you go back far enough."

Now it is my turn to laugh, though less enthusiastically. "So this is, like, spinning my evolutionary clock, kinda."

He nods.

"And the others who have gotten gills," I say, "they've got some of this Atlantean DNA in them, too?"

"Yes, but they are not pure, like you. Every human has some amount of the ancestry, and these other gill people you speak of likely have more than most. Their proximity to this skull will produce effects, but only you are the true Atlantean. The only one that heard the skull's call."

By *call* I think he must mean the siren. "But Lilly," I say, "my friend out there, heard it, too."

"I see her in your mind," says Lük. "Well, *this* skull is only for you. *I* am only for you, but she may well be one of the three, in which case, there is a skull for her, at another location."

"The three?"

"Yes. There are three Atlanteans. That is how we designed the skulls, to find the three with the most pure version of the code, within parameters such as age.

Only a youthful brain is elastic enough to handle these transformations. And your body is young and strong, which will be necessary for what's to come. Also, the skulls are tuned to specific aptitudes. So, not only do you have to be pure enough, but you must also possess the right skills."

I think that I should feel fear, or more frustration at being told all this, because none of this is my choice. It's completely beyond my control. Instead, what I feel is peace. Again, it's as if I have known this already, as if a part of me, a purpose, is waking up for the first time in my life. "Okay, and what's to come?"

"There is a legend," says Lük. "Like this: 'Before the beginning, there was an end. Three chosen to die, to live in the service of the Qi-An, the balance of all things. Three guardians of the memory of the first people, they who thought themselves masters of all the Terra, who went too far, and were lost to the heaving earth. To the flood. Three who will wait, until long after memory fades. And should the time come again, when masters seek to bend the Terra to their will, then the three will awaken, to save us all.'"

The words sound like truth to me, like something I'd known all along.

"Now that you have been awakened, it is your destiny to return home. You must protect the Heart of the Terra. It is in danger."

"In danger from what?"

"From the very machinery that we built. Someone has

discovered our sin, and seeks to use it. If they do, humanity will near extinction once more. And this time it may plunge over the edge."

"Who found this . . . sin that you're talking about?"

"I am unaware of the exact events that have taken place out in the world, only what they must mean if you have arrived here. If you are here, talking to me, then the Sentinels were activated. How to describe this . . ." He checks me. "Okay," says Lük. "Think of the Sentinels as sensors that were tripped. The sensors activate the skulls, and the skulls find and activate the Atlanteans. The Atlanteans return to the Heart of the Terra to protect it. How this all happens I can and will explain to you, but not now. We have to go slow. Even your young brain is only so elastic."

"Okay, sure, but . . ." I am already feeling exhausted. He's right: it is more than enough to know I'm an Atlantean, descended from an ancient culture. "Where am I supposed to go? Like, where is this Terra? Wait, are you going to tell me it's inside all of us, or something?"

"No, it is very real and had a location. But finding it is the job of the Mariner."

"The who?"

"Each Atlantean has a purpose: there is the Mariner, who can locate the Heart of the Terra; the Medium, who can speak to it; and the Aeronaut, who can get you all there."

"Which one am I?" I ask.

Lük looks at me for a moment, then he glances up.

I follow his gaze. "What?" All I see are the heavy cloud bottoms, dark, raining ash.

But then a light. A craft drops down out of the black, arcing on the wind. It is large, triangular, with sails billowing off its central mast. It reminds me of a bigger version of the craft outside the skull room. A blue light glows from its center, like a power source.

"Wait, you guys could fly?" I ask.

"You don't map the earth and build a worldwide culture by boat," said Lük. "That would take ages. Now, look at the ship and tell me: Why is he listing like that?"

"He's battling probably a thirty-knot crosswind from the southeast," I answer immediately. Then it occurs to me that I knew that, just like I'd been sensing winds the last few days.

Lük is smiling.

"I'm the Aeronaut," I say.

"There is a craft in this temple," says Lük.

"Wait, you're telling me I'm going to *fly* that thing?"

"Yes, but I will help you. That's why I'm here. I trained to be an Aeronaut. And that learning will awaken inside you. Now that you've connected with the skull, I will be able to join you in your mind."

"Like you're going to download into me?"

"More like I have always been there, like memories you didn't know you had. Other things will happen, too. More effects of your awakening."

"Oh," I say, "more of *that*."

"Yes, but what's important is that we can work on your training without the skull present."

"Yeah, about the flying . . . ," I say. "I know you can read my thoughts, so you might want to picture what I'm thinking about right now."

Lük closes his eyes, then frowns. "That looks like some sort of giant dome structure."

"Yeah. It's going to be kind of a problem."

"I'm afraid I won't be any he—wi . . ."

Lük's mouth is still moving, but his voice is cutting out.

The world around us flickers from dark to white.

"Hey," I say to him.

"Y . . ." His mouth moves. "To make th—"

The world around me brightens. I brighten. The vision is fading. I am leaving the skull.

Everything turns to white, but then suddenly to black.

I feel myself returning, and time and space begin to solidify.

So does pain.

18

I LANDED BACK INSIDE MY BODY, FILLING ITS spaces, feeling my heart pumping, my feet on the floor, my hand burning, and my breath—

Stopped. Pain around my neck. Tension. Everything squeezed tight.

My eyes opened and the room was dark except for light beams. Flashlights. In their sweeps I saw Lilly, held with an elbow around her neck by one of the two Security Forces guards we'd seen earlier.

There was an arm around my neck too.

The lights caught the skull, but its inner glow had gone dark.

"This is fascinating." Cartier appeared. He walked over and picked up the skull, holding it in both his gloved hands, making little bouncing movements with his arms like he was testing its weight. "Mr. Jacobsen will be very pleased to know about this." He looked at his officers. "His orders are to bring these two and the skull to his lab. Let's go."

I glanced over at Lilly. Her face was red. There was no way we were breaking these holds. I tried to say to her, with my glance, *It will be okay,* or something like that, even though I didn't know how it could be.

But even though we were caught, I felt fuzzy, only loosely connected to the outside world after my time inside the skull. I could barely make sense of my limbs to walk, couldn't quite pay attention. Despite the danger, it felt like my brain was busy with other things.

Gather round, everyone, a technician was calling, waving his arms. The yellow suits clustered around a bank of consoles, looking at screens full of spiking meters. *You know those data vaults we've always wondered about?* There were murmurs among the others. *Well, they're coming online.*

I shook my head, trying to focus. Through the brain fog, at least a couple things were clear from all that had just happened.

The Nomads had been after the skull, and me. Did that mean they knew that I was an Atlantean? And they wanted to get me away from Project Elysium. So, was that what Lük was talking about? Was Project Elysium the thing that was going to destroy the Heart of the Terra, if we didn't protect it?

My captor loosened his grip and pushed me through the narrow back-and-forth passage. I came out on the walkway above the little airship. He grabbed me by the arm, moving me ahead.

They marched us up the spiral stairs, back to the map room. There, Cartier pulled the jacket off the dead Nomad. When he yanked it loose, her arms flopped. Her head thudded on the marble floor. He took the jacket and wrapped the skull in it.

We climbed up the ladder, back into the mine tunnels, up and up until we were in the long hall with the concrete floor.

Ahead, I saw the side tunnel where Lilly and I had entered. Beyond that was the next ladder, the one that would likely lead us up into the Aquinara, and right to Paul. As I passed our tunnel, I thought halfheartedly about making a break for it, but I could barely process how to do that, and I was so tired, the exhaustion of the entire week overwhelming, and on top of that was this fuzzy-headed way my mind seemed to be so distracted.

Lilly, though, had all of her energy, and she had something I didn't.

Her captor suddenly shouted in pain.

My guard was already spinning around as I did, and there was Lilly, holding out the Nomad's knife, its end glistening in blood. Her arm was extended toward the next guard, but it also seemed like she was trying to get the knife as far away from her body as she could. Her eyes were wild, looking as scared by what she'd just done as fierce because of it.

I had to move. I slammed my hands into my guard's back, doubting what good it would do, but it sent him face-first into the nearby wall.

"Gah!" he shouted, collapsing to his knees and grabbing at his nose as blood poured out.

My eyes locked with Lilly and we spun and sprinted into the side tunnel. Out of the corner of my eye I saw Cartier rushing back toward us, but his careful grip on the skull slowed him down, and then we were flying down the dark passage.

"Have to get to water!" Lilly shouted, her voice at a higher pitch than I'd heard before.

Shouts and footsteps behind us. Lilly was getting ahead of me. I told my legs to go faster, but they didn't seem to get the message. Again, it was like all of my circuits were busy.

Lilly turned back. "Come on!" She grabbed me by the wrist and dragged me, and I barely kept my feet underneath me. Down the hall, around the wall at the end, into the chamber. I could barely see in the dark, needed the siren, but Lilly's memory was true. She kept pulling me and running and then our feet splashed into icy water and we dove. Air out. Water in. My skin seemed to scream at the cold, and it shocked me back to reality. Kick. Pull. We shot through the tunnel, two fish finally thrown back into their sea.

We jostled through the listless koi and reached the opening and were back out into the green of the lake. We angled up and caught the push of the outflow current. Swimming, owning the water, and it was amazing to me that it was still daytime. How long had we been in there? It had felt like days, years maybe. I'd gone in looking for answers, trying to understand what I was. Now I felt like I knew more than I could even grasp.

'Owen!' Lilly shouted as she waited for me to catch up.

'I'm trying,' I said, kicking harder, because even though we were in our medium again, everything still felt off, slow, like my body was trying to do two things at once.

'Where are we going?' I asked Lilly.

'Don't know yet.' She was kicking furiously.

I noticed that she was still gripping the knife in her hand. The water had washed off the blood, and now the blade snared and respun little shards of sunlight with each of her swim strokes.

We stayed deep, crossing the lake. Then, there was a new sound. We looked up and saw the bellies of motorboats sliding by above, two together.

'They're looking for us,' said Lilly.

'We have to go deeper,' I said, starting to pull down into the darker layer.

'Not good,' said Lilly. Above, the boats were circling. She passed me. 'Faster, Owen!'

'I am,' I said, but something was wrong. I was trying to swim, trying to go harder and faster than I ever had, and yet I was falling behind again.

Wow, look at that . . . , said one of the technicians, like there was brand-new equipment suddenly in place.

Well, this is unexpected, said another. The whole group of them were ignoring their usual posts.

And meanwhile I was slowing down. Everything felt weak. My arms were coming to a stop, my legs hanging loose, and my lungs starting to twitch—

Wait. The fluttering in my neck . . . There was stillness where there had been movement. I tried to swallow water, but the flow had stopped.

'Hey!' Lilly looked up at me from the deep shadows.

My gills weren't working, and I was just hanging there in watery space, nothing happening . . . except now a tickle in my throat, a heaving feeling, something was coming up, out. Oh no . . .

I coughed out that little bubble of air from my lungs. Suddenly they were awake, and wanted to breathe, to take over. What had happened to my gills?

I grabbed at my neck, pressing on the folds, causing stabs of pain, but still nothing worked, the flesh soft, dead. And I was drowning again. Thrashing and trying to move, and down was up and I couldn't understand what had happened or why now, after everything I'd been through, all I'd learned. Now I just needed air, air . . . *air*!

Lilly was coming toward me, but it was too late. My mouth opened. I was swallowing water and there was that cold again, the icy pain searing out from the inside. That feeling of safety, that comfort of water's pressure, like this was my world—all of that was gone. The freezing liquid poured down my throat, into my trachea, and the pain and the cold and the dying happened all over again.

I tried to move. There was no moving. I tried to scream or close my throat, but nothing worked, nothing, all systems off-line, sinking. Lilly was fading into a blur of green, and it was all going to black, and even as I clawed weakly at the liquid—final desperate movements—the technicians were still huddled around something new, mumbling with fascination, like they didn't even notice what was happening to me, like they barely even cared.

PART III

And should the time come again,
When masters seek to bend the Terra to their will,
Then the three will awaken, to save us all.

19

YOU WOULD HEAR THEM FIRST. VIBRATIONS IN OUR
walls, making the coffee mugs dance on their perches above
the stove.

Mom counted the seconds; the closer together the
booms, the stronger the storms. And the bigger they were,
the more excited she seemed to get. They usually came at
night, when I'd be lying in my bed, the one lamp in our
single bedroom buzzing low because of the power rationing.
I liked to sleep with my back up against the wall, and when
the walls rumbled, I'd feel it in my spine.

"One . . . two . . . three . . . four . . ."

Another rumble. Mom looked over at me, and maybe
my six-year-old eyes looked scared, because she smiled and
said, "Here comes the giant." She got up, putting down
the reader tablet, whose weak charge she'd nearly used up
reading to me. She shrugged off her fleece shawl and made
big steps around the room. "Boom boom boom," she said.

A message blinked on the desk monitor. Mom stopped

and slipped on her glasses to read it. "Ooh," she said softly. "Owen, they're here. Want to go see?"

No, I thought. I didn't really want to go see. I wanted to stay in bed. "I thought we were supposed to stay inside because they were dangerous?"

My mom smiled at me in a way that was maybe supposed to make me think I was being silly, except it also always made me feel like she was disappointed in me, in my caution, my fear. Dad wouldn't have wanted to go out either, but Dad was at work. He worked a lot of nights, managing the battery storage of the geothermal energy charge. The batteries were always having problems.

"Nah," my mom said, still smiling. "We'll be fine." She looked away as she said it. I'd seen her do that when she was talking to Dad, like having to deal with someone as fearful as me was trying for her. I got the feeling that, if I resisted anymore, she'd start to get frustrated. And with Mom, it always seemed like if you made her too mad, or disappointed her too much, she'd tune you out. Those moments scared me, as if even at that age I could sense that they were little auditions for when she really would leave us.

"Okay," I said, and slipped out of bed.

She handed me my jacket. I put it over my pajamas and wondered if she'd notice and tell me to put clothes on, but she was too busy finding her camera and putting on a scarf and a cowboy hat, like she was getting ready for a night on the town. Mom always did that, as if every place she went was a stage.

We left the apartment and walked up the main cavern road through our neighborhood. The booming sounded again. Dust drifted loose from the cavern walls with each concussion. I put up my hand for Mom to hold, but at that moment she was busy waving to a few neighbors.

A small crowd had formed in the street, heading in the same direction as we were. In a way, everyone had been waiting for this moment for over a year now, even while we'd hoped to avoid it. There were other kids walking with their parents. Some carried flashlights and blankets to sit on. So my mom wasn't the only one who felt this urge that I didn't share. That only made me feel more inadequate.

The elevators up to the city concourse were closed for power rationing, so we had to take the stairs. The narrow metal flights switched back and forth up the rock wall. They shook and whined with the crowd of people on them.

We emerged on a flat rock ledge, on the inside rim of the Yellowstone caldera, looking out over a wide, flat plain. It was dark, starless. The leading clouds of the storm were already overhead. More thunder. Hot wind whipped our hair and clothes, bullied its way through the dry evening cold. The slender windmills atop the ridge were spinning furiously, making a droning hum.

"There," said Mom. She and others were pointing to the west, where a dark-orange glow lit the underbellies of the clouds. A spear of lightning zigzagged down, causing a flash in the distant pine trees. The orange light illuminated gaps in the cloud columns, canyons rising high into the sky. They were called pyrocumulus clouds. Dry thunderstorms where, though there might be rain falling somewhere thousands of meters up, the little amount of water evaporated while it was still in the sky. The storms got nicknamed lightning rains because lightning was the only thing that made it to the ground.

This one was different though, bigger, fueled by the smoke of the Three-Year Fire, which had finally found us.

I didn't like being out there. In fact, it might have been the most scared I'd ever been. All I wanted was to be back inside, and yet, there was my mom, Nina, her face to the scalding wind, holding on to her hat, watching the ridgeline with the same anticipation that I had watching a breakaway in soccer.

The orange grew, and then the flames appeared, their brilliance reflecting off the white poles of the windmills along the ridge.

The fire had been moving around the American West for two years. For the first year and a half we'd counted its age in months like it was a toddler, but then it was too old for that. There were no resources or people to fight it, so it just burned and burned. Nobody knew how long it would last. It was a question of fuel. How many years would it take to burn every last tree in the American West? The answer turned out to be three years and one and a half months.

Aside from a near miss in month six, this was the first time it had ever come to us. Maybe, in a way, we'd felt left out.

It moved like some vicious, primitive predator, a swarm of ants, a herd of velociraptors leaping over the caldera rim and devouring the pine trees in bright bursts of sparks. The flames looked fluid, streaming down the hillside, and soon they were flooding the whole valley. When I saw it the next morning, all the green and yellow was gone, the land painted gray, the trees brittle black twigs, the river choked with ash.

All by our hand, someone would say, or said, long ago.

As the fire stampeded by and brittle gray flakes snowed down on our hair and eyelashes, Mom rested her hand on my shoulder. "Isn't it amazing?" she said. I knew she didn't mean amazing like strictly good, but her voice was low with awe, if not excitement. Others around us seemed struck too, maybe because we had heard so much about this terrible thing, and now here it was, its marauding demon gaze finally falling on us.

I didn't know if I thought it was amazing, or if I was terrified or what, but I looked up and saw Mom's expression, and it was one I remembered many times after she left, not a year later: her eyes glassy and wide with wonder, her mouth slightly open, like seeing this, being this close to it, was spiritual for her. I don't remember her ever looking at Dad or me that way.

The trees began to pop. Big, terrible cracks as trunks exploded, branches collapsing into the flames.

I started to cry.

Mom looked down at me, and I tried to hide it. I didn't want to ruin her moment.

"Owen, it's okay. You're okay. . . ."

"Owen, you're okay."

I opened my eyes to find Lilly on her knees beside me. Her hand was on my shoulder. The heat of the Yellowstone fire was the SafeSun on my face. I looked around and saw that we were in the little clearing on Tiger Lilly Island.

It took me a second to understand where I was, or when I was. I'd really felt like I was back in Yellowstone, with Mom, six again. And I had a sinking feeling now. That night when the fires came had been terrifying, but it had been a relief to be back there, like none of what came next had ever happened, like it would never happen . . . except it all had. I was never going to be six again, and my life from then to now was never going to be undone, or redone. It just was.

My brain shuffled again, like it couldn't quite find the present. I pictured the world inside the skull, Lük's city under ash skies, that night at Yellowstone. That was what linked the two memories: that weird sense of being witness to the end, and the real acceptance that the world you knew wasn't permanent, that it was fragile and temporary and could be destroyed at any moment. My genes had seen it before, and again.

"Try to breathe," said Lilly.

I looked up at her, the recent past finally cementing itself. We'd run from the temple, swimming away, but then I'd stopped, things had stopped. I hadn't been able to breathe.

I tried now. It worked, but it hurt. I tasted the metal lake flavor. Remembered it pouring into me. "Okay," I croaked. "That's the last time I'm doing that."

I heard Lilly laugh quietly. Felt her fingers brush across my neck. "It's your gills."

"What?" I reached up and touched them, only to find that they were barely there. The slits, which had been deep, had connected my throat to the water, now felt like shallow indentations. "They're gone," I said vacantly.

"I had to drag you out of there," said Lilly. "Pump your chest all over again. And you shivered like crazy all night, sweating, too, but I wrapped us both up in the blanket and held you, and by this morning you were warm again."

I listened to this. Looked at Lilly sitting there in her baggy sweatshirt and shorts. I had spent the night wrapped in Lilly's body . . . and I didn't remember it. "Thanks," I managed to say. "Again."

Lilly shrugged. "You know me, professional Owen saver." She smiled, but only for a second. "When I was pulling you, I saw that your gills were moving less. I think they gave you just enough oxygen to keep you alive until we got here, but . . . why are they gone?" She touched her own gills.

"Lük said they were a side effect of activation," I thought out loud, "of everything reorganizing. . . ."

"I don't think I understood any of that," said Lilly.

"Oh, right." I struggled to sit up, and then told her about the time inside the skull: Lük, the Atlanteans, the Qi-An, and the Terra.

"Well," said Lilly, sounding a little shocked by it all, "I guess it wasn't the bug juice. Marco will be disappointed."

"Yeah," I said. "And so I think my gills disappearing is maybe just part of the changing."

"Leech should have called you Frog-boy instead of Turtle," said Lilly.

"What's that mean?"

"Sorry"—Lilly pointed her thumbs at herself—"one of my CIT duties is leading nature walks. But so when frogs change from tadpoles to adults, they lose their gills and tails and grow giant mouths in, like, a single night. You're not going to grow a giant mouth, are you?"

I smiled, but also felt around my face. "I don't think so."

"So, you're one of three Atlanteans," said Lilly. "The Aeronaut."

"Yeah," I said, "at least, I guess I will be." I saw that she was frowning, looking away. "You're one, too," I said. "You're either the Navigator or the Medium. We'll know when we find your skull."

Lilly's lips were pursed. "Right," she said.

"What," I said, "you don't believe me?"

"No, I do." She turned and rummaged through her red bag. "Here." She handed me half a chocolate bar.

"Thanks." My throat hurt with each swallow, but the chocolate reminded my body about food.

"It's just a lot," she said.

"Yeah," I said.

"I mean, I know I'm the one who was all, 'We have to get out of here and figure out what's going on,' but," Lilly said slowly, "I stabbed someone. I could have killed him. Taken a life." She stared at the ground beside me. "I keep hearing the sound the knife made when it tore clothing and skin. I keep feeling how it caught on his ribs when I pulled it out. . . ."

I reached out and rubbed her knee. "You were brave," I said. "You got us out of there."

She shrugged. "Maybe."

I shook my head. "All of this is hard. I mean, these changes are happening to me, and I can't control any of it. It's like I'm just along for the ride."

"Like puberty wasn't hard enough," said Lilly. She managed to smile. "But you did make a choice, Owen. When you ran, back in the Preserve. You made the choice to find that skull, to know why this is happening, to take control. All we can do now is try to find out what's behind all this."

"I guess." That made it sound a little better. "So, now what?"

"We can't go back," said Lilly, gazing off in the direction of camp. "The boats were out searching for us all night. And I saw flashlights in the woods. But even if they weren't looking for us, I mean, what we saw down there . . ."

Lilly gazed toward the dome roof. "This whole place is built on a lie—its history, its purpose, even its location."

"Yeah," I said. "Paul's probably got the skull by now. That's where Cartier said he was taking it."

"But you're the only one who can use it, right?"

"Right."

"And so once Paul figures that out, finding you is going to be his number-one priority."

"Project Elysium's number-one priority," I said. "I want to know what that is."

"Yeah," said Lilly. "And also, I swam back just before dawn to look for Marco or Aliah, or even Evan. I figured after we didn't show up at the ledges, they might have been out at the raft, but they weren't there. I need to make sure they're okay. Paul will know they're lying by now. And, I think anyone with these"—she pointed to her gills—"is in danger."

"So what should we do?" I asked. I was trying to come up with something, but my brain still felt foggy, slow, like my body was still distracted. It had gotten rid of my gills. What was it busy with now?

"The ledges," said Lilly. "Marco and Aliah might have left us some word up there, about what was going on in camp, or where to meet next."

"If they ever got up there," I said.

"Yeah, well"—Lilly was suddenly almost snapping at me—"we can't just sit here until the security teams find us. Stand up."

I did and she took the blanket I'd been lying on and stuffed it into her waterproof bag. She pulled off her sweatshirt and stuffed it in, too. Then, she zipped it closed and started rolling down the top to fasten the big metal buckles.

As she was doing that, I found myself staring at the long grass that was matted in a flat rectangle where the blanket and our bodies had been. I tried to picture us lying there together, curled tight, but my mind was more concerned with something else. Something else I could do . . .

I picked one of the long, flat strands of grass. It snapped free. I held it up and pinched it in the middle and made a loop. I ran the bottom end under and back up through the loop, then around the back of the top half. Back down through the hole . . . I pulled the grass down, cinching it tight. I looked at my work.

Lilly clicked the buckles then knelt on the bag and wrenched the straps tight. She looked up. "What's that?"

"A knot," I said.

It's called a bowline. The voice in my head was familiar. It was Lük, a part of my mind now that we'd joined inside the skull. And yes, a bowline, that's what it was. I knew more, too. "You can use it for tying off sails."

"Is this more Atlantean Owen?" asked Lilly, almost suspiciously.

I gazed at the knot. I was a little bit proud of it. "Yeah, guess so." I had a weird impulse and held the knot out toward her. "Here."

Lilly's eyes narrowed at the little twist of grass. "What?"

"For you."

Lilly took it between two fingers. "What am I supposed to do with this?"

"I don't know. It's just a little gift."

A slight smile dawned on Lilly's face. "You made me a knot out of grass." She didn't sound convinced, but then she stuck the little knot back in her braid. "Thanks," she said, and then business Lilly returned. She stood up, hoisting her bag over her shoulder. "Ready?"

"Oh, sure," I said, a little surprised that the moment had ended so fast. "You're bringing your bag?"

"Yeah, this is everything that matters to me. And I don't think we'll be spending any more nights here. I still have this, too." She indicated the knife at her waist.

We left the clearing. The only evidence of Lilly's time there was the dried wax pools on the rock, ancient artifacts for future generations to try to decipher.

We pushed through the birch branches, to the water channel on the back side of the island. It wasn't far to shore, but I felt a hesitancy that I hadn't felt in days. If my gills were really gone, then I was just a land creature and water was an enemy again.

"You can do it," said Lilly. She waded in up to her hips.

I started after her, missing the way that the cold on my legs used to bring my gills to life. There was a faint tingle, like the ghost of something that used to be there, but that was it. My feet felt unsteady on the rocks. I was tense all over and I could almost feel my cramp beginning to lock up.

I reached chest level and pushed out, swimming slow, keeping my head up. Lilly dove under, the bag dragging along the surface behind her. I paddled along, wishing I could keep up but feeling the lameness of my side, the protest of the muscles keeping my head above water, keeping me tied to the surface. I looked down into the green and missed that world.

By the time I got to shore, Lilly had her bag open again. Her gills were tucking away. She looked at me. "Nice work," she said, and I felt like she was CIT Lilly again and I was just the little student, like our time together was being undone.

I climbed out of the water, through a little forest of water grass. As I did, something buzzed and landed on my forearm. I looked down to see something like a butterfly, but with a long, shimmery green body and four flat, iridescent wings. I raised my other hand, thinking if this was a robot like the butterflies, then we couldn't afford to be seen—

"Don't!" said Lilly. "It's a dragonfly."

Its long tail twitched.

"Is it fake?" I asked.

Lilly rolled her eyes. "No. Dragonflies aren't fragile like butterflies. They've been around since, like, the dinosaurs."

I held my arm close and looked at the ancient creature, thinking that maybe Lük had seen these in his world, too.

"You're kind of like one," said Lilly. "More than Frog-boy, actually."

"Huh?"

"Dragonflies start life in the water as these swimmy things, and then they crawl out and turn into the flying guys. You know, metamorphosis, like you. And they're one of the fastest flying animals."

"Oh, cool." I started climbing up the bank, and the little creature zipped off.

"'Course, once they fly they only live a few days. Just long enough to mate, then they die."

"Thanks, Counselor Lilly." I smiled at her, but she wasn't looking, instead digging in her bag. I felt like yesterday, when we both had gills, we would have laughed together about that.

She pulled something out and tossed it to me. A bundle

of sky-blue-colored fabric. I unrolled it and found that it was a T-shirt, a lot bigger than one I'd usually wear.

"It's Evan's," said Lilly, still rummaging around. "But it should work for you."

"Sure," I said. More spells being broken. Why did she have Evan's shirt in her island bag? Had he left it there one time after they'd hooked up? Had shirtless Evan been on the very blanket where Lilly had introduced me to rain, had kept me warm? I hated this.

She stood up, holding an armful of clothes. "Now turn around, and no peeking."

I felt a little twitch of excitement that almost brushed away my Evan jealousy, but not entirely. I turned around and tugged the T-shirt over my still-wet body. Despite my recent muscles, it was huge on me, Evan-sized.

"Okay," said Lilly.

I turned back around. She'd changed into jean shorts and a tank top. She had a bottle of NoRad in her hand and was shaking some into her palm. She reached up and started wiping it onto her shoulders.

"Do you—?" I started, but paused.

"What?" Lilly asked.

"Um, do you want me to do that for you?" I asked.

"Nah, I got it," she said. She tossed me the bottle. "You should put some on, too. Up on the ledges we'll be exposed."

"Right." I tried not to sound disappointed, but it seemed

like everything was off, weird. There was some distance between us. Was it just because she was worried about the CITs? Or was it really because I was no longer a gill breather? But we were both still Atlanteans, so what was the problem? I couldn't tell.

"Trail's this way," said Lilly. She was heading off to our left.

I finished putting the NoRad on and caught up.

"Now this." Lilly traded the NoRad for a small package. An energy bar. "Tastes like bedsheets, but I don't think we'll be dining with the rest of camp today."

"Right," I said. "Thanks." I tore open the package. I devoured the mealy, tan-colored bar, barely noticing the taste.

We hiked up through the pine trees, angling back toward camp. Soon, we hit a dusty trail that ran steeply up the hillside. We followed it as it switched back and forth, climbing steadily.

We started to be able to see out through the trees, to the sparkle of the lake and the distant gleam of the city. The trail became more uneven, and soon we were climbing up triangular rocks that formed a natural staircase. The trees were shorter up here, their branches tucked in tighter. The canopy gave way and we were in the bright SafeSun. It felt way hotter than down by the lake. I squinted and could see the lowest banks of globe-shaped lights, not that far up the wall. Their heat felt more direct, less like the sun. Back home, we'd had a pet lizard a few years ago that lived in a little aquarium with a heat lamp on top. That was what this felt like.

The trail opened up onto a short slope of crumbled rock, mica flecks sparkling within the dark-gray and brown boulders. Above, I could see the naked ledges of Mount Aasgard's summit, like a collection of kids' blocks piled quickly. Behind the small peak was the gray curve of the dome. A single ladder, painted to match the dome, ran up the wall. It was surrounded by a cylinder of bars for safety. I followed it up and saw that it became a staircase as the dome curved inward, and then a catwalk that led all the way out to the Eye.

From here we were close enough that we could also see the enormous triangular panels. This part of the dome looked nothing like the section over by the elevators. The panels were scarred with brown-and-red streaks from dust seeping through their seams. Black, spiderlike cracks zigzagged this way and that: radiation burns. Even the unscathed panels looked worn, beaten. This was definitely not a view that EdenWest would ever want its inhabitants to see.

We climbed up the scree slope and came out on the first of the ledges. I was breathing hard, Lilly less so. The ledge was long and narrow. A five-meter wall of angled rocks led up to the next one.

I noticed a long, straight cut in the rock by my feet, about a hand's length wide and only a couple centimeters deep. It crossed the ledge, ending at the wall. There was another one to my right, the same width, running parallel. "Are these the Viking markings?" I asked Lilly.

"Yeah." She whistled toward the higher ledge, making three short sounds, each curving from a lower to a higher note. "Just in case they're here," said Lilly. "Don't want to barge in on them making out."

We waited. No reply.

Lilly moved to the left side of the wall in front of us. There was a narrow crevice. She slid inside it and climbed, pulling up on fingerholds while bracing her feet between the two walls. I slid into the tight space below her. It was stuffy and smelled like hot rocks. I started up, wondering if I could do it and hating that I was back to worrying about things like this, and then I promptly slipped, raking my knees on the rough stone.

"You okay?" Lilly called down.

"Fine," I mumbled. I had to focus! I wasn't all the way back to being the turtle. I was just a dragonfly, changing. I gritted my teeth and started again, this time making it fine.

We crossed the second ledge, and I noticed more Viking lines carved in the rock. Looking down, I saw that these picked up where the ones on the ledge below left off.

We headed toward a low overhang of rock that created a black space beneath. Lilly stopped at the edge of the shadow. "You guys in there?"

There was silence for a second, then an answer, but it wasn't Marco or Aliah.

"Who's there?" a voice whispered.

"Who are *you*?" Lilly replied.

I touched her shoulder. "Wait." I thought I knew the voice. I stepped into the shadows. "Dr. Maria?"

20

"OWEN?"

My eyes adjusted to the shade. Dr. Maria was sitting against the back wall of the small, low-ceilinged space, beyond a little fire pit made of blackened rocks that were sprinkled with ash.

She was wearing a black jacket, jeans, and heavy brown boots, all coated with trail dust, as was her tangled hair. Her black backpack sat open beside her, the medical kit spread out on top.

Across her lap lay the Nomad bomber from two days before. His face was blotchy, old bruises and scrapes turned a rotten brown, his tan skin now a sallow gray. His eyes were closed.

"His name was Carlo," whispered Dr. Maria. She stroked his hair, only the hair didn't move. It looked wet, but her hand made a coarse sound across it. There were spots of burgundy crusted on his ear and temple, deep stains on his collar. "He died this morning. I knew it was bad, but he was still able to walk, and talk, enough that I thought if we just kept moving . . ." Her words dissolved into quiet sobs.

"What happened?" I asked.

"After the attack in the Preserve, Cartier tortured him for information. Drugs, and . . . other methods. He wanted to know what Carlo knew about . . ." Dr. Maria looked up at me.

"About us," I finished. "The Atlanteans."

Dr. Maria nodded sadly. "I'm sorry, Owen, that I didn't tell you more. I couldn't . . . I mean, at first I wasn't sure if you were even really the one, but, once I knew, I did what I could to help get you out. It wouldn't have done you any good to know what was really going on here, before you understood what you were. I thought my people could get you to safety, and get the skull. . . ."

"It's okay," I said. "I know, now. I went to the temple. I found it."

"I heard," said Dr. Maria. "Paul flipped out when we realized you were gone from the Preserve. When Cartier radioed in that he had found the temple room and the crystal skull but had lost you two, I knew Paul would be on the rampage. I also knew they'd have found your blood sample with the Nomads, and they'd know I was the one who'd been helping them. So I grabbed Carlo while everyone was searching for you. Marco and Aliah told me you were going to meet up here—"

"You've seen them?" Lilly asked.

"Yes, they came to see Evan at the infirmary yesterday. They told me they'd been waiting for you up here, but you hadn't shown up yet."

"Where are they now?" Lilly asked.

"I don't know," said Dr. Maria. "I grabbed Carlo and ran right after that. I thought I could heal him. . . . So many complicated things I've done," she whispered, "but I couldn't save a simple life. . . ." Fresh tears fell.

I had a thousand questions for her, but I tried to hold them back, to respect her loss.

"I wanted to bury him," she said. "His body deserves to be returned to Terra."

"You know about that?" I asked.

"Yeah," said Dr. Maria. "There are those of us among the Nomads who follow the teachings of Heliad-7, based on the words of the old ones. Well, not follow strictly; I mean, Dr. Keller herself is as crazy as Paul, but her teachings follow the Atlantean way."

"Pyra said there's another skull down in the south," I said. I looked at Lilly. "Maybe it's yours."

"Maybe," said Lilly.

"Pyra," Dr. Maria moaned, like she'd known them, too. Then she looked up. "Wait, what do you mean—" but she didn't finish.

We all heard the dogs, yelping, heading this way.

Dr. Maria gave a long sigh, a terrible, resigned noise.

"Adios, Carlo." She slid out from beneath him and then laid Carlo's head gently down on the rock.

She stood and grabbed my arm. "Listen, Owen, take this." She reached into her jacket pocket and thrust a small object at me. It was a round, orange plastic case. A sequence of numbers was handwritten across the top in black marker. Something rattled lightly in it. I took it and popped it open. Inside was a little plastic disk. "It's a thumbprint," said Dr. Maria. "The code on the top will get you into the lab, and that will get you into my computer files. You need to know what Project Elysium is."

"But—"

Dr. Maria brushed past me. "Aaron, in the Eye, is a friend. He may not seem like it, but he helped me get the Nomads in. He can help get you out, okay? But first, go to the lab, behind the red door. Promise me."

"Um, okay," I said, "but what about you?"

"I have to go."

The dogs were closer. We could hear their claws scraping on the rocks, their panting breaths between barks. The clap of boots now, too.

"And Owen . . ." I found Dr. Maria looking at me with big, sad eyes. "I'm sorry." She glanced at Carlo one last time and started out.

"For what?" I whispered, following her into the sunlight.

She spun around and held a finger to her lips, then smiled at me gently. "For all of this . . . what I've been part of . . . for what you'll soon learn. . . . Now go!" She waved me away like a child, then turned and sprinted across the ledge and out of sight among the high boulders.

Lilly emerged from the cave. "She left this." She handed the black backpack to me.

There were scraping rock sounds from the ledge just below us. I looked toward where Dr. Maria had run. "We should—"

"No. She doesn't want us to go with her," said Lilly. "Come on, this way." She ran across the ledge in the other direction.

I knew Lilly was right. I slung Dr. Maria's bag over my shoulder and followed. We hurtled down the rocks and dashed into the pine trees on the back side of the ledge. We headed downward and circled around to the side of the scree slope, staying in the safety of the trees, then looked back up at the ledges. There was the Security Forces team, scaling the same crevice we'd used to get up to the cave.

"Owen!" It was Paul. He'd stepped out to the edge of the ledge. "There's no reason to hide!" he shouted. "I know what you are! We need each other!"

Lilly's hand fell on my arm. "Don't listen to him." She pulled me back further into the shadows.

"I know it's confusing, Owen, but it doesn't need to be! I can explain everything that's happening to you. And no one else has to get hurt! You don't want any more blood on your hands, do you?"

I hated hearing him, and wasn't he right? Blood on my hands. Dead Nomads, Evan, even Colleen. If I was the reason for the temple, then I was the reason for EdenWest, and for all that had happened here.

"Look, we're going to find you, either way!" Paul shouted. "Come out now, and I'll guarantee that Miss Ishani is protected!"

I glanced at her. Paul knew just what to say.

"He's lying," Lilly hissed. "You know it."

I nodded. I did.

A moment of silence passed. We stayed still.

"Have it your way, then!" Paul shouted. "But be prepared for the consequences!" He disappeared from the ledge.

"Let's go," said Lilly. We continued down, staying in the trees, until we were back at the base of the fallen rocks. We started sprinting down the trail.

Something began to drone overhead. We stopped. The sound grew quickly. "Duck!" Lilly shouted. I saw her leaping off the trail. I did the same, just as two small hover copters, like the ones we'd seen putting out the dome panel fire, buzzed over our heads.

I scrambled back onto the trail and turned to see them rising toward the mountaintop. High above that, I saw a figure racing up the little ladder along the dome wall. Dr. Maria.

The copters rose until they were parallel with her and hovered. A voice blared from a speaker on one of them.

"Turn around and proceed down, now."

"They've got her," said Lilly.

"I repeat, turn around and head down—"

There was a crack. A gunshot. A flare of smoke from Dr. Maria, her hand extended outward. A glint of sunlight on the weapon she'd just used.

One of the copters jerked, angling away steeply as black smoke trailed from it. It wobbled in the air but stabilized.

The other copter fired back, a burst of machine gun fire.

I saw Dr. Maria's body convulse, whipping back and forth like it was made of rubber. We were too far away to see the details, but we knew.

My fists clenched. My teeth ground together. No. Not another death, not our ally. *Be prepared for the consequences.* Paul's words echoed in my head. How could I possibly be worth these lives?

"Let's go, Owen. We have to keep moving." Lilly tugged my wrist gently.

But I couldn't. I stared for another second. Dr. Maria hung limply in the metal bars. I turned away, felt the backpack on my shoulders, and then I realized: "She knew. That's why she left us her bag."

"I think so," said Lilly. "She also gave us a head start."

I felt something fall away inside. Some floor, and from beneath it boiled up something dark, black and bitter, craving vengeance. "Then let's take it." I burst past her, leading the way now, running down the trail.

21

WE RAN, WALKED, RAN MORE, AND THE TRAIL
eventually brought us back to the ropes course, and then
along the lake to the cabins. We cut wide up the hill around
the Spotted Hyenas cabin, but it was quiet. I looked through
the windows, didn't see anyone in there, and felt a strange
longing to go inside and see my stuff, even lie down on my
bunk. Maybe it was just fatigue.

Another thought occurred to me: "There's a tablet in
our cabin," I said, pulling Lilly to a stop by her elbow. "We
could send a message out. To my dad, or something."

Lilly rolled her eyes. "O, all those messages are
monitored by the camp staff. Paul would know."

"Oh. I wonder if my other messages ever even got to him."

"Doubt it. Come on."

We passed the other cabins, and then heard the distant
sound of cheering.

"Perfect," said Lilly. "Everyone's at flagpole."

I could see them out there in the midday sun, a blur of

T-shirt colors and skin. One of the cabins seemed to be standing up in front, probably doing a skit about something. All of them so unaware of the world they were really in. And yet it still felt weird to be outside of that group. Not like I wanted to be over there, pretending to be in a happy little camp, except maybe I did a little.

The flapping of the flag caught my eye. The Eden logo was whipping hard. *Northwesterly, up around fifteen knots,* I thought. *We'll need secondary thrust to fight that—*

"Hey, snap out of it." Lilly pulled me along as we left the paths and cut through the woods, working our way around toward the dining hall. We emerged from the trees by the building and we were two steps out when I saw the kids coming up the path on the far side.

"Around back!" Lilly hissed, and we ducked and ran for the side of the building.

"Think they saw us?" I asked.

"Probably not," said Lilly. We ran through the underbrush by the wall, out to the dirt road. We checked for people, didn't see anyone, and crossed over toward the offices. We paused at the door, listening. It didn't sound like there was anyone inside.

"Owen!"

I turned and there was Beaker, running toward us from the dining hall's back door.

"Get out of here!" I hissed at him, waving my hand like he was a stray dog.

"I snuck away from our table!" he said, either not hearing me or ignoring me. "I saw you when we were coming up the hill, but don't worry, nobody else did!"

He reached us, panting, his little chest leaping. He had a big purple bruise below his right eye.

"What happened to your face?" I asked.

"Oh, yeah, that. The guys had me stuffed in a cubby for an hour yesterday."

"Leech," I muttered. "He's such a—"

"It wasn't him. He wasn't around. It was Jalen, because I told him to stop calling Bunsen a bed wetter and maybe I threw a dodgeball and hit him in the face. But it's fine, 'cause we have to stand up for each other, you know?" He looked at me like he was my soldier, waiting for my approval.

"Sure. Listen, Beaker," I said as nicely as I could, "get out of here."

"But where have you been?" he asked. "Everybody's been looking for you! We heard that you were off with—" He stopped, almost like he'd just noticed that Lilly was there, and he jumped back at little, like she was an alien. Then his eyes narrowed. "Are you guys okay?"

"Yes, we're fine," I said. "Just go back inside."

"And don't tell anyone you saw us," Lilly ordered.

Beaker looked down. "Oh, okay. But . . . can I help? I mean, we heard you got attacked by Nomads, and then you ran off, and the Arctic Foxes said that, this one time, they saw you out in the morning acting all weird, and—"

I glanced around, then cut him off. "Look, I know, but the way you can help most is to go back inside before someone notices you're gone."

"But what's going on? What happened to you?"

"I can't tell you. Sorry."

Beaker's face fell. "You're not coming back to the cabin, are you?"

"I don't think so."

"Well, that stinks. I mean, whatever, but . . ."

I hadn't realized that Beaker thought I was, whatever he thought, his friend or something. Then again, maybe I had. That to Beaker, I was his CIT. He'd seen me take on Leech and it inspired him to stand up for himself. But now I was abandoning him.

I wondered if there was something I could tell him. "You know what," I said, "if you want to help, here's what you can do: go back inside and tell our cabin, and especially Todd and anyone else who's around, that you were just outside and you saw the two of us running across the fields like we were heading toward the docks. Can you do that for me?"

"Okay," he said uncertainly, but then his face brightened. "Like a diversion . . . I can do that!"

"Thanks, Pedro."

"Yeah," he said. He kept standing there.

"Okay, go!"

"Right!" He ran back toward the dining hall.

"You know you're his hero," said Lilly.

"I don't know how that happened," I said.

"Come on, Mr. Swimming-into-temples-ancient-Atlantean. You might need to get used to being a hero." Lilly rubbed my shoulder. I felt a surge of electricity from her touch. Finally, some connection between us again.

I smiled at her and turned back to the door. "Okay, let's go in."

We stepped into the lobby area. All the doors were closed. We headed into the infirmary. The hall was quiet, but Paul might be back at any time. We ran to the red door.

"No sign of Evan," said Lilly, peering into each exam room as we passed.

We reached the door and I pulled out the little orange case. I punched the five numbers written on the top into the keypad. Locks turned. A hissing sound. The red door swung open an inch. We pushed through.

Beyond the door was a metal hall, its sides draped in plastic. A single long light beam stretched along the ceiling, shining down cold, harsh light.

The hall led to a room. It was dark, low-lit in blue and white. It was almost like the light of the siren and the skull down in the temple, only this flickering came from modern devices, not ancient: monitors and sterile lights. The floors and walls were all covered in plastic.

There was another door at the opposite end of the

room. To our left was a desk. It stood atop the plastic, as did the other objects in the room. Its top was covered in a glass monitor. Behind that was a long counter, lit in pale white light. It was covered with steel machines, and a set of refrigerator cases with racks of vials inside.

The wall to the right was paneled with flat glass monitor screens, showing views of other rooms, other labs almost identical to this one. One screen was black, the one labeled South, just like up in the Eye.

"So, all the Edens have labs like this," I said quietly, looking at the similar rooms. Even though there was no one here, something about this place made me want to keep my voice low.

The labs on the screens were mostly empty. In one, a white-coated technician seemed to be working with a set of vials, putting them in some round device that started to spin.

"This is not very summer campy," said Lilly. "So, this means that all the Edens are up to the same thing, yes? Are they searching for Atlanteans at these other sites, or what?"

"Something like that, I guess."

Lilly peered at the screens. "Hey, what's EdenHome?"

I realized now that not all the screens were the same. The one in the bottom right corner was different. It showed a bleak landscape, hardpan with patches of loose dirt and crumbled rock that was a burned rust color, the sky hazy with dust and tinted amber.

"I don't know." Lily was right. There were six screens instead of five, and this one was labeled EdenHome. "Looks like it's in a desert. Must be sunset or a dust storm or something."

"So, that means there's a sixth Eden somewhere, like, that nobody knows about?"

"I wouldn't put it past them."

"I am not feeling good about this," said Lilly.

"No." I moved away from the screens, around the desk and over to the refrigerators, peering through their clear glass doors. There were racks of blood inside, hundreds of vials, each with a label similar to the one Dr. Maria had used for me. But the number of vials was small compared to the racks of tiny plastic slides on the bottom shelves, each with a single strand of hair coiled in the center. These were marked with similar numbers. And also birth dates.

And then I remembered: "We had to submit a hair sample with the application to Camp Eden."

"Huh?" Lilly joined me.

What had it said in the application? That it was to screen for allergies and compatibility with Eden's unique environment. "Okay," I said, my heart starting to race. "I think I know how I 'won' the drawing to come here."

Lilly stepped beside me. "You think you were selected?"

"Yeah, and not just me." I opened one of the cases and reached to the back of the shelf, pulling out a tray of slides. I pointed to the birth date on the front one.

"November nineteenth, 2046," Lilly read. Her voice slowed as she understood. "I was born in forty-eight. These . . . these are the Cryo kids."

"This is why you got in, too," I said, feeling pieces click together. "If they had DNA from every applicant, they could screen it. Like, to see if we had the Atlantean code. Maybe they already had a profile, like, a sample from some other site. Maybe they found a skeleton or something, and they were trying to match us to it. And they selected the candidates who fit."

"So, they used the Cryo program to screen for possible matches first," said Lilly. "And then expanded it to the camp program? And then what, brought us here to see what happened? Like if any of us grew gills?"

"I think pretty much."

"If they were choosing the Cryos based on the genetic match," said Lilly, "then that means from the start, like as far back as the domes go, they've been looking for . . ."

"Us," I finished for her. I turned away from the samples, feeling a heaviness from all this information, almost like this whole place was going to come down on me, crush me. I tapped the glass desktop. A white box appeared in the black:

[AUTHENTICATION REQUIRED]

Below the words was a circle and a blinking picture of a thumbprint.

I flicked open the orange case and pulled out the

semiclear oval. I picked it up with my fingernails and pressed the mold onto my own thumb, holding it for a second. When I let go, it stayed in place. I pushed it against the spot on the monitor. The box blinked.

A voice spoke from the screen. "Welcome back, Dr. Estrella."

The screen jumped to life, folders appearing on top of a background photo of red rock mesas. Somewhere Dr. Maria had been, maybe.

The folder in the center had the title *For Owen.*

I tapped it.

There were two more folders inside, one titled *DI Index Monthly Report*, and the other titled *PE Quarterly Report to Eden Board.*

I tapped the DI file. It opened and a chart filled the screen. There was a scroll bar on the right. The chart was long. There were columns of data, by date, most recent at the top. Normal things like temperature, humidity, pressure, and then on the right, the dome integrity rating.

I read the numbers. "Whoa."

"What?" Lilly asked.

I pointed at the chart. "Look at the DI levels for each week."

Lilly started reading. "Fifty-seven percent, fifty-five percent, fifty-two percent . . . Um, those are *way* lower than what they tell us. The Nomads were right."

I scrolled down. "And look: they're like that for the

other domes, too. And . . . six months ago the results were in the sixties." I kept scrolling. "Last year near seventy." I turned to Lilly. "It's going down, fast."

"EdenHome isn't on that chart," said Lilly.

I looked at the columns. "No. Maybe it's a different kind of facility."

I scrolled to the bottom and found a final row of numbers, titled *Time to Integrity Compromise*. For EdenWest it was 238 days. The others were in the same range. I pointed to the numbers.

"That's, like, eight months," said Lilly. "Eight months until these domes start to fail. Wow." She peered at the screen. "Look at that."

There was another table below this one. The first column was each Eden name, and then columns labeled *Yearly Expected Mortality Percentage*.

I ran my finger across the EdenWest line, watching the numbers rise. "Fifteen percent a year from now . . ."

"Meaning fifteen percent of EdenWest's population will be dead?" Lilly was almost whispering.

"I think so." I kept reading. "Thirty-five in two years, seventy-four . . ." My finger reached the end. "Everybody in here will be dead in three years."

"If they stay."

"And there's nowhere for them to go."

I remembered the boy with the burns the other day. "Nobody here has any idea how much danger they're in."

"It's . . . it's just like we thought. . . ."

"Only way worse," I finished.

Lilly sighed, like she'd picked up something heavy. "Everybody needs to get out of here."

I scrolled back up to the top of the file. "Look at the date of the latest reading," I said. "Four days ago. This must be what got Paul so upset. I heard him freaking out in his office the other day." I thought of that dome panel bursting into flames. "So, Project Elysium must have something to do with this. *We* must have something to do with this, and Atlantis."

"Yeah, but wh—"

Lilly didn't finish. She was stopped by a scream in the distance, a muted, desperate sound.

I looked up. "What was that?"

Lilly had turned toward the door on the far wall. "I think it was that way. Come on." She rushed over to it.

I looked back at the screen.

"It needs the thumbprint," said Lilly, examining the door lock.

There was another shriek. It was eerie, high-pitched but muffled, not just by the door, but like through a gag. And definitely made of sheer terror. Maybe someone was tied up down there. At this point, I wouldn't put anything past Paul.

"Come on, Owen!"

I glanced from her to the files. "But Dr. Maria wanted us to see these!"

Lilly scanned the room, then pointed toward a video sheet printer. "Download them!"

"Okay, yeah." I tapped out of the folders, and dragged them to the printer icon.

The printer buzzed to life in the corner. I found a Log Out button and clicked it, gave Lilly the orange box, and hurried over to the printer.

A video sheet was slowly emerging, the files embedded in its silica fibers. I looked around the table for one of the chargers you needed to read it, little batteries that clipped into the base of the sheet and provided the current, but I didn't see one.

I heard a beep and a thick hissing behind me. Lilly had opened the door.

"Owen! Let's go!" Lilly's panicked tone matched the feeling I was getting inside from having heard those screams.

"It's almost done!" I said. "What's the—"

Another shriek, and this time, with the heavy door open, the sound was much more horrible than I could have imagined, the note warbling and frayed. It sounded like an animal as much as a person, something terrified and alone, and it made a knot in my gut.

"No . . ." Lilly's voice trembled. She launched out of sight.

"Wait!" I looked back at the printer. The sheet was still printing. And . . . done.

I grabbed it, rolling the smooth, clear surface as quickly

and gently as I could, and then slid it into the backpack before I hurried to the door.

On the other side, a steel staircase led straight down. I could see another plastic-covered floor at the bottom. "Lilly?" I called quietly.

I started down the stairs, my feet clanging on the metal. There were sounds down there. Mostly machines. Humming. But also something rhythmic like breathing.

I neared the bottom. Another sound. Like a low voice, speaking to someone else.

Closer.

The voice bubbling, something miserable and lonely about its edges. I thought of the way that mourners spoke quietly to the tiny cinder piles after funerary ceremonies back home, just before setting the ashes free on the night breeze.

I reached the bottom step.

Another agonizing scream clawed at my ears.

The room was perfectly circular, almost like the Atlantean room, everything bathed in white light, reflecting off shiny surfaces.

Brilliant white. Only this room had a very different purpose. . . .

And I felt myself lose touch with my skin, like I'd come unstuck inside, a floating thing, tethered only by the images appearing in my eyes. Things I could never have imagined.

But this was not the dream inside the skull.

This was a nightmare.

22

I AM ON A BEACH. STANDING IN A GRAY MIX OF pebbles and sand. Bright morning sun makes the water blinding. The lake is surrounded by an amphitheater of jagged mountains, their peaks topped with snow.

In front of me is a little ship crafted of dark wood beams, brilliant copper plating at its joints.

"No, no, no, oh God, no . . ." The voice is behind me somewhere. Back in reality.

Don't listen to that. I look beside me to see Lük. He stands before his own similar boat. And there are others to either side of us, in a line, all about my age. *Stay here,* says Lük. *See this.*

Are we in the skull? I ask.

No, Lük replies, *we are in your head, inside our shared memory.*

I look back at the craft before me. It is like the one in the temple: single mast, metal triangular object in the center with the oval-shaped clay pot on top. The curved metal poles arch over the front half from one corner to the other.

"No, it's okay. It's going to be okay. . . ."

Cast out! a voice calls from behind us. I turn to see a teacher in a maroon robe ushering us away. He is large, bald, with a curving pattern of black tattoos across his face that makes him look more like a warrior than a teacher.

Behind him, stone buildings ascend in levels back toward the city. Our city. The sky is blue. This is before the ash and darkness. In the midday sun I can see the shining mosaic tiles on walls, the copper frames around windows and roofs, the brilliant gold-plated tips of obelisks and domes, the arched bridges spanning from one cluster of buildings to another. I can see the white globes that burn eternally around the square top of the central pyramid.

Like this, says Lük. He steps into his craft with one foot, pushing away from the beach with the other. Everyone is doing the same. So do I. The craft wobbles laterally as I get in. I steady my balance. With a gritting sigh, the craft leaves the sand and drifts over the lapping waves.

Where is the wind? Lük asks.

I know this. I feel it. *To our right, a westerly. About ten knots?*

Yes. So run a port-side sail.

Okay. I pop open the seat on my left and pull out a rolled bundle of fabric. Find the corners, marked by copper rings. I rummage back in the box for the short rope lines. They are smooth and stretchy, woven of silk. I tie anchor-hitch knots to fasten the three points of the sail to the junctures of the curved pole structure and the mast, my fingers twisting the rope without thinking, then throw the sail up to the left side of the boat. It billows into the air, catches a full breath, and the craft shoots off away from shore.

"Stay with me, just stay, okay? Stay. . . ."

Steer with the pedal rudder! says Lük. He is pulling ahead of me. I look down and see a wooden plank sitting on a metal fulcrum. Pressing it down left or right will control the rudder. I turn the craft to grab the wind.

We have to get enough speed to generate a charge for the heat cell, says Lük.

Heat cell?

That clay pot. It gets its charge from turbines. Look over the side.

I do and see a blur of spinning metal beneath the waves, some kind of small wheel attached to the side of the craft.

We're close. Now put up the thermal! I look over to see Lük, and others spread out over the water, arranging large pieces of fabric. One of them billows full, creating a spherical balloon above the craft.

I open the other seat, pulling out a large bundle. I run it through my hands until I find the triangular opening. This needs to be positioned directly above that little copper nozzle on the clay pot.

"Please, please . . ."

That voice is tugging too hard. Though I want to, I

can't avoid it. The other craft are beginning to rise from the water, taking flight, but the image is starting to wash away.

Owen! Lük calls to me. I see him looking down, through bright sun, but it is fading into white and blue. *Stay here! Learn this!*

I can't, I say.

I have to leave. I have to go back and face what I've seen.

23

"COME ON, JUST HANG IN THERE, I'LL GET YOU out. I swear."

I blinked. I was back in the cylindrical lab. Around the wall there were metal exam tables on wheels. Five of them. Each had a tent of plastic, stretching up from the edges of the table to a point at the ceiling. The air smelled like strong chemicals, alcohol and ammonia, burning my nostrils.

In the middle of the room, there were three more exam tables that had been tilted to vertical. In the very center was a little round table. There was nothing on it except for an old brown jacket, draped there. On the floor were three thick cables, weird clear tubes stuffed with twisting, multicolored wires, and with large, clear suction cups at their ends. These ran up into the air, to the three vertical tables, where they connected to clear masks. Masks over the faces of Evan, Aliah, and Marco, who were strapped to the tables, hanging there, heads slumped forward, eyes closed. Their heads had been shaved in spots to allow little electrodes to be affixed to their scalps. Banks of monitors blinked beside them.

It was the Nomad's jacket in the middle of the room. The skull had been here. And the CITs had been tested to see if it would work for them like it did for me. But that wasn't where Lilly was.

"It's okay, it's okay."

Her voice was coming from my right, by one of the flat metal tables. I could see the cloudy shape of a figure through the tent. Lilly was leaning through a rectangular hole in the plastic. She had unzipped a panel that now hung down like a flap of skin. Her hands were in there, working feverishly. I could see the wet gleam of her eyes, the tears falling, the tremors running down her arms and legs.

I moved over to her. I didn't want to look, but then I followed Lilly's arms into the brilliant white light inside the tent, down to her wrists, where the blood began. To her hands, which were soaked, to her fingers, which fidgeted furiously at a buckle.

A buckle strapped over a clear plastic piece.

A plastic piece that covered a chest.

A chest that had been opened, that lay open now, skin peeled back, ribs separated.

Lungs inflating.

Heart beating.

"It's okay, Anna, it's okay."

Anna.

And it was worse. Even worse than all the tubes and wires running down into her open torso. Little white dots, sensors, were stuck to organs. Little spray jets, misters, were mounted to the plastic piece, sending down a fine spray to keep things moist.

The incision ended at her collarbone, but then her neck, her gills, had been pried open, skin shaved away around them. Bumpy muscle and veins exposed. Two thick plastic tubes snaked down into her mouth from machinery above. One was foggy with condensation, from air, the other dotted with bubbles, from water. The water flowed out of her gills, being caught by curved funnels. There was a steady sound of falling water.

She screamed again, a shriek that was muffled by the tubes, but still agonizing.

And there were other tubes running everywhere, some filled with clear liquid, some with red. Multicolored wires running out of her body. Towers of monitors blinked and beeped beside her.

And her eyes were open. Green eyes in a pretty face; hair that if it hadn't been matted with months, years of grease would have been blond. It flowed out chaotically behind her, strands knotted in the tubing.

Anna stared at Lilly. Her eyes couldn't have been wider.

"Just gonna get this off," Lilly was saying, her voice shaking. "Unhook all this, and then get you out. Oh God, Anna, I'm so sorry."

Anna blinked, leaking tears. She made a quieter sound now. "Uuuu." Her eyes flashed to the bank of machines. "Uuuu."

I stared at the body, this girl, now a science project. This was a girl named Anna, a girl who had smiled and laughed and swam with Lilly, only now she was just insides, systems and organs dissected and turned into a living archaeology site. She had been torn apart by Paul and Eden in their search for the secret code . . . for me.

"Uuuu," Anna moaned. Her eyes fluttered back in her head.

"Almost there," Lilly assured her softly, her fingers flicking open the buckle. She threw the straps aside and pulled away the protective plastic piece, dropped it on the floor with a hollow thud that reverberated around the room. Her fingers twitched for a second. "I don't—," she said like she was talking to herself, and it was edged with a sob. I wondered what she was going to say, but then she started reaching gingerly down among Anna's insides, pulling out the little electrodes.

"Uuuu."

I looked back at poor Anna's pretty eyes, the edges red and crusted, surrounded by rings of bruising. The searing white lights reflecting in her green irises. Again, she was looking up as if into her own skull, then down, then back up. Was something happening to her? Or maybe she was trying to say something.

"Lilly, wait," I said. Peering behind Anna's head, through the plastic . . . I ducked my head out of the tent and looked to the wall. A thick power cord snaked up to a socket. "I think she wants us to turn it off."

"What?" Lilly snapped, sniffling. Her blood-soaked fingers were still working to untangle wires.

"To turn off the machines."

Lilly kept working. I wondered if she'd heard me. Then she stopped. It seemed to take a lot of effort for her to look Anna in the eye. And doing so made her cry again. "Unplug it? Should we do that first? Before I take these off? Will that make it hurt less?"

Anna's eyes welled again, big rims of tears, and she nodded.

"Okay, okay, and then we'll finish getting you out." Lilly turned toward the plug, but I caught her arm.

"Hey," I said quietly, "I . . . I don't think she wants us to get her out." I couldn't be sure, but that was how it seemed. I imagined myself like this. Like *that*. And it wasn't like we could carry her out of here, not in her condition.

"What are you talking about?" Lilly jerked away from my arm.

"Wait." I stepped in front of her. Held her shoulders. "I think turning it off will let her die."

"She—" Lilly started shaking her head, almost like she wanted to keep the idea from sticking in her mind. "But, we can't, we need to—"

"Lilly. Look at her."

I did. Lilly didn't for a moment, then finally did, too. "Is that what you want?" she whispered.

Anna nodded at us, slight movements of her head against the tubes. More tears, but also something like relief in her eyes.

"Oh, God," Lilly sobbed. She backed away. "I can't."

I took Lilly by the shoulders and turned her to Anna. I knew what I had to do, and I hated it. "You stay with her."

Lilly was frozen, like this had broken her. But then she nodded. She reached into the tent and put one hand behind Anna's head. With the other, she rubbed a thumb on Anna's cheek, wiping away the tears. "It's going to be okay," she said, her voice getting thick. "You hear me? It will all be okay in just a minute. . . ."

I stepped over to the wall. Took hold of the plug. The attachment was tight. I held my breath and tore it free.

The machines around Anna went dark. Humming cycled down to silence. Anna's breathing stopped.

"I love you," I heard Lilly whisper.

I thought about going back to her, to hold her, or something, but thought I'd leave her last moment with Anna for her. Besides, I didn't want to see that again.

I took a deep breath. Let it out slow. Now I knew what Paul, Eden, even Dr. Maria had been capable of. *This* was what she'd been apologizing for up on the ledge.

I looked around this dim subterranean lab, the evil

doppelgänger of the Atlantean room. This, right here, beneath the cheery camp, the TrueSky, the SafeSun lamps, the entire dome, this was the heart of EdenWest, a chamber of blood and suffering. And now of death. In this place, they'd been searching for what was inside me. I ran my hand over my chest, imagined the ribs being sawed open, fibers tearing as the covers were spread apart, cold air on my bare organs. . . . He would do that, if he thought he needed to. He would do it without hesitation.

Yet even knowing that, it was still almost impossible to really imagine someone cutting open a girl and stuffing her insides with tubes, like she was nothing more than a piece of equipment.

I walked, dazed, over to the next tented table. I could see the outline of a body. I looked through the clear plastic window. He was a younger boy I didn't know. Probably one of the missing kids that the CITs had mentioned. This was where they'd all really gone. To be pried open and dissected, studied, *understood*. Lilly and Evan had talked about scientists growing ears on the backs of mice, of clones. None of that had ended. It had just gone underground, followed the money. Everyone knew EdenCorp had tons of money.

The next table held little Colleen, her insides on display. Her eyes were open. Wide, innocent. She looked at me. A soft moan from her tubed mouth. I could barely look at her, remembering her little pained voice the other day in the infirmary. Inside, I felt things closing up, locks going on chambers of feeling.

Let's just put these away for a while, said the technicians solemnly.

Then I stepped to the wall and pulled her plug.

Went around the edge of the room, from one tented table to the next.

Pulled all the plugs.

Humming slowing down to silence. Little lights going dark. Tortured lives ending.

When I was done, I slumped against the wall, cockeyed because of the pack on my shoulder. I felt heavy, too heavy. Slid down, and finally acknowledged the feeling in my gut. Threw up on the floor. A splat of liquid. Closed my eyes. Needed there to be nothing for a while. . . .

But another sound began. A voice through a speaker. Coming from behind me. From Dr. Maria's backpack.

I pulled the pack off my shoulder, knelt, and dug into it. Under the medical kit, there was an extra shirt, flashlight, some soymeal protein bars, and a subnet phone.

"Is, um, anyone hearing this?" On the little phone screen was Aaron. "Oh, hey, it's the gill boy, I mean, Owen. Maria gave you the phone, I take it."

"Yeah," I said. "Dr. Maria said you were a friend."

Aaron nodded. He looked past me. "Oh, looks like you've been down to the chamber of horrors." I didn't know if that was supposed to be humorous or what. If it was, then Aaron had a sick sense of humor, and right then, I couldn't find a response.

Aaron glanced over his own shoulder. "Listen, we need to get you out of here," he said quietly, "as soon as yesterday. There's a maintenance hatch due south of the boys' cabins. Number six. How soon do you think you can get there?"

I tried to measure the distance in my head. "Half an hour?" I guessed.

"Okay, good. I can tell Robard and the Nomads to send a team to meet you there. And I can disable that door, provided you don't get caught before then. But, near as I can tell, Paul is back down in the temple, so you should have some time."

"Okay," I said. "We—well, Dr. Maria is—"

"I know, kid, I saw it happen live on the cameras. Just get to that south maintenance door, number six, okay? I'm opening it in thirty minutes and it can't be open long."

"Okay."

The screen went blank. I stared at it. Yes, leaving now. No special flying craft, no skull . . . no ending up on one of these exam tables.

There was a zipping sound. Lilly was closing the plastic window above Anna. She moved back to the middle of the room, to Evan, the closest CIT. I watched her check his pulse and nod. "Still there," she said. "I checked them when I first came down."

"Good," I said. "Hey . . ." I slung the backpack onto my shoulder. "Aaron says he can open a door for us, but we have to get there in thirty minutes. Which means, now."

"Okay," said Lilly. "Just help me get them down, and we'll go."

I looked at the bodies, felt the clock ticking. We had to move. "Listen, Lilly, Paul's not going to do what he did to Anna, to these guys. Now that he knows about the skull and us—"

Lilly spun at me. "They're my *family*, Owen!" She was screaming suddenly, just screaming at me. Her face twisted. A furious animal. "You still have one. I don't!"

"We're going to end up like *that*"—I pointed to Anna— "if we don't get out of here!" I couldn't help yelling back. I could almost feel the knives slicing my chest open, looking for the Atlantean inside.

"Then *go*!" She turned and started unstrapping Evan. "I'd rather die than lose them, too."

Her words echoed around in my head. *Lose them, too.* She'd already lost one family.

I looked again at the CITs and then I realized I was wrong: Paul might not cut them open, might not need to, but now that they'd been down here, seen all this, was he really going to let them go back to lifeguarding? I felt pretty sure that once you ended up in this room, the only way you were getting out was the way Anna just had. "I'm sorry," I said. "You're right. It's just, the time—"

"Then start helping."

I did. Lilly pulled a needle carefully from Evan's elbow. We unbuckled straps, and he crumpled into our arms. "Evan, wake up," Lilly whispered in his ear.

"Nnnn," he moaned. We dragged his hulking body over to the wall and propped him there.

We did the same with Aliah and Marco. By the time we were done, they were coming to.

"Man." Marco was coming out of it the fastest. He rubbed the back of his head. "Security Forces busted in while we were visiting Evan in the infirmary. All I remember after that is something white. . . . What *was* that?"

"A skull from Atlantis," Lilly said matter-of-factly. Marco looked at her. "No time for all that," she said. "We're getting out of here, but we have to move. Can you guys walk?"

"We can try." Marco started pushing himself up the wall. He helped Aliah.

"Guh, what happened?" Evan's eyes blinked open. He saw me and frowned. "Last thing I remember, I . . . you . . ." He squinted at me. "Isn't that my shirt?"

"Yeah," I muttered, and switched topics. "Paul brought you here and tested you," I said. "To see if you were like me and Lilly. But you're not." I couldn't help feeling a little bit of satisfaction saying that.

"What does that mean?" Evan asked. He slowly got to his feet, too.

"It means," said Lilly, "that Paul and Eden have been

looking for someone with a lost genetic code that connects them to Atlantis."

"Atlantis?" said Aliah. "Wait, you mean like Plato and the sunken city and all that stuff?"

Everybody just looked at her.

"What? I read my classics in school."

"Something like that," I said.

"Point is," said Lilly, "they've been looking all along. It's why we were selected as Cryos. And . . ." She bit her lip, inhaled slowly like she was gathering strength. "I need to show you guys something."

She took Evan's arm and put it around her shoulder. I felt a knot form inside to see them like that, but this moment, what Lilly had to show them, it was theirs, not mine. I had to respect that.

I stayed where I was as Lilly led the CITs over to Anna. I heard Aliah gasp. Heard Marco curse. Then they were silent. I heard a kissing sound and saw Lilly take her fingers away from her lips and reach into the plastic tent. The others did the same. Then they whispered their good-byes and turned away.

"Paul never had to study us," said Lilly, leading Evan toward the stairs. "He had his lab rat in Anna. So he left the rest of us alone and just watched, to see what we'd do. Watched until the real Atlantean arrived."

Evan looked at me. "You mean *him*?"

"Yeah," said Lilly. I felt their eyes on me as we headed

back up the stairs. Lilly gave them the short explanation about the temple, the skull, Dr. Maria, and the Nomads, as we returned to the lab and then the cheery infirmary hallway. At each door, we paused, looking warily for Security Forces, but there were none.

We left out the front door, squinting against the bright daylight. There was a distant din of plates and forks. Lunch was still in progress. We headed around the dining hall and back down through the woods. The CITs slowly regained their legs, and we moved faster, rejoining the trail to the cabins.

"Hey, look." Marco was pointing out toward the fields. A squad of Security Forces was jogging down the path toward the boathouse.

"Good job, Beaker," I thought aloud.

We ran on until we reached the first cabins.

"We need to turn south," said Lilly.

"So, we're just heading out into the barrens of Radland in our bathing suits?" Marco asked.

I looked down at Evan's shirt. "We can stop by my cabin. Some of those clothes should fit everybody. And you can have your shirt back." I pulled the subnet phone from my pocket and checked the time. "We have to hurry, though. I told Aaron a half hour, and it's already been twenty minutes."

"So," said Aliah as we jogged over to the Spotted Hyenas cabin. "I have to wear sticky boy clothes? And by the way, I'm totally kidding, but still . . ."

We entered the front door. The subnet phone beeped. "This is Aaron."

"Hey," I answered.

"I am not seeing you on the wall cameras. Are you at the door yet, or what? Everything is set."

"Yeah, we'll be there, maybe a couple minutes late."

"Okay, well"—Aaron's mouth turned down like I was something bitter tasting—"a couple minutes is going to be shaving it real close, especially when it comes to the neck that is stuck out to help you, that being mine. Make it fast, got it?"

"Got it," I said, stuffing the phone away.

"Man, dude, this place completely smells," said Marco as we entered the bunk room.

I looked around. It seemed like forever since I'd been here. I hurried to my bunk and changed into a shirt and jeans. I stuffed an extra shirt, underwear, socks into Dr. Maria's backpack. It was too full to add any more.

Marco and Aliah were digging jeans and long-sleeved shirts out of cubbies and throwing them on. I tossed Evan his shirt.

"Anybody see a pullover that's not gross?" Lilly asked as she rummaged around.

"Here." I gave her mine, then considered the other cubbies. I remembered Wesley having a fairly nice sweatshirt, and he was about my size. I rounded the beds in the middle of the room and checked Wesley's cubby. It wasn't there. His bunk was below Leech's. I looked there and found the sweatshirt lying among other clothes and his blankets. It didn't smell terrible.

I stood up, slipping it over my head. As I did, I caught a glimpse into Leech's bunk. The things he'd taped to the wall: his Trilobytes poster (they were a super-popular band that toured the Edens and the Northern Federation), and his signed photo from the previous camp session with a big pink heart drawn in the corner around Paige's name. There was also a drawing in black ink, with the title *The Preserve: Secret Routes*. It was a map showing the whole Preserve in amazing detail. It had all the trails, animal pens, and here and there, dotted lines and arrows that were labeled with things like "good shortcut" or "ambush spot." So, that was how he'd known where to leave the trail. He'd been keeping track from his previous games. The map even had a compass rose in the corner. And there were funny things, too. Like, he'd drawn a little bear in its enclosure that was standing on its hind legs, fangs bared, holding a terrified camper in its paws. There was a curving monster like a sea serpent in the little pond where the CITs had surprised us.

The drawings were really good. Maybe that shouldn't have been a surprise, since he'd often had that sketchbook with him, but I guess I hadn't wanted to think of Leech as having any talents other than being a jerk. Did knowing this change how I felt about him?

"We good?" said Lilly. I turned to see her by the doorway. The others had left.

"Yeah." I took a step.

But I stopped. I turned back to the wall.

The map. Leech's map. Something about it was sticking in my brain. Something familiar about that little sea monster . . .

And then I knew. The black cylinder case he took on his trips with Paul. It wasn't a fishing pole.

"Oh," I said quietly.

"Owen, what?" Lilly asked.

Everything was swimming. I thought about sitting down. Or, falling over. But there it all was. He'd been here the longest . . . his injured hand that one morning . . . he and Paul finding me in the water by the Aquinara. . . . They hadn't been fishing at all.

I stared at the little map on the wall, and said, "I know who the third Atlantean is."

24

"WHAT?" LILLY ASKED. SHE STEPPED OVER TO MY side. "You do?"

I pointed at the little map. "It's Leech," I said. "Those maps we found in the temple. Paul didn't draw them. Leech did." As I said it I thought, *No way,* there was no way, and yet I felt like I knew it, for sure. "Paul knew. He even had Leech try to open the skull chamber. That's why his hand was bandaged the other day. He must be the Mariner."

"So what does that mean?" Lilly asked.

I sighed. "It means we can't leave without him."

"Let's go tell the others," she said. We headed outside.

"*That* kid?" said Evan when Lilly broke the news. "It was bad enough when it was just *him,*" he added, pointing at me, "but that little runt, too? Why them?"

Guess it wasn't based on who had the biggest shoulders, I thought to reply, but instead I just pointed. "And Lilly."

"Well, yeah, but . . ." Evan trailed off and looked at the ground like he really was disappointed. Maybe he'd just realized that everything that had been happening here wasn't about him. That he was basically a side character in someone else's story. In *my* story. That was something I still wasn't used to, either.

"It wasn't a contest, idiot," Lilly added, scowling at him.

"So now what?" asked Aliah. "Don't we need to get to that south door if we're gonna get out of here?"

"Yeah," said Lilly. "You guys should get going."

"Wait, what about you?" Marco asked.

Lilly looked at me. "We're going to find Leech. Then, I don't know."

I thought about how Lilly had called the CITs her family. "You can go with them, if you want," I said to her. "We can find each other outside."

Lilly's mouth twisted, like she was considering it. Then she shook her head. "I'm going with you," she said. "We'll find another way out," she told them.

"That's stupid. You guys should come with us now while we have the chance," said Evan.

"Listen to you," said Lilly, "Mr. I'm-never-leaving-Eden."

"Yeah, well." Evan glanced at me, and looked around. "Things changed."

"They did," said Lilly. "And they just changed again. So get going."

"Maybe we should help you?" said Evan, almost like he was asking himself.

"No," said Lilly. "Look, someone needs to get to the Nomads and tell them what's really going on in here. If we don't make it out, then, well, I don't know, go tell the ACF if you have to, and come back for us. Now go, and don't ask me if 'I'm sure' or any of that. This is the plan, got it?"

I listened to her and felt like I was falling for her all over again.

"Fine," said Evan.

"Good luck," said Marco.

"Yeah," Aliah added.

I saw Evan catch Lilly's eye and make a little motion with his head, like he was saying, *Be careful.*

Lilly made it back. I made sure not to react.

Then, the three CITs turned and ran into the woods.

Lilly took my hand. We started back down the path toward the fields. "Now what?" she asked.

"Not sure," I said. My heart was pounding, though. We wove through the trees, and stopped in the shadows just before the fields. No one was out playing. It was early afternoon. They'd all be at electives and free swim.

I stared out at the sunny field, a moment of exhaustion rushing over me, my thoughts spinning around.

I felt Lilly watching me. "Tell me what you're thinking."

"Ha," I said. "Nah."

She grabbed my arm and twisted it, like she was going to break it if I didn't tell her. "Or, yes. Spill it, Parker."

"Well . . . honestly, I was thinking that I wanted to run

back and join the others and get out of here. And then, I don't know, just take off. You and me, like . . ." I stopped, because I knew we needed to keep moving, needed to keep our guard up, and yet, everything was so dangerous now, and what if there wasn't ever going to be the perfect opportunity to tell her the things on my mind? What if all our quiet moments, like on the island, our chances to really talk, were already gone? "What if . . . ah, never mind."

"Excuse me, you can't say that and then *not* finish." Lilly was doing that thing again where she was staring at me and her eyes were being all blue and white and too much to look at.

"Fine. Well, it doesn't matter now, 'cause my gills are gone, but I had this whole idea where you and I could run off and find our own little bay somewhere, you know, just us, a place where the coastline was clean, and there were still fish, and stuff. And we could catch them, and, I don't know, just be there."

Lilly smiled. "You want to catch me fish? Like, with a spear?"

"Sure, or, you know, a net."

She stepped toward me. "So underneath that quiet exterior, you're a romantic."

I shrugged. "Who knows what's under here anymore?"

Closer. "I'm starting to think I do."

"Okay," I said. Heart starting to sprint. Fingers tingling. But this time I was going to be the one who took that final little step, the one that made our bodies press together. I put my arms around her, and even as our faces were closing in on each other, I was still having that old thought like, *This can't be right! You* must *be doing* something *wrong—*

But then we were kissing. Lips moving in waves. Her tongue found mine, two warm creatures playing, and I tried to sense what hers was doing and do the same, and make the same lip movements too. And it worked, at least I thought it did, because we were still kissing, and it was amazing, and seconds were passing, now a minute. . . .

"Hello? Hellooo?"

The phone. The damn phone.

I pulled away. "Sorry." I dug the phone from my pocket. Aaron was on the screen, peering frantically into it. He didn't look happy. "Hey," I said, "this is Owen."

"Owen, Owen, Owen," Aaron muttered. "Why is it that I'm sitting here, or should I say huddling in an empty office corner to avoid detection, and watching a team of Nomads sneaking between the solar panels on their way to hatch six, while simultaneously keeping this fact a secret from the rest of EdenWest, mind you, only now I'm noticing on the hatch camera that there are *three* young people approaching the door, not five. Please tell me this is because my above-average vision has suddenly and inexplicably deteriorated, and not, I repeat, *not* because you and that girl are still inside somewhere."

"You're not going blind," I said. "Lilly and I are looking for Leech."

Aaron's face darkened. "You're looking for Leech."

"Yeah," I said, "he's the other Atlantean."

"Oh." Aaron rolled his eyes. *That.*

I stared at the phone. "You *knew*?"

"Obviously," said Aaron.

I felt like screaming at him. "Why didn't anybody tell me?"

"Well, for starters, so that you wouldn't feel compelled to do something inane like go find him instead of heading for the nearest exit like I *told* you."

"Well, sorry, that's what we're doing. You can see inside the temple, right?"

"The Eye sees all," said Aaron. "Actually, that's not completely true. The cameras in that temple place are still down. And, it's not like there are cameras in any of the showers or bathrooms in camp. I swear." He made a noise like he was amused by his own joke.

"You're creepy and disgusting!" Lilly shouted toward the phone.

"So, you don't know where Leech is," I said.

"Not only don't I know," said Aaron, sounding angry now, "but I'd have zero reason to tell you even if I did."

"We can't leave him," I said. "He's the third Atl—"

"Kid, spare me. I know the whole deal already, and what I also know is that we can get Leech out later, some other way, but the best way to get *you* out is currently arriving at the south hatch. So, turn around and get moving."

"But—," I started to say, except then I heard a soft footstep. And a click.

I looked up at Lilly and she was looking right back at me. Her face had gone cold.

The soldier was a few paces away, rifle raised at us. "Don't move!"

I heard Aaron swear to himself, and the phone went black, then suddenly sprouted sparks in my hand, the screen cracking. I dropped it, smoking, to the ground.

More Security Forces arrived, breaking cover from the trees and sprinting toward us.

"And here we are, finally," said Cartier, following close behind. He held up his own phone. "Mr. Jacobsen, it's me. We have them."

25

THEY TOOK OUR BAGS, TOOK LILLY'S KNIFE, AND marched us out across the fields to the swimming area. A long, sleek-looking motorboat was tied up at the dock, right where Lilly and I had first met. There were younger kids and CITs all around, stopping what they were doing to watch us go by.

"Owen!"

I glanced over to see Beaker on the far side of the dock, sitting in his bathing suit with his feet dangling over the side. The rest of my cabin was scattered in the water, their heads turned.

"I'm sorry!" Beaker shouted. "I did what you wanted!"

"It's okay!" I called to him.

"Quiet," said Cartier.

"Owen!"

I saw that now, of all people, it was Mina, looking over from a group of Arctic Foxes who had conquered the floating trampoline. "Are you okay?" She had this worried look on her face like she hadn't recently hated me. For a second I considered that somehow, by blowing her off and then being missing, and now being captured, I seemed to have won back her interest. None of it made any sense to me, and none of it mattered now.

I wondered what they all must have been thinking, what they'd figured out. Did any of the others in my cabin, in the Foxes, have even a clue what was really going on here? Seeing them there, just doing their normal camp thing, I shouted, "It's all a lie!"

"Quiet!" Cartier snapped again.

"They have Leech, too—" An officer's gloved hand fell over my mouth. They shoved me into the boat. The motor revved to life, and we curved away from the dock, speeding out of the inlet.

Lilly and I were seated side by side, the wind slamming our faces. We crossed the wide body of the lake, between sailboats and yachts, even a water-skier, all of them oblivious. I wanted to shout at them, too.

I wondered what we were headed for, and if this was the beginning of a terrible end, if by this time tomorrow we would be on tented tables, Paul searching our guts for our big mysteries. I remembered what Aliah had said about test animals, and thought that the worst part would be not understanding why. Anna, Colleen, they probably never even knew why they were being subjected to such horrible things. And for as much as I knew, there was still so much more that I didn't understand, and maybe never would.

Come on, think! I told myself. The boat was nearing the Aquinara. We were headed back into the temple. There had to be something I could do to escape.

You should check out the new memories, advised the technicians. *We think they're fascinating!* They all turned back to a flickering screen.

Then show me! I shouted at them. I closed my eyes and slipped back inside my head, looking for that memory that I'd been unlocking, of learning to pilot the craft with Lük. I gazed into the spotted darkness behind my eyes, and then light swept around me and I was back there, almost like restarting a video that had been on pause.

I was in the boat on the sunny afternoon, cold wind whipping. Lük was above, his craft rising. Others were already higher, lifting up into the clear sky.

Put up the thermal! Lük shouted.

I looked down at the pile of fabric in my hand, but put that aside. I was looking for something else on the ship. *Where is that button?* I asked.

Button? Lük asked. *There is no button. Just put up the thermal so you can fly!*

I looked around some more. He was right. But there was a button on the ship in the temple. That little gold one.

And these things, they always start in water, I asked, *right? Just with wind?*

Lük looked confused. *You need wind to generate the*

initial momentum that activates the hydroelectric charge. That's what ignites the heat cell. I've heard that some have been adapted to roll across desert plains and produce the same effect.

Okay, I said. *Thanks.*

But the thermal is only for achieving initial lift, said Lük. *There's a second system—*

"Out."

Back on the surface of my senses, I felt myself being grabbed. *Gotta go.* I could hear Lük protesting, but I pushed forward from the memory, back through darkness, and opened my eyes. We had arrived at a dock beside the Aquinara. Cartier led us inside, through wide glass doors, and across the plant's main floor, where pipes and tubes of water twisted around in a huge space above us, the guts of Eden's breathing system. Workers in white jumpsuits walked along catwalks, checking monitors and panels. I thought of how I imagined my insides. It was weird how similar this was, just on a bigger scale.

We entered a hallway, passed through keypad-locked doors, and took a staircase that dropped down five or six levels. A final door slid open into a large lab. The walls were covered with projections of maps, photos of ancient artifacts, and aerial shots of ruins. Pieces of rock were placed on tables, under giant microscopes. I saw holographic projections of rooms and mosaics, being rotated and studied by technicians.

At least there were no tented tables.

In the center of the room was the round hole in the floor that Lilly and I had seen from below, a ladder leading into it. The officers climbed down.

"After you," said Cartier.

We descended into the cement-floored tunnel. We followed the same route, down passages lit with strings of bulbs on the ceiling, down more ladders, until finally we were back in the Atlantean map room. It looked like it had before, except for the other Nomad body being gone. The table of hand-drawn maps was still there, and Leech's black cylinder case was now lying on top of it.

They marched us down the spiral staircase. As we crossed the catwalk at its base, I glanced down at the little Atlantean craft, lying on its dry stone floor. No water or wind for starting it. I glanced up at the black sphere and pedestal suspended above, that strange umbrella of copper beneath it, and then all the way up to the marble ball in the ceiling, trying to figure out what it all meant.

Hands pushed me in the back. "Keep moving."

They'd strung lights around the dark walls, and through the narrow zigzagging passage. A thick tangle of power cords snaked along the floor. We squeezed through, back into the tiny skull chamber.

"Well, there he is."

The light in the chamber was blinding, white coating the walls. There was a steady electric buzz, and snapping sounds of sparks. I couldn't see the skull because it was on the other side of a silhouetted figure who eclipsed its light.

Paul stood to the right of the pedestal, wearing welding goggles to shield his eyes, gazing at the skull. The silhouetted figure was short, leaning forward, an officer on either side holding his arms.

"Okay, he's done." Paul motioned to the two officers. They started pulling on the figure's arms, and it seemed to take a great effort, but then they had Leech free, and as they turned him to the side, we saw that they'd been holding his hands to the skull. "Nnnnaa!" he shouted. His face was wrenched in a knot, eyes closed, teeth bared. A shorter man in a white lab coat, also wearing goggles, appeared in front of Leech and held a square device up to his forehead like Dr. Maria had. The little glass ball glowed a greenish yellow, like a color in between how it had glowed for me, and for Colleen.

"Give him a breather," said Paul, waving his hand toward a cot against the back wall.

Leech slumped weakly in the officers' arms. There were electrodes stuck to his head in shaved spots, like there'd been for the CITs. Wires were attached to the crystal skull, too. Its hollow eyes gleamed at me, but I watched Leech as they laid him down on a cot behind the pedestal. Machines there were monitoring his vitals. His arms were twitching, his legs too, and for the first time, I felt something like bad for him. Leech, the camp favorite, the bully, who'd been controlling us all with nicknames and jokes, when all along he was being controlled.

"Well, Owen . . ." Paul turned around, lifting his goggles as he did.

For the first time I saw his eyes, finally saw what had been behind his tinted glasses, and regretted ever wanting to know.

They were seared, scalded, the whites a sickly blood crimson, threaded with black-burned veins. Except the irises were blue, an electric blazing blue, and I could see crisscrossing lines in them, geometric patterns, with little sparks of light flashing, and I realized his eyes were fake, circuitry, and his pupils were glass camera-lens holes. He must have seen my reaction, because he smiled. His pupils whirred open wider, the machines adjusting their focus. And while I'd found his smile strange with his glasses on, with them off, it was something soulless and cold that I felt sure would live on in my nightmares, if we ever made it out of this.

"Yes," he said, waving a hand toward his face. "This is what happens when you stare into the face of the Gods. Or, in my case, a Sentinel created by the Atlanteans to alert their chosen children. Luckily there's a doctor in EdenEast who makes excellent eyes. They even have direct holotech input, if I cared for such things. But I don't. My eyes are for truth only. And you, Owen, you are truth."

The eyes burned into me, sparks flickering. He motioned to the skull. "And this is yours, I take it?"

I didn't answer him.

"That's okay. I already know that it is. And knowing that, I feel an apology is in order. I should have come right out and told you what I suspected about you from the moment I saw your DNA sample, but . . . just like with the others"—he waved dismissively at Lilly—"I thought I'd let the truth reveal itself."

"Why couldn't you just tell us?" asked Lilly bitterly.

Paul sighed. "I *could* have, but think it through: You're probably smart enough to have figured out at this point that we're using Camp Eden to find the Atlanteans. But what would have happened if I'd sat everyone down at the start of the session and announced that we were looking for the genetic descendants of an ancient race, and that everyone had been selected based on their potential match, and that we expected those who were top candidates to exhibit odd symptoms? We would have had kids drowning themselves, making fake gills, and who knows what else. And for you, Owen, for the true Atlantean, it's such an enormous concept, such a huge change, that I thought you had to discover it on your own, organically. But, either way, you know now, so we can move forward. And I feel like a proud parent, seeing you all come this far."

Lilly made a hissing sound.

"Now, now," said Paul. "Anyway, the timing is perfect. I was running into a wall with Carey." He motioned toward Leech, who was lying still on the cot. "He was the very first one to have the symptomatic gills, all the way back when this place was still Camp Aasgard. It was his condition that brought my team here. And when I saw his drawings, that's when I knew we were close. We Cryoed Carey while we established the dome here, and excavated the navigation room." Paul motioned to the ceiling. "When we brought Carey down, that room really ignited his powers, and since then, he's been making all these maps. I thought it was that obsidian star chart that was activating him, but all along it was this skull, hiding beneath my feet. *Your* skull. Which means there's one out there for him somewhere, I gather."

I didn't respond.

Paul glanced at the skull again. "Just amazing. It makes sense, now. You know, my father was the one who found the first Atlantean city, up in Greenland. It had been covered in glacial ice since about ten thousand years ago, after a sudden and cataclysmic natural event that changed the entire earth. The crust of the earth moved; there were massive tsunamis, floods—I mean literally the ones that ancient myths speak of—and the world was plunged back into an ice age until, well, technically just a few hundred years ago.

"My father's team of climatologists was drilling the Greenland ice sheet for ice cores, trying to understand past climate changes, trying to find a way to stop the Great Rise. I was thirteen at the time, traveling with them. The ice sheet had already receded farther than any modern human had ever seen, and then one day, there was a massive glacial calving in one of the fjords, and there it was, this ancient city. It was made from the same stone as the great Pyramids, and yet it was thousands of miles north. And as if that wasn't amazing enough, there was all that we found inside once we'd tunneled through the ice, including a temple not unlike this one, only larger.

"There were three tombs inside," Paul went on. "Three young bodies, well preserved in the ice, their throats slit. And there was a message inscribed in the rock that my father translated. It took him months, sitting in a tent up there, running the symbols through ancient Sumerian, cross-referencing them with the earliest Mesoamerican codices. It said:

"'Before the beginning, there was an end.'"

I finished for him, "'Three chosen to die, to live in the service of the Qi-An, the balance of all things.'"

Paul's eyes clicked wider, the circuits flaring. "You know it." His mouth fell open almost like he was hungry. He rubbed his palms and sighed. "And you know about the city?"

I nodded. "I've seen it."

He sighed. "I can't imagine what it must be like for you. To be connected, to be the conduit to the ancients. To know that *power*. I mean, for almost forty years I've been studying this temple and the others we've found, translating texts and unpuzzling megalithic structures. I probably know the Atlanteans better than anyone else, even better than my father did. But you . . ." Paul's voice lowered almost to a growl. His mouth moved and I almost expected to see him lick his lips, a predator stalking its juiciest prey. "You *are* the one. *You've* been on the inside looking out, haven't you? You've seen their world. And now, Owen, I need you to tell me everything. You'll do that, won't you?"

I didn't answer him.

"I mean, the skull just will not talk to anyone else. Believe me, I've tried."

"I know," I said, thinking of the CITs strapped to those tables. "I saw."

"Ah yes," said Paul, "because you were in the lab. And so now we both know that this skull is only for you, am I right?"

Hearing him, I realized that maybe there was a chance here. . . . "Yeah, only me. I'm the only one."

"Yes," said Paul, like this was exciting him to his core. "And has it told you where to find it?"

"Find what?"

"The Brocha," said Paul.

I tried to remember if Lük had mentioned that, but I was pretty sure he hadn't.

"Ah, so your skull didn't tell you about that," said Paul. "I'm talking about the Brocha de Dioses. Well, that's what *we* call it. It's Spanish, from a priest's translation of an ancient Mayan codex. I'm sure the Atlanteans would have a different name for it."

"What is it?" I asked.

"Well . . . that's the mystery," said Paul, "the big one. Brocha de Dioses means Paintbrush of the Gods. That was the priest's translation anyway. It's been very hard to piece together, but we believe it's a machine, an ancient machine, one that could, well, save us all. And it's located in the Heart of the Terra."

Lük had talked about that. And, listening to this, I remembered what he'd said: *Someone has found our sin, and seeks to use it.* Maybe *this* was what I was being called to defend. To protect this Paintbrush of the Gods from Paul and Project Elysium.

"What do you mean, save us?" I asked.

"It's fascinating, really," said Paul, and it sounded like he really was fascinated, "and we can get into it more once we start the journey, but the Atlanteans found a way to control the forces of the earth, to literally change it to suit their needs. Their civilization was global and very advanced, in some ways not quite to the level of ours, but in others vastly superior.

"About ten thousand years ago, they were facing a climate change event, something like the Great Rise, which isn't that uncommon if you look over a long enough record of history. But the Atlanteans were the first living creatures on earth with the intelligence to do something about it. They were facing a dramatic warming period, and, also like us, these were a people who lived primarily on the coasts, since they were master seafarers."

I realized that this was the first thing I knew that he didn't. Paul didn't know about the airships. He probably thought that craft here in the temple was a boat. Which meant he didn't know exactly what I was meant for, either.

"They were watching their cities submerge," Paul continued. "So, to save themselves, they fought back. They created this Paintbrush of the Gods, and they used it."

"But it didn't work," I added, remembering the ash-filled sky in Lük's world.

Paul smiled, like I was his star pupil. I couldn't help being interested in what he was saying, in the story of my people, and there was something intriguing about all this knowledge that Paul had. How much more could he teach me? But then I looked over at Leech. He was still out cold, his face pained even in unconsciousness, and I had to remind myself that he was Paul's last star student.

"It might be more accurate to say that it worked too well," said Paul. "Based on the evidence we've found, the Paintbrush of the Gods caused a cataclysm so great that it became the basis for all those flood myths around the world.

"The Atlantean civilization collapsed, and the greatest technology the world had known until this millennium was lost to ice and ruin. And yet . . ." Paul spread his arms. "Here we are, on the verge of discovering it once again. Only this time, think of it, Owen: we can apply our modern technology to the Atlantean model, and succeed where they failed. Do you see what I'm saying? We can *fix* the earth. We can save humanity."

He smiled at me so wide, eyes sparking, that I could feel the infectiousness of his enthusiasm, like a virus that could get inside me, change me, but I fought to hold it back.

"Don't you want that, too?" Paul said to me. "Think of your father, your life out there at Hub. Think of all the people suffering outside the Habitable Zone." He glanced at Lilly as he said this. He must have known about her parents. "The diseases, the malnutrition. All those who have died. Even those living in the Edens. I'm sure you know that the domes won't last forever. In fact, there's precious little time left. Our species is at a crossroads. We can die out, or we can persevere."

I stood there. I didn't know what to say. Did I want that? Maybe. Lük had said that trying to use the power of the Terra had destroyed their civilization. That I was supposed to protect it and keep that from happening again. But Lük couldn't know about modern times. If Paul was right, and this Paintbrush could be improved . . . I thought of my dad, the nebulizer, his coughing, only getting worse the more time he spent underground. What did Lilly think? I wanted to ask her.

As if giving me her answer, Lilly suddenly hissed at Paul, "You killed Anna!"

Paul frowned at her. "Actually, I heard from Cartier

that *you* killed her when you pulled the plug on her life-support system."

"How could you do that to her? To those other children?" Lilly spat. I could hear her anger raising the pitch of her voice, could feel her shaking beside me.

Paul shrugged. "They were necessary sacrifices in the pursuit of knowledge," he said coldly. "We had to understand the mechanism of the gill growth. Had to understand what other changes were happening inside. We knew that Anna and the others weren't *the one*, and we had no idea when, if ever, our Owen would appear, so I decided to enlist their help as trial cases—"

"She wasn't a *trial*!" Lilly shouted. "She would never have agreed to let you do that to her!"

Paul winced and made a motion to Cartier, who grabbed Lilly, putting a gloved hand over her mouth.

"Lilly, dear, you remind me of my *father* with your small-minded belief in some moral code. He was a founder in EdenCorp. Finding Atlantis was his thing, but when we discovered the existence of the Paintbrush of the Gods, and the board of directors asked him to lead the search for it, he refused. He said it was wrong to tamper with the earth, to muddle with nature. He thought that we should listen to the ancient warnings. When, the truth is, everything we *do* tampers with the earth. We are part of nature, its crowning achievement. We *are* nature."

Paul stepped close to Lilly, his electric eyes reflecting

in her own. "Do you know, my father *refused* to open the antechamber we'd discovered in Greenland, the one where his evidence pointed to the Paintbrush being located? All that knowledge, right *there*, and he wouldn't do it, because he thought it was too dangerous. He was *scared*. So you know who did it? His son. I went into the temple and opened the antechamber myself and came face-to-face with a Sentinel and lost my eyes. And that's when the board of directors knew I was the one who should lead the search. Because I would do what was necessary.

"Like with your friend Anna. By the way, a lovely girl, full of life—too much life, it turned out. She *hated* what was happening to all of you. So she came to me and wanted to know if there was anything she could do to help figure out what was going on. It was nice of her to offer, I thought."

Lilly surged free of Cartier's hold. "She didn't know you were going to do *that* to her!" Her eyes were watering, her voice thick with rage. Cartier grabbed her again.

Paul turned away from her. "Probably not." He looked back at me. "But what's one life when billions are at stake? And Owen, you don't have to worry, I'm not going to cut you open or any such primitive thing. I want to *follow* you. I want you to say you'll help me, say we'll do this together. And then we can start our journey, to find the Terra, the heart of Atlantis. We need to stop letting *nature* do whatever it wants and *be* nature. Please. Don't you want to do the right thing here and save the human race?" His mouth turned down in a strange way, like he was trying to look like he cared, and yet his mechanical eyes were still boring into me, as if he was trying to see through my skin to the Atlantean inside.

And I *did* want to save humanity from the Great Rise, be the savior of our species. I did want better lives for everyone, my dad, even me.

"You'll be a hero," Paul added.

I felt the energy draining out of me. And I wondered: Paul was making this sound like a choice, but was it? I couldn't really say no to Paul, could I? Wouldn't he just force me to do what he wanted anyway? Though Lilly would never agree, it seemed like there was really only one answer. If I said yes, if I worked with Paul, I could keep us both safe. And as we figured out what the Paintbrush of the Gods really was, then we could decide what to do. Saying yes would buy me time. Buy us time. But what if the chance never came? What if I provided Paul with information, and it was all he needed to get to Atlantis and that was that?

"How do I know I can trust you?" I asked.

Paul smiled. "Fair question. Here's the answer: because I've never lied to you."

"Mmmm!" Lilly thrashed her head free of Cartier's grip for just long enough to shout, "This whole place is a lie!"

Paul sighed. "Technically, it's more like a distraction, to allow the discovery of a greater truth." Paul looked at me again. "You'll find, in the big game, that sometimes this has to be the case. But it doesn't change the fact that I never lied to you directly. And you have my word, Owen, if you say yes, I will keep you informed, protected, and well taken care of from now on."

I thought back, and he was right. He'd never lied, not to me, not directly. But the story about Colleen, and the camp as a whole . . . The lies were everywhere else.

"Well, Owen?" asked Paul. He put his hands out toward me, palms up. "Time to choose."

Owen.

The siren had appeared. She floated on the far side of the room, behind Paul. I glanced at Lilly. She was staring at me with wide eyes.

I looked back at the siren. She gazed at me, intently. *You must be true to the Terra.*

What does that mean? I thought to her.

Qi-An is always two. All states occur in pairs. To know truth is to know both.

To know both sides?

To see both.

I didn't know what she meant. What two sides? Was this about the choice to work with Paul or not? About Lük telling me to stop Project Elysium, and Paul asking me to help it? So, me saying yes, or me saying no . . . Or maybe this was about Paul. About seeing both sides of him. Because I knew what I'd see if I said yes. He'd treat me like his new favorite son, and I'd use the skull and tell him everything.

And as terrible as it sounded, part of me actually craved that. I really believed that Paul would protect me if I was his most valuable asset. And I could even understand his rationale for the gruesome things we'd seen in the lab, how he saw it as hard science in the quest to save the planet. And yet . . .

What was the other side of Paul? Had I really seen it? Could I trust him? Did he really have such noble goals? He wouldn't tell me, and I couldn't make him, but I could say no, and see how he reacted.

And maybe more than that, there was Lük, my . . . brother? Telling me not to help this man. Telling me that I needed to do the opposite. It was what Lilly wanted, too. What did I want?

I wanted to be true. I wanted to see truth.

Yes, said the siren, and I thought I saw approval in her eyes. Looking at her right then, I suddenly wondered something else. Because Lük had never talked about her. . . . *Who are you?* I asked her.

She disappeared.

Paul's hands were still out in that helpless gesture. Had even a second passed? It felt like it, and I thought about what I'd say. *Yes* was a deal with the devil, but also safety, at least for a while. *No* was . . . what? The only thing I was sure of was that it was truth.

"Well," I said, "I think my answer is no." And then I watched.

Watched Paul's eyes flicker at me, the pupils getting smaller. Watched him sigh and shake his head slowly. Watched his expression turn hard. His gaze left me, like I was no longer important. He looked at the officers beside me and made a slow single nod.

They grabbed me by the arms and moved me toward the skull.

"Hook him up," said Paul with a wave of his hand, and just like that, I had become another object, a test subject.

"No!" I shouted again. I struggled, but it was no use. Each officer had me by an arm, and they moved my hands toward the skull. The white-coated technician appeared and started attaching electrodes to my forehead. I thrashed my head, but he grabbed me by the chin and held me firm.

I'd said no, and seen the truth: that there really was no choice, after all. No was really yes. But at least by saying no, I had been true to myself, true to the kids who died. True to Lilly.

"Administer the sedative," said Paul. "Let's bring in the board. They'll want to see this." He turned to the wall, where a video screen hung dark. He touched the corner and it illuminated. A message blinked:

[ESTABLISHING LOW-ORBIT CONNECTION]

And then a room appeared, the camera at the far end of a desk, and the seven gray-haired heads of the EdenCorp board of directors all leaned forward.

"Is this the one?" asked the wiry man at the end of the table. He was framed by a window showing a wide view of the night sky.

"This is Subject Two," said Paul. "We are about to synch him to the crystal medium."

"Excellent," murmured a board member.

"Very impressive," said another. Heads bobbed toward one another and spoke in low whispers. They moved slowly, almost like they were floating in air.

The soldiers moved me closer. I tried to fight. I would keep fighting, no matter what, and at least in the skull, I'd be safe for a little while. Maybe I could figure out some way to resist Paul, from in there.

The technician returned with a needle. He dabbed my arm with a cotton swab.

"Get the girl ready, too," said Paul. "We'll want to see if anything lights up in there."

My hands were almost on the skull, my secrets about to be laid bare. Its glow brightened as I neared.

"Fascinating," said Paul, watching the monitor screen beside him. "I don't even think we'll need the electrical current."

The needle pressed against my skin. About to break the surface . . .

Something pierced the air. A flash in the corner of my eye, glinting in skull light. It seemed to have arrived as a blur but was now frozen in space.

"What was that?" asked a board member.

"I think we have a weak connection," complained another.

The hands that were holding me loosened, and I looked over and saw a silver bead of light. It hung still, and I could see that it was the glowing metal tip of an arrow. An arrow, protruding from black cloth, from Cartier's chest.

26

THE ARROW HAD COME FROM BEHIND. LILLY
thrashed free of Cartier, his body spasming, and she shoved
him in the back. He toppled forward, coughing up blood
and slamming into Paul, who had only just started to turn
around. They crashed over onto the monitor console.

The arrow protruding from Cartier's back had tricolor
feathers. It was from the archery range. I looked to the
doorway. Evan stood there, bow in hand, another arrow
ready. As he stepped in, Marco and Aliah followed.
They had weapons. Rifles. Probably from officers they'd
surprised above. They were soaked, leaving wet footprints.
Creatures from the deep, come back for their own.

"Nope!" Evan shouted. He waved the bow and arrow at
the officers beside me. They'd let go of my arms to try for
their own weapons. "Get against the wall," Evan ordered.
Standing there, dripping wet, his shoulders tensed with the
bow at the ready, he looked more intimidating than ever.
His eyes caught mine, and I couldn't help wondering if he

was about to finish what he'd started in the Preserve.

"Come on," he said to me instead.

The two officers were obeying, especially with the sight of Marco and Aliah training rifles their way. The white-coated technician joined them.

Paul had rolled Cartier off of him and was scrambling to his feet. Evan spun and aimed at him. "You too." He motioned with the bow. "Against the wall."

Paul started to smile, to put up his hands. "Now, kids, listen—"

"Shut up, butcher," snapped Aliah. "We know what you are." She waved her rifle in Paul's direction. "Just give us a reason."

Paul's eyes narrowed, his pupils flicking coldly. "I urge you to reconsider what you're doing."

No one responded. Lilly was busy grabbing our bags from the officers. "Get Leech," she said to me.

"Right." I stepped to the bed and started shaking Leech. He stirred, his eyes half opening. "Hey, we're leaving, come on. Can you get up?"

Leech winced and started to sit up. "Yeah," he said groggily.

His fingers fumbled at the electrodes on his head and under his T-shirt. I helped him pull them off, then I hoisted him up and pushed him toward the door.

Paul had joined the officers along the wall. Lilly stood before them. "Guns and phones, please." She took the officers' gear and handed them to Marco and Aliah. "I'll take this, too," she said, pulling her Nomad knife from an officer's belt. She shoved Paul's phone into her pocket. "Thanks," she hissed. Then, she turned and grabbed the skull.

"Listen," said Paul, "all of you, there's another way to do this—"

Lilly uttered a teeth-clenched growl and spun. She had the skull in two hands, and she slammed it into Paul's temple and jaw. His head cracked back against the wall and he collapsed to the floor. Lilly looked down at him. "That's enough from you." He rolled onto his back, one of his eyes shooting sparks.

We moved toward the door. I passed Evan, his bow still drawn. "Thanks," I said.

"Yup." He kept his gaze on the officers.

"This way," I said to Leech, and we squeezed through the passage and back out onto the platform.

Lilly had started left with Aliah and Marco, heading for the stairs.

"This way!" I called to her. "We're taking the craft."

"What?" She looked at me like I was crazy.

"Trust me! It will work!" I tried not to show that I maybe thought it was crazy, too, that I barely knew what I was doing. I ran around the platform and down the stairs, Leech trailing behind me.

"What's this?" he said, like he was looking at a piece of junk.

"You draw maps," I said. "I fly this."

I saw Lilly hugging Marco and Aliah, then Evan. "Be careful!" she called to them over her shoulder as she ran around and joined us. We crowded into the little craft. Lilly uncinched her bag and stuffed the skull and the knife inside.

"This thing looks like a rowboat," muttered Leech. His attitude bothered me.

"Owen . . . ," said Lilly. She pointed up. The officers were emerging from the skull chamber, supporting Paul between them. They glanced at us but headed up the stairs.

Above them, the CITs were nearly to the top. "They'll be fine," I said.

"Yeah, but what about us?" Leech asked.

"Watch," I said. I held my finger over the tiny gold button. I looked again at the little razor-edged ring in the center of the fingerprint shape, its hollow middle, then at the tiny copper tube leading down through the bottom of the hull.

I looked up. From here, that copper umbrella hid the giant marble ball in the ceiling from sight. The officers and Paul were just reaching the top of the staircase.

"As soon as they get out of these tunnels," said Lilly, gazing up with me, "they're going to send the whole complex after us."

"Yeah," I said. I put my finger to the button, felt the sharp edge. "The key is inside me," I repeated, hoping the siren meant this too. I jammed my finger down. White-hot pain shot up my hand, but I kept pressing. It would take time for the blood to drip down the tube. . . .

"What are you doing?" Leech asked, sounding unconvinced.

Everything began to rumble. The craft shook. Dust sprang from the walls.

I looked up. "You figure, with all those tunnels we took, that we're somewhere under the lake, right?"

The rumbling increased, like there was giant machinery in the walls. The stone catwalk above us started to slide into the wall. The spiral stairs too.

There was a high-pitched grating sound from above. I leaned out from the side of the craft. So did Lilly. "Owen, that ball of rock in the ceiling is moving," she said, "and . . ."

I saw it rising, and then Lilly's voice was drowned out by the deafening roar of water gushing in through the hole in its place. It poured down in a giant cascade, hit the copper umbrella, and sprayed out in all directions, creating a curtain of water falling all around us, filling the chamber while we sat there, mostly dry.

"Wow," said Lilly. "Okay, this could work!"

We started to rise, the water lifting the craft from the floor. The mast hit the umbrella and there was a loud click as it locked into the center. The copper rods snapped away. The umbrella rose with us, deflecting the spray.

Something slammed against the copper and then tumbled by us. I saw the obsidian ball from the map room disappear into the frothing water.

"Ah," said Leech, sounding disappointed. "Good-bye, star chart."

"Did you need that?" I shouted to him.

Leech stared at the water. "Well, it was helpful, but I'll be all right."

We were already parallel with the platform. Water rushed into the skull chamber.

We rose, cresting the walls of the lower chamber, rising up into the map room. The water swirled everywhere, and among the bubbles were papers.

"Your maps, too!" Lilly yelled to Leech.

He looked down and I thought he would freak out to see the wet pages, their ink bleeding away, but he just smiled. "It's okay," he said in his old cocky Leech way. He tapped his head. "It's all in here." But then his smile faded as he scanned the room. "I think Paul got my case, though. Those were the best ones. But he can't make too much sense out of them without me."

The room filled. We bobbed on the frothy water, nearing the curved ceiling. Water was sloshing all over us, now. Spray in our eyes. The craft was getting tossed around. Its rear corner slammed into the roof. We were nearing the top, starting to rise up into the hole where the marble ball had been. The craft began to spin. Water everywhere.

"Hang on to something!" I shouted.

The craft lurched and reeled. We surged upward, spinning faster. The cascade roared against the copper umbrella. Waves drenched us. Everything was lost to spray and bubbles, light and shadows. But I could feel that we were still rising. There was brightness above us. And in a final thrust and deafening roar, we shot up out of the sunken temple, up the center eye of the whirling water, to the surface.

Waves slapped around, then calmed. The craft settled. We were drifting on the lake, not far from shore, off to the side of the Aquinara. Breeze. Birds. Warm sun on our wet skin. We sat there for a moment, breathing hard, but amazed by the sudden peace around us.

"Wow," said Leech, "that actually worked."

Lilly started scanning the water. "They'll get boats out here soon," she said.

"Yeah." I stood and popped open the seat compartment. I could feel the usual westerly wind coming from the direction of the city. I pulled out the sail and the short coils of rope, as I'd seen Lük do in the memory. The materials were stiff, but the fibers were amazingly still in working shape. How long had they sat down there, waiting for me?

I put my feet on the pedal rudder and angled so that we would be running downwind. I tied a guideline to a hole at one corner of the triangular sail, and then I stood and tied the sail straight off the front of the copper poles and mast with anchor-hitch knots that my fingers tied without thinking. The sail grabbed the wind, billowing out in front of us, and yanked us straight down the lake.

"How did you learn how to sail when you drowned during the swim test?" Leech asked. "Was it on all your secret nights out?"

He did know about those. I just tapped my head like he had. "No, in here."

"So, you really are the other Atlantean," he said.

"Yeah, it's the three of us."

"Great," said Leech.

Right then I wondered if this could really work. Given all we'd been through, and all the danger we were in, I still couldn't help wondering if I could possibly survive being with Leech.

"Here they come!" Lilly shouted. She was pointing to the jetty by the Aquinara. Two speedboats were peeling away from it, toward us.

We were gathering speed, a frothing wake behind us. I leaned over the side of the craft. There, beneath the waves, I could see the spinning disks of metal. With enough speed, they'd create the charge for the heat cell.

I grabbed the line and pulled in tighter on the sail, creating more resistance. We surged ahead.

"They're closing!" Lilly shouted. "They're probably going to have guns!"

I looked down at the clay pot, the little copper nozzle.

Nothing there yet. I adjusted the sail and rudder. We needed more speed.

"This isn't gonna happen," said Leech, watching the boats approach.

"Move!" I pushed his shoulder and opened the compartment where he'd been sitting, pulled out the thermal and started unfolding it. I threw it up on top of the copper poles and started tying lines. There were three holes around the triangular opening in the thermal, which corresponded to a gap in the poles.

I dropped back to the rudder. The boats were coming from our left. Our speed was increasing, but slowly. Too slowly.

"Can you angle right?" Lilly called. "Look!"

She pointed ahead, and I saw other boats coming toward us. Five small sailboats tacking up the lake. If I moved right, they would get between us and the speedboats. I pulled in on the sail and angled the rudder.

"Hey," said Leech.

And then we heard the shouting. Arms were waving from the sailboats. As we closed, we saw their faces. Noah, Jalen, Beaker, Paige, Mina . . . all the Hyenas and Foxes.

"Cut them off!" Leech shouted, waving his arm toward the approaching speedboats.

Something started to hum in the craft. Vibrations in the floorboards. Almost there. I hauled the sail in close and tweaked our angle. "We're almost there!" I shouted over the wind.

The camp sailboats were cutting at an angle past us. The speedboats were closing in, but the sailboats crossed their path. The speedboats swerved hard. I saw Jalen yank the rudder of his sailboat and send it spinning right in front of one of the speedboats, which had to throw itself into a chaotic turn.

But the other boat was already roaring around them.

"Great! That only got us a couple seconds," said Leech.

A spark flashed on the heat cell. Then another. Popping sounds, and a little blue flame jetted from the copper nozzle on the pot, flaring to orange. "That might be all we need!" I shouted. The thermal sail began to rise, filling, forming the small hot-air balloon.

The roar of the motorboat grew behind us. I glanced back and saw it gaining, getting too close.

But then we began to skip off the waves. The balloon was growing. Two big bounces . . . and we were up! Airborne. We rose, the wind still filling the sail and propelling us ahead. I looked down to see our cabin mates waving and cheering, and the speedboats rapidly shrinking.

Lilly rubbed my shoulder. "Nice."

"Yeah, but"—Leech was looking up at the obvious question, far above—"now what?"

"Just a sec." I closed my eyes and reached back into my head, found the training memory. Back at the mountain lake, my craft was now up in the air, rising alongside Lük and the others. *Now what?* I asked him.

Like this, he said. He'd moved the sail off to the side and added a second, so that they were both on angles off the mast. He had one line in each hand, and was pulling on both to steer.

Okay, sounds good, I said.

His craft banked on the wind and arced away from me. I noticed that the other pilots were making a line in the sky and heading for a tall obelisk-shaped building in the Atlantean city. It had some kind of metal rod extending from its top.

What's that? I asked.

That's the second power system, said Lük. As I watched, the first craft passed over the tower. A jagged flash of lightning leaped from the tip of the tower to the mast of the craft. There was a burst of blue light on the ship, like something had ignited, and the ship suddenly darted away at incredible speed. *An electric charge similar to lightning activates the second system, beneath the heat cell. That black metal unit is a mercury vortex turbine. It uses electromagnetism for antigravity.*

Wow, I said, watching one ship after the next receive its flash of lightning and then explode off toward the horizon in a glow of blue.

Obviously real lightning will work if you can get near it, said Lük, *though that can be tricky. What's the weather like where you are?*

Well, it's kinda always sunny where I am.

Ah, right. Then for now just worry about using the thermal and the sails. They should be sufficient. He soared over and joined the line.

I pushed back to reality and reached into the compartment for a second sail. I untied the first one. Our forward speed slowed, but we were still rising from the balloon. I attached the two sails side by side off the mast, each angled off-center. Then I took a line in each hand. When the sails caught full, I practiced changing the tension, testing the interplay between the two. Suddenly the ship was diving and turning, sweeping back and forth in long arcs that made my stomach drop.

"Wooo!" Lilly shouted.

I smiled. There was a feeling of freedom in these movements. And unlike in the past, I had no fear of how high we were. This was like swimming below the surface, fluid, only even more so. Lakes had boundaries, but the sky had none. Well, except this sky.

"Ha! See those?" Leech was pointing down over the side of the craft.

We looked and saw the summit of Mount Aasgard a couple hundred meters below us.

"The cliffs?" said Lilly.

"No, the lines!" Leech made up-and-down motions with his hand.

"You mean the Viking etchings?" I could see that those lines on the cliffs were really straight when seen from above, and ran toward each other, like they were making an arrow. They came nearly to a point at the inside of the ledge Lilly and I had been on. Above that, there was another etching on the very top ledge, higher than where we'd been. It was a crude version of the same symbol I'd seen etched in the Camp Aasgard sign and the tunnel leading to the temple.

"Not Viking!" called Leech. He looked back with an actual smile. "Atlantean! Us! Those mark a ley line! They show the bearing we'll take to the next marker!"

"And you know what all that stuff you just said means?"

"Totally." Leech pulled his sketchbook and pen from the pocket of his jeans and began sketching furiously.

"Okay, then we just have to get out of here." I looked up. We were even with the lowest SafeSun banks. The triangular pattern of the roof panels was clearly visible. "We need to call Aaron."

"Aaron? In the Eye?" asked Leech.

"Yeah," I said. "He's on our side."

"Our side . . . ," said Leech skeptically. "You sure about that, Tur—"

"Stop! Not Turtle. It's going to be Owen from now on."

Leech nodded. "Okay then." He looked away, and I wondered if he was thinking the same thing about being with me as I had about him.

Lilly dug Paul's phone from her pocket. "How do I get in touch with him?"

"That I can do," said Leech. He took the phone and

started tapping quickly. "Paul let me use this a bunch. . . ." The phone started to beep. "Yeah," Leech said into it, "need to talk to Aaron. Tell him it's *Owen* and company."

I guided the craft into a wide, banking turn and started tacking to the southwest. We were passing over the EdenWest city itself now. Down below the haze of atmosphere, I could see the building tops, the blinking neon SensaStreets, the parks and little tram cars buzzing along.

"Owen!" Aaron's voice blurted from the phone. "What are you doing out— Or in, I guess . . . in some kind of ship. Are you *flying*?"

"Yeah," I said as Leech held the phone toward me. "Listen!" I shouted over the flapping of sails and wind. "We need you to open one of those emergency vents! The ones I saw you open that day when—"

"Yeah, I know the ones you mean. Um . . ." Aaron rubbed his hand over his mouth, then up through his hair. "Here's the thing: How big is that craft of yours?"

"I think it will fit," I said.

"No, not that." He glanced around. "I mean, as in, do you have room for one more passenger? If I open a vent, there is going to be no way they *don't* know it was me that did it. So, unless I leave with you, I'm going to be very dead."

"There's room," I said. "But how are we going to get you?"

"Okay, can you see the Eye from where you are?"

I strained to look up and behind us. "Yeah."

"On the southwest side there's a door. Catwalk out, the one with no tram. You see it?"

"Yeah."

"You meet me there. I can control the Eden systems remotely once I'm on board. You pick me up, and we all soar to freedom. Sound good?"

"We're on our way." I was already turning the craft, the sails luffing, now catching the wind again. We flew back toward the Eye, still rising.

I took the sails in one hand and reached down to the heat cell. There were no buttons or levers on it. Just that nozzle, a blue-orange flame above it. There had to be a way to adjust the strength of the flame. I touched the clay exterior and found that it was cool. I slid my hand up, closer to the copper: still cool. Touched the copper with my finger. It was cool, too, somehow. I clasped it with two fingers and twisted. Counterclockwise lowered the flame. The hiss of the jet quieted and we rose more slowly.

"I don't think we want to slow down," said Lilly.

"Why?" I asked.

She pointed off the starboard side. "I guess it was only a matter of time before they showed up."

The two hover copters were still distant, but speeding toward us.

I spun the nozzle. We surged upward, but that made the wind harder to control, and we swung back and forth.

Up near that catwalk and the ceiling, we'd need to be more precise.

We were rising past the giant antenna that hung down below the Eye, its thorny sides threatening to pop the balloon with each wind gust. I made a slow upward spiral, keeping my distance. Up in the Eye, I could see faces in the lower ring of windows, fingers pointing at us, getting others' attention.

The air was starting to swirl unpredictably as we met the heat that rose naturally from below and billowed against the top of the roof. The craft swayed and bounced.

"Whoa!" said Leech, getting tossed around.

"Doing the best I can!" I snapped.

I could hear the hum of the copters now.

"Hey there!" The shout came from above. We looked up to see Aaron out on the metal catwalk, maybe twenty meters above, closing the door behind him. He had a bag over his shoulder, a jacket tied to his waist, large sunglasses on.

"What does he think this is, a vacation?" asked Lilly.

"Here," I handed Leech the sail lines and opened a compartment. I found another rope, stepped up beside Lilly, and tied it to a copper ring on the bow. "Okay, when we get close, throw him this."

I took the lines back from Leech. "This is going to have to be fast," he said, watching the copters close on us.

We lifted to parallel with the catwalk. I turned the nozzle down to barely a flame. We rose another couple feet and hovered, swinging back and forth. The balloon whined, its fabric rubbing against metal beams of the roof.

"Here!" Lilly threw the rope. Aaron jumped to catch it. He pulled us in. I eyed the superstructure of the catwalk, making sure the balloon didn't snag. It was going to be tight.

Aaron leaned over the railing. He reached out and grabbed the bow of the craft. "No steps or anything?" he asked, looking at the dizzying drop.

"Throw your bag over!" Lilly called.

"Right." Aaron slipped off his bag and tossed it over. Lilly grabbed it and threw it to Leech. "Careful!" shouted Aaron. "My remote pad is in there! That's our ticket out!"

"Just hurry up and jump in here," I said.

"Faster," said Leech, watching the copters closing.

Aaron reached out, but a gust of air shoved us to the side. I pulled on the sails to right us.

"I'll tie this rope to the railing!" said Aaron. "Then we can cut it once I'm on."

"Okay," I said.

Aaron knotted the rope, then leaned back out. He grabbed the swaying bow, but lost it again. "Can I get a hand?" he shouted.

"Ugh!" Lilly grabbed the mast and leaned far out of the craft. Another gust made us sway. She got a hold of the catwalk railing, her whole body stretching out over space. My stomach lurched at seeing her like that. "Come on!"

she barked at Aaron, holding out her hand.

"Okay, okay, okay . . ." Aaron gritted his teeth and took Lilly's hand—

Then grabbed her braid with his other hand and yanked her off the craft.

"Hey!"

Aaron fell back, dragging Lilly onto the catwalk. The door slapped open. Paul burst out, his glasses back on, flanked by two guards. He grabbed Lilly and pulled her to her feet.

"Lilly!" I shouted.

Paul had her.

"Sorry about that!" said Aaron, grinning.

I saw it instantly now, and felt like an idiot. Aaron had set us up, even helped Dr. Maria to make it seem real, but it was all an act. Just another lie to trap us, a backup plan in case we escaped the temple.

"That's enough, Owen!" said Paul. "Now, I have *her*, so bring that craft down to the Aquinara and we'll pick up where we left off."

The craft bobbed up against the scaffolding. I yanked on the sails but also took a step toward the bow and had no idea what to do except to yell, "No, let her go!" Except inside I felt myself deflating. This was hopeless.

And Paul knew it, too. He laughed. "Absolutely not! You and Carey belong with me, Owen! We were meant to do this together!"

"Go to hell!" Leech suddenly shouted, his voice thick with hate.

Paul just ignored him. "Owen, if you care about Miss Ishani, and you want to see her safe . . . come down!"

"No!" Lilly called. Paul tried to cover her mouth, but she struggled against him. "Owen, go! Leave!"

I stared at her. There was no way that was happening. It was over.

"Yes, Owen, go! Now!"

"Lilly—," I started, about to tell her it was pointless, but she cut me off.

Lilly's eyes were red, wild, tear-filled. "I lied!"

"What?"

She kept struggling, grabbing the catwalk railing and pulling free of Paul and the guards for another moment. "I lied about the siren! I never saw it! I just wanted to go with you! I'm *not* the other Atlantean! Now go!"

27

I THOUGHT, *NO*, EXCEPT, I KNEW IT WAS TRUE THE moment she said it. I remembered her being quiet in so many moments when we'd talked about being Atlante-ans . . . and how she hadn't followed me that night that I first swam after the siren. And I wondered if, in a way, I'd known this all along, but had been ignoring it. Because if Lilly was an Atlantean, then we *had* to be together. It was destiny. But if she wasn't . . .

"You heard her!" Leech hissed at me. "Let's go! We can still outrun those copters."

I looked at Lilly, struggling against Paul, and felt frozen. Lilly . . . my Lilly. *She lied to me.* But I didn't care. Did I? She'd lied so she could come with me. I never would have made it this far without her. How could I face whatever came next? No. I wasn't leaving her now. No way.

But Paul had her. And the copters were hovering below. There had to be something. . . .

"Tick tock, Owen!" Paul called.

I looked down at the craft. Thought back to the training memory, to Lük showing me the features, the mercury vortex and the ships shooting off into the distance. How had they done that? That's right. . . .

I glanced at Aaron's bag. "Hold on to that," I said quietly to Leech. Then I looked up at the catwalk.

"Okay, fine," I said to Paul. "I'm turning off the heat cell, and then we can lower down."

Paul smiled. "Good."

I reached forward and flicked off the nozzle. The flame died out. The balloon still held us in position. It would be slow to cool. I bent over, out of Paul's view, and reached for the knife tucked in the top of Lilly's bag. Then, I took Lilly's bag and Dr. Maria's backpack and stuffed them into a compartment. When I stood, I shouted to Paul, "Okay!"

I caught Lilly's eye, then glanced at Aaron. Then back to Lilly, trying to point to him with my eyes, so that she'd understand.

Then I stared at her hard and shouted, "Tandem!" and hoped she knew what to do.

I swung the knife as hard as I could at the lines connecting the thermal balloon.

"Owen, what—?" Paul shouted.

The knife hit the first line, snapped it clean, and nicked the second. It unraveled then tore, and the third line popped from all the weight. The balloon leaped free, bouncing up against the ceiling.

And we started to fall.

But the line was still attached to the catwalk, and as we dropped it caught, jerking the entire craft and making us swing to vertical, the bow of the craft pointing straight up. I gripped the sail lines as tight as I could, and saw Leech hanging on to the edge of the craft as our feet left the floor and we hung in space, the lake so very far below.

The force of the craft yanking on the railing made the catwalk buckle, not much, but enough for Paul and Lilly to lose their footing. Lilly slammed an elbow into his stomach and jerked free of the other guards. She lunged, grabbed Aaron by his arm and looked down at me. Our eyes locked.

"Hey, what—," Aaron began.

"Come on!" Lilly jumped, dragging Aaron over the edge with her.

She hit the right sail, and her arms slammed against the sideways mast. She slid over it and for a second I thought she might fall right by, but she fell against me, and I grabbed her with my free arm, my other gripping the sail lines and feeling like my shoulder socket would tear apart.

"Bah!" Aaron slammed against the bow of the boat and toppled over.

"Grab him!" I shouted to Leech. He stuck out an arm and pinned Aaron against the mast.

"You got me?" I said to Lilly, and felt her arms wrap around my torso.

"Yeah!"

There was a blistering snap from above, as the line holding us to the catwalk frayed and broke.

We plummeted toward the lake. Someone screamed. Maybe all of us.

The craft righted itself and for a moment we found ourselves level. Lilly slid off me and I grabbed the sail lines, trying to hold us steady. I jammed my feet against the rudder, but it didn't help. We started to pitch forward, but the sails caught, billowing back at us, and keeping us from nosing straight down. Still, we were falling fast toward the glistening water.

"Aaron!" I called over the wind. "You need to fire the deionization!"

"What?" He looked up at me from the floor of the craft like I was speaking another language.

"Set it off or we die!" I screamed.

Aaron's confused look stayed on me for another half second, then he glanced over the edge of the craft and his eyes got wide and he seemed to get it. "My bag!" he shouted.

Leech shoved it into his chest.

Aaron fumbled with the clips, his fingers shaking.

"Faster!" Lilly snapped.

Wind crushed against our faces.

Aaron got the bag open and slid out his computer pad. He slapped his finger at it. "Stupid password!" he muttered to himself.

"Shut up and do it!" Leech barked.

"I am, I am!"

I glanced from him to the sight of water growing larger. I could feel fear starting to paralyze me. We were all going to die, killed on impact. I'd miscalculated, or been an idiot to even try to time this—

"Okay . . . got it!" said Aaron.

There was a hum and a momentary feeling of energy tickling our skin, then a brilliant flash from above us. The huge antenna discharged with an explosive crack of electricity. My body shuddered in the current, almost like my bones were heating up from the inside out. There was a wicked hissing sound as the lightning, instead of leaping down to its grounding tower far below, was attracted to the nearest metal object: the mast of the craft.

The mast lit up, momentarily glowing hot white, and then there was a flash of blinding blue, and a whirring of motion inside the triangular metal unit. The ceramic heat cell exploded, shards flying everywhere. Shrapnel sliced my cheek but I barely noticed. I was scrambling forward to see inside the black unit. There was a circular hole in its center, and inside, blue light swirled like liquid. There was a high-pitched hum as the light spun faster, the ship vibrating like it might break apart.

Still we hurtled toward the water.

I closed my eyes, traveled inward, found the memory. Lük was distant, in line for his own lightning charge. *How do I fly it?* I shouted to him.

Use the sails to steer. The pedal rudder will apply electromagnetic charge. You'll learn to feel the repulsion of gravity over time.

I have about ten seconds, I said, and swept forward to my senses, saw the lake rushing at us. I put my feet on the rudder, pulled in on the sails, heard the engine whirring faster, felt it starting to slow our fall. We began to arc, leveling, slowly leveling, but we were going so fast, the lake getting closer. Closer. Too close.

"Now!" said Lilly.

"I know!" I pulled harder, jammed my feet against the pedals. We leveled more, finally almost horizontal. I could see the individual waves below.

And we flattened out. Wind caught the sails and yanked us forward. The bottom of the craft skimmed the surface. I screamed. We all did as the craft slipped along, racing above the water at incredible speed.

"Whoa!" Leech shouted.

I turned to Lilly, exhaling hard and meeting her eyes.

"Nice work," she said, her gaze still wide.

I nodded. Then thought about what had to happen next. I pressed the pedals, pulled the lines, and we arced up, rising away from the water and shooting ahead. When we were about twenty meters above the surface, I leveled off. "Can you hold these lines for a minute?" I asked Lilly. "And put your feet just like mine on the pedals."

I slid over and let her take my seat. "Like this?" she said.

"That should work."

"What are you going to do?"

I didn't answer, but turned and lunged at Aaron. He was leaning out over the edge, gazing at the water, his pad clutched tight to his chest.

"Hey, what—?" he started.

I grabbed him by his shirt collar and yanked him to his feet, pushing him out over the side of the craft. "Now open the vent!"

"Come on—"

"Open the vent or I throw you out!" I shouted, spit flying in his face.

Aaron looked down at the waves. We were high enough for a painful impact. "Okay, okay, fine, sheesh."

I let go and Aaron slumped down and tapped at his pad. "Here we go . . . and . . ." He looked up. "There."

I saw the giant triangle sliding open in the roof, far in the distance. I nodded to Aaron. "Good."

"So, okay, now what?" he said, panting. "I helped you guys out just now, you know? Discharging that lightning, opening the vent—that should be payback for everything. So, you're gonna let me go, right?"

I felt my jaw clench. "Yeah," I said, and shoved him over the side.

"Whoa," said Leech. "Dude." He sounded maybe impressed.

Aaron screamed as he fell, and I watched to see him

righting his body and hitting the water feetfirst. He disappeared, then his head popped up, arms thrashing. Alive. That was good, except in the moment I'd pushed him, I'd felt like I didn't care. If Aaron had died, that still wouldn't have evened the score, but I didn't want to think like that. If he had broken a few bones, though, that would be fine.

"Here come the copters," said Leech, pointing skyward.

I moved to the back, and Lilly slid out of the way. I looked at her and she nodded. "He's lucky that's all he got."

I yanked on the lines and pressed the pedals. We pulled into a steep angle and shot back toward the roof. We rose above the SafeSun, the wind blistering at our velocity, the ceiling of the southwest wall closing in. Brilliant light spilled in through the open vent.

"They're getting closer," said Lilly. I turned to see her pointing off to starboard. There were little cracks, and bullets splintered the side of the craft. "Guess they're not worried about our safety anymore!" she added.

I started banking the craft back and forth. Zigzagging. A bullet tore through the port sail. But we were nearing the open vent.

"We're gonna do this!" yelled Leech, squinting his eyes against the bright triangle of sky.

I thrust us into one more sweeping arc then straightened out. More pops of gunfire . . .

And we burst through into daylight.

"We're out!" I shouted.

The curve of the dome fell away beneath us, the rings of thousands of solar panels reflecting like a crystal forest. And above, a pure, searing white sun burned in a cloudless afternoon sky. The ground below was stepped rock and barren plains. To our right, the bed of Lake Superior was ringed with different shades of dried sediment. The tiny green sliver of its remaining water was visible far off.

I looked back and saw that one of the copters had risen through the dome but was just hovering there, watching us go.

And just like that, EdenWest was already distant, its entire monolithic form in our view, shrinking fast. Soon it was only a little bubble on the world.

Lilly threw her arms around me. "You just did that," she said.

"Yeah," I breathed. A week after sinking to the lake floor, I'd flown out the dome roof, my dragonfly change complete, I was something different now, something more. And not alone, but with Lilly, and with this tiny group of people, knotted together, *my* people. "We did," I said.

The sky was the deep blue of late afternoon. The engine hummed and I used the pedals to keep us high and straight against wind gusts. The air was hot, sweet with the smell of baking rock, the dry that I knew from back home. That humid clinginess was gone; so was the feeling of being enclosed. Suddenly we were out in the vast, vacant world, and who knew what we would face next?

"Cool," said Leech. He was looking down. We were passing over a barren town.

I watched the little model world slide by. The empty, crumbled brick buildings clustered around dirt-covered streets, the sun-bleached cars tossed here and there—it looked like the remains of an ancient civilization. Some mysterious people had once lived here, when the world was different. And we were the gods from an even more distant past, now come back from the future.

Soon, EdenWest was only a glint of reflected sunlight on the horizon.

We sped on, bearing west across the wasteland.

28

NIGHT FELL, COLD AND DAZZLING WITH STARS. I brought the craft down low, a few hundred meters above the ground. The dark was complete, the way it would get outside of Hub, though now and then we did pass over some little light flickering in a gully or a window. A solitary family, a band of travelers. I wondered if they noticed our ghostly blue light speeding overhead and puzzled over what we were.

We decided to wait until morning to figure out where we'd go next. Leech needed to draw some maps. I'd suggested we head for Hub, to get supplies, and to see Dad. Lilly wasn't sure yet. So, for the night, we were just flying due west, based on Leech's reading of the stars.

A silence settled over us for a while, the magnitude of what we'd done, and what we'd left behind, sinking in.

Later, I looked over to Lilly, who was lying back, staring up at the stars. She noticed me noticing her.

"You're right," she said.

"What?" I asked.

"The stars are brighter out here. I can't even find Orion."

"You actually can't see it in the summer except right before dawn," said Leech, like he had a star map in his brain. "Aaron just kept it out all the time 'cause he liked it."

"Oh," said Lilly, sounding a touch annoyed or disappointed. But then she added, "Thanks." She turned to me. "Speaking of which . . ." I felt her hand slip into mine, her fingers rubbing my knuckles. "Thanks again for saving me."

I smiled. "How many times did I drown? I owed you."

"What we just did was crazy."

"Yeah, but it worked."

"Unless we actually hit the water back there and this is just the pleasant journey to nirvana," said Leech from the front of the craft.

"I think we made it," I said.

Lilly took my hand and put it to her face, to her cool, smooth cheek. She smiled, but her eyes were serious. "You should have left me."

I shook my head. "No."

"But"—Lilly sat up on her elbows—"you heard what I said. I never saw the siren. I'm sorry I lied."

"It's okay," I said. "I'm just glad you're here." I thought to lean in and kiss her again. Started to—

"What's this siren you keep talking about?" asked

Leech. I glanced at him and saw that he had a little smirk, like he knew he'd been interrupting. Having him around all the time was going to get old fast.

"You know," I said to him. "The blue girl, the vision. Underwater, or in the temple." Leech's brow scrunched. "You might have seen her somewhere different," I added.

"Or," said Leech, "I have no idea what you're talking about. I just grew gills and knew how to draw maps of the world the way it looked ten thousand years ago. I never saw anything like your siren girl. You sure she wasn't some little fantasy of yours?"

"I didn't make her up," I said, but now I had to wonder. Was I really the only one seeing her? And so was she even real? "Hey," I said to Lilly, "if Leech hasn't seen her either, maybe she's just a part of my awakening. You might still be the third Atlantean."

"Maybe," said Lilly, "but I've never felt like one. Not the way you have. The way both of you *know* things? That hasn't happened to me."

"Well, but, maybe it will, the closer we get."

Lilly just shrugged. She sat up and closed her eyes at the breeze. "Man, this air is so dry. Sweet-smelling, too. Free air. I love it."

She turned toward me. We kissed. It was already a little familiar, the taste of it, the movements, and that only made it better.

"Ugh, this is going to be unbearable," Leech groaned.

We kept kissing just to spite him but then stopped because we could feel him watching.

"Um . . . ," said Leech.

Lilly pulled away. "What?"

"I'm not going to kiss either of you," he said, "but thanks for coming back for me."

"Sure," I said.

Leech's expression darkened. "I thought I knew Paul. He was so patient with me. We'd been working on those maps for years, me drawing down in that navigation room. I thought I was important, like part of the team. But then when you guys found that skull, it was like everything changed. He had me try to talk to it, or whatever you do, and when I said it didn't work, he hooked me up to those machines like I was one of his lab rats or something."

"We know the feeling," I said. I also thought back on how Leech had acted toward me, and realized that at least some of it was because he'd been feeling left out himself, something I could relate to.

Lilly was gazing out behind us. "You can't even see it," she said. "It was my whole world, for so long, and now it's not even on the horizon." She sighed. "Feels good."

"Yeah." I wasn't sure what I felt. We'd escaped, but that only meant that we didn't know what came next.

"Good luck, guys," Lilly said quietly. I figured she was thinking of Evan, Marco, and Aliah.

"I'm sure they'll get out," I said, but I also realized that if Aaron wasn't on our side, that south hatch might never have been open.

"Yeah," said Lilly. "We have some contacts in the city that could help them. I'm not worried. They're my people."

I rubbed her back as her gaze stayed distant.

"They're gonna be after us," said Leech. I'd had that thought, too. "Paul and his team. We're the key to his entire plan, and he's not going to stop until he has us."

"Do you know what the Paintbrush of the Gods is?" I asked him.

Leech shrugged. "Not specifics. Only that it's something Paul thinks can save the world, or whatever."

"What if he's right?" Lilly asked.

"Then we find out on our own," I said. "We find Atlantis, the Heart of the Terra, and we decide."

"Sounds good." Lilly slid up beside me and put her arms around my shoulders. She leaned against my back, and I was glad to protect her from the wind, and glad for her warmth.

We watched the shadow world slide by below, the stars above. After a while, Leech dozed off, curled into a little ball in the bow of the craft. I was exhausted, but determined to keep going until dawn.

"Ooh!" Lilly whispered into my ear.

"What?"

She was looking up. "Shooting star," she said. "My first one."

"Cool. Did you make a wish?"

"Nah."

"Why not?"

She kissed my cheek then pressed hers there, our faces in the wind together. "Because right now is what I want."

I leaned my head into her. Soon, she fell asleep, and sometime after that, the moon slipped up from the horizon, dimming the stars with its brilliant white. It was wide and full, just like it would have been on the dome wall, but brighter and more stunning than that projection had ever been.

I thought about waking Lilly to see it, but she was deep asleep, breathing lightly in my ear, her chin on my shoulder.

So, I read the wind's changes and pulled in on the sails—the Aeronaut, keeping us heading west, over the dark earth. The moon arced overhead, painting the ground in silver and black. I felt the frigid breeze on my face, the warmth on my back, and thought that I agreed with Lilly. Tomorrow we would deal with what we were, and where on earth we needed to go, but for tonight, right now was what I wanted, too.

ACKNOWLEDGMENTS

ANY BOOK THAT INVOLVES KIDS GROWING GILLS at a summer camp full of robotic butterflies inside a dome that sits atop a ten-thousand-year-old temple is probably a work of fiction. That said, to create Owen's world I did read a number of fascinating books about climate change. If you are interested in what scientists think may happen in our lifetime, you might like reading *The Weather of the Future* by Heidi Cullen, *The World in 2050* by Laurence C. Smith, or *The Flooded Earth* by Peter D. Ward. I also read a number of astounding books about ancient civilizations and what Atlantis may really have been. Again, if this kind of thing interests you, check out *Fingerprints of the Gods* by Graham Hancock, *The Atlantis Blueprint* by Colin Wilson and Rand Flem-Ath, and *Technology of the Gods* by David Hatcher Childress. With either subject, these books are just the tip of the (melting) iceberg.

When it comes to thank-yous, I feel like pretty much everyone I've ever known has in some way played a role in this book's existence, but a few people stand out.

To my family: my parents and my brother and all the Emersons and Petersons and Cloughertys and Hubers, who are always so supportive and excited to hear what I'm working on; Willow and Elliott for letting their dad go off again and again to toil at the coffee shop and for being bundles of magic when he returns; and Annie, most of all, who through thick and thin continues to think all this is a good idea, whose love and effort makes every sentence possible, and who is always first reader.

To George Nicholson, who always listens patiently to my wild ideas, and also to Erica Silverman, Kelly Farber, and everyone at Sterling Lord Literistic for their heroic work finding wonderful homes for my stories.

To Katherine Tegen, who took a chance on me and has been a thrill to work with, as well as Katie Bignell, Amy Ryan, and the rest of the team at Harper for making this lovely book from my words!

To Margery Walshaw, whose tough questions and good ideas on a long drive between Beverly Hills and Burbank led to the key plot breakthrough of this series.

To my Seattle writing community: Liz Gallagher, whose prose inspires and who gave this book its first vote of confidence; Martha Brockenbrough, whose keen eye illuminates potential I didn't even know was there; the gang from SCBWI WWA, who have welcomed me into their inspiring group; Suzanne, Christy, Tegan, and the rest of the passionate and wise Seattle booksellers who have been so supportive; and all the fabulous librarians I've met in the Northwest.

To the amazing educators, whose work is so vital, and who I am so lucky to work with: Kylie Kypreos and the talented, dedicated teachers at Catharine Blaine K–8, whose seventh and eighth graders astound me with their writing and teach me about my audience in the process; Rebecca Hoogs, Jeanine Walker, and the staff at Seattle Arts & Lectures, as well as the dazzling teaching artists of Writers in the Schools; Margot Case and the team at Richard Hugo House; and Teri Hein and the exceptional volunteer crew at 826 Seattle.

And finally: Approximately 95 percent of this book was written at a small round table (or one of the four other suitable window seats if that table wasn't available) at the Caffe Ladro in Fremont, Seattle. Many thanks to Carolyn, Jessica, Joe, Sarah, Alana, and Keegan for cup after cup of "drip" in the special mug (are those apples or cherries?) and for humoring this regular.

This too: 80 percent of this book was written to a playlist of Aimee Mann, Elliott Smith, Beck, Ben Folds, and Neko Case, 10 percent to a Pandora station based on Perez Prado, and the final 10 percent to Medeski Martin & Wood's Radiolarians albums. Most of this book was revised to the New Pornographers.

100 percent of the original "ideas" in this book owe heavily to prior genius, mainly the work of Joss Whedon,

Lucas and Spielberg, the writers of *Lost*, Kurt Vonnegut, Poe, and I could go on and on. If you think of one I missed, drop me a line. What's more fun than geeking out about influences?

Oh, and one more thing: if you were in my mind, you would see that Camp Eden, temples, sirens, and secret labs notwithstanding, looks just like my own summer camp, Camp Jewell, in Colebrook, Connecticut. Some of the more down-to-earth things that happen in this book happened there, and, I don't know, I just think that's kinda cool.

BEWARE THE GODS AND THEIR HORRORS . . .

Read on for more of Owen's adventures in

THE
DARK SHORE

BOOK TWO OF THE ATLANTEANS

IT WAS DAWN WHEN WE DESCENDED OVER THE FIRST city of the dead: Gambler's Falls, in what had once been South Dakota, at the western reach of the Great Mississippi Desert. We'd flown over other towns during the long night. They'd all looked the same: ghostly geometric sketches in moonlight, the buildings intact, the cars in orderly lines along streets or neatly parked in driveways. You could almost imagine the people still sleeping peacefully, except for the dark streetlights, the open car hoods and gas tanks, and on everything, the thick crust of blown sand.

What made Gambler's Falls different was the wall.

And the corpse.

We were dropping out of a vacant blue sky. The sun had just risen behind us, orange and fiery, and though the wind on our faces was still the hollow cold of night, I could already feel the lethal heat on my back. Lilly was asleep, curled beside me. Leech sat in the front of the triangular craft.

We'd been going for fourteen hours since escaping from

EdenWest, and we needed a place to hide from the sunlight and EdenCorp. I'd spotted a narrow canyon on the far side of town that might work.

As we lowered, I cast a glance behind us, looking for any sign of Paul's forces, but as it had all night, the horizon kept its secrets. At first, I'd thought that Eden would be right on our tail, but Leech and I had discussed it and figured that actually it would take Paul some time to get a team together to come after us. His hover copters would need modifications for the real sun, and fuel and supplies. They were probably on their way by now, but we had a head start, and I figured we could afford a few hours of rest.

"You sure we have time for this?" Leech asked skeptically as we flew over the outskirts of town. "We're already so far off the bearing."

"I've got to sleep," I said. It had been more than twenty-four hours since I'd slept at all, and days since I'd had anything more than a few meager hours. "Otherwise, there's no way I'm going to get us to your marker."

As the night had gone on, this had become the latest tension between me and Leech. He'd been sketching maps, and, using the lines we'd seen etched in the top of Mount Aasgard back in EdenWest, he'd come up with a bearing that pointed southwest. Leech believed that this bearing would take us to some kind of Atlantean marker, the next stop on our way to the Heart of the Terra, the place we had to get to before Paul.

I trusted Leech's idea. He was the Mariner. It was his job to plot our course, and my job as the Aeronaut to get us there. But instead of following Leech's bearing, I had been flying due west, toward Yellowstone Hub, where I was from. All through the night, Leech had noted that we were getting farther off course and adding to our time. My point was that going to Hub made more sense as a first move, because we knew we had my dad there, and we could get supplies to stock up for the longer journey.

"I get that you need your beauty sleep," said Leech begrudgingly, "but— Whoa . . ." He leaned over the side of the craft. "Check that out."

I looked down and in the shadows between buildings, I saw the wall. It was maybe ten meters tall, an uneven pile of stacked furniture, sandbags, bricks, and chunks of concrete, all stitched together with barbed wire and telephone lines. Its spine was lined with jagged shards of glass. It undulated like a serpent through the streets, past the overturned, blackened hulks of cars and trucks; the spills of furniture and trash; and sometimes right through collapsed buildings.

"Dude, look out!" Leech shouted.

I'd gotten distracted by the scene, my exhausted brain in slow motion, and now we were too low. Directly in front of us, the wall crested to a high point. Perched at the top was a cockeyed lookout tower, a square wooden platform with a blue plastic tarp over it. The tarp had been shredded by wind, but the aluminum poles were still standing, including the one sticking up through the middle.

That was where the body was.

I slammed down on the pedals in the floor of the craft. The vortex engine, a black triangle of polished stone with swirling blue light in the center, hummed at a higher pitch. Its glow increased and I felt a teeth-rattling vibration as the antigravity propulsion kicked in. We leaped skyward, barely clearing the body.

Lilly jolted awake. "What happened?" She pulled up on my shoulder.

"Dead guy," Leech reported.

Lilly craned back to see. "Jesus," she muttered.

"I don't think Jesus was involved," said Leech.

The body was mostly bones, with some stretches of cooked, leathery skin still spanning joints. A few tatters of brown clothing fluttered in the breeze.

"There are more," said Leech. He pointed to a heap of brown bones and clothing at the rubble-strewn base of the wall. "Looks like they were trying to get in."

"What do you think *they* were, warnings?" Lilly was looking over my shoulder at the tallest building in town. It was brick, and about twelve stories. Incomplete letters on its side suggested it had been a bank. Brilliant sunbeams silhouetted skeletons, one displayed in each window.

A decorative border had also been constructed around the roof that gave the building a castlelike appearance, only these miniature battlements were actually stacks of skulls. Lots of skulls.

"I would take those as warnings," I said.

"Looks like that's what they were trying to protect." Leech pointed in the other direction.

The wall made a rough circle through the town, and at its center, just beyond the downtown blocks, stood an enormous building, a giant expanse of flat, sand-covered roof. A tall sign beside it, white with faded blue letters, read:

WALMART SUPERPLUS GAMBLER'S FALLS

"I used to go to one of those, back before I was cryoed," said Leech. "It had pretty much everything. It makes sense that they defended it."

There was another body strapped to the flagpole outside the front entrance, and all the glass doors had been covered with plywood. The body looked similarly leather skinned and old.

I banked the craft and headed out of town, toward the canyon I'd seen.

"What happened here?" Lilly asked quietly, watching the streets slide by. Most of the buildings and houses were flattened. A few beams and remnants of walls stuck up from the sand, along with the skeletal stalks of scorched trees.

She'd been asleep all night, except for one period where she'd stirred, whimpering softly to herself. The one word I'd been able to make out was "Anna." She'd said it in a despairing way that took me right back to the secret lab beneath Camp Eden, where Lilly had found her best friend pried open and turned into a cruel science experiment, one that had been done in search of the Atlantean code that we had inside us. The image of Anna, of her ribs and her organs, the tubes, and her wide, terrified eyes . . . I couldn't shake it.

"Like," Lilly added, "who were these people?" I remembered her wondering about this very thing back on the raft at camp: Thousands of years from now, what would future beings think about this lost society of the twenty-first century, this *us*? Of course, on the raft, she'd been talking about an empty swimming pool in her old backyard in Las Vegas. Here we were talking about a massacre.

Maybe this was more than Lilly had bargained for. It was definitely more bleak and violent than anything I'd seen back at Yellowstone Hub, but I had at least heard tales of the things that happened out in the wild lands.

"Holdouts, probably," said Leech. "That's what they were called back in the Rise."

"Yeah," I agreed, suppressing a flash of annoyance. Even though we were out of Eden and back in my part of the world, Leech still liked to act like he was the expert on everything. But he was right in this case, so I let it go.

This whole part of the continent had once been fertile cropland, but during the middle of the Great Rise, the river system dried up. It had been one of the cruel jokes of climate change. The warmer the atmosphere got, the more water vapor it could hold, and so even though the oceans were rising, the land was drying out.

There had been time for people to evacuate, but not many places left for them to go. Aside from the lucky few who could buy their way into EdenWest, the other options had been grim. A family could either head for the coast and pack onto a tanker bound for the employee prefectures of Coke-Sahel, or make the migration north to the Borderlands of the Habitable Zone, where visas into the American-Canadian Federation were already rare and disease and crime were common.

"Instead of leaving," Leech explained to Lilly, "they fortified, and tried to make a go of it, like at Hub or Dallas Beach. Those groups sometimes can get support from the ACF."

"Most of them fail, though," I said, "from plague or infighting or starvation. Sometimes all three."

"Mmm," said Lilly, still gazing at the wreckage below.

She shook her head and leaned into me. The warm press of her melted through the chill of the long night.

"Hi," I said, glancing over. She was huddled in my LoRad pullover, her long, dark hair matted from sleeping. Her eyes were as clear and breathtaking as ever, sky blue with tendrils of pearl white. A curvy pattern of pale lines snaked down her almond-colored cheek, indentations from using her red waterproof bag as a pillow. I reached over and traced one of the lines in a slow S from her eye to her chin. "Funny sleep marks," I said.

She smiled and kissed my cheek, her nose pushing into

my cheekbone. I felt her eyelashes on my temple. The sensation was already something familiar. Even though it had only been two days since our first kiss, I had this feeling of knowing every detail of it, her lips—her breath, how it smelled a little salty—and I couldn't imagine that I had ever not known that. Each kiss was like a dust storm across my mind, wiping everything else out.

But then she pulled away sharply. "Ow," she groaned. She rubbed at her neck, at the slim red lines of her gills.

"What's up?" I asked.

"They're really sore," she said, scratching lightly. "They feel dry."

"Mine used to feel that way before I'd come down to the lake at night," I said, "like they needed water." There was barely any trace left of my gills. Not even two days since they had stopped working, and now it was almost like they'd never been. Another in a series of changes so complete that I could barely remember what had been before. Had I really swam for hours in the dark of Lake Eden? Had I really felt at home in the pressure and cold of water, felt stronger there than on land even? And now air was my home. Instead of water currents, I reacted to wind speeds. Instead of the pressures of different depths, it was the tension of sails against the breeze.

Lilly ran a finger over the faded lines on my neck. It caused only a faint echo. "I can barely see them." She frowned and turned away.

"Hey," I said, wanting to reach for her shoulder, but the

morning thermal breeze was picking up, so I had to keep both my sore arms on the sail lines. Ever since my gills had faded, things had been different between us. Not bad, just . . . off. I'd lost my gills because I was an Atlantean, one of the Three. Leech was, too, but Lilly . . .

It didn't seem likely. Her gills hadn't faded like Leech's and mine had. She'd also lied about seeing the siren, except Leech hadn't seen her either, so that didn't prove anything.

I still didn't know why I'd seen the siren. I wondered if maybe it was because the skull beneath Eden had been mine. Maybe that was also the reason my gills had come and gone so quickly. Leech's had probably faded because of prolonged contact. He'd been around my skull for years, working in the underground temple right above it. Maybe being here in the craft with my skull would be enough to make Lilly's gills fade. . . .

Or maybe she just wasn't one of us. And if that turned out to be the case, what did that mean for the rest of our journey? It had already crossed my mind that there might come a time when I could go and she could not, where the difference in our destinies would separate us. Maybe she felt that, too, like a cloud over us, despite the relentlessly clear sky. The idea caused a cold squeeze of adrenaline in my gut.

"It will be okay," I said. I didn't know if I meant the pain in her gills, or us, or even the unknown that lay ahead of us. Either way, I worried that I was lying.

Lilly sighed. "Yeah." She rubbed at her gills again. Her

gaze stayed distant, like she didn't quite believe it, either.

The sun was getting hotter by the minute, making my skin itch even through the heavy sweatshirt I was wearing. It was a product of EdenWest, though, with no UV Rad protection, and out here, it wouldn't be enough. We'd spent a few hours in the late afternoon sun the day before, and I already had a sore feeling on my scalp, and worrisome pink blotches on my legs and hands.

"How about we rest inside that Walmart?" asked Leech, gazing behind us. "Then we could check it for supplies."

"There's nowhere to hide the ship," I said. "I think that canyon will be safer, and, besides, ten more hours and we can be at Hub. We just have to hold out a little longer."

"Yeah, but I'm hungry now," said Leech. "And what makes you think your dad can even help us?"

"Who else can we go to?" I asked. Our only other option for supplies seemed to be tracking down a Nomad pod, but we had no idea where to find one, and Leech still liked to go on about how they were savages, even though Lilly and I knew otherwise. Before finally succumbing to sleep last night, Lilly had scanned the gamma link for the Nomad Free Signal but hadn't found it.

Leech had a good point about my dad, though. Because really, it was hard to imagine what his reaction would be to my story:

Hey, Dad, listen. I know I only left for Camp Eden last week but I'm back and some things have . . . changed. And now I need help getting supplies without alerting anyone that we're here because, oh, did I mention we're on the run from the EdenCorp? They want me because I'm a genetic descendant of the ancient Atlanteans, one who can help them find the Brocha de Dioses—sorry, Paintbrush of the Gods—which is ancient technology that can reverse the course of climate change? You know, save the world.

No, I know, saving the world sounds great! But there's one problem: we don't trust Paul and his board of directors and their Project Elysium, because they did a bunch of terrible things to our friends, not to mention how they've been running the search for Atlantis and us Atlanteans in secret for over fifty years. I know, right? If their reason was really as simple as saving the planet and the population, why would they be keeping it such a massive secret? Yes, that is pretty suspicious.

What? Oh, right, What exactly is MY plan. We're going to find the Paintbrush of the Gods ourselves and then decide what should be done. No matter what, we'll protect it from EdenCorp.

This craft? It's mine. I know, cool, right? Yes, I can fly it. How? I learned from a dead kid named Lük, whose consciousness—well, technically his Qi-An life force— was trapped inside a crystal skull.

So . . . does all that sound good? Okay, great! Now, we just need a bunch of food, a tent, and some other supplies, and then I need you to go ahead and let me fly off into the sunset with no word of where I'm going . . .

Just like Mom did.

I probably wouldn't add that last line. But even without it, how exactly was Dad going to react? When I tried to picture it, I could only imagine him freaking out.

And even if, somehow, he thought this all sounded fine—that it was perfectly okay for me to fly off to who knows where while being pursued by EdenCorp—then what? I was assuming that my dad, who had trouble with the two flights of steps up from the cavern promenade to our apartment because of his breathing issues, who could barely cheer on the Helsinki Island soccer team without breaking into wicked phlegm-filled coughs, was going to be able to ferry us supplies without collapsing?

Not likely.

But I hadn't mentioned all this to Leech. I didn't want to give him any more ammunition to add to his argument for bypassing Hub and heading southwest. Maybe going to Hub was dumb, but I couldn't help wanting to go.

And it was more than just supplies: I also really wanted to see Dad. The feeling surprised me. We weren't all that close, and yet as last night had passed, the feeling had come on strong. So much had happened in the last week, from drowning to my Atlantean awakening to our escape. All of it played in my mind like some brightly colored and impossible dream, and it was like, What had my life even been like back at Hub? It felt so distant, which was ridiculous because I could clearly remember the quiet nights on the couch with Dad, the lonely days walking to school and sitting more silent than not among my little class, the dank subterranean light, the smell of sulfur and rock. It was all right there in my mind . . . and yet it seemed like there was a gulf, a vast space, between that old version of me and this new one. And while new Owen, with a purpose, with Lilly, was definitely a big improvement on who I used to be, I also couldn't help feeling unstuck somehow, like I had left my old reality and was floating outside it now, slightly out of sync with time and space.

I fiddled with the leather bracelet that I'd made back at camp. Crude stamps spelled out *Dad*, followed by a coarse etching of what, at the time, I'd thought was just a funky symbol for Camp Aasgard, but that I now knew was an Atlantean symbol, maybe for Atlantis itself.

It was the old me and the new. And so maybe I just wanted some concrete connection between the two, like before I could go be this crazy thing, this Aeronaut, I needed to make sure I was still old Owen, too. A week ago, I wouldn't have imagined wanting that, but now I found that I did.

All of which was why I said to Leech, "You haven't *lost* your bearing, have you?"

"Of course not," he replied.

"So after Yellowstone, we'll correct our course."

Leech gave me a weird look: less annoyed, more serious. "Look, I just think it's wasting precious time." He almost sounded worried.

"Well," said Lilly, "I vote with Owen. So deal with it." She started rubbing her back. "It's getting hot, fast. Is that where we're headed?"

"Yeah." We were coming up on the small canyon. It was narrow and curvy, its walls striped in every shade of brown.

"Looks homey," Leech muttered.

"It's concealed," I said, "that's the point."

On its bank was what had likely been a park. There was a wide expanse of cracked pavement, a flat area with picnic tables awash in drifts of sand, the skeleton of a playground poking out. Beside it, the canyon opened into a wide mouth, like there had been a waterfall. Below that was an empty scoop of land; maybe it had been a pond. Kids had probably gone swimming there, way back when.

But as we passed over the park, we saw that now the dry pond was something very different.

"Aww, man!" said Leech.

"Uh . . ." Lilly breathed, sounding nauseated.

The dry depression was piled with bodies.

Their journey continues. . . .

Now that they've escaped from Camp Eden, Owen,
Lilly, and Leech have to cross a wrecked planet in hopes
of finding Atlantis. Along the way, they will witness
unspeakable horrors, and Owen's love for Lilly will be
challenged by an exotic girl who is the third Atlantean. . . .

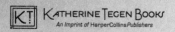

KATHERINE TEGEN BOOKS
An Imprint of HarperCollins Publishers